7 FREE PRELUDES

AT

FreeFantasyFiction.com

STONE & TIDE

STONE TIDE

Z.S. DIAMANTI

GOLDEN
GRIFFIN

For Crystal,
Since you had to wait the longest.

FINLESTIA

LAND OF TARRINE

CHARTOK
TUNDRA

ICE LAKE

TANDAL SEA

BORORA   DAK-TAHN

D R E L E K

RENJAK   RUK

PORAK   LAKJO

EANT
SEA

CROSSDIN

EHUN-RA   CALROK

EALIUM

KANE HARBOR

LORALITH   WHITESTONE

HILL STOP

ELDERWOOD
FOREST   WHITESTONE
FOREST

EANT SEA NARROWS

PALORI RUINS   DAHRENPORT

STRANDED COAST

TELRO

TAMARIA

EANT

ROTTING

MARON   BLACKMAR
FOREST   LAKERUN

PEARL
LAKE   VANDOR

PALORI   STALFORD

WILDLANDS   SEA

LASTTOWN

LAST LAKE   MOON
BAY

KALIMANDIR

NARI
DESERT

LLAMPORT

ELENPORT

SORELLO   PAW ISLES

VERFIN   TARN   ARELON

LETTO   DIRK

DENRUS

LAND
OF **KELVUR**

SEA

CRAE
WASTES

G R A E
FELL KEEP

VENTOLI

EASTERN
KNOLLS

DUSKWOOD

LAKE KNOLL

ELINGO MINING
CAMP

ZORS

THE
PALISADE

AIDEN'S DELL

ZOR LEDI

THE SHOALS

ANTALON

FOREST OF
WIRRA

ZOR TOREIS

SEA

ZOR VELNIS

ELAIN'S SHOULDER

TALVIN

LANT

LAKE TORI

LOD MORAZ

SOLREB

ZOR PLEMR

LOD ZIM

LAKE
NEL

ZOR LANTI

LORNASB POINT

LOD KELPIO

FAR

LOD LAKE

FAR
COVE

LOD POINT

LERIAN SEA

LOD METO

CHAPTER ONE

THE SHOALS

S creams from the village ripped Shorlis from his quiet contemplation. His sea green eyes snapped open, and he turned quickly to his father. Anthanar heard it too. Shorlis found it strange that his father would hesitate rather than sprint toward a potential threat.

Of course, Shorlis wasn't eager for something to interrupt the quiet time with his father. When he was younger and his shell softer, getting up before sunrise had been a daunting task, but he'd grown to look forward to his father's deep wisdom.

"Discipline might sound like a harsh word, my son, but it is the discipline of quiet that allows us to hear the world that surrounds us. Finlestia has much to say, if you are willing to hear it," his father would say.

Every morning they emerged as the sun's glow kissed the horizon. They walked to the beach and felt the sand, still damp from the night's tide, squeeze between their green toes. They stretched their lank limbs and enjoyed relieving pops inside their shells.

Other people groups often compared chelons to tortoises. Unlike the slow four-legged creatures, chelons stood on two legs, as tall as men. Their shells were much thinner than those of common sea and land turtles. As a result, chelons weren't able to retract their limbs or heads into their shells but were surprisingly agile.

Regardless of their agility, chelons had no magical ability to overcome a surprise attack.

Anthanar ran a hand over his bald green head, speckled by the sun as most amphibious skin tends to be. His eyes danced while he calculated something Shorlis could not see. The old chelon launched from the sand and hoisted his grown son to his feet.

The initial screams had woken the rest of the village, and cries of fear echoed from more huts as the two chelons hustled through the sand.

"Hurry!" Anthanar shouted to his son as they ran along the beach toward their village.

Several huts blazed with fire, and chelons young and old shouted. At first, Shorlis could not see the source of the chaos. When they had fires break out in the past, the whole village united to douse the flames with sand and water. Shorlis noticed the panicked villagers ran frantically without order.

Suddenly, Shorlis was tackled from the side. Landing hard in the sand next to an outcropping of beach roses and trying to catch his breath, he rolled over, spitting sand from his nostrils, hoping to glimpse his assailant.

"Stop!" Anthanar hissed in a whisper.

Shorlis blinked the sand away, confused by his father's aggressive actions. The old chelon pressed his son to the ground while he peered over the beach rose bush that concealed them. Shorlis raised his hands slowly, indicating he understood the necessity for quiet and slow movements as he rolled up to peer past the leaves.

"What is it?" he asked. Before Anthanar could answer, Shorlis saw.

Geldrins!

Geldrins were brutish creatures that stood a head taller than the tallest chelon. Their dry skin was crusted with an appearance of jagged mountain stone. They had no hair, but moss grew on them in strange patches and in a variety of shades. They wore furs and skins of beasts from the Eastern Knolls and were protected by armor made of metal rings.

"What are geldrins doing in the Shoals?"

"I do not know," Anthanar answered, examining the scene.

Shorlis watched as a stony monster muscled Tenzo to the ground. Tenzo was one of the strongest chelons, but he looked as though he'd been pummeled by a couple of the attackers. He rose to his knees, swaying to one side, obviously dazed. Another geldrin tied Tenzo's wrists together before hefting the heavy chelon to his feet and pushing him toward the far side of the village.

Shorlis's hard jaw clicked as he gritted his rounded beak. His fists squeezed tightly as he watched the geldrins take his friend.

"They're capturing us." Anthanar's words startled Shorlis out of his rage. "We need to get to the hut. I need my staff."

Shorlis gave his father an incredulous look. The old chelon held the wooden staff that he brought with him every morning. "You have your staff!"

"Not this one," his father answered. Shorlis sensed that his father was suddenly sad, as though he were about to change his son's view of him forever. Perhaps his father had greater secrets than the younger chelon knew.

Shorlis had always known his father was peculiar. While they were growing up together, the other children teased Shorlis with that accusation. Over the years, he watched his father share kindness with all the people on their little island in the Shoals. Whenever anyone needed something, Anthanar would be the first to help. Shorlis's father was a gifted healer and seemed wiser

3

than any other person he had ever met. He did not think the positive light in which he viewed his father was out of some compulsion or duty to believe the best of his father. No. It was more than that.

Unlike any other hut on their island, theirs was filled with books and scrolls from faraway lands. Villagers would regularly borrow from the knowledge hidden in those parchments and tomes. Their home had become a village library of sorts. As a result, it had been specially built to protect the contents inside. Many chelons had aided in the reinforcement of the hut when Shorlis was only a softshell.

"I have another staff," Anthanar explained. "It is hidden under the reed floor in my sleeping room."

"What? I don't understa—"

"We do not have time, my son." Anthanar gripped his son's strong shoulder. "I will explain everything later. Right now, we need to get that staff. It is unlike any other."

Shorlis did not understand, but he trusted his father. If Anthanar needed that staff to stop whatever was happening in their village, they had to get it.

"Alright then." Shorlis nodded with determination. "Let's get that staff." The younger chelon heaved himself into a ready stance but paused, turning to his father. "If you're not going to use that one, though ..."

Anthanar surrendered the wooden staff and a proud smile to his son. "Of course."

Shorlis knelt beside a bank in the sand, watching his father move into position behind a copse of sea oats. The long yellow stems waved in the morning breeze. The younger chelon didn't think the oats concealed his father very well but knew the geldrins were busy rounding up other villagers.

Anthanar shot him a silent signal with a prolonged look from his green eyes and a slow nod.

Shorlis hesitated. He didn't care for this plan.

Anthanar intended to dash toward the nearest hut and weave his way between, around, or even through others to get to their own. If all went accordingly, he'd reach their hut and retrieve the important staff that Shorlis had never seen nor heard his father speak of before that morning. The greatest challenge to the plan was the geldrins actively searching for and snatching villagers from their homes.

"Get over here!"

Shorlis froze as he watched Anthanar disappear behind the sea oats. He turned slowly to peer in the direction of the center road through the village where the geldrins were binding their captives before dragging them away. A large geldrin with grey-tinted, cracked skin barked at a younger soldier.

"You going to let these weak turtles crack your face like that?"

The young soldier bowed, embarrassed. He pulled a hand away from his face, revealing a bloody mess. Someone had done some work on his already crooked nose.

"Which one of these little crusts did this to you?"

The soldier pointed to an elderly chelon woman.

"No ..." Shorlis whispered under his breath. It was Tellen. Shorlis had known her his whole life. Tellen would sit with Shorlis and talk with him as a chelon mother would do. She had no children of her own but bestowed upon Shorlis great love and kindness. Shorlis had never known his mother. She had been a chelon from a land in the far south of Finlestia and died just after he was born. He was thankful for Tellen's motherly goodness toward him.

"This old crab?" The geldrin commander balked. Tellen gingerly lifted herself onto her knees with a defiant grimace. The commander shook his head. "She'll be no good in the mines."

In one swift move, the big grey geldrin brandished his sword and stuck old Tellen in the chest. A sickening *Cthunk!* revealed the weapon had penetrated her shell and found its mark.

"No!" Shorlis yelled, realizing his folly as the gathered geldrins turned on him.

Shorlis inadvertently turned to check his father's progress only to lead the gazes of the geldrins to fall upon Anthanar, frozen in place between two huts. The geldrin commander sneered and ripped his sword from Tellen, who fell to the sand, unmoving.

He pointed his sword toward Anthanar and growled, "Get him!"

Shorlis bellowed a primal cry as he launched himself over the sand bank into a sprint at the commander. The geldrin's eyes squinted, and his face contorted into a wicked smile. Shorlis's legs were on fire as he ran through the sand, his heart pumping blood through his body in a frenzy. His eyes widened at the commander's smirk.

I'll kill him! Shorlis thought. The young chelon swung the staff around in a mighty arc. His tunic, light linen like most chelon attire, rippled in a dazzling flourish as he struck at the geldrin.

The commander, however, proved that geldrins, though stonelike, were more agile than expected. He side-stepped the lunging chelon, swinging his sword sideways and slapping away the wooden staff. Shifting his weight on his feet like a well-trained soldier, the geldrin swiftly brought his sword around, cutting through the back of Shorlis's shirt as he stumbled past.

For a moment, Shorlis locked eyes with a young chelon girl, Lani. Tears fell off her quivering chin as she gripped Tellen's lifeless hand.

"Take another charge, turtle," the commander chuckled behind him. "I like to see strength. Should make for a hard worker."

Shorlis wheeled to face the smug geldrin. "I won't be going anywhere with you."

Another wicked grin cracked the geldrin's stony face, but he did not move. He merely waited.

Shorlis heaved himself forward, swinging his staff in from the left, the right, whirling it overhead and bringing it down hard, met every time by a parry of the commander's sword. They danced in circles in the sand, their weapons colliding with uneven *thunks*.

Finally, the geldrin commander parried and spun away in a flashy move that appeared to be for show. He was playing with the chelon.

Shorlis gasped for air, his lungs trying to catch up to his great efforts. He couldn't beat the commander, and he knew it. As he looked past the great geldrin and caught sight of their ship's sails in the distance, he decided he would rather die than become a slave to their ambitions. The muscles in his legs twitched, and his grip tightened around the staff.

The geldrin commander chuckled again, readying his own stance.

"Shorlis, no! *Gackk!*"

Off to the right, a geldrin held up Anthanar. The gravel-faced monster pressed his twisted dagger tighter to the chelon's throat.

"Father ..."

"Father?" the commander mocked. "Oh, then I am saved! Surely, a mighty warrior such as yourself would have bested me. But so noble a creature as yourself wouldn't put his own father in harm's way. Right?"

Shorlis's sea green eyes leveled with the geldrin commander's gaze. *What am I supposed to do?* the chelon thought. He was at a loss. While he would gladly give his life to save the people of his village, he would not so idly throw away his father's.

"Rragh!" Shorlis screamed a wild cry and snapped the staff across his knee, breaking it into two jagged and splintery pieces.

"Good choice," the big geldrin said with a smirk. He turned to bark more orders at his soldiers. "Alright, enough games! You grab that pain in my—"

His words were shortened as everything around him went into motion. Anthanar was shoved to the ground beside little Lani. As the older chelon hit the sand, Shorlis bolted for the commander, throwing one of the staff halves directly at him. The commander barely had time to whip his sword up to send the piece flying off, landing quietly in the soft sand. Shorlis dove forward with the remaining half, ramming the jagged point at the commander's head. The big geldrin didn't have time to whip his sword around again but pummeled the chelon in the side as he attempted to spin away from the attack.

Shorlis rolled to the side, his breath gone from his lungs, as another geldrin jumped on top of him to subdue him.

The commander screamed in rage, pawing at the great gash on the left side of his face. It looked like a fissure that opened up just before lava erupts. Instead of lava, the geldrin's face erupted with blood. He cursed at the pain in his eye, unable to see anything out of it.

"Shall I gut him?" one of the geldrins asked, swinging his sword with anticipation.

"No!" the geldrin commander yelled. "No. No. He doesn't get off that easy. Death would be a release from what he has in store."

Shorlis lay still under the weight of the heavy geldrin. He scowled at the commander, who glared back while covering the left side of his face.

"Knock him out."

Shorlis shifted, trying to find some room to fight back before the pommel of a sword hammered down on his bald head.

The clinking of chisel and shovel against rock resounded around the camp. The season brought a late heat, which made labor almost unbearable. Shorlis tried to wipe the sweat from his brow but, instead, only created a muddy paste in his green hand. He was covered from head to toe in dirt, an all-too-common occurrence.

How is it so dry here?

He'd asked himself a million similar questions over the past year while toiling in the open mine. The miners weren't allowed to converse with one another during the long work hours that lasted from dawn to dusk. They weren't even allowed to speak to each other during the midday meal—the one break they received each day. The meal, Shorlis knew, was given more out of necessity to keep production up rather than actual care for the miners. The geldrin guards were not reluctant to abuse the captives should they step out of line in some way. Shorlis himself had been beaten many times.

When they'd first arrived, Shorlis carried an obstinate attitude, fighting back any way he could. Even rebelling in little ways made him feel as though he still had some control over his life. People can only be beaten and treated like animals for so long before they begin to break.

He used to wonder what would have happened if he had managed to kill the geldrin commander—whose name he learned was Chol—back in the Shoals. He even used to dream about getting another chance, but those dreams eventually faded. Shorlis assumed that his body was so tired when he racked out after a hard day's labor that he couldn't dream anymore. No doubt, he felt the exhaustion in the depths of his shell. If he was honest with himself, he knew that, had he managed to kill Chol back then, it would have changed little. Perhaps he wouldn't be in the mine. Perhaps they would have killed him and left him in the sand next to old Tellen. Sometimes he wondered if that would have been a better fate.

The sun beat down, casting strange beams of light through the dust that swirled around the mines. The Glinso Mining Camp ran an open air mine, meaning the miners worked in tall ditches, only shaded from the hot sun in the early mornings and the late evenings. Sometimes, Shorlis wondered what it would be like to work a deep mine, always covered by tons of rock above, never feeling the sun's unwavering heat. He imagined it would be cooler, but the smell of sweaty laborers would probably be unbearable in the confined spaces.

A small dwarven boy approached, carrying a pail with a ladle bouncing around the rim.

"Water," the boy said, lifting the ladle toward the chelon.

Shorlis took the ladle with both hands and tipped his head back to drink. The water was cool as it sloshed into his mouth, an indication that the dwarven boy had just refilled the bucket from the well. Grime stuck to his tongue as the water mixed with the dust that had collected in his mouth while he was working. He peered around to see whether the geldrin guards would hear his gratitude. "Thanks, Doran," he whispered.

The dwarf took the ladle and scooped another half full, looking to either side to make sure he wouldn't be caught before quickly handing it back to Shorlis. The chelon sipped more slowly.

"What happened to the dragon?" the dwarf asked.

"Which dragon?"

"Gundorbil, of course," he whispered with more fervor.

"Shh," Shorlis quieted him. "You'll find out tonight."

"Ahh …" Doran complained, a look of pain on his face.

"Go now." Shorlis shooed him, barely hiding his entertained smile.

"Oy! Don't make me come down there!"

Shorlis gestured with his hands that the dwarf boy was merely bringing him water as Doran hustled to the next laborer.

The geldrin guard was high on a rise above him and didn't seem too interested in coming down to discipline a captive in the heat. His skin appeared more cracked and drier than usual for a geldrin. He glared and grunted at the chelon to make sure Shorlis knew who was in charge before swiveling to overlook another section of the mine.

Shorlis turned back to the stone and dirt before him, working at it with his hammer and chisel. He had grown strong over the last year. When he'd first arrived, he didn't think he could make it through a week. As time went on, his muscles grew accustomed to the work, and he'd grown into a sturdy chelon—not something he could say for all of them.

He shot a glance to his left. Doran had just finished and moved on from another captive. Anthanar smiled back to his son through the grime that caked his face. The old chelon was quite taken with the little dwarf. Every night, when the guards locked them in the sleeping chamber, Anthanar told stories to the other captives.

Their nights weren't always that way, of course. The first couple of months, Shorlis and his father spoke in hushed whispers to each other, then the geldrins brought in another mix of people, including the young dwarven boy. One night, Doran overheard the two chelons and inserted himself into the conversation. Anthanar could not help his delight at the boy's presence and told him a story to help him fall asleep. The old chelon had a way of telling stories with a certain gusto, and soon enough, everyone in the sleeping chamber was invested in the ending. But that, as he said, would have to wait for another night, for they needed their rest.

Since then, Anthanar told stories to all the captives every night before they went to sleep. Some of the legends Shorlis remembered from scrolls read when he was younger, but many more he did not. He witnessed no shortage to his father's tales. One night, Shorlis asked why he continued to tell stories.

"They see little hope in all that surrounds them. There really is not much to see." Anthanar had laughed. "If I can tell them of a greater world, they will live with hope to see it one day. Do not underestimate the power of hope in the hearts of people."

And hope he had given them. Shortly after the tales began, captives started to wake up early to join Anthanar and Shorlis in their morning routine. Anthanar taught them to stretch their aching muscles, move their bodies in controlled flow, and even find stillness before their captors would come to wake them for the day.

Over the last couple of weeks, however, Shorlis had seen his father's age assault him. The old chelon had seemed to be of infinite youth back home in the Shoals. Many times, Shorlis had heard others comment about his father's surprising vibrancy for his age. Most of his spots and the variations in his green skin had still not greyed.

As Shorlis observed his father's struggle with his shovel, the younger chelon thought he looked greyer than a week earlier. In fairness, the dust coating everyone made them appear far less vibrant. He still worried about his father.

Though Shorlis had long given up on the hopes of escape, he was suddenly filled with a resurrection of the idea. He did not want his father to die in that place.

CHAPTER TWO

KINGLY DUTY

The afternoon breeze blew a revitalizing warmth through the market square of Whitestone. People buzzed about between the various stalls to trade or acquire tools, food, linen, or whatever resources their families needed. The white and blue sails that provided shade and relief from the sun billowed and settled with pleasant gusts of wind. Trained griffins sat atop the stone archways and walls that provided the border for the market, while guardians from the city's fabled Griffin Guard intermingled with the people. It was a good day in Whitestone.

Ellaria smiled as Tam shifted awkwardly in his guardian armor, emblazoned with the crest of Whitestone—a blue shield flanked by white wings with a silver griffin in the middle. He carried a large sack of potatoes slung over one shoulder and a small barrel of grains under his other arm. Tam laughed at himself as he blundered over to the cart under the lopsided weight of his haul.

Guardian armor was not cumbersome. Its layered design was intentionally made with mobility in mind. Riding and fighting on griffin-back was a difficult discipline; it didn't need to be more difficult because of restricting armor. The unwieldy packages, coupled with his layered attire, though, put Tam at a mobile disadvantage.

"You look ridiculous," Ellaria said as she watched the struggling man walk toward her.

Tam stopped and tilted his head to the side with an unamused look on his face. His short black hair blew in the wind, and his eyes narrowed, nearly closing. "Any help you care to offer would be appreciated."

"And miss the show?" she teased.

Tam stood defiantly until Ellaria laughed again and sidled over to help him. "Thank you," he said sarcastically.

"Glad I could save the day."

Tam let out a short laugh. "You kill me!"

"I mean, if we ever were battling each other for real ..." She let the words hang on the air between them.

"One time!" Tam burst out in defense. He looked both ways to make sure he hadn't drawn any attention to the two guardians. In a lower tone he continued, "It was one time. And the next time we spar, I've got a couple tricks of my own. I was going easy on you since you're so new."

"Oh! I'm sure that's it," Ellaria mocked.

"Seriously!" Tam continued. "I didn't want to make you feel bad when you're still so new to the guard. You didn't go through the same training as the rest of us, and it's important that we all believe in the guardian next to us. Believe they have our backs. Believe they will come through for us in the midst of battle."

That kind of deeper thinking made Tam a good wingman among the ranks of the Griffin Guard. While Ellaria liked to tease him, she respected him a great deal and considered him a good friend.

He was right, though. She hadn't grown up in the rigorous training through which the griffin guardians are raised. Many of them had gone to Whitestone's Grand Corral, the home and training base of the Griffin Guard, at the young age of eleven.

They lived in the training barracks as they grew into highly capable defenders of all the people of Tarrine. Ellaria, on the other hand, had arrived in Whitestone through a sequence of strange and inexplicable events that she could only chalk up to destiny.

She was the daughter of a huntsman named Grell from the great plains city of Tamaria. She'd spent much of her growing years learning to cook, clean, and most importantly, how to heal. Her father and older brothers would return from their hunts banged up with injuries, and she and her mother would employ their healing knowledge to fix them up. She got plenty of practice with her younger brothers as well. They were always coming home, having fallen off a wall they'd been balancing or sporting an impressive gash from a play sword fight.

Ellaria, however, wanted more. Eventually, she had convinced her brothers to take her hunting, and when they saw she could hold her own, they never hesitated to take her again. That was, until one hunt when they ran into a savage plains bear. Her brother Greggo distracted the beast while her other brother Merrick grabbed her and ran them to safety. Greggo's death had been a turning point for them. Merrick no longer took her along on his hunts. He went into the city on his own to sell meat and furs. He hunted in the forests and plains around Tamaria with none but his falcon, Rora. Ellaria used to feel as though she'd lost two brothers that day.

Then, many months ago, a battle raged between the wyvern-riding orcs of Drelek and the Griffin Guard closer to Tamaria than anyone could remember. Ellaria went out to help bury the dead, only to find a guardian alive. Finding Orin changed everything.

They embarked on a wild adventure, discovering a dragon on their journey to return Orin to Whitestone. The turn of events was funny to her as she thought back on them. Their group hadn't returned to Whitestone before they battled the dragon alongside the dwarves of Galium. Her griffin—for Silverwing was certainly hers as much as she was his—had arrived just in time during the battle. She had been working with him for weeks before their journey, healing him of his own injuries from the battle near Tamaria. However, he was still on the mend, and one griffin to five travelers is not good math. So, he'd been left back in Tamaria.

She smiled, thinking of him at the Grand Corral with many other griffins. How she loved that silly boy. They had forged a bond like all guardians do with their griffins. Her and Silverwing's connection was unusual, however. In all the Chronicles of the Griffin Guard, no mention of a griffin bonding with more than one rider could be found. For that reason, Ellaria was part of the Guard under the strict supervision and personal training of the leader of the Guard's special missions unit, Talon Squadron.

As the breeze blew her wild red hair sideways, she thought how strange it was that she felt so at home in Whitestone. She smiled at the noise of people chattering in the market square. The sound reminded her of the hubbub in the larger city of Tamaria.

She and Tam loaded their haul onto the cart. The pair had been assigned to provision procurement duty for the week at the Grand Corral. Tam would take the cart back to the Corral while Ellaria saw to another task at the castle.

"So, you really think you can beat me, then?" she asked as Tam moved to the side of the cart, stepping into the box at the front and sitting.

Tam laughed again and shook his head. "You are relentless."

"I know," Ellaria confirmed with a smile. "I hear it's one of me greater qualities."

Tam huffed a chuckle and said, "I'll see you back at the Corral when you're done in the dungeons."

He snapped the reins and clicked to the horse who lurched into action, drawing their cart out of the market square. Ellaria watched the guardian drive the cart back toward the Grand Corral, the wheels making soft clicking noises as the wood connected with the cobblestones. She smirked and wheeled toward the castle.

Pernden leaned over the balcony and took a deep, resigned breath. They'd been at it all day, and the afternoon was growing late. Pernden's hands traced the white marble railing that kept him safely in the tower. While the day's breeze was pleasant, stray gusts posed a danger at such a height. The castle at Whitestone had been built many years ago with all care and consideration for the surrounding feats of nature.

The new king overlooked the greater Whitestone area, taking in all the hustle and bustle as people milled about their daily tasks. He still found it hard to believe himself in his position. He'd never expected to be king of Whitestone, nor had he ever held such ambitions. He had loved being the captain of the Talon Squadron.

Pernden silently cursed his blood, for his lineage was the reason he'd been removed from the Guard to stand as king. That, and the fact that his cousin Garron had been manipulated by a wicked sorcerer from Kelvur across the sea. The sorcerer had tangled his cousin's mind and tricked him into handing Whitestone over to their enemies, the orc nation of Drelek. Further revelations uncovered that the sorcerer was manipulating the orc king of Drelek as well. In a strange twist of fate, Drelek and Whitestone became allies, and Pernden became king of the latter.

He thought about Garron below in the dungeons. His heart ached. The crown of Whitestone had been passed to Pernden because the people could not trust Garron to fulfill the duty. Thus, Pernden stood in the late afternoon breeze on the balcony outside the council chamber.

"My King." A calm voice behind him stole Pernden away from his brief respite.

He turned to greet Mistress Leantz, the former Mistress of Whitestone's library. She'd been elevated to a council position after the great distress that Whitestone had undergone when the sorcerer attacked with an army of goblins and orcs. Once they'd learned the sorcerer had come from Kelvur, the council decided the wisest course of action was to bring Mistress Leantz into the fold. She was a highly respected member of their community and, with her many years in the library, had read more from the tomes and scrolls than anyone. Though their historical records on anything concerning Kelvur were limited to the ancient scribblings of wizards, she would be the one to find any information.

Pernden appreciated her presence more because she had compassion for his predicament.

"I'm sorry. Just another moment." Pernden nodded to her.

Her wisdom-wrinkled face twitched with a sympathetic smile. "I will let the others know."

Mistress Leantz gave a slight bow and disappeared beyond the heavy curtains into the council chambers.

Pernden inhaled another deep breath, looking up into the sky. *Oh, how I'd rather be flying with Rocktail right now.* He chuckled and shook his head. He had gotten far less time with his griffin of late than he liked. Kingly duties require different sacrifices than those of guardians.

With a resolved exhale, he patted the stone railing, spun around, and strode into the council meeting.

Nera sat across the large wooden table from Pernden. The knotted wood used to craft the table made the furniture a work of art. She wondered if the people gathered around her thought the same. The Council Chamber was not lavishly decorated, nor was it cold. The walls, built from the white stones the city was named after, were decorated with tapestries, woven by former residents of the castle to denote stories from their times. Nera recognized many of the fables.

She especially appreciated the one where Tally Lomern, one of the first guardians, faced a mighty giant. The impression was well conceived: Lomern raised her sword against the towering giant that squeezed her griffin in one hand and her love in the other, a look of anguish on his face. That was back when giants roamed Tarrine. Most people thought that to be more myth than fact. Giants certainly made for good stories.

Next to Nera, High Commander Mattness leaned heavily on her elbow and scratched at her brow, clearly frustrated and ready to move on. Nera nudged the High Commander. In a private conversation between the two women, the captain of the Talon Squadron had been given permission to alert the High Commander if she ever looked particularly grumpy in one of the council meetings. Mattness adjusted her position, retreating from her propped slouch and straightening backward into her seat.

As the High Commander of the Griffin Guard, her duty and responsibility was to discuss the issues of safety and war for the people. Aside from the fact that she didn't feel the need to hear about the merchants of the city and their goings-on, she didn't care for the Merchant Master, Feink. He was a rotund, balding man who always appeared sweaty, even when Mattness had interacted with him in the cold of winter. She judged him to be undisciplined. While it was said that he kept a finger on the pulse of the people's lives, she thought him to be more of a gossip.

Nera agreed with her High Commander on that point but showed greater patience for the meetings. She noticed Pernden's eyes glazing over, no longer registering Master Feink's words. Nera smirked at the king, who noticed out of the corner of his eye and shot her a disapproving look. She shook her head at him with a playful scolding.

Pernden rolled his eyes, ran his hands through his long blond hair, stretched his back, and crossed his muscular arms on his chest. "Master Feink," he interrupted the man's droning. "I think that's enough about the merchants for now."

Feink looked disappointed, as though he could have shared for another couple hours, yet he nodded to the young king and shut his mouth.

"And what of the new settlement on the Gant Sea?" asked Edford.

Pernden flinched at the man's direct question. That particular mission had not been going as well as they'd hoped. Every time Edford brought up the subject, Pernden felt the reminder like a barb poking at his inadequate abilities as king. In fairness to the elder man, Edford's responsibility was to manage communications between the parties involved in the upcoming settlement intended as a joint city for men and orcs to live at peace as a united front against outside threats.

"I have, of course, continued correspondence with Jalko, of the fisher-orcs in Calrok," Edford stated. "He assures me of their preparations to join our new combined settlement north of the Gant Sea Narrows."

"Yes, of course." Pernden nodded to the elder man as if his report were expected.

"What news of your brother in the south?" Edford prodded.

"We received a pigeon from Dahrenport yesterday. Orin expressed his deep regret at the difficulties they've faced trying to convince some people to relocate."

"Should we send someone with more experience in negotiating? Someone who would be better suited to convincing the people?"

Pernden's shoulders twitched as he held back his mounting anger. His brother Orin had faced plenty of challenges, especially in the last year. If anyone could overcome the difficulties his team faced, Orin would. Pernden could brush off much of Edford's badgering, but he would not tolerate the elder man speaking in such a way about his only living brother.

"Orin, Coal, and Ezel will accomplish what they set out to do," the king said through clenched teeth.

Nera recognized Pernden's building frustration. *I better step in,* she thought. She jumped into the conversation before Edford could continue his probing. "When I was last in Dahrenport, I found the people to be quite firm in their ways. The fishermen's guild has strict thoughts on sailing through the Narrows. Most avoid getting anywhere near them with their vessels. Aside from that, many of them have known the orcs of Drelek to be enemies all their lives. How quickly do you think they would jump to sail north of the Narrows that have protected them from the orcs of the north for generations?"

Edford sat back in his seat, raising his eyebrows as though he didn't have a good argument against Nera's logic.

"Right," Pernden affirmed, giving her a thankful nod. For a moment he took in her countenance. Her ebony skin was smooth, and the single braid all her hair twisted into was the most regal of manes. She blushed under his gaze, and her reaction to his attention shocked him back to the moment. "And anyway," he continued. "Orin said in his note that they wouldn't stay in Dahrenport much longer if they couldn't find anyone to join our cause."

Edford perked up at the news. "And where will they go? Stalford? Vandor?" He spoke the last name incredulously.

"If they must," Pernden said with finality. "We're asking people to believe in a fledgling alliance with an orc nation that has been our enemy as long as the eldest of elves have been alive. Surely, few of them even remember a time when we were not at war with Drelek, if any. These are unprecedented times."

Edford's shoulders slumped slightly. "My King. Please. I only meant to suggest that we must choose the people for the new settlement ... carefully."

Pernden couldn't believe the elder man's words. They were too much.

"Please, Edford. Please tell me how important this joint venture is for our young alliance. Where were you when we flew to Galium to fight off the sorcerer's dragon? Where were you when we fought side by side with the orcs of Calrok? Where were you when man and orc and dwarf and elf mourned our fallen comrades at the feast of Galium?"

"I meant no disrespect, my—"

"Of course you didn't! You only mean to question my every action!"

The room fell silent. Nera stared at Pernden, her brows stitched together with concern. He caught her look, and she could tell he was cursing himself for letting his frustration get the better of him.

For Edford's part, the elder man breathed deeply and sat forward. "My King," he started carefully. "I only mean to say that Jalko has expressed great pleasure with the way his people have adjusted to having the huntsman and the elf in their city."

"Merrick and Ralowyn," Nera corrected him.

"Yes." Edford quickly made the correction. "Merrick and Ralowyn have represented our peoples well among the orcs of Calrok. They are well respected."

"I imagine Merrick's friendship with Gar Karnak has a lot to do with that," Pernden said, keeping his breathing steady.

"Yes, I imagine so," Edford agreed. He took the moment of common ground to voice his true concern. "If the people we bring to build up the settlement are from less quality stock ..." Edford paused to rephrase. "If they are less respectable than Merrick and Ralowyn have proven to be, it could cause problems for our fragile alliance."

Pernden drew in a deep breath as he looked toward Nera again. She gave him a slight shrug, indicating it was a fair concern for a man in Edford's position.

"Thank you for your concerns," Pernden said to the elder man. "We shall keep them in mind."

"Thank you, my King." Edford bowed his head.

"Let it be known," Pernden continued, intentionally looking around to all who sat on the council. "I have fought and bled alongside these allies. Know that battle forges something within warriors that is not easily broken. This alliance is not as fragile as you all may think. This council session is over. Thank you for your time."

As everyone stood from their chairs and made their way to the door, Nera stole a glance back at Pernden. He mouthed, "Thank you." She flashed a brilliant smile and nodded and winked to relay that her assistance was nothing.

Pernden placed a hand to his heart as though he were catching the wink and drawing it near to comfort him in her absence.

Nera turned out the doorway and quickened her pace to catch up to High Commander Mattness. Her heart welled as if it were about to burst, and she couldn't wipe the silly grin from her face.

Parchment ruffled in the breeze that slipped through the dungeon's high window. Garron gripped the tome in his lap, holding the pages flat. Such a breeze through the window that illuminated his cell was rare, but the gust was quick and bothered him little. He scratched at his head and rolled his shoulders to crack his neck before settling back into his chapter.

A moment later a *Clink!* reverberated off the dungeon walls. Garron didn't immediately look up; he was trying to finish his page. And anyway, it would be either Dona, the woman in charge of his care, or Pernden, his cousin. Ellaria had already come by that morning, and his other cousin Orin was off to the south somewhere. They were his only visitors.

"You must have half of the Whitestone Library down here," Pernden laughed.

A low chuckle escaped Garron's lips. "I think Dona prefers it this way. If she brings me books and scrolls, she doesn't have to spend all her time entertaining me."

He heaved himself up from the small bed to greet his cousin. Garron scanned the area. Pernden was right. It did seem a rather humorous sight. He had books stacked next to the bars, while scrolls and parchments lay neatly on a small table in the corner next to some well-burned candles. Even outside his cell, Dona had stacked several more tomes and fresh candles within reach should he need to grab another and pull it into the cell with him.

"What are you reading today?" Pernden asked, leaning on the bars.

"*The Lost Notes on Nari* by Kel Joran," Garron replied with a shrug. "It's a copy of the notes found by the travelers from Last Town. Kel Joran and his company were never found, so the book is incomplete. I should like to know what happened to him."

"Sounds like a fascinating mystery," Pernden said with a half-smile.

Garron furrowed his brow, noting Pernden's demeanor. "Tell me, cousin, which of us is imprisoned?"

The prisoner smirked at his notion. In all honesty, he did not begrudge Pernden's situation, and as far as prisoners went, Garron was living quite well. No other prisoners had a dedicated caretaker like Dona, even if she frustrated him sometimes with her doting. No other prisoner was granted luxuries such as books and scrolls, candles, or even a table. Truly, he recognized the benefit of his cousin's nepotism, and he was thankful for it.

Pernden let out a long sigh. "Do you want to trade?"

Garron laughed. "I think it should be nice to walk under the noonday sun again. Or stare at the stars far above." There was an air of fond memory in his voice.

"I'm sorry," Pernden said, shaking his head. "I'm a fool."

"Well, I wasn't going to say it."

Pernden laughed. "It's just ..."

"Being king isn't all you'd hoped it would be?" Garron finished the thought.

"No. It's not that." Pernden waved off the question. "I never wanted to be king. I was happy being the captain of the Talon Squadron."

"I am sorry the burden fell to you," Garron offered, a distinct sorrow in his timbre.

Pernden grabbed his cousin's hand, which rested on the bars between them. "The blame cannot be all yours. A sorcerer from Kelvur with the power to twist the minds of men is something none of us could overcome. I fear my heart would have been weaker than yours, and I might never have been recovered."

Garron flinched. It took everything in him to keep his hand on the bar. He relished the touch from his cousin—the small show of affection proving to him that he was not completely lost and alone. In the back of his mind, though, a shadow grew. He wasn't sure he really had recovered, nor did he know if he ever would. With his other hand, Garron brushed back his shoulder-length brown hair, scratched at his stubbly beard, and reached for Pernden's shoulder.

"I thank you for this small kindness," Garron said.

"Imprisonment?"

"For my traitorous crimes? Death would have been the more reasonable punishment."

"How could I do that? So few of us are left."

Garron couldn't help but agree. All of his siblings had been killed in battles with the orcs of Drelek prior to the sorcerer's appearance. They had thought Pernden to be the last of his brothers as well, until they discovered Orin was alive. Yes, they had seen far too many of their own blood off to the Halls of Kerathane.

"Perhaps it is time to start making more of us. How is Nera anyway?" Garron teased.

Pernden pulled away from the bars. Garron regretted the comment, already missing the contact. When Pernden turned back toward him with a suppressed grin on his face, Garron continued. "She is a fine woman. A fiery warrior."

"Stop," Pernden pleaded. "With everything going on, it's been difficult to get any time alone with her."

"Are you saying she has an eye for someone else now because of your absence."

"No," Pernden blurted more defensively than he meant to. "It's just ... the responsibilities that come with being king have left little room for things such as romance."

"Not even room for a spar?" Garron gave his cousin a wry smirk. "A king must keep up his practices. He would lose his ability as a warrior if he didn't. It would be hard for the Guard to follow a king without a warrior spirit."

Pernden caught on. "Yes, you're right. That would leave Whitestone in a terrible state."

"And anyway, some sparring at the training ground might help you loose the chains of responsibility that have imprisoned your spirit."

The cousins, new king and old, sat and talked and laughed like they had when they were young. Eventually, Dona brought Garron his evening meal, more than happy to see Pernden visiting with him. Though it was a reminder of how late the day had gotten, Pernden stayed while Garron finished his meal, offering to take the dish back to the kitchen to save Dona the trouble.

Garron thanked his cousin for the visit and tossed out one more reminder for Pernden to get to the Corral for some "sparring."

When he was alone again, Garron laid his head down on his small bed and closed his eyes. A flash of light streaked across the inside of his mind. He shot up, eyes wide, murmuring to himself, "No, no, no, no, no ..."

He punched the feather pillow several times before resigning himself to another sleepless night. He sat near the small table, pulled open *The Lost Notes on Nari,* slid a candle closer, and hunched over the book in the dark cell.

Garron read two full pages of Kel Joran's transcription of an ancient Nari script before he realized he should not understand the language of the Nari. He stared hard at the unfamiliar letters inked on the page. He recognized them to be of the Nari, but he had never known the language. None had for centuries. And yet, somehow the combination of letters formulated words in his mind that he understood as clearly as the common tongue.

Confusion etched the man's face as he leaned closer to the tome and drew a candle nearer.

What magic is this?

CHAPTER THREE

THE SONS OF SILENCE

T he sea that battered the rocky slope smelled the same as it did in Kelvur. Hazkul Bern sniffed the air and tasted the salty moisture in his mouth. The waters swirled and spat foam upon the rocks where he stood. The mist produced by the heavy waves crashing into the larger rocks ahead sprayed him with cool droplets. The elf's dark hair danced in the night's breeze while he waited patiently for his spy to return from her reconnaissance in the city.

Two others sat quietly throwing dice in the bottom of their boat. If they were spotted together in Calrok, they would probably seem an odd group. Hazkul had sent their only orc into the city to watch their prey. Gilk was the only one of them that had any hope of blending into the crowds, though the tall, slender orc had covered herself almost entirely in a hooded cloak.

Hazkul watched the other two, a woman and a geldrin, play their game. Most wouldn't give them a second glance, but Hazkul knew them to be capable assassins with skills far superior to many he'd worked with in the past. That's why they were chosen for their mission—at least the woman, anyway. The geldrin was forced onto Hazkul's team, a necessity of the current state of affairs that he was not particularly pleased about.

An assignment across the sea had never been attempted before, and he needed the best with him. Well, the second and third and fourth best, if he could give them such credit. None of them matched his own caliber.

Hazkul had been a notorious assassin for half a century. His notoriety had made other would-be assassins gather to him. Thus, the Sons of Silence was born. His elite group of assassins—if they could be called that anymore, for they were an army, even having their own castle—had been well known for their ability to perform a job and keep the secrets of their benefactors. Those were the good old days, before everything in Kelvur had changed.

Hazkul gritted his teeth and tried to change the path of his thoughts. *The sun is descending,* the elf thought. *Gilk should return any time now.*

The woman, Chadwa, cursed under her breath, though it was more a growl than actual words.

"You lose again," Jilgor, the geldrin, whispered.

The sound of the crashing waves against the rocks covered any noise they made, so Hazkul had no need to correct the two. And anyway, they had anchored themselves far to the south of Calrok, knowing the fishermen would not come so far as to spot them.

Hazkul looked out to the sea, knowing where their impressive ship lay in wait. It amazed him that he could not see the mighty vessel. It was hidden by an intricate array of massive sails. They were painted the color of the sea and imbued with magic that tricked the eye. They were of no use for sailing, of course, but ran along the ship on ropes and pulleys for quick concealment and removal, which made the vessel stealthier than any he'd previously seen.

"Fwt-Foow! Fwt-Foow!"

Hazkul's pointed ears barely picked up the agreed-upon bird call from the rocks. He turned and searched the formations, looking for Gilk. It took him longer than he liked to spot the orc. *She is one of the best,* Hazkul reminded himself, granting slack for the extra time he took to put eyes on the orc.

After paddling their boat around a rocky outcropping, the crew brought the vessel close to the shore so Gilk could join them.

"So?" Hazkul cut straight to the point.

"The city is almost entirely populated by orcs." Gilk shook her head in disbelief.

"As we were told," Hazkul replied as though it were obvious.

"Right. I saw only a few goblins among them and no trolls."

"And the towers?"

"They won't be a problem." Gilk waved off the notion. "I'm not sure this city has ever been under attack."

Hazkul nodded. Gilk's assessment made sense. Calrok sat in a perfect valley where the mountains met the sea. To the north, the Scar Cliffs jutted straight into the ocean. To their west and south were impressive mountains. And to their east, the Gant Sea roared. The elf was no slouch when it came to military strategy, and even he couldn't imagine the force it would take to overcome a city so well protected by natural elements.

"And what of our prey?" the elf leader asked.

"He was easy to find. He stays in a house on the slope. Rather plain place, I thought."

Hazkul rolled his eyes. "Can we take him?"

"It should be easy. We can do it tonight."

Karnak released a hardy laugh that sounded like a roar to Merrick. The big green orc slapped the huntsman on the shoulder, nearly knocking him off the small porch.

"You better get to that cottage," he said boisterously. Realizing he was still being loud, Karnak peeked over his shoulder. Tanessa had gotten onto him only a few moments earlier. The big orc hunched and lowered his voice. "Before you get me in trouble!"

Merrick snickered as he slipped across the grass to the small cottage on the edge of the property. He settled himself into one of the chairs that sat on the even smaller porch of the cottage and waved good night to Karnak after the orc gar composed himself enough to go quietly back into the house.

Karnak's little son, Gernot, had gone to bed shortly after dinner. He gave everyone hugs good night, attempting to prolong the inevitable conclusion that he would land in bed while the grown-ups enjoyed further fellowship. The little orcling's tuft of black hair bobbed as he waddled from person to person. Merrick earned a disapproving scowl from Tanessa, Karnak's wife, for riling up the young orc. Eventually, Gernot was swept up and taken away for tuck-ins.

Tanessa and their elven guest, Ralowyn, had both turned in shortly afterward. That left Merrick and Karnak to their own devices. Merrick was a man living among orcs, and Karnak, the orc gar of Calrok, took it upon himself to show the huntsman everything that was great about his people. Merrick had enjoyed his time in the orc city immensely.

Merrick shook his head and gazed down the slope over the city of Calrok as it spread toward the Gant Sea. He had taken to sitting on the porch in the evenings, breathing in the cool evening air and smelling the sweet aroma of the pasture flowers and the coast. He always took stock of the things for which he was grateful. There was Karnak's friendship, of course. Never in Merrick's wildest dreams, sleeping under the open sky on his many youthful hunts, did he imagine he would be friends with an orc of Drelek—let alone a gar.

There was also Ralowyn, of course. Beautiful Ralowyn. Merrick glanced around quickly as though someone might have heard his thought. She was surely beautiful. Merrick was often struck by the presence of the slender, pale elf with silvery hair from Loralith. He was glad she was in Calrok with him. More than glad.

He had grown fond of her. He did not know how to tell if she reciprocated his feelings. How could she? He was a simple huntsman from Tamaria—a nobody, really.

And she is ... His thoughts trailed off. He had no words to describe her.

He was also thankful for Valurwind. The giant astral falcon from another plane came to mind as he absently thumbed the cool stone figurine in his pocket. Over the last month since their arrival, Merrick had been able to train with her, and the two had grown closer, becoming quite the duo. When he'd first ridden her, he found soaring through the air a clumsy and terrifying event. He and Valurwind had enjoyed a marked improvement in their abilities together training with the Scar Squadron, Drelek's elite group of wyvern-riders. The Scar Cliffs provided the perfect training ground to produce fierce orc warriors and a confident astral falcon-rider. Merrick finally understood the way Valurwind moved and leaned comfortably into her turns. He trusted her. She wouldn't let him fall.

Merrick's ponderings on gratitude wandered to Karnak's household. They made Merrick feel part of their family. Tanessa was as patient an orc as the man had met in Calrok. Furthermore, she was kind and showed him and Ralowyn overflowing hospitality. She had said many times that their stay in the cottage was of no imposition, and she proved her generosity by having Merrick and Ralowyn at the house for meals every day. Gernot was a rambunctious orcling who reminded Merrick of some of his little brothers. The orcling would race to Merrick, his hair tuft waggling on top of his head, and jump into the man's arms, ready to wrestle.

The man gripped the armrest of the old wooden porch chair and stood. He breathed deeply, inhaling the night, and smiled as he took a final look over the pasture of the lovely home.

Yes, he thought, thumbing the ridged wood of the door as he slipped inside, ready for rest. *I've got it pretty good.*

The scream tore through the night and ripped Merrick from his sleep. He stumbled to his feet and staggered toward the door in a drowsy stupor. The first noise could have been the result of a nightmare. Merrick had experienced them off and on since the battle in the orc capitol of Ruk.

A booming roar snapped him fully awake. He had no doubts in the reality of that mighty cry. Merrick grabbed his spear from beside the door and burst into the night.

Outside, all seemed calm, until a crash resounded inside Karnak's home. Merrick rushed across the grass. Just before he reached the porch, the door exploded outward. A body flew in his direction, and Merrick whipped his spear around instinctively, cracking it against the head of the flying body with an awkward *Cthunk!* The creature fell to the ground, unmoving.

Merrick had never seen such a being. It looked about the size of an orc but had an appearance of stone. The huntsman reached down and rolled the creature over to get a better look at its face. It too was like stone, with orange and white patches of moss growing where hair should have been. He knelt there, no less confused than when he was startled awake. When he hit the creature, it hadn't felt like cracking his spear against stone. He carefully prodded at the creature's face. It had a certain crunch to the touch but still had give, as if the skin had dried and cracked, leaving stony layers.

"Wait!"

Merrick snapped his head in the direction of the house. It was Karnak's voice, but he wasn't outside, and he wasn't speaking to the huntsman. Ralowyn ran up beside the huntsman as Merrick hopped to his feet and bolted into the house, leaving her to ponder the strange creature lying on the ground.

As Merrick rounded into the main room, he stopped short when Karnak raised a hand to halt him. The huntsman had always known Karnak to be a fierce orc. He'd gotten to see the big orc gar's friendly side in their time together as well, but the look on Karnak's face was one he'd never seen before.

Fear.

The huntsman followed his friend's unwavering gaze. There by the table stood a tall, dark-featured elf. His long black hair blew out the edges of his hood, disappearing against his even darker garments. What the elf held in his grasp made Merrick's heart sink.

Gernot ...

The elf looked surprised at Merrick's entrance. Then his eyebrow lifted, and a smirk scrawled across his moon-white face. He glanced past Merrick, seeming to answer his own question about the huntsman's appearance. The elf bobbed a quiet chuckle and shook his head.

"Gilk and I will have to have a conversation later," he said lightly.

"Let go of my son!" Karnak growled but stayed perfectly still.

The tone of his father's voice scared Gernot even more. A heartbreaking whimper escaped the little orc's lips.

Merrick reacted with a single step forward before the elf said, "Now, let's not get hasty," and pulled Gernot closer. It was then that Merrick noticed the intruder's posture. He held a dagger close to the young orc's throat, but the weapon must have been painted black, for Merrick saw only a glint of light shimmer on the sharp edge of the blade.

Karnak tensed, shooting a desperate hand out to stay the huntsman. "I don't know what you want here, elf, but my son has nothing to do with it."

The elf let out a half chuckle, shaking his head. "How is my friend out there?" he asked with a nod toward the open door. He let a brief silence fill the room, while Ralowyn stepped in through the door with a quiet gasp. Her fists curled around magical staff. Purple energy buzzed and swirled from the pinnacle of the silver staff.

"I see ..." The intruder shrugged. "In fairness, he wasn't really my friend—more of a necessary acquaintance. You know how that is."

Merrick heard Tanessa suppressing terrified sobs behind him in the hallway. The rest of them stood in a silent showdown.

The elf intruder's face twitched as he regarded his current predicament. It appeared that much of the night hadn't gone the way he'd hoped. He clearly didn't like the odds with which he was currently presented. After a moment, he grinned again.

"Well, this has been quite the eventful evening, eh Tyke?" he asked, leaning over Gernot. The intruder glanced toward the door that opened up to the cool night. "It appears this night wasn't going to go my way no matter which way we sliced it." He gave a slight chuckle. "Lucky for me, you were out of bed, Tyke. Why is that?" he asked with a frown.

"Wait—" Karnak started.

"At-tat-tat," the intruder scolded Karnak, halting him. "I think we'll be going now."

"Wait!"

In a flash, the elf twirled, reached into his pocket, and threw a jar to the middle of the room. Ralowyn raised her staff to launch an attack at the fleeing elf who dove out the nearby window with Gernot. Before she could loose the magical energy, the jar exploded with a concussive shock and filled the whole house with thick, black smoke.

The blast knocked all of them back into walls and sent the table and chairs flying in all directions.

Karnak came to, his vision blurred and his head ringing. He rolled to his side as best he could, his head lolling heavily. As he felt along the floor, he squinted to clear his sight. Everything was covered in a thick black dust. He crawled as fast as he could to the hallway and found his wife.

"Tanessa! Tanessa!" Karnak roared.

He lifted her close to himself, shaking her.

"Mfff ..." she let out. "Wha—"

"Are you alright?" Karnak hollered over the ringing in his ears.

Tanessa shook out the daze. "I'm ... I'm okay," she said, but then clarity struck her. "Gernot! No! No, no, no, no!" she whimpered, groping at Karnak in an attempt to get up and find her son.

"I know. I know," Karnak said, squeezing her tighter in his comforting embrace. He was unsure if he were trying to comfort his wife or himself as they knelt in the dust and lingering smoke. "I'll get him back. I promise."

Karnak kissed his wife's face, streaked where tears revealed her beautiful green skin beneath caked dust. He stood and padded toward a side table in their room where he retrieved his battle axe, *Dalkeri,* Fire Storm. He cursed himself for not grabbing it when he initially heard Gernot scream.

What could I have done even if I had? Karnak had barely fought off the creature that looked like stone before the elf emerged from the shadows with his slimy hands holding the orcling. Karnak was sure of one thing: he would bring a storm down on the heads of those who had taken his son.

He hurried to the other room where Tanessa was trying to wake Merrick. Karnak knelt beside his friend. "Merrick! I need you to wake up!"

Karnak shook his friend back to consciousness. Merrick opened his eyes and tried to regain control of his head. The huntsman looked at the orc gar blearily, trying to focus in the dark. Karnak gripped the man's shoulders tighter. "Brother, I need your help."

Events flooded back to the man, and his eyes snapped open. "Gernot!" he coughed.

"Yes," Karnak nodded. "I need your help to find him."

They looked toward the doorway as a purple light shone through the opening. Ralowyn was outside, working some spell over the fallen creature. Karnak hurried to join her.

Merrick blinked wildly and shook his head. Tanessa stayed to help him up.

"What is this creature?" Karnak asked Ralowyn.

"I do not know," she said. "But it is still alive."

"Can you wake it?"

"I do not know."

"What do you know?" the orc roared.

"Karnak ..." Tanessa said from behind him.

The big orc took a deep breath and balled his fists. He released them and ran them through his dark hair before tightening the knot on top of his head.

"I need information. I need to know where they took him," he said, doing his best to stay calm.

"I do not know how to give you that," Ralowyn said. The pain on her face was sincere. She would have given anything to help him.

"Over here!" Merrick shouted. The huntsman had wandered around the house. "I've got tracks in the mud here."

Karnak sprinted to him. "Elves are so light-footed, how did you—"

"These tracks are big. Like our friend over there. If we can figure out what direction he came from, maybe we can find which direction the elf went."

"Yes!" Karnak agreed, looking about.

"Wait!" Merrick said, raising a hand to halt the orc. "Let me look before we make more tracks."

The big orc hunched impatiently. He knew Merrick was right, of course, but it didn't relieve the anxiousness that threatened to burst from his mighty chest. He watched the huntsman move slowly and methodically scan the ground. The man followed the tracks out of the mud. Somehow, Merrick perceived more tracks through disfigured blades of grass. Were the circumstances less dire, Karnak would have been enthralled by the huntsman's ability.

"I think they went this way."

"Let's go!" Karnak blurted. He yelled over his shoulder to Ralowyn and Tanessa, "Tie that one up. Use a lot of rope. He was strong!"

Karnak ran after Merrick. They sprinted through the darkness, following an unknown trail that led southeast. They slowed occasionally as Merrick traced the ground to ensure they hadn't lost the tracks.

As the sun teased the horizon, painting the sky in pinks, Merrick stopped. Karnak's heart sank in his chest. "Did you lose the tracks?"

"No," Merrick said, not looking up from the ground. "There were more."

"More?"

"More people."

Karnak watched Merrick walk in what seemed to him a random circle.

"One followed the coastline. Multiple times," Merrick observed. "Ah!" He shuffled closer to the rocky ridge ahead.

Karnak followed. "What is it?"

"They all seem to come from over the ridge," Merrick shouted as he hustled up the slope.

When they reached the other side, they found where the Gant Sea met the cliffs that formed the eastern edge of the continent of Tarrine.

"No ..." Merrick whispered.

"No!" Karnak roared.

They saw a small rowboat floating away in the distance. Karnak gripped *Dalkeri* as the axe blazed to life in a ball of orange flame. The orange stone in the center of the axe hummed with power. Karnak mustered all his strength and hurled the axe as far as he could over the water.

The axe flew a great distance but nowhere near the boat that paddled out toward open sea. *Dalkeri* soared through the air like a magic missile before it finally slowed and dipped toward the waves. Just before it plunged into the sea, the axe slowly floated back toward the orc who knelt in defeat on the edge of the cliff. Karnak heard the hum of Fire Storm as it flew back to him. Not looking up from the ground, he lifted one hand into the air and caught it.

"Where are they going?" Merrick asked under his breath.

Karnak looked up. The huntsman was right. *Where could they be going?*

He saw no ship in the distance. The small boat could not be trusted for a voyage on the open sea, especially if they were going south toward the Gant Sea Narrows. They'd be swallowed by the waves or crushed against the many islands. Karnak looked down over the waves that crashed into the rocks below them, imagining his poor son being smashed on a similar one somewhere in the Narrows.

Karnak bellowed a mighty roar. "We need to get back. I need to get Ker!" the orc said, speaking of his wyvern.

"I'll call Valurwind and follow the boat so they don't disappear," Merrick nodded.

"Good idea! I'll run as fast as I—"

The bushes to their right rustled. Karnak lifted *Dalkeri* in front of him as it blazed to life again. Merrick slid alongside the great orc, taking up his own ready posture.

Whoever was hiding behind the bushes was about to have a very bad morning.

CHAPTER FOUR

TAVERN TALES

O rin slumped into his chair at the table in the corner of the tavern. The place wasn't bursting at the seams by any means, so his companions likely heard his entire conversation with the two sailors that just left the tavern. The smells of biscuits and breakfast remnants permeated the room. Orin groaned and rubbed his temples, preparing himself for his friends' questions.

"Not so good on that one either, eh?" Coal asked, sitting across from Orin.

Another sigh pressed out of the man. Orin ran his hands through his close-cut hair and shook off the disappointment. "Not so good," he replied to the black-haired dwarf.

Coal pulled at the braid in his long beard, his other hand gripping an empty mug firmly planted on the table. "I'm not thinking we're going to be finding the folks you were hoping for here," the dwarf said.

A scrawny gnome sat in the chair beside him. Unlike his bearded friend, the deep gnome was hairless—bald to the top. An assortment of runic tattoos covered his greyish skin. The gnome's hands swirled in a quick flurry.

"Aye," Coal nodded. "Ezel says that—"

"I know what he said." Orin stopped the dwarf.

When they started traveling together, Orin discovered that Ezel was a mute. For a long time, Coal had translated for the gnome. Though, having spent so much time together, Orin had learned much of Ezel's sign language.

He still wondered what had happened to Ezel. The griffin guardian had met few gnomes, and all of them had been surface gnomes at that. The couple he'd met before Ezel had been able to speak just fine. Orin assumed it had something to do with the scar across the gnome's neck, though the man had never pressed for information about that either. Ezel was a jovial companion, and Orin figured that if the gnome wished him to know about his past, he would tell the guardian.

Orin leaned forward. "He's right. We can't stay here in Dahrenport. We need to move on. No one here is willing to go north of the Narrows. Why would they?"

"The promise of trade with Whitestone seems a good enough reason to me," Coal said, finally pushing away his empty mug. "They'd be building a city where their fish had buyers lined up—like Crossdin does for Galium in the west."

"They're scared," Ezel signed.

"I know that," Coal flourished back stubbornly.

"Most of these folks have lived their entire lives avoiding the Narrows," Orin put in. "Living so near to rocky islands, these people know their dangers better than any. Sailing straight through the Narrows must seem quite the gamble for them."

"Not to mention, they're afraid of orcs," Ezel added.

"Yes. That does present a challenge," the man admitted. "These people have no idea what we went through in the north. The idea of an alliance with Drelek sounds like a tall tale to most of them. Too many have met my words with laughter."

Orin leaned on the wooden table, feeling a knot poke the bottom of his left elbow. His right elbow rested in a sticky spot, but he was too worn out to care. He pressed his face into his hands.

"I'm telling you; these ones don't have a proper understanding for the opportunity," Coal said, swinging around on his chair looking for a tavern aide to bring him another drink.

"Did you find us a vessel?" Orin asked, not looking up from his hands.

"Aye," Coal replied. "We leave in an hour."

Coal finally got the attention of a young woman who was passing out mugs to a table in the middle of the tavern. Most of the tables were empty as the fishing boats had gone out early, but several workers enjoyed their breakfast at the north docks tavern.

"An hour?" Orin popped up, eyeing his dwarven friend.

Coal turned back to him sheepishly. "I didn't expect that last one to go well."

"Thanks for the confidence," Orin said, grabbing his own mug that sat in front of him, untouched.

"Well, you can't blame me," Coal said, raising his hands in defense. "This town is filled with captains who have bigger ears than brains. They'll listen to a good plan, but you can't make them know it's good."

"That's not fair," Ezel scolded him.

"You're right. You're right." The dwarf's hands rose in surrender. "All I'm saying is you need to find folks that need it as bad as we do."

"Someone who needs to join hands with orcs from Drelek to establish a new city by the sea? Orcs who, according to most of them, still star in monster stories they tell their children?"

46

"I didn't say they wouldn't be desperate," Coal shrugged. "Ah, thank you, lass!" he said, taking a huge mug from the tavern girl.

She peeked past the dwarf and cocked an eyebrow to Ezel. "You need anything, honey?"

"No, thank you," Ezel signed.

Orin was pretty sure she had no idea what that meant, but Ezel gave enough visual cues that she caught the gist. She smiled and sauntered off.

"How does he do that?" Coal said, dumbfounded. "All the girls like him."

"He's better looking than you," Orin said, taking another swig.

"What? Look at this beard! This is a glorious dwarven beard. Among my people, I'm a highly desirable bachelor!"

"Yikes," Orin said, scrunching his face in pity for all the dwarven women out there.

"They think I'm cute," Ezel signed with a smug grin. He used both hands to lift the mug to his lips, his wide eyes squinting with amusement.

"He's hardly bigger than a halfling female, and most of them could lift his scrawny hide with one arm. Might not be an ounce of muscle on him," Coal argued.

"Like he said, he's cute," Orin laughed.

The three friends had a much-needed good time around the table. Their mission to find people willing to settle a new city near the sea in the north was not going well. In that moment, they enjoyed a reprieve from the disappointment. They joked with each other and laughed heartily.

Coal even called the tavern girl back to tell her stories of their exploits. The dwarf got so into it, others around the tavern listened in. Ezel, always a good sport, used some of his magic to accentuate the tales. His runic tattoos burst into a blue glow, matching the faery fire in his eyes. Blue wisps of magical energy floated around, lifting mugs and plates into the air and creating a spectacle for the onlookers, while Coal battled the imaginary beasts.

Orin watched his friends entertain the tavern folk. With nothing more they could do in Dahrenport, having a little fun was in perfect order.

Their trip following the coastline south to Stalford had gone as smoothly as one can, skirting through the Gant Sea's unpredictable waters. Coal and Ezel were seasoned sailors and jumped into an easy rhythm with the crew of the *Lorna*. The crew didn't require payment since the captain was happy to escort a member of the fabled Griffin Guard of Whitestone—surely eager to let everyone know how special his vessel was if it was good enough for the Guard—but Orin and the others were happy to pitch in where they could. Unlike the other two, Orin had little experience on a boat—his only time ever having been on Coal and Ezel's river boat, the *Lady Leila*—and that had not been the smoothest of sailings.

Arriving in Stalford, however, was something he wouldn't soon forget. The ships there were huge compared to the ones in Dahrenport. They seemed massive to his untrained eye. They were real sea vessels, designed to brave the wild waters around Vandor and the open waters east of Half Moon Bay. Orin thought some of them were sturdy enough to cross the sea to Kelvur, but he was no sailor. He wasn't sure that trek was possible for anyone. The only Kelvurian he knew about had used magic mirrors to enter Tarrine.

Soon enough, Orin found himself in the same situation as he had in Dahrenport: frustrated at his efforts and sitting across the table from his friends. The tavern in Stalford, *The Weary Whale*, despite its name, was much livelier. They sat at a table crammed into the corner. Boisterous conversations filled the room from the crowded tables. With so many patrons, the place had a musty smell that made Orin push away his drink.

"Not going to finish that?" Coal asked hopefully.

"No." Orin shook his head. "I'm done."

"That was a loaded 'done,'" Coal said as he traded his empty mug for Orin's.

"I feel like we've been here before," he replied.

"We have. Yesterday. And the day before that. And the day before that. And the—"

"He gets it." Ezel stopped the dwarf with a quick flick of his hands.

Orin rolled his eyes. "It's the same thing over and over again."

"We're going to find someone," the gnome signed, his face full of optimism.

"If we look in the right place," Coal signed to the gnome.

"What's that supposed to mean?" Orin asked.

Coal flinched. He and Ezel had spent years having side conversations. Sometimes he forgot Orin understood them.

"All I mean by it is that you're looking for people in the wrong place."

"Where else should I find fishermen and dock masters to help establish a new fishing city?" Orin leaned forward, his irritation evident.

"He means that these folks already have a life here," Ezel jumped in.

"Right," the dwarf nodded. "Like I said before, you need folks who need it."

"Desperate," Orin muttered to himself, recalling what Coal had said back in Dahrenport.

"Right. Desperate folks are willing to make drastic changes, hoping that desperate measures will change their fortunes," the dwarf said matter-of-factly. He took a long draw from his mug, leaving thick foam on his black mustache. He smiled when he came up for air, thinking himself rather wise in that moment.

"And where do we find these desperate people?" Orin asked, genuinely hoping Coal had an answer.

"Well, I've been thinking about that," the dwarf said, shooting a glance at Ezel.

The gnome looked at him as though he were crazy, but as he realized Coal's line of thought, Ezel's face contorted. "*No. Absolutely not!*" he signed at the dwarf.

"They've got nowhere else to go," Coal shrugged. He turned to Orin. "I think I may know of some folks who would be just desperate enough for our mission."

"Who?" Orin asked slowly, not sure he liked where the possibility was leading.

"I think it's time we introduce you to some old friends of ours."

CHAPTER FIVE

SHOWDOWN AT THE GRAND CORRAL

S hadows danced across the training field at the Grand Corral as griffin guardians flew through the sky in training patterns and aerial sparring. The bright sun formed contrasting silhouettes into dreamlike action sequences on the patchy grass below.

Nera soared through the air on the back of her griffin, Shadowpaw. She wasn't the largest griffin in the guard, but she had a fierce heart—a quality she shared with her rider. Nera believed, when the two had been paired years before, that exact feature bonded them. Shadowpaw's raven-black feathers ruffled as her wings cut through the air and twitched ever so slightly, sending the duo into an unexpected dive. Nera leaned into it without reservation. She'd given Shadowpaw her complete trust years ago.

With a few flaps of her powerful wings, Shadowpaw lifted into a diagonal angle, shooting to the right.

Nera looked over her shoulder, her big black braid whipping in the wind, and laughed. She saw Ellaria and Silverwing gaining on them, but Shadowpaw's erratic maneuvers kept their pursuers from lining up a shot.

Ellaria glowed with a magical energy, an arrow of pure green light nocked on her bowstring, poised for the moment her aim lined up with Nera. The Talon Squadron's captain rolled her shoulders, adjusting the round shield that protected her back. Ellaria had learned to form her magical arrows with blunt tips, but the impact still hurt if one took the full force without armor or protection. Nera didn't plan on getting struck at all.

The game was simple. Nera and Shadowpaw needed to fly to a marked white stone jutting high above the tree canopy at the edge of Whitestone Forest and then return to the Grand Corral without being hit by one of Ellaria's magic arrows. Ellaria's goal was to hit her captain with a faux killing blow before Nera reached the Corral.

It seemed simple enough, but Nera had years of experience flying with Shadowpaw, while Ellaria had only been flying griffin-back for a few months. She and Silverwing had a strong bond that they'd formed through adversity. It was the strongest way to bond guardians with their griffins and the reason training new guardians was filled with rigorous challenges. Much could still be said for experience, though.

Shadowpaw twisted again, sending the pair careening to the left. Nera smiled. She loved the feeling of flying. She and Shadowpaw merged as one in their movements when they rode the winds. Nera glanced back, catching a determined look on Ellaria's face as Silverwing adjusted his angle.

The more experienced guardian turned toward Whitestone Forest, isolating the designated rock formation. The monumental slab of white granite rose high above the trees, as though it were king over the forest. The captain chuckled at the notion. It wasn't even the largest of the stone giants that peppered the forest and the surrounding hills of Whitestone, but its unique face and its proximity to the Grand Corral made it the destination for many such chases.

Silverwing had been injured in battle and hadn't regained his previous speed. Likely, he never would. Prior to the griffin's injury, though, he had been the fastest in the Guard, so he remained a force to be reckoned with. Knowing that Silverwing was faster than Shadowpaw and that Ellaria was a capable bow-woman even without her enhanced magic, the duo couldn't dash straight for the monument.

Nera jerked sideways as an arrow of pure magical energy sizzled past her right shoulder.

"Time to move," she said to Shadowpaw.

The black griffin banked right, and they dropped like a sack of stones. As soon as Silverwing began his dive, Shadowpaw flared her wings out wide and flapped with several mighty beats shooting her and Nera high into the air.

After a few more dodging, acrobatic moves, they drew near to the edge of the forest. Nera smirked. It was time to show Ellaria a new trick—or rather a very old one. Shadowpaw dipped low as if they planned to fly directly into the trees.

Ellaria hesitated, forcing Silverwing to slow. Nera and Shadowpaw disappeared into the tree canopy. Ellaria's jaw tightened, her blazing red hair blowing across her face in the wind. A moment later, she leaned into the dive with Silverwing. Once they entered the trees, they could see nothing. Shades of green bounced around tree branches and the forest floor.

Meanwhile, Nera and Shadowpaw flapped up the opposite side of the giant white stone. Shadowpaw clicked her front talons on the top of the monument, the requirement before heading back to the Corral. With a push of her back paws, the griffin launched through the air at a renewed speed directly toward the Grand Corral.

By the time Ellaria and Silverwing realized the deception and popped up to the top of the monument, Nera and Shadowpaw were halfway home.

Nera laughed at the team far behind them. Ellaria had done well in training. She was capable, and at this point, Nera had no problem taking her on any mission that might come up.

While Ellaria had proven to be a capable woman, humility always makes a good lesson for a guardian. When soldiers think they're invincible, they make mistakes.

Nera sat back in her saddle as Shadowpaw carried them into the Grand Corral in a relaxed glide.

As the large gates to the Grand Corral opened before him, Pernden released a sigh of relief. One of the trainees on guard duty watched the king curiously. Pernden nodded to him with a grateful smile. "Smells like home," he said.

"Welcome home, my King," the trainee said.

Pernden heard a *Thwap!* behind him as another guard hit the one who'd spoken to him.

"Are you dumb? The king lives in the castle."

"He said it smelled like home to him."

"So you say, 'Welcome home'? I can't believe ..."

Pernden chuckled as the young guards' voices faded. He strolled across the grounds, taking in the precious sight. His kingly duties had kept him away from the Corral far too long. He watched the shadows dance across the field for a while, and then he saw her.

Nera swirled her spear, *Santoralier*, Lightning Rider, over her head and spun closer to the wild redhead defending herself with a thin, slightly curved sword. It was a standard issue sword, but hers glowed with a green aura.

Crack! Boom!

The strikes and parries sounded like thunder as the two magics collided. Pernden neared, watching the spectacle.

Nera dove to the right and, in the same motion, swiped her spear across Ellaria's calf, dropping her to her knee. Before Ellaria could stand again, Nera pounced on the woman and pressed her spear against her back. Ellaria's green magic dissipated as she scrunched her face in disappointment and blew her red hair out of her face. She looked up from her defeat, her emerald eyes falling on the nearby king. Ellaria quickly shifted herself to regard him.

"No, please," Pernden said. "None of that now."

Ellaria stood to greet him while Nera eyed the king.

Pernden advanced. "How is our new guardian doing?" he asked, eager to greet his friends.

Ellaria shifted uneasily; the green stone tied around her neck glinted in the sunlight. "As you can see, I still have much to learn."

"Ha!" Pernden responded with a laugh. "I'm pretty sure everyone feels that way when sparring with Nera."

His eyes shifted to the captain, falling on her with an entirely different look. Her dark skin glistened with a light misting of sweat. He always wondered how she looked so beautiful after sparring. *Maybe it's the sparring that inclines my eyes toward her,* Pernden thought. As he studied her, though, he knew his attraction was multifaceted. She was a beautiful woman. Her smile widened as he stared at her.

"What brings the king to the Grand Corral?" Nera asked, trying to stop his gawking.

"Ah, yes. Well," Pernden composed himself. "My cousin thought it would be good for me to get some exercise."

"Oh?" Nera gave him a sideways glance. She slowly stepped to the side, adjusting *Santoralier* in her grasp.

"Yes," Pernden continued. "I could hardly disagree with his logic. It wouldn't be prudent for a king to lose his battle readiness, after all. What kind of leader would that make him?"

"That seems a fair point," she said, circling wide to the king's side and nodding sympathetically to the notion. "Should I call a sparring partner for you, or did you have someone specific in mind." Nera gave him a sideways shrug.

Pernden turned to face her and keep her in front of him. "Well," he started. "I thought I might spar with you. If you were available for such a thing, of course."

Ellaria slowly stepped away from the two, shaking her head and rolling her eyes in amusement.

"Oh, I see," Nera said, pressing her lips together as though she finally understood. She lowered her golden spear into a comfortable ready position. Vibrations emanated from the yellow stone in the center of the finely crafted weapon. Arcs of electrical energy bounced from it. "Fortunate timing for you then."

"And why is that?" Pernden asked, sliding his sword, *Wintertide,* from its sheath.

"Well, I am already tired from a hard day's training," Nera smirked.

Pernden laughed inwardly, tightening his jaw to avoid showing his amusement. He stared at her again. *Why does this woman charge me so?* he wondered.

Nera continued, "I'll try to take it easy on you."

"Give me everything you've got," Pernden said with a glint in his eyes.

Ellaria sat on the patchy grass to watch, enjoying their banter.

The two stood absolutely still, the only movement being the slight pulsations of their magic-imbued weapons.

Pernden moved first, not wanting to lose the advantage since Nera recovered her strength with every passing second. He lunged forward, point first. Nera batted his sword away and stepped to the right, bringing her spear into an arc and swiftly driving it downward. Pernden swiped his thin curved sword upward to meet the counterstrike. The weapons collided with a spray of ice and lightning before the two spun away from each other.

Nera jumped forward reaching her spear out, shooting arcs of blinding yellow energy at him. Pernden swirled *Wintertide*, catching the energy with an icy shield that shattered into flakes. In a flash, Nera's spear was upon him. Pernden sliced sideways and rolled. Nera didn't let up. She attacked with a combination of sweeping strikes, jabbing and delivering arcing swipes. Pernden parried away every single one, his feet dancing in the grass while he deftly maneuvered into a better position.

Upon the last parry, Pernden smiled.

"Not bad for a rusty king," Nera teased.

"It seems you may have overstated your fatigue," he shot back.

"Let's find out."

Pernden returned to the fray with his own set of strikes. He sliced right and stepped closer to Nera while her spear was out wide to block. Pernden tucked his sword in under the spear. Nera attempted to bring *Santoralier* back in while she danced out of the way of the king's flurry—and a flurry it was. *Wintertide* let off icy blades that crashed against her leg and then her side.

Nera grimaced. She dove to the side, rolling away from another incoming blade of ice that flew through the air. The captain raised *Santoralier* high above her head, magical energy buzzing through the spear, and then slammed the point down.

Electric arcs shot out from the spear lashing at Pernden like whips.

Pernden raised *Wintertide* in front of himself, holding it out like a shield. He focused all his energy on the weapon as it formed a barrier of pure ice. The enchanted sword drew most of the blazing yellow arcs toward itself, but one snuck past the barrier, striking the king.

"Ahh!" Pernden hollered.

Nera snatched her spear from the ground, halting its magical outburst. "A-are you okay?" she asked as she ran to his side.

The king held his shoulder, rubbing and rotating it with a wince. The ice barrier had fallen to the ground, and he held his sword at his side.

Nera stepped close and reached for his shoulder, inspecting him as the golden yellow light flickered from her eyes. "I'm sorry," she said. "I didn't mean to—"

"It's alright," Pernden comforted her. His words faded as he recognized their closeness.

Nera's hand slipped from his shoulder to his chest as she pressed closer. A deep smile surfaced.

Pernden smiled back, his own hand unconsciously sliding to Nera's back and drawing her even closer.

When their faces were only inches apart, Nera whispered, "Did I win again?"

Pernden breathed out a slight chuckle. *How are you so beautiful?* he thought. But he said, "It seems to me that I'm the one winning right now."

Nera's grin grew, and she bit at her bottom lip. "Is that so?" she inched closer.

"Oh, it's so," Pernden whispered back.

How many times had they been in such a moment? Pernden had loved this fierce woman for years. They had danced around their feelings for so long. *I've been such a fool*, he thought, staring at the gorgeous woman in his embrace. *Not this time*. He meant to kiss her, right then and there, and he didn't care who saw.

"Ahem!"

The sound jolted the king from his trance. He pried his eyes away from Nera's, pulling on all the strength he had to turn toward the sound.

Edford stood several feet away, bowing slightly, looking rather embarrassed.

"I'm sorry to interrupt, my King," Edford apologized.

Suddenly, Pernden was flooded with emotions. He remembered the last time he and Nera had been interrupted in the Corral. Then, it had been Master Melkis, a man who had held Pernden's deepest respect, who had essentially raised him. The old bearer of *Wintertide*.

A sickly feeling rose in his stomach as rage overtook the ecstasy he'd been experiencing with Nera, before sadness at the memory of his old mentor toppled both emotions.

"I ..." Pernden couldn't get any words out.

Nera straightened, still holding onto him. Concern etched her face.

Pernden shook his head as though he were fine. "Yes?" he continued. Then he shifted. "How did you find me?"

"Again, sir, I apologize for the intrusion. Dona was in the kitchen, and I asked if she had seen you for lunch. She told me you had chosen to skip the meal because you wanted to get some sparring in at the Grand Corral. Of course, I remember how your cousin had withered during his time under the scourge of the sorcerer from Kelvur. I partly wanted to ensure that you were, in fact, well and practicing here at the Corral and—"

Pernden waved a hand at him. "Please, Edford. What is it?"

"I've just received a raven from Calrok. Jalko has some questions about details for the unified settlement that require a swift response."

Pernden sighed. His shoulders slumped, and he turned a pleading glance toward Nera. The only help she offered was a sympathetic smile. *Why does this always happen?* Pernden thought.

She leaned close to his cheek and whispered, "Don't worry. I'm not going anywhere."

Her gentle touch and her breath on his cheek made his heart flutter. She turned and walked away from him, looking over her shoulder with a coy smile.

That woman may just stop my heart from beating, Pernden thought with a shake of his head. His long blond hair flipped in the breeze as he turned and marched past Edford toward the Corral gate.

"Let's get this over with then," he grumbled, and off the men went.

Nera caught Ellaria's wry grin out of the corner of her eye and checked herself. She pushed Ellaria with a playful elbow.

"That was quite the display," Ellaria teased.

"Stop," Nera said brushing past her.

"Should I have been taking notes?"

"Stop." Nera turned with an embarrassed grin of her own. She didn't slow her pace.

"Was I supposed to be paying attention to the sparks of *Santoralier* or the sparks between you and Pernden?"

"Stop!" Nera's command was accompanied by a laugh.

"A bit shy on it, eh?" Ellaria teased as the women made their way to the dining hall.

The sun sank outside the dungeon's high window as Garron transferred the flame from one candle to another. Dona had been by only moments earlier to take his plate and light a candle for him. Transferring the flame was deliberate work. If he messed it up and accidentally lost his flame, he'd have no light to read by for the rest of the night and would likely give into his exhaustion and fall asleep. He couldn't do that. Plus, though it was his prison, Garron did his best not to get wax all over the place. He took pride in caring for his cell. As strange as the notion was, it was his home.

Before he even settled into the chair next to his small table, he heard the metallic *clunk* of the dungeon entrance ring through the place. Garron leaned against the bars, awaiting whoever would appear around the corner. He smiled at his cousin.

"Why do you look so disappointed?" Garron asked. "Did you spend all day cooped up in the castle again?"

"No," Pernden shook his head with a laugh. "I took your great advice and went to the Grand Corral for some sparring, but the crown duties followed me!"

Garron laughed along. "Strange how many men would think the crown some great treasure, but the one that wears it views it as shackles."

Pernden scratched at his head and ran his hand through his hair. "I keep doing that," he said sheepishly. "Sorry."

"No," Garron said, tightening his chin and shaking his head. "You're not alone, cousin. I read some time back about a king who hated the crown so much, he no longer wore it. He wanted

61

people to see him as a man like everyone else. Is that why you don't wear it?" His eyebrows cocked as he eyed his cousin.

Pernden shook his head. "I don't wear it because it doesn't feel right—like it's not mine. It was never supposed to be mine. I should still be flying on griffin-back every day. Out there," he waved his hand to indicate the whole sky. "I should be with the Talon Squadron. Training in the Corral. Working on our formations. I should be with the Guard."

"With Nera?"

Pernden's expression turned stony. "I'm serious."

"So am I," Garron said with a pop of his brow.

The king took in a deep resigned breath, drawing nearer to the cell and dropping into his usual chair. He rubbed his temples, clearly overwhelmed. Garron was sympathetic to Pernden's plight, just as his cousin was for his own.

Garron remembered a similar tension while he was still the prince and a member of the Griffin Guard. Honestly, he had not figured out a way to sever that tension, and whether his cousin knew it or not, Pernden would not likely be the first to come up with a resolution. Warrior and king or king and warrior? The crown or the helm?

"Did you at least get to see her?"

Pernden's shoulders bounced with a chuckle. "You are relentless, you know?"

"I sit in this cell all day, every day. I do some training. Ellaria comes for her daily visit. I read. I talk to Dona. I read more. I train again. I eat whatever Dona brings me. I read some more. And I ponder about my dear cousin's love life so I can torment him when he visits me. It's more fulfilling than you might expect."

Pernden laughed. "I'm beginning to think you might be more trouble down here left to your own devices."

Garron grinned for a moment, but his face grew grim. *If you only knew ...* He quickly shifted his thoughts. "So, did you spar with her?"

"Yes," Pernden replied, brushing off the question.

"Did you kiss her?" Garron teased.

That time, Pernden's face grew dim. "No." His answer was short, but Garron knew there was more to it.

"Did you try?" he asked, watching closely for Pernden's reaction.

"I had every intention to ..."

"And what happened?" Garron encouraged him to continue.

Pernden shook his head. "I think we might be cursed."

"Cursed?" Ellaria repeated in disbelief.

Nera chuckled. "Yes. I can't tell you how many times we've been so near, locked in some tender moment, and then *Bam!*" She slapped her hands together. "Something interrupts us."

"Does it have anything to do with him being the king and you being a captain in the Guard?" Ellaria asked, picking up her mug of tea. She blew on it and took careful sips.

Nera adjusted herself in the wingback chair. The dining hall was nearly empty. Most of the other guardians had left shortly after the evening meal; only a few remained scattered throughout the place. Nera and Ellaria sat alone near the great stone hearth, enjoying the low crackle of the fire with their evening tea.

"No," Nera said, picking up her mug again. She inhaled the honey- and chamomile-scented steam. It was her favorite tea, and sitting in front of the glowing hearth was another one of her favorite things. "We've been dancing around this for years—long before he was king."

"Have you ever talked about it?"

"What?"

"About your feelings for each other," Ellaria explained as if her question were obvious.

"Well, no," Nera replied honestly.

"It can't be that you think he doesn't love you back."

"No," Nera shook her head, holding the mug with two hands in front of her. "I think he feels the same way about me. I mean, we've been doing this for so long ..."

"He does. I saw more sparks than I've ever seen from Lightning Rider," Ellaria laughed and nodded at the spear that leaned against the stone wall nearby.

Nera rolled her eyes. "I know he does. Of course. I feel it too. I just ..."

Ellaria watched her friend and captain chew on her thoughts. When it seemed Nera wasn't going to finish, Ellaria jumped in. "You know what I think? I think you are two warriors, stubborn and competitive, and both so hardheaded, thinking you're winning some contest by not being the first to break."

"Really?" Nera's brows shot up in surprise. The huntsman's daughter from Tamaria was as fiery inside as her blazing red hair.

"Yep," Ellaria said, nodding at the fire and settling into her chair. She seemed pleased with her astute observation.

"Well, I ..." Nera trailed off again. The more she processed that bit of insight, the more she realized how true the words might be. She knew it was more than that. She had lost her father as a girl and had been devastated, erecting protective walls around her raw heart. Pernden had broken down those walls over the years, so was stubbornness the only thing holding them back?

"Well, you ... want to kiss the king?" Ellaria guessed Nera's thoughts.

Nera's head dipped to the side in shock. Her friend was quite brash with her words.

"Just do it, then," Ellaria finished.

Nera sensed her friend's mirth. "You are relentless."

"I'm a griffin guardian now. Of course, I am. But it's more than that."

"Oh, yes? What is it then?" Nera asked, genuinely curious.

"It's simple: I'm right."

CHAPTER SIX

HOOK, LINE, AND SINKER

Gernot pushed his way out of the bushes. Giant tears streamed down the little orc's face, and his pudgy cheeks and chin quivered. Merrick stood dumbfounded, but Karnak dropped his mighty axe to the dirt and dove to his knees, scooping his son into his big arms.

"It's okay," the orc gar repeated over and over to his son—or maybe to himself. Merrick could not tell, but he was certain that Karnak was filled with a mix of emotions. Tears of joy escaped Merrick's own eyes as he watched the reunion.

The sea breeze blew upon them as they paused to breathe. The morning light was reaching the cliffs, and the waves continued their relentless crashing against the rocks below.

Merrick turned and spotted the small boat, continuing its paddling to nowhere. *Where are they going? Why would they leave Gernot?* he wondered.

"Karnak," Merrick said.

"What? What is it?" the orc gar asked, holding the little orc on his hip as he stood. Karnak wiped tears from his face and approached Merrick's side.

"What was the point of all this? Where did they come from?"

"I don't know," Karnak growled. "But I intend to find out."

"I can call upon Valurwind," Merrick suggested, speaking of his astral falcon, and removed the stone figurine from his pocket. "I can follow the boat to wherever it goes."

"No." Karnak's tusks adjusted into a snarl. "No. This ends now."

Merrick looked the orc over, the black knot of hair on his head flopped with the wind while loose hairs blew freely. Tanessa and Gernot were Karnak's family, and they extended their love to him and Ralowyn. Someone had attacked them in their home. Merrick would not sit by while Karnak pursued justice on his own; he would follow whatever path Karnak chose.

"So, what do we do?" he asked resolutely.

"You take Gernot back to Tanessa."

Merrick looked at the orc as though he were crazy. "What?"

"With Valurwind, you can get him back to the house and send Ralowyn to get Ker from the Scar Cliffs," the orc continued.

Merrick nodded his understanding. "Ralowyn can summon Ker, and then we can fly out to catch the fiend together."

Karnak grunted a response. "I'll watch them so they don't disappear on us. They don't seem to be going anywhere fast."

"Fair enough," Merrick said. He held the falcon figurine out in front of him. The stonework of the figurine still fascinated him. At first glance, it didn't seem much more than a rendering of a falcon carved out of smooth stone and crystal. The huntsman found it odd how such an inconspicuous trinket could be the key to call upon the astral falcon. "Valurwind," he whispered.

Immediately, a strangely hued mist formed in the air before him. The otherworldly mass swirled and grew until great wings opened wide. Just like that, Valurwind, the great astral falcon, stood before them. Aside from her massive size, her breast was a strange shade for a falcon, resembling speckled stars. She clicked happily at first but quickly sensed something was amiss.

"Come, Gernot," Merrick said, taking the orc child from his father. Gernot went readily, though Karnak hesitated. "I've got him," Merrick assured his friend.

"Find swiftness," Karnak nodded back. "Gernot, my son, you will be alright. Merrick will get you home. I'll see you soon."

Gernot whimpered slightly, but Merrick embraced him tighter.

Merrick and Gernot hopped on Valurwind's back, and with a great heft of her wings, she launched them into the morning sky and zipped off toward the northwest. Merrick turned over his shoulder and watched Karnak grow smaller with the distance. The great orc stood stoically on the cliffside, staring over the Gant Sea.

By the time Merrick arrived at the house, Ralowyn was leading Henry from the stable. The pegasus followed the she-elf into the pasture, seemingly happy to do so. Tanessa emerged from the stable as well. The two watched with puzzled looks on their faces as Valurwind descended. The falcon beat her wings as they slowed to land, sending ripples through the field of tall flowers, still half closed in protection from the cool of the receding night.

"Gernot!" Tanessa cried as she rushed to greet them.

Merrick lowered the little orc to his mother, who squeezed him into a tight hug. "Ralowyn, you need to get to the Scar Cliffs. Get Ker and fly to the southeast. The attackers are on a small boat heading out to sea. I'm heading back there now."

"How far south?" Ralowyn asked, mounting the pegasus. Henry had grey and white dapples on his coat and a kindly demeanor. The pegasus stole a nibble of grass while the elf was distracted.

"Hit the coast south of the city and follow it south even more. Karnak is on the cliff, watching so we don't lose them."

Ralowyn nodded as she turned Henry to the side. They galloped several feet before the pegasus spread his wide wings and lifted them into the morning air.

"Are you alright?" Merrick asked Tanessa.

She held her son to her chest, and Merrick wondered if the poor orc boy had enough room to breathe. "Thank you," she said through her tears.

"And the creature?" Merrick asked as Valurwind shifted to prepare for the flight back to the sea.

"It's tied up in the stable," she confirmed.

"Lots of rope?"

"Lots."

"Good," Merrick said as he turned to join Valurwind's gaze to the east.

"Merrick!" Tanessa stopped him with a shout. The huntsman turned back to regard her. "Take care of my husband. Bring him back to me, too."

"I will," he assured her.

Valurwind took to the sky again, flying at a blistering speed. Merrick's hair whipped about his neck, flicking his shoulders as they flew. He was not sure what Karnak planned to do. Certainly, they would descend on the boat, and the occupants would have little way of defending themselves. But then what? They'd be able to question the creature when it woke, though Merrick wasn't sure if it had language or not. It might be wise of them to capture another of the crew that attacked them.

He knew the elf spoke, at the very least. Maybe they could get answers from him.

Merrick glanced to the left. The city of Calrok, bathed in the pink light of the rising sun, stirred. The early risers began their daily routine. He couldn't hear them with the wind whipping by his ears, but over the months he'd spent there, he'd grown to know the orc city by the sea. He'd go so far as to say he'd grown to love it and that it almost felt like home to him.

He returned his gaze forward, petting Valurwind's neck feathers. "Make haste, Valurwind. Our brother needs us!"

Karnak sat on the edge of the cliff, keeping watch over the sea. He ground his teeth as his tusks swayed slowly back and forth. The orc's muscles twitched as he gripped *Dalkeri* in his big hands. He watched the boat drift farther and farther away, laughing at the lunacy.

When Ker gets here, we will tear you up from the water and rip you apart, Karnak imagined. *Where do you think you can hide from me?*

He watched the boat, his intense gaze never wavering. The rising sun seared his eyes as he watched them paddle almost directly east. Unlike most of the orcs of Drelek, Karnak's eyes were well adjusted to the sun, but they still burned to look straight into the brilliance. He squinted, trying to watch through welling tears. He tried to blink them away without changing his line of sight. When he opened his eyes after a few blinks, the boat was gone.

Karnak leapt to his feet, peering across the water. He strained his eyes in a panic. *Where did they go?*

He squinted hard, hoping to boost his ability to find them again, but saw nothing.

The big orc gar paced along the cliffside, staring east. The changing of his position proved fruitless and gave him no sight on the escapees. He cursed his orc eyes.

Where did they go? he thought again. He felt the blood inside him rise as though his heart were pumping too fast. *Where's Merrick? How long has it been?*

He couldn't remember how long they had sprinted through the night. Even if he could, he wasn't sure how that would translate to flight for the speedy Valurwind or his wyvern, Ker. All he knew was that he'd lost sight of the boat—the one task he had. And he wasn't sure if they'd get back fast enough for them to find the dinghy again.

He dared to hope and looked northwest for any sign of his friends. He spotted the outline of the great astral falcon and her rider in the distance. Relief flooded him so quickly he got a sick feeling in his stomach. Karnak blinked furiously, trying to keep the tears in, but they fell anyway down his quivering chin.

The wild night left him exhausted. His emotions had been raw and inconsistent, but none of that mattered. Like most elite warriors, Karnak would turn them all into a focusing fuel for himself. He would use the unbridled power that would erupt from his roiling emotions to his advantage.

Shortly, Merrick and Valurwind came screaming into a landing nearby.

"Where is the boat?" Merrick yelled to Karnak, not dismounting.

"I don't know. I only lost sight of it moments ago!"

"How is that ..." Merrick didn't finish his thought. He peered across the sea, squinting into the sun. "Gernot is safe with

Tanessa, and they have the creature tied up in the stables. We can question him later."

Valurwind flapped a few powerful beats and lifted up from the cliff.

"What about Ker?"

"Ralowyn and Henry flew for the Scar Cliffs. They shouldn't be far behind. I'm going to search for that boat."

Karnak turned back toward the northwest to search the sky. Sure enough, he saw the elf on her pegasus and Ker, his wyvern, approaching quickly. His gaze didn't linger on them, knowing it wouldn't increase their speed.

He turned back to the east. Valurwind hurriedly swooped over the waves as Merrick searched for the small vessel. Karnak couldn't see the boat, but he would stop at nothing to find them.

Valurwind dipped close to a mountainous wave that rolled lazily as though the concerns of people were of no consequence to the roiling mound. *Where could they have gone?* Merrick wondered in frustration. He looked back toward the coast, a great distance away. Ralowyn was nearing Karnak, and they would join the search soon.

The huntsman turned back toward the sea, unable to extrapolate any clue as to their prey's escape path. He was skilled on the ground, but having grown up near the plains city of Tamaria, he had little experience with the sea, save for the few times Karnak had taken him on one of Calrok's fishing ships. Those trips hadn't gone well. Merrick had been sick the first couple but had stomached through the third. Still, he deemed himself a sorry seaman.

Valurwind shifted, and her left wing dropped in a quick bank. "What is it, girl?" Merrick asked. "What do your falcon eyes see?"

He stared over the rolling waves trying to follow the astral falcon's heading. He saw nothing. The waves continued to move, and nothing seemed to break their rhythm. Occasional whitecaps sent spray high into the air, misting them as they flew.

Suddenly, Merrick's head cocked to the side. "What is that?" he muttered.

In the distance, what appeared to be a wave shivered to life. Merrick first wondered if it was some great whale breaching the water. He'd been fortunate to see the magnificent creatures on one of his jaunts with the fishermen. What he witnessed below wasn't the same.

"Let's see what that is," Merrick said. Valurwind swooped closer to the waves, gaining speed as she did.

The shivering wave remained the same distance away from them as they flew toward it.

What? Merrick couldn't believe what his eyes told him.

As though someone had ripped a hundred cloths from a hundred paintings to reveal some spectacular work of art, the shivering wave dismantled itself to reveal a ship at full sail.

"Hurry!" Merrick shouted.

Valurwind beat her wings furiously to gain altitude. Her speed was incredible, and Merrick gripped tighter so he wouldn't plunge into the sea.

The ship was unlike any Merrick had ever seen. It was larger than any in Calrok, and though Merrick had never been to the port cities in southern Tarrine, he doubted any its equal were there. The vessel plowed through the water, undaunted by the forceful waves. They had a favorable wind to back them, and they sailed east toward open sea.

Where are they going? Merrick wondered as the wind whipped his brown hair wildly. He smiled. The wind might fill their sails, but it was also a tailwind for Valurwind. He would bet on the falcon's great speed over that of a sea vessel every time. Suddenly, it struck him. What would they do once they caught up with the ship? He had no idea how large a crew it took to sail a vessel so large. Certainly, he and Valurwind couldn't take the ship by themselves, but they didn't have to. Karnak and Ralowyn would show up soon, and they could formulate a plan. At the very least, Merrick could get close enough to do a couple low passes and get a read on the ship and its crew.

Valurwind shifted into their descent, speeding up as they gained on the vessel. Merrick could see the ship had strange sails that gathered into tight bundles on the sides and back of the giant boat. The fabric was painted in a strange hue that tricked Merrick's eyes. After a couple of minutes, he guessed they were some form of disguise for the ship. *Maybe that's why we couldn't see it,* he thought. *What clever magic is this?*

Shouts from the upper deck tore Merrick from his thoughts. He spotted crew members running about as the ship plowed through the roiling waves. The huntsman nudged the great astral falcon. He wanted a better look. Valurwind maneuvered and swooped toward the ship's starboard side. As they passed the center sail, Merrick's eyes widened.

Another of the strange stony creatures pulled back and aimed what looked to be some sort of mounted bow on the rail of the ship.

Before Merrick could react, the launcher propelled an object that ballooned into a wide net, completely enveloping the pair.

Valurwind released a wild cry as she and Merrick sank into the salty water below.

They flopped around, unable to find any opening in the net. They were stuck. Merrick coughed water from his lungs as he pulled at the ropes that tangled them. Valurwind nipped the ropes and flapped her soaking wings.

Something slithered in the water nearby. Valurwind screeched, and Merrick tried to see what the slithering thing was. *Is that a rope?*

Suddenly, the net jerked forward after the vessel. The tangled webbing tightened on the pair as they were submerged and dragged along behind the fast ship. Merrick could hardly think. Water pressed against them, and the net pulled. They were caught in a deadly trap and couldn't breathe.

Pressing his hands against the falcon, who flailed against the conflicting forces, Merrick believed they would drown.

He had seen Valurwind heal from gnarly injuries before. Once, he sent her back to her astral plane with a gash along her leg. They had gotten too confident in their flying skills, attempting to copy a move Karnak had shown them on one of the more jagged ridges of the Scar Cliffs. When Merrick had called her back from her plane, her injury was nearly healed. After another trip, she was completely healed. He knew she recovered better in her own plane. She certainly couldn't recover from death in his.

Merrick pulled himself toward the great falcon's head. Valurwind recognized he meant to connect with her and settled at his touch. He faced her, and though the seawater stung his eyes and his lungs felt as though they would explode, he looked her straight in the eyes and gave her a nod. Valurwind understood, and in a strange flurry of bubbles, she dissipated and disappeared.

Without the bird's great mass, the net rose to the surface. Merrick gasped a quick breath between holes in the net before he was forced back under the current of the boat. He could do nothing. He watched the light shimmer through the ripples above him. He held onto the net and wanted to cry out, but there was no use.

His only hope was Karnak and Ralowyn, flying through the air he struggled to reach.

Ralowyn cried out as she watched Valurwind and Merrick plummet into the Gant Sea. Karnak roared, and Ker flapped her great membranous wings, lurching them even farther ahead of the elf.

"With all haste, Henry," Ralowyn said, her eyes ablaze with a lavender flame.

Henry neighed in response, galloping with his legs through the air as though it would help him fly faster. Ralowyn held the Staff of Anvelorian ready at her side. The artifact buzzed in her hand. She felt the magic flowing from its pinnacle through her. She was connected to Henry. The pegasus would fly anywhere for her, and she was thankful for his loyalty and effort.

They pressed forward trying to catch the great orc atop his wyvern. He was increasing distance on her, Ker's great wingspan wider than Henry's.

"Karnak!" Ralowyn yelled for him. "Karnak, we must be careful and work together!"

The orc could not hear her. She feared his rage had consumed him at the sight of Merrick and Valurwind dropping into the sea.

Henry sped through the sky, giving her every ounce of effort he had. Ralowyn watched the water where she'd seen Merrick vanish. She could see no sign of him. After careful inspection of the waters behind the ship, she thought it was dragging something.

No... Her heart sank. If she didn't reach the vessel quickly, Merrick and Valurwind would certainly drown.

Karnak thought he heard Ralowyn yell to him as Ker ripped through the winds above the raging Gant Sea. The wyvern pushed herself, her long neck stretched out with her legs and tail streaming behind. Her great leathery wings sliced through the air. Her horns sleeked back over her smooth scales. She was flying at full speed as they chased the ship farther and farther out. A thought struck Karnak: he'd never been out this far from the coast. This was where the Gant Sea was deep and held great mysteries.

"Ker," he said, rubbing one of his hands along her scaly neck. "We need to help Merrick. They've got him."

The wyvern glanced back at the great orc, her friend since she was very young. They had flown together almost all her life. Karnak had grown much over the years, but so had she.

Ker clicked at him and pressed harder.

"Let's get him," Karnak replied to her increased effort, grateful for her. How many times had they found themselves in dire circumstances over the years? Through them all, Karnak and Ker had survived. She was the most loyal companion he could ask for, and after his family had been attacked and his friend dragged down by this unknown enemy, Ker was ready to fight with him once again.

Ker twitched her elongated neck and flourished her wings, raising the duo high as they approached the fleeing vessel.

Karnak lifted *Dalkeri* high above his head. The orange stone radiated mystical energy, awakening the battle axe into a fiery weapon of death. Karnak felt the hum rattle his bones.

His muscles tensed as he raised it high and hurled it with a mighty roar.

The axe spun with deadly speed, hurtling toward the back of the crewman steering the large ship from the upper deck. A woman clambered up the steps to the sterncastle moments before the axe collided with the helmsman. She whipped out a rod of wood the length of her forearm and swiped it across the front of her body. *Dalkeri* bounced off an invisible force and spun at an odd angle toward the ship's fore portside. The axe chopped into another crew member, sending him flying overboard and skipping across the waves.

Karnak recoiled. *They have a mage.*

Suddenly, he noticed men on the starboard side pulling a heavy rope and dragging a huge net up the side of the vessel. "Merrick!" Karnak yelled, though only Ker heard him.

The wyvern whipped sideways and adjusted into a nearly vertical dive toward the vessel. Karnak's eyes narrowed. A man on the deck looked up in terror at the descending wyvern, expecting to be eaten whole. Karnak stretched his left hand out wide reaching for *Dalkeri*. He needed the axe to loose itself from the fallen enemy and fly back to him. He intended to smash it down on the center of the ship, taking out its mainmast.

Another sight caught his attention. A stony-looking brute, like the one bound and waiting in his stable, wheeled into place behind the mizzenmast. The creature eyed Karnak with a wicked grin and held back the strings of what looked to be a giant four-armed bow. Karnak's eyes widened.

No!

Before the orc could react, a great bolt was released from the mounted bow, blasting into Ker's chest. She uttered a horrific screech as Karnak felt the bolt pierce her with a sickening *Kathunk!* underneath him. The sudden impact sent Karnak flying into the sail and tumbling uncontrollably as *Dalkeri* lodged into a crossbeam above him.

Karnak flipped awkwardly toward the deck before cracking his head against a large barrel. The massive orc leapt to his feet, ready to take on any enemy that came within range, then wavered. His head throbbed, and his vision blurred.

The large orc gar wobbled sideways and collapsed on the deck.

"Karnak!" Ralowyn cried out again.

The orc and his wyvern had flown down to attack the crew without her. She pressed Henry even harder; the pegasus glistened with a foamy sweat. She had to reach that ship. Karnak was a fierce warrior, but Ralowyn had never seen a ship so large and assumed it hosted a large crew. Though Ker could certainly do damage to a foe, her movements would be hampered by the many ropes on the vessel.

What is he thinking? the elf thought. Knowing Merrick had been downed on the starboard and not wanting to also be trapped, she guided Henry's flight in tight to the ship's portside. She raised the Staff of Anvelorian, drawing upon the magic of the ancient artifact. She couldn't just start lobbing fireballs over the bow and risk hitting Karnak or Ker.

A woman leaned against the tall railing and whipped a wand over her head, launching a ball of magic at Ralowyn as they passed the sterncastle. Henry deftly dodged the orb, but the woman didn't stop. She launched ball after ball, each searing through the sky. The projectiles crackled as they zipped past them. Henry flapped and twisted and turned, avoiding the barrage.

As he dodged the attack, they drew closer to the vessel, within range of a wicked-looking mounted bow. By the time Ralowyn saw the evil mirth on a stony creature's face, it was too late.

A massive harpoon, likely designed for some massive sea beast, shot through the air and blasted into Henry's side, throwing Ralowyn off, as the two spiraled toward the sea below.

They hit the water hard, sinking deep beneath the waves. Water assaulted Ralowyn's nose, making her nostrils burn and her lungs revolt. Her ribs felt as though they had exploded. She and Henry had still been connected when the pegasus took the harpoon. Though she didn't feel the full pain of the impact, she still felt like she'd taken a harpoon to her ribs.

As the bubbles around her dissipated, she opened her eyes. Stinging from the salty water, they desperately sought the surface. Ralowyn flailed her arms and legs, trying to get her bearings. Finally, she saw the sunlight warping through the water in a myriad of refractions and swam toward it.

Breaking the surface of the Gant Sea's ever-shifting waters, the elf coughed and retched, her body expelling the seawater that had violated her lungs and stomach. Ralowyn searched the massive waves that surrounded her. They curled and rolled in an endless dance. Some waves dipped and split in front of her, and she glimpsed the great vessel forging onward, farther and farther away.

Her mind reeled. Henry was gone. Not many creatures would have survived a blow like that. Merrick and Valurwind were captured, if not drowned. And Ralowyn had not put eyes on Karnak or Ker while she and Henry were dodging the projectiles from the ship's mage. How had this all ended so badly? Ralowyn shifted her mind to what she could control, which wasn't much.

She was floating in the middle of the Gant Sea. The elf turned toward what she knew, judging by the sun, was west, but she could not see Calrok—or any land for that matter. Karnak and Ker were likely far too distracted with the crew of that ship and wouldn't notice she had dropped into the waters. Even if they did, who knew how long it would take them to find her. Ralowyn was a speck in the vast sea. She treaded water as she bobbed with the rolling waves. She was very much alone.

An acute realization overcame her: she no longer held the Staff of Anvelorian.

CHAPTER SEVEN

OLD "FRIENDS"

O rin's initial hesitation about Coal's plan seemed to be proving itself justified as they walked through the alleys of a dank part of Stalford. The buildings there were constructed from wood, weather-stained by the regular rains that poured off the Gant Sea. Most of the people that lived in the area were already at Stalford's bustling docks starting their work or fishing in vessels that had cast out to sea before sunrise. The companions walked past a grubby blacksmith who stopped hammering and eyed them curiously, and Orin wondered how lost they looked.

Coal marched onward, never slowing. Though the sun was rising, the fog rolling into the big bay between Stalford and the island of Vandor was thick and wispy. Orin thought he could divide it with his hand, but when he tried, the fog swirled, evading his grasp.

Ezel did not look happy about the situation. In fact, the normally cheerful deep gnome hadn't smiled since Coal mentioned their "old friends." Judging by their surroundings, Orin wondered what kind of characters they would be.

Orin knew, of course, that Coal and Ezel had spent time on the Gant Sea years before he knew them. The guardian had noticed they only shared fun stories, leaving out any raw details.

He wasn't even sure why Coal and Ezel had shifted to being river boatmen.

Ezel padded along on the damp cobblestones alongside Orin. The deep gnome's solemn visage was even more pronounced on his greyish skin.

Orin tapped him on the shoulder as they walked. "*Are you alright?*" he signed.

Ezel hesitated. He hadn't realized he wore his emotions so close to the surface. He straightened, but his countenance remained sullen. "*I'm fine,*" he signed back with a shrug.

"*Are these 'old friends' trouble?*" Orin asked.

"*We ...*" Ezel's hands paused as he tried to formulate his response. "*It's been a long time.*"

Orin examined the gnome, trying to read him. Even under normal circumstances, the gnome was hard to read. Ezel, half the guardian's height, dipped his head, making it harder for Orin to observe him. The guardian tapped his shoulder again. "*What is—*"

Coal's sudden stop interrupted him. The dwarf grumbled, looking left and right down the alleyways.

"Are we lost?" Orin asked.

"No," the dwarf replied stubbornly. "We're just turned around a little."

"*That means lost,*" Ezel signed to Orin with a smile.

Orin laughed.

Coal wheeled around. "Now hold on a minute," he scolded. "You can't be making jokes when I don't know what they are."

"I'm pretty sure you did that for a long time before I understood what you two were saying," Orin pointed out. His eyebrow was raised, and he regarded the dwarf with a wan smile.

"Well, that was different," Coal grumbled. "I—"

A ship bell chimed, and the dwarf swiveled.

"It's that way," Coal said with a sheepish shrug.

Orin shook his head in amusement. He loved Coal. The hearty dwarf was generally good-natured, if not brash at times. After everything they'd been through, they had forged a bond that could not be easily broken. They squabbled like brothers sometimes, but their love remained strong.

They walked through another alley that led them to a cracked stone street running along the docks. Coal turned south, following the coastline, until, after a short time, they left the southern docks behind. The group passed the last buildings on the south side of the city. The road became a dirt path. Orin and Ezel followed Coal around a bend.

As they crested a small hill, another dock came into view farther down the coast. This one was far less grand and in desperate need of repair. Crew members ran along the docks shuffling barrels and woven sacks onto various boats. The size and shape of the vessels varied widely. One, however, caught Orin's attention. It was larger than the rest, its mast standing nearly twice the height of the next largest.

Orin nearly toppled over Coal, who'd stopped to take in the sight himself.

"Now these folk," Coal said. "They are the folk that need a new day." A distinct sadness coated his voice.

Orin scanned the scene, shifting his gaze from the docks to the lopsided buildings that sprinkled the hill slopes running toward the water. The buildings were hovels, making the weather-stained wooden structures in south Stalford look like fine establishments by comparison. Several people milled about, starting their early mornings. The fog that hung thick in the air made the scene all the more dire.

"What happened here?" Orin mumbled to himself.

Coal inhaled deeply and released a resigned sigh. Ezel appeared to have no reaction to the sight whatsoever. The gnome stood stoically beside his companions. His runic tattoos appeared blacker on his grey skin, as though they had lost all color and light.

A rather glum-looking elf ascended the dirt path. He paused when he spotted Ezel, and his eyes widened. His gait changed, and he rushed past them.

"Good morning," Orin said quietly.

The elf didn't respond. He left the path to give them a wider berth and hurried along toward Stalford's south end.

"What was that all about?" Orin asked.

Coal and Ezel shared a look. They didn't sign, so Orin had no idea what unspoken conversation passed between them. He was getting the feeling that these "old friends" might not be as keen to greet them as Coal had hoped.

After another person sidled off the dirt pathway to pass the trio, eyeing them nervously, Ezel pulled Coal aside to have a conversation—more accurately, a heated disagreement. The dwarf and the gnome argued about the wisdom of the plan in bursts of rapid hand motions. Orin could only stand by since the two didn't include him in their quarrel. The guardian watched the flying hands and marveled at how either could understand each other with the rapid, overlapping pace. They stood in aggressive stances, and the runes on Ezel's hands lit, glowing blue several times in what Orin assumed was an attempt at emphasizing his point over the dwarf's counterarguments.

Orin had seen them squabble before but never so intensely. The guardian paid close attention, trying to catch any explanation about the root of the disagreement. However, neither of them gave any detail about why he was right. Orin caught phrases like, "*There is too much history here,*" from Ezel, and "*That was a long time ago,*" from Coal.

Ezel swiveled on his heel, his scrawny hands firmly planted on his hips. He looked deeply annoyed. The gnome turned back to the dwarf and signed, "*This is foolishness,*" and waved a dismissive hand at Coal.

"*Then* we'll *go and talk to them,*" the dwarf signed, indicating Orin. "*We have some gold from Whitestone. You can procure supplies from the Stalford markets for the journey back,*" Coal's hands flashed.

"*If there even* is *a journey back.*"

"*Ezel,*" Coal signed then swept his hand wide over the squalid scene. "*How could there not be?*"

The gnome stared over the hovels and haphazard docks. His eyes glassed with tears before he blinked them away and turned back toward Orin. The guardian's face scrunched with compassion, not knowing what ailed his friend but wanting to support the little gnome. Ezel's eyes dropped, and he shook his head in defeat.

"*I'll return to Stalford and find fair merchants,*" the gnome signed.

"Aye," Coal said aloud, nodding.

"*But,*" Ezel turned on the dwarf again. "*I won't purchase anything until we're officially agreed with them. I still think this is a bad idea.*"

With that, the gnome was off, his boots padding softly on the dirt road north to Stalford.

Orin watched Ezel go, thinking how impressed he was by the deep gnome. Most folks had never seen a deep gnome before, and the fact that Ezel was a mute added to their surprise. The guardian thought it fascinating how the deep gnome put great effort into finding ways to connect with people. He had watched Ezel work his magic to communicate with merchants, moving items through the air to the delight of many. Orin found his little friend capable of just about anything the gnome set himself to doing.

As he watched Ezel walk around the bend and out of sight, Orin felt a pang of disappointment shoot through him. He would rather they stuck together to approach this community, but he didn't understand his friends' argument. He spun to find Coal staring into the dirt a few feet away, grabbing at the braid in his thick black beard.

"I don't understand why Ezel doesn't want to go with us," Orin stated plainly.

The dwarf grunted, gripped the braid, and yanked a couple of times. His usually white nose was red with frustration. "Let's just get this over with," he growled through gritted teeth.

As they set off down the dirt path, Orin realized they'd been stopped for so long the morning fogs had dissipated. The sun's light that bathed the dock community did not make it appear any less hopeless.

Few people remained around the docks when Orin and Coal drew near. Up close, Orin noticed the docks were barely held together by an overabundance of rope. He wondered if the docks were more rope than wood. Most of the lumber was weathered and worn with an occasional newer log contrasting the rest.

A small open-faced building stood at the south side of the docks. Orin saw a man with grey hair and a scruffy face milling around a table. As they approached, the man looked up with squinted eyes, surveying them. Once he got a good look, his shoulders drooped, and he shook his head. His grey mustache wrapped around the side of his face and grew into the mop of hair on his head. The stubble of beard looked as though it had been shaved a week or two earlier. His skin was sun-cooked and spotted.

"As I live and breathe," he called.

Coal flinched, and his step slowed. Orin grew more wary of their surroundings, but no one else seemed to notice their arrival. Most of the movement in the small community was in and among the hovels. Orin only saw one other person near the docks; a young woman rolled rope into a round pile. Her wavy blond hair blew sideways in clumps as she worked.

Orin turned back toward the man as they walked into the open structure. Coal's arms swung out to the side and came back together for a few hesitant claps. The dwarf took a deep breath, and his lips pursed. "Befors," he addressed the man.

"Coal."

Silence fell between them. The older man wiped his hands on a rag that looked as though it would likely make his hands dirtier. His eyes flitted to the guardian, standing tall next to the dwarf, then glanced down at his hands, noting they had not gotten any cleaner.

Orin looked from dwarf to man, waiting for one of them to speak.

Finally, the older man laughed to himself. His shoulders bobbed, and he shook his head again. "Ezel got bigger," he said but couldn't finish the thought with a straight face. Coal laughed with him. The older man's eyes watered, and he coughed as laughter overtook him.

Orin couldn't help but chuckle softly. Whether it was his nerves or the fact that the other two were just that humorous, he could not tell.

When the older man composed himself, wiping the tears from his face with his stained hands, he released a loud sigh. "It's been a long time, my old friend," he said.

"Aye, that it has." The tinge of sadness in Coal's response was not missed by the men.

Befors breathed deeply and scanned the hovels and broken-down docks. He pressed his lips together in a half smile. "Not exactly how you expected to find us, eh?"

"Not exactly," Coal admitted, but he looked up to the man and chuckled. "I didn't expect you to get so old."

This made Befors laugh again. "Well, a hard life makes a man age faster, and we can't all live as long as a dwarf."

Coal nodded his agreement. He and Befors were near the same age: the man in his sixties and Coal in his seventies. A long-lived dwarf could reach the ripe old age of 350 years—nowhere near the lifespan of an elf, but one can lose many friends over such a span.

"And what of our humble home?" Befors asked, dragging Coal back into the conversation. The older man's eyes squinted as though he were inspecting the dwarf again.

"Aye, it's ..." Coal's words trailed off as he looked around. He couldn't find the words to describe it.

"Not much. I know," Befors finished the thought for him, scratching at the grey mop on his head. "But we've made something of it. You saw our ships before they left dock, eh?"

"Aye." Coal nodded.

"Did you see the galleon?"

"Aye," he said again. "She was hard to miss."

Befors laughed. "She's new. Well, new for us." Befors corrected himself. "It's taken us all these years to acquire another full-size galleon. We'll finally be able to bring in greater loads. The winds may be changing for us."

"Oh ... that's good to hear," Coal said, though he sounded slightly disappointed as he remembered the mission at hand.

Orin shifted. Maybe they weren't as desperate as Coal initially thought. They may not want to go north.

"You seem disappointed," Befors said, his brows furrowed in disbelief. "Did you think we would wait for you to come back? You left us years ago when we had nothing. We couldn't sit around and do nothing. We would have starved long before now."

"I ..." Coal started again, but the dwarf struggled to find his words.

Befors shook his head. "Nothing to say after all these years, eh?"

They stared quietly at each other.

Orin realized the conversation wasn't going well. The guardian looked back and forth between the two, wondering who would speak first, but neither did. When Orin couldn't take the tension anymore, he spoke. "Sir."

"Sir?" Befors laughed. "I'm no knight!"

"Befors, then," Orin nodded. "We've come all the way from Whitestone on a mission."

"Wow," Befors mocked, appraising Coal again. "You made it all the way to Whitestone? Classy."

Orin pressed on. "We're seeking a group of people who are looking for a new opportunity. We want to establish a fishing city on the sea, north of the Gant Sea Narrows."

"North of the Narrows?" Befors laughed even harder. "Opportunity? For madmen, maybe."

"This would be a joint effort. My brother King Pernden has endorsed this mission to see that the new city will be a success," Orin pressed. Based on Befors's reaction thus far, the guardian withheld the details about orcs from Drelek also being involved. "This is an important settlement that will have the full weight of Whitestone's support."

Befors squinted at Orin, scratching at his mustache. He seemed to be trying to figure the man out.

"Why is this important enough to Whitestone to send a prince?" Befors asked.

"I'm no prince," Orin corrected him.

"I've always been pretty good at math, young man; that's why I'm the dockmaster here. I can put two and two together. Brother to the king is a prince, is he not?"

"That's ..." Orin hesitated. How could he explain to the man that his brother took over the crown of Whitestone out of necessity when his cousin was incapacitated by a wicked sorcerer? If he did, would that instill confidence in Whitestone's ability to keep the new settlement safe? He decided to advance the conversation. "As you know, there hasn't been a settlement on the sea north of the Narrows in hundreds of years."

"Aye, because the orcs of Drelek burned the last one to the ground."

"Hundreds of years ago," Orin emphasized.

"Remembering tragedy helps us avoid it in the future." Befors's tone was grave, and he looked directly at Coal.

Orin tried to reel him back in. "Certainly, learning from our past helps us to forge a different future, and that's what this is about. A new future. A future hope."

"Hope," Befors grumbled.

"Yes, hope." Orin untied a sack from his belt, lifting it and dropping it on the table for emphasis. The bag did exactly as he'd hoped: it clunked heavily and fell open. A few coins slid onto the rotting wooden table.

Befors's eyes widened, and he stared incredulously. "You're serious."

"Very much so."

Befors shook his head, trying to gather his senses. His eyes fell on his old friend. "After all these years, you think you can just come back and save us. But you left. You left ..." His words trailed off.

Coal stepped forward, but Orin raised a hand to stay him. "This is not Coal's doing; this is an offer of Whitestone. We need men and women and families that know the sea. The people in Whitestone don't know it. We're not fishermen. We don't know how to run ports or even how to build docks, but we do know how to protect."

Befors huffed a laugh. "Spend more time in the sky than the sea, you lot."

Orin smiled back at him. "That is true."

"I ..." Befors stopped, eyeing the coins on the table.

Orin straightened and glanced around, inspecting the hovels and the dock. "You've built all this from nothing?" he asked with an impressed tone.

"Aye, nothing."

"Imagine what you could build for your families with Whitestone's resources behind you."

Befors's eyes glassed as he surveyed the hovels again. If Orin could see the possibilities, surely the older man could, too.

"But why?" Befors asked quietly.

Orin had made it to this point in the conversation with many others in their travels down the eastern coast of Tarrine.

This part had always been where the conversations ceased. Orin couldn't lie to the man. *Why bother coating it with sugar now?* He had grown tired of beating around the bush. It did not make the information any more palatable for his hearers.

The guardian cleared his throat. "Because we're building the first joint settlement between man and orc." The plainness with which the words slipped out surprised him.

Shock screwed up Befors's face, and he rocked back slightly. "Man ... and orc?" He repeated the words to make sure he'd heard Orin properly.

"Aye," Coal cut in, and Befors shot a glare at the dwarf. "We fought alongside the orcs against a mad sorcerer that came from Kelvur with a dragon."

Befors looked as though he struggled to piece together the information they gave him. "No," he said, pushing the coins back into the mouth of the bag. "No, we're doing just fine here."

"Listen," Orin leaned in. "I know it's scary to think of the possibility. In our letters with King Pernden, he's been telling us the orcs are scared, too. Our peoples have been fighting for centuries. And now, for the first time in history, we're trying to do something that's never been done."

"It's never been done because it's not a good idea," Befors scolded the younger man. "I don't think you've learned from the past."

"Oh, but I have. I've learned that the way we used to do things only led to bloodshed on either side. I carry the blade of my brother who spilled his own blood in that war." Orin indicated the sword on his belt. "I've learned in recent times that when our peoples work together, we can overcome great odds. And that people, even from different places, can often surprise you."

"Aye," Coal agreed.

"And what would you know of that?" Befors hissed the words. He turned back to Orin. "You don't even know that you've befriended someone who will leave you at the direst time of your life. How are we supposed to know that Whitestone won't abandon us if things with our orc 'friends' go awry?"

Orin looked to Coal. The dwarf seemed wounded by the comment. "Coal and I have fought side by side through some horrible things. We rode out together on the field of battle with the War Hog Cavalry of Galium. He has never abandoned me. I don't know what history the two of you have, but I do know that Whitestone will not abandon the settlement. This is a chance to forge a new future for yourself and the families of this community—a new life that will bless generations to come."

"We're doing fine here," Befors said angrily.

"No, we're not!" a voice yelled back from nearby.

They all turned, searching for the owner of the voice. The young blond woman appeared from behind some barrels she'd obviously been hiding behind to eavesdrop on their conversation.

"Aless," Befors scolded.

"Don't you start with that!" she scolded back. "We are not fine here. We have barely survived. What about last year, when the fishing was stale and even the crews of Stalford were having trouble? We didn't have enough food to eat or enough wood to keep everyone warm. We lost seven people during the winter."

"Aless, you don't know what this man is offering."

"Oh, don't I?" she asked, eyeing Orin. Her blue eyes were stark against her tanned skin, and Orin found her quite stunning. She brushed her wavy blond hair from her face. "You offer us the chance to start a new life, in a new bay, with new equipment and resources to build new homes and new docks. Is that right?"

"Well," Orin paused to make sure he heard all of the things she listed. "Yes."

"But—" Befors started.

Aless cut him off. "But we have to make friends with some orcs who are also nervous and worried about us?"

"Yes." Orin nodded.

"But they are willing to make friends with us?"

"Yes."

"Well, they sound better than the folks of Stalford who want nothing to do with us and wish we'd all die of starvation so they can have their bay back."

"Aless," Befors scolded again.

"No," Aless snapped at the older man. "You don't get to scold me for wanting a future away from this." She waved her hands wide, indicating their surroundings. "You don't get to do that just because you're still angry about something that happened years ago. I lost my parents back then, and I've grown on. Learning from the past is one thing, but I refuse to live in it."

Everyone fell silent. Orin glanced between the young woman and the older man, not wanting to get caught in the middle of whatever silent battle the two fought. He turned slightly to see Coal's reaction. The dwarf stared at the beautiful young woman, tears pouring down his cheeks into his thick black beard.

"I cannot make the decision alone," Befors conceded. "Tinothe and I will need to discuss it when he returns to the docks."

The young woman's hard stare softened, and she nodded her approval of his intent to discuss the opportunity further.

Orin was suddenly filled with hope. Perhaps they had finally found a group of people who would be willing to establish a fishing city in the north.

"But I have one more question," Befors said gravely.

"What is it?" Orin asked.

Befors didn't look at the guardian. Instead, he faced Coal. "Where is Ezel?"

CHAPTER EIGHT

ADRIFT

The Gant Sea roiled around Ralowyn as she treaded water to keep herself afloat. The slender elf shifted her weight to tread the water primarily with her legs. She would not be able to stay afloat forever. The great swells of the Gant Sea would eventually swallow her, and not a soul would know her fate. She decided she would not give in easily to such an undesirable end to her life. Her arms stiffened, reaching her hands below the surface for the Staff of Anvelorian. She'd unfortunately dropped the artifact when she was propelled from Henry's spiraling body after the pegasus had been struck down.

She reached into the deep, hoping beyond hope to feel the artifact through the dense waters. She had been able to pull the staff toward her through the air many times in the past. It was an act that had become almost thoughtless for her. It was easy because she had always been connected to it with an invisible tether. But then, it had always been nearby. Reaching through the salty waters, she could not sense its presence.

Ralowyn spluttered and coughed as she accidentally slipped beneath the surface. Several tears escaped her eyes and joined the rest of the saltwater. She was unsure what she could do.

The elf thought about her memories with Merrick. She recalled the way his eyes looked at her when he smiled. She saw his shoulder-length brown hair tousled by the wind as they crossed the paddock overlooking the city of Calrok.

She had grown fond of the huntsman. Though he still had a boyish way about him and liked to have fun, she found him to have a deep side that surpassed his years. Like her, he'd experienced deep heartache. People who've lost loved ones share an inexpressible understanding.

Her vision flashed to an imagined sight of him struggling in a tangled net with Valurwind unintentionally crushing him and pushing him deeper under the water while they wrestled for air.

Ralowyn's eyes snapped open.

She didn't know if Merrick was alive, but she would not succumb to the deep, nor to despair. This would not be how their story ended, and she would not resolve herself to such a fate.

The elf centered her breathing and extended a single slender hand through the waters. As her head slipped under the surface of the water and she began to sink, she reached with all her might, focusing her mind and will on a singular point. Her heart pounded in her chest, reverberating through her limbs and head.

There.

She felt something far below the surface cutting through the water, hurtling toward her. In a moment, she saw a lavender light rippling through the dim. The Staff of Anvelorian broke the surface of the water in an exciting fashion, like a whale breaching in a celebratory leap.

A whale, Ralowyn thought. The pinnacle of the silver staff burst with magical light, and her eyes blazed with a lavender hue. She reached out with her heart and mind for help. Shortly, she heard the haunting echo of whale song. The great vibrations resonated through the water and into her body.

The elf shed more tears, but these were filled with joy. Her silvery hair splayed out in the water like some strange tentacled sea creature as she peered below her to view the great mass of whale that drew near.

With the Staff of Anvelorian firmly in her grasp and her new friend there to help, Ralowyn's outlook shone brighter. She still did not know what was happening on the enemy ship or whether Merrick had even survived. She did know two things: she would stop at nothing to find the huntsman and she needed help.

When Tanessa had burst through the door of Calrok's modest mage library, Smarlo had been in the middle of reading a rather fascinating excerpt on the innate magical properties of celeris crystals in old Master Kanjor-Pukra's tome *Magic of Mines, Their Monsters, and Minerals*. She'd startled him, and his first reaction was to laugh. He was no longer laughing.

Tanessa hurriedly explained what had happened in the middle of the night at their home and started weeping. The slender orc mage could hardly process what she told him. As he rushed with her back to his gar's home, he hadn't been sure what to expect. As Smarlo observed the stone-skinned creature, unconscious and tied up before him, he knew he couldn't have expected the reality he faced.

The sunlight beamed through the opening of the stable, landing on the creature's form as it slowly rose and fell with the rhythm of its breaths. The smell of hay and leather permeated the area. The sun was warming the world, and the wind rustled the long grass in the paddock outside the stable.

Smarlo's eyes darted to Tanessa at the entrance. She watched the house carefully, not paying attention to the strange creature whose deep breathing made the only noise inside the stable. Smarlo's long ears twitched with sympathy. Tanessa had always been good to him. He and Karnak had been best friends, even when they were young. Long ago when Karnak had fallen for the charming orc woman, Smarlo had felt a hint of jealousy at losing his friend's attention. That was short-lived. He had grown to love Tanessa as a sister.

"And there was an elf, as well?" Smarlo asked gently.

Tanessa didn't look away from the house. "Yes. Dressed in black."

"And what did he say about our stony friend here again?"

"Just that they weren't even really friends, like their working together was some sort of necessary inconvenience for him."

"I see." Smarlo nodded, staring at the creature before him. "And Karnak, Merrick, and Ralowyn went after the elf?"

"Yes." Tanessa sighed. She seemed as though she were trying to keep herself from breaking down into another fit of sobs. "But they've been gone for so long."

"And you said Merrick flew back to retrieve Ralowyn and Ker?"

"Yes. Merrick came back and shouted for Ralowyn to get Ker from the cliffs. Then they were off again." She crossed her arms in front of her chest, hugging herself closely.

Smarlo strode to her and placed a long hand on her shoulder. "Tanessa, you're tired. It's been a horrible night. You should get some rest."

"How can I rest? Karnak is out there, and I have no idea what's happening."

Big tears escaped her eyes. She scrunched her face, trying to fight them back.

"But your son is safe. Gernot is unhurt. He'll be shaken, I'm sure. But for now, he rests, and you should too. Go be with him. I will watch this one," Smarlo said, jutting a thumb toward the unconscious prisoner. "Karnak and the others are probably trying to sort this all out. By now I'm sure they've already caught up to the fiend and are questioning him. I sent Taglan to find Belguv, and he'll rally the squadron. I'm sure they're already in the air and flying our way. I'll have them look for Karnak. If we still haven't heard from the others by nightfall, we will start to worry then."

"You should already be worried." A coughing laugh resounded behind them. "Her husband is already dead."

Tanessa picked up a nearby shovel and charged toward the prisoner. Smarlo grabbed her and held her back.

"No! What do you know?" she shouted.

The stony face turned into a jagged smile.

"Tanessa, wait! We can get information from him." Smarlo struggled to explain while the enraged wife fought to get at the prisoner.

"Information won't help you." The creature sneered. "A shadow is rising. It already looms over Kelvur. The world you know is coming to an end. It will be dashed upon the rocks like the waves. The tide of war will wash you away, and you can do nothing to stop it."

"Kelvur?" Smarlo asked.

"You know nothing!" The stony prisoner laughed and shook his head.

"What of my husband?" Tanessa growled at him.

The prisoner clicked his tongue. "He is most likely dead. He wasn't even the one we wanted. The sorcerer sent us for the—"

Suddenly, the stony prisoner stopped speaking and expelled an odd guttural sound. His eyes widened, and his mouth gaped.

Pain and surprise crept across his face, and he hunched over again.

Smarlo and Tanessa looked at each other, confused.

The orc mage took a step closer to inspect the creature. He wasn't breathing. Smarlo grabbed at him and shook him. "No. What?"

"What is it?" Tanessa asked in a quiet panic.

"He's dead," Smarlo said. He indicated a small feathered barb that protruded from the prisoner's neck. "Someone killed him. Someone's here!"

Tanessa didn't hesitate. She bolted from the stables, straight to her house. Smarlo followed her into the sunlight, trying to spot the attacker. He saw no one.

He ran into the house, finding Tanessa rocking Gernot in her arms, tears streaming down her face.

Smarlo's heart dropped, but when Gernot pushed at his mother, trying to escape her tight squeeze, relief flooded the mage.

"Is everything alright in here?" Smarlo asked, his heart thumping so hard he felt it in his long green ears.

"Yes," Tanessa managed to say through her sobs.

Smarlo made a quick sweep through the house to ensure no unwanted parties were present and ran back outside.

The sun was shining like a normal day in Calrok. The outside warmth and the smell of the paddock flowers contrasted the dread that Smarlo experienced within. Something was very wrong in Finlestia.

Targ, the youngest among the Scar Squadron, was assigned to guard Tanessa and Gernot. Members of the squadron had buzzed around the place throughout the day. The squadron had found no sign of Karnak or the others, despite the long day of searching. Smarlo had received regular reports on the flight patterns of the wyvern riders searching for their friends as they tackled the areas around the city in planned patterns. Their searching had thus far resulted in nothing, but Belguv pressed the squadron on, expanding their search area.

Master Tan-Kro, the elder mage of Calrok and the keeper of the city's modest mage library, was informed of the situation and joined Smarlo in the stable. By the time the older mage arrived at Karnak's house, Smarlo had searched all the stone-skinned prisoner's pockets for any clue as to its identity but had found little.

Laid out before the orc mage were a couple of items, seemingly of limited informational value. A small pouch held a couple pieces of dried meat. Smarlo could not guess the source of the meat. Three coins were emblazoned with indistinguishable markings. They didn't appear to be very valuable in Smarlo's estimation. The strangest of the items was a small piece of blank parchment.

Smarlo had shifted the stony corpse into a prone position to get a better look at him. His build was not so different from that of an orc. His muscled arms and barrel chest were larger than Smarlo's, but the mage was a tall and slender orc. The creature had more the build of a large orc like Karnak. It had eyes and teeth much like theirs, and where hair should have been, strange patches of moss grew. As odd as those were, the stony skin perplexed the orc mage most. In all his years, he'd never read anything about such a creature.

When Master Tan-Kro entered the doorway into the stable, Smarlo was jolted from his speculations.

"What in Finlestia ...?" The old orc mage trailed off.

"It's good you're here," Smarlo half-greeted him. "I've found little on his person, just some small things."

"Even small things can be big if you look at them the right way," Tan-Kro said quietly as he circled and inspected the stony corpse.

"A pouch of dried meat, some coins, and some blank parchment," Smarlo said flatly.

"And the markings on the coins?" Tan-Kro asked like a teacher quizzes a pupil.

"Vague, hard to make out. They seem old, worn—like they've been used for centuries. They don't look familiar."

Smarlo handed the coins to Master Tan-Kro. The old orc examined them with his long, knobbled green fingers. A white eyebrow shot up, and for a moment, Smarlo thought the Master might be able to tell him something about them.

"They do not seem very valuable," Tan-Kro said.

"I didn't think so, either."

"But they also don't look like they're from Tarrine."

Smarlo paused. In his mind, that conclusion made sense. The creature had mentioned Kelvur, and nothing about this creature had been familiar. Why couldn't it be from Kelvur or somewhere else outside Tarrine? The problem was that the only interaction they'd had with someone outside of Tarrine was the dark sorcerer Jaernok Tur. If their stony-faced attacker was from Kelvur as well, it meant they may be in for a whole lot more interaction with Kelvurians, and they had proven to be anything but friendly.

"Kelvur," Smarlo replied.

Master Tan-Kro appraised the corpse again, placing the coins back on the ground where Smarlo had organized them before his arrival. "Why Kelvur?" Tan-Kro asked.

"The creature spoke of a shadow that covers Kelvur, and he mentioned that the sorcerer sent them. Jaernok Tur is the only Kelvurian we've seen here in ... who knows how long. Records of Kelvur are limited. Also, we followed Karnak and Merrick's tracks to the cliffs down the coast. It seems they pursued the attackers out to sea."

"And no sign of them?"

"No," Smarlo answered. He was frustrated by their lack of results. "Belguv took others with him to fly over the sea. They will likely find nothing. There won't be any footprints on the waves."

"True," the old orc agreed airily. "But there is always something to find if one looks hard enough."

Smarlo scratched at his long green ear to fight his growing irritation. He loved Master Tan-Kro. The old orc mage had been a fine mentor to him all these years. But, he didn't have time for the mage's ambiguous colloquialisms. They'd been at this all day. The night was coming, and they had little to show for their efforts. They had no information to put into action. With Karnak gone, oversight of the Scar Squadron rested on Smarlo, the second-in-command. With no information, what command could he give? He felt stuck, with a growing tightness in his stomach.

"You look tired," Tan-Kro said bluntly.

Smarlo laughed. "I am."

"Have you eaten?"

"No." Smarlo admitted.

"Perhaps we get someone to help us bring all this to the library where we can protect and inspect it further. We can get some food to renew our strength. It may be a long night."

Master Tan-Kro sounded like a compassionate father. In truth, he had been like a father to Smarlo as he'd grown up under the older orc's tutelage. He appreciated that Tan-Kro still cared deeply for him.

"You're right. I'll have someone bring the corpse to the library. I'll take these with me." Smarlo picked up the pouch of dried meats, the coins, and the parchment and tucked them in an inner pocket of his robes.

When they stepped outside, one of the orcs that had gone with Belguv's search party was just dismounting from a distressed wyvern in the paddock. As the orc ran over to him, Smarlo assumed he'd worked the wyvern to a great speed in order to get there. Hope rose in the orc mage.

"What is it? What have you found?" Smarlo asked.

"We found ..." The orc gulped a breath. "We found the she-elf!"

"Ralowyn?" Smarlo asked to clarify, though Tanessa had told him the attacking elf had been a male.

"Yes," the orc said, shaking his head in disbelief. "She was atop a ... a whale!"

"Atop a whale?" Smarlo's facial features contorted.

"The creature was bringing her to the coast."

"Where is she now?" Smarlo pressed him.

"Belguv sent me to tell you. He flew out to talk to her. They are coming back to Calrok."

Smarlo turned to Master Tan-Kro who'd been listening with great interest. "Kelvur," the younger mage stated as though there could be no doubt that all signs pointed to the lands across the sea.

"Perhaps," Tan-Kro replied.

"We may need to reach out to our friends. I sense this is going to be bigger than we expect."

Master Tan-Kro nodded thoughtfully.

Smarlo whipped open the side of his cloak and sifted through the layers until he reached the pocket he was looking for. From it, the orc mage procured a small abalone seashell.

He whispered something to it, and a small orb of light flickered into existence, floating just above the shell in his hand. The light licked the colorful shell, dazzling the messenger orc still standing nearby.

Smarlo paused under the dusky sky gathering his thoughts and looking at the scene before him. He'd always loved the view from Karnak's home. He'd spent many evenings there with his best friend, gazing over the city of Calrok and out to the sea. He worried for his friend, wondering where the big orc was, but dared to believe that Karnak was still alive and well.

CHAPTER NINE

KINDNESS OF A STRANGER

Karnak tightened the knot of black hair on the top of his head but winced as he pulled. The blow he'd taken to the head ached constantly and shot spikes of pain when he forgot he was injured and touched it. He couldn't be sure how long they'd been at sea because time had been a blur between unconsciousness and sporadic moments of lucidity.

The ship groaned as a wave tilted the massive vessel. Items hanging from chains nearby clinked together. The movement made Merrick shiver in the corner of the cage in which they were kept. The huntsman hadn't vomited in at least a day, and Karnak thought perhaps he was getting his sea legs—or at least his sea stomach.

They'd never be able to tell, though. Their captors fed them sporadically and not every day. When they last brought food, a crew member had given them stale bread and the carcass of a fish to share. That had done little to satisfy their hunger, and the poor huntsman had been so sick he'd hardly touched it.

Smart, Karnak thought. *Keep us hungry. Keep us weak.*

And weak they were. Merrick lay sleeping in the corner of their cage. He looked withered from frequent retching, and the fetid stench in the bowels of the ship wasn't helping the man overcome the sick. The big orc had always been much larger than the huntsman, but the man, curled in the corner of the cage, seemed just plain small to him now. Karnak's jaw quivered—with rage or heartbreak or some combination, he was unsure. He felt weak as well, though he did not look so pitiful as the man.

Worst of all, they had no prospects of escape. Karnak assumed, though he had no way of knowing, they were far out to sea at this point. Neither of them had their mounts. While they'd been unconscious, the crew had taken their weapons and everything from their pockets, including Merrick's statuette of Valurwind.

And then there was Ker.

A soul-deep sadness welled within the big orc. Ker had been killed instantly when the harpoon struck her. Karnak could still feel the impact of the massive bolt that impaled her. He'd been in dire situations before, but he'd always had Ker. The wyvern had always been there, fighting alongside him. But now, she was gone.

Karnak's teeth ground together, forcing his tusks outward in a furious grimace. He felt a warm twitching in the creases of his scrunched nose as his eyes threatened to release a flood of tears again. *Ker*, the orc thought. *I'm so sorry.*

He cursed his impetuousness. How foolish he had been to dive down on the ship ill-prepared. The only friend he'd had longer than Ker was Smarlo. *How could I lead her to such a death?* he scolded himself.

Merrick stirred and mumbled. His stirring became more violent as he tried to escape whatever dreams terrified him so. Karnak had witnessed them a couple times since they'd been captured.

The big orc carefully moved across the cage as another wave swayed the floor of the ship beneath him. He placed a large green hand on the shoulder of the huntsman, waking him. Merrick rolled over. A bead of light poked through a hole on the upper deck and illuminated the man's face. He squinted the painful light away.

"Merrick, wake up. You're alright. Take this," Karnak instructed, handing him a wooden bowl. It was only water, but at least they had that. Someone from the crew would descend to the cage occasionally to check if they had water. If they needed any, the crew member would take the bowl and refill it.

Karnak helped Merrick sit up to drink. The man took a short sip. They'd learned to ration the water as the appearance of crew members to replenish it had been irregular, and the pair could never be sure when they'd come.

"It's day again," Merrick croaked. He took another small sip.

"Yes. There's been a lot of activity on the upper deck this morning." Karnak filled him in. "Something is different. We may be coming into port."

Merrick's body shifted. His relief was visible, even though they had no idea where their captors had taken them. Karnak let an ironic smile creep across his bruised face. The huntsman understood the orc's thoughts. Merrick mirrored his friend's look and shrugged as he said, "It's got to be better than the belly of this ship."

"Well, if we get out of this, I bet you'll do much better on the fishing boats back in Calrok." Karnak gave him a wry look.

"*When* we get out of this," Merrick corrected him. "I would like to never step foot on a ship again."

Karnak patted his battered friend on the shoulder.

A clunk of metal and the creak of hinges signaled that someone was coming. Karnak pushed the bowl of water back at Merrick, who drank it down quickly. They'd gotten into the habit of doing so in order to get more water whenever someone came to inspect.

Someone new entered the dark underbelly of the ship—a human woman. She was tall and lean. Her tight core was visible in what appeared to be seaworthy garments. She had a wicked grin on her face as she closed in on the cage. Karnak and Merrick watched her approach out of the shadows and into view. No one said a word.

A rage boiled in Karnak. They had barely survived this journey. They had been taken away from their home. They had been ripped away by people who attacked his family in the dead of night. *Cowards!* He was not amused by the game this woman played. The big orc stood to his feet, trying to appear as steady as possible in the bobbing ship. He loomed tall above her as he strode to the bars.

The woman's eyes flicked to the huntsman sitting behind the orc. She surveyed him for a moment and returned her wicked grin to Karnak, undaunted by his size. He wavered. He fought every urge not to look back at Merrick. The orc knew the poor state his friend was in.

A low growl escaped his lips vibrating his tusks.

The woman raised an incredulous eyebrow, pulling from her side a wand that started glowing, illuminating the dark lower deck.

"What do you want with us, witch?" Karnak growled. He hadn't meant to speak. He knew her action was a power play—a move to discomfort them. Unfortunately, Karnak didn't particularly like magic, and her play had worked.

She drew nearer to the bars. Karnak wondered for a split second if he could reach out and grab her. Then he thought better of it.

"That's enough, Chadwa." The voice came from the shadows. "Didn't your mother teach you not to play with your food?"

The elf emerged from the shadows, his dark features having hidden him exceptionally well. He pulled back the hood of his cloak, revealing his pale face and long black hair that poured around his pointed ears.

Karnak's eyes narrowed.

"Not that she's going to eat you, of course. She might be strange." The elf glanced over to the witch and shook his head with an amused grin. "But she doesn't eat orc. You don't, right?"

Karnak turned toward the woman. He waited for her answer. She said nothing; she only continued to stare at him.

"She's a real talkative Tally." The elf shrugged. "And you? Karnak?" The big orc winced at the mention of his name. "You're quite the talkative Tally yourself. Though admittedly, I found our previous conversation was rather one-sided. Don't you agree?"

Karnak's muscular arms twitched as his big hands coiled around the bars.

"You can't hold that against *me*, of course. I was rather forthright. Though admittedly, I can see how the situation was uncomfortable for you. Your little tyke did throw a knot in my plans."

Karnak banged his arm against the bars. "You won't speak of him again, or I'll rip that tongue right out of your face." Karnak's body heaved up and down with the exertion of his lungs. In an instant, Merrick stood beside the big orc, a hand on his shoulder.

"Now, now," the elf said with mock surprise. "I understood the people of Tarrine to be brutish, but I expected more than this outright barbarism." The elf clicked his tongue, disappointed. "Can we not have a civilized conversation?"

"How can we?" Merrick stepped in.

The elf gave the huntsman a sidelong look. "I don't understand your question, Merrick."

Karnak did not miss the elf's purposeful use of Merrick's name and the huntsman's subsequent nod. The orc caught on to what his friend was doing. "Yes. How can we?" Karnak echoed. "You seem to know who we are, but we know nothing of you."

"Oh, dear me." The elf laughed, looking over to Chadwa, whose gaze never left the large orc. "You're absolutely right!" He twirled to make his cloak billow, bowed, and said, "I'm Hazkul Bern, original assassin and leader of the Sons of Silence!"

The two prisoners stared blankly at him.

"Oh dear, I fear Tarrine is even less cultured than we were told," he said toward Chadwa. "Our exploits are known far and wide. Though, as the Sons of Silence, not many know them to be our exploits, of course. You see, that's our thing. We're well known for not letting our benefactors' secrets become ... well, known." Hazkul grinned at his accidental turn of phrase.

"Of course, we're not all sons." The elf waved a hand toward the woman. "Our Chadwa being a prime example. But alas, a name change was not in order. The 'Sons and Daughters of Silence' doesn't really have the same ring to it. Don't you agree?"

Karnak and Merrick continued to stare.

"Oh, well," Hazkul Bern said, straightening. "Here I am, rambling about how great I am and not letting you get into the conversation again. Some might say I'm prone to such monologuing, but they usually aren't great conversationalists and don't live long anyway."

"Why did you attack my family?" Karnak growled.

"Oh, straight to the point, this one." Hazkul smiled to Merrick and jutted a thumb toward the big orc.

"Why did you attack his family?" Merrick echoed.

"Wow." Hazkul stepped back, nodding in mock approval. "You two really are quite the pair. 'How can we?' 'How can we?' 'Why did you attack my family?' 'Why did you attack his family?'" The elf mocked. When the prisoners didn't respond, he said, "So serious, too. I'm sorry. I shouldn't mock. It's rather unbecoming."

When they didn't answer him again, he continued, "Alas, the world is not as it once was. You see, there was a time when an assassin could get good honest work. You know, someone would pay you coin to kill someone else. Simple transactions usually. Very lucrative, as you might guess."

"And now you have to capture people?" Merrick asked, not really getting where the elf was going.

Hazkul Bern released a dramatic sigh. "Well, that's one way to put it." He leaned nonchalantly against an upright wooden beam. "You see, the people that pay are usually the ones in power. And if they are the ones in power, they also become targets themselves. It's a nasty cycle really—profitable, but nasty."

Karnak grunted. His frustration was evident. *I'd rather them send another crew member to fill our water and let us wallow again,* the orc thought. Hazkul didn't miss the orc's annoyance.

"Anyway," the elf continued as though Karnak's grunt had been a very rude interruption. "Usually, someone would hire us for a grievance or vengeance or something of the like. Normal things, you know? But things have changed over the years. A new power has risen, and well ..." He paused for a chuckle. "We go where we'll continue to get paid."

"So, you're mercenaries then," Merrick said bluntly.

"Oh, no." Hazkul laughed and looked to Chadwa as though Merrick had said something stupid. "Assassins." He emphasized each syllable. "Well, more like an army of assassins for hire." He paused and put a finger to his chin and nodded contemplatively. "You know, when you put it that way, we definitely sound like mercenaries. The man has a fair point, Chadwa, though we're still not changing the name. Don't get any ideas."

Chadwa said nothing, her unwavering eyes glinted at Karnak. The orc started to get nervous, wondering if she was laying some unspoken curse upon him. "And who sent you to capture us?" Karnak asked.

"You? No." Hazkul clicked his tongue with a chuckle. "You were a happy coincidence. No. No. We were tasked with the huntsman. Ironic that we were hunting a huntsman, I grant you. There is a poetic way about the world that is often missed by those who don't take the time to see it. I would—"

A bell high above them rang several times.

"Oh," the elf started. "That'll be it then. I meant to come down here to tell you two to be on your best behavior as the crew shackles you. We're about to make port, and it would be a right mess if you made a scene in front of all the miners. Their spirits are already broken. We wouldn't want to hurt them by giving them any unfounded semblance of hope. The geldrins would have to beat it out of them all over again."

"Geldrins? What are geldrins?" Merrick asked as the elf walked away.

"And who sent you?" Karnak yelled.

"Now, now." Hazkul shook his head. "Karnak, we do have to work on that temper of yours. And for now, you'll both have to wait. If you're well-behaved, we'll have another conversation soon. I did so enjoy this one."

With that, the elf and the woman disappeared into the shadows. Karnak and Merrick heard the familiar creak of hinges and the clunk of metal as the lock slid into place.

The two looked at each other; neither of them knew what to say.

Finally, Merrick spoke. "They were after me," he said quietly.

Karnak placed a big orc hand on the huntsman's shoulder. "Then let us count it fortunate that I survived and I'm here with you."

They didn't say anything after that, both lost in their own thoughts, wondering where in Finlestia they could be.

The sun beat down on the slaves all morning, doing their geldrin overlords' jobs for them. For some reason, it seemed a hotter morning than those of the past couple weeks. It was dry, and dust blew about the mining trenches in clumpy clouds. The dust caked the inside of the chelon's nostrils, making it impossible to smell even his own sweaty body. Shorlis couldn't understand how the place was so dry, considering its proximity to the sea. Nevertheless, it was.

He sighed in relief at the clanging of the midday bell. For a moment he leaned on a nearby cart and thought about the Shoals. He'd been thinking about them a lot. The Shoals teemed with life. The Mines of Glinso were a place of death. Just yesterday they'd lost an elderly woman from a city near the Eastern Knolls. Shorlis knew she'd been a slave to the geldrins for a few years and that her city had been one of the first to fall to the wicked creatures.

Shorlis gave his father a nod as Anthanar walked up to him and gave him a pat on the shell. The younger chelon took the tools from his father and placed them into the cart where they wouldn't get lost. Misplacing tools was just another of the many reasons a worker could get beat. In a strange way, Shorlis was thankful for the blistering heat. The geldrins felt the heat like any other, maybe more so as their stony skin soaked up the sun. When that was the case, they were less prone to beating the prisoners. It was more effort than it was worth.

Anthanar led his son toward the line of other dust-coated people climbing out of the trenches toward the camp for the midday meal. It was never a luxurious meal. Usually, it consisted of some form of broth and bread. If they were fortunate, vegetable chunks would float in the soup. If they were even luckier—or the commander wanted to see more production out of them—they would find the occasional piece of meat.

The geldrins were particular about what the slaves worked out of the stone, as though they were looking for something specific. They were always inspecting anything that could be perceived as an oddity. The slaves had worked hundreds of different crystals and unique stones out of the mine. They had found gems of many shapes, sizes, and colors. But none of the items uncovered had been rewarded with any excitement. Occasionally, someone would unearth a red stone or crystal. That worker would be brought to the main building so the geldrins could inspect it closer. But like every time before, the worker would be sent back into the mine to find more. Shorlis often wondered what their captors were looking for.

A strange air filled the camp that day. The geldrins seemed in a rather odd mood for a day with such an unbearable heat. They seemed more arrogant. They talked amongst themselves with a haughty attitude. Shorlis scanned the tables lined with workers who'd already made it through the serving line and sat eating the best meal they'd get all day. Most of them ate with their heads down.

Anthanar made it to the end of the line, where Doran scooped water out of a large barrel. He handed the ladle to Anthanar who took it thankfully.

"When Thanaris rose up to fight the evil warlock of Malodran, did Romis and Laro go with him?" the dwarven boy asked in a hushed whisper.

Anthanar chuckled quietly. "There is a right time for everything."

"I know," Doran said sadly, having been corrected with this same phrase from Anthanar on other occasions. The dwarven boy's eyes widened, and he asked, "Just a little hint? Please?"

"We shall see tonight," the old chelon said, winking one of his blue eyes.

"You need to be more careful," Shorlis said as his father moseyed away to find a place to sit. "They probably let you get away with a little bit because you're the water-bearer and just a child. But they are less lenient with adults."

"But we're not going to be here that long, right?" Doran asked, handing Shorlis a refilled ladle.

"What?" Shorlis hissed at him, looking around to see if anyone had heard the foolish young dwarf. "Keep your voice down. Where did you hear such a thing?"

"I heard you and Tenzo whispering the other night."

"We were discussing the graveness of our situation," Shorlis whispered.

"Yeah, but why couldn't we fight back? The heroes in the stories always fight against the wicked forces. Maybe we can be like the heroes."

"Stop. Doran, you mustn't say such things. If anyone heard you speaking—"

"Oy, move along!" A geldrin several paces away scolded Shorlis.

The chelon raised an apologetic hand and downed the ladle. Handing it back to Doran, he whispered, "Say nothing of this."

A sudden ripple of murmurs ran through the camp as a horse-drawn cart approached the eating area. Several guards laughed victoriously.

An elf at the front of the parade dismounted and handed his horse's reins to a guard who took it around a nearby building. The other riders followed, leaving the caged cart sitting before the eating miners. The elf glanced around, a strange look on his face. Was it disgust?

Shorlis watched as Commander Chol exited the building to greet the elf with more diplomatic poise than he'd ever seen from the geldrin.

What is this? Shorlis wondered.

A woman joined the elf. She carried a large bag that wrapped around some large unknown object. *A large hammer, maybe?* Shorlis guessed. *Perhaps it's a gift for Commander Chol—a new weapon for him to assert his power over us.*

As the three disappeared into the building, Shorlis's sea green eyes landed on the cart. It was a reinforced cart with an iron cage over the top. Inside sat two ragged prisoners. The miners had never seen someone transported in such a way. Why were they so special? When Shorlis and his people were brought to the mines, they were chained together and forced to walk.

There was something different about these prisoners. They looked like they'd been dragged on a long journey. A strange sympathy for them rose inside Shorlis. Stranger still, one of the prisoners was an orc—a large one at that. Orcs were rare in Kelvur. Shorlis had never actually seen one before. He knew that most of them resided in the northeast, but they were rare enough that the chelon was captivated by the sight. And so was everyone else.

Most of the workers had stopped eating, stunned by the arrival. The guards were so caught up with themselves that they didn't even yell at the slaves to hurry up. The appearance of the caged cart had changed the environment of the camp.

Shorlis's eyes met the pathetic look of the caged human. He looked as ragged as any of the other humans Shorlis had met during his time at Glinso Mining Camp. Shorlis shook his head and moved to the table. Just before he sat, Anthanar rose and walked past him. Anthanar retrieved a full water ladle from Doran and moved toward the cart.

"Father ..." Shorlis tried to say quietly.

Anthanar did not stop. All eyes of the workers watched as the old chelon approached the cart and handed the ladle to the man. The orc sat up as well. They shared the ladle, sipping from it.

"Thank you," the orc said.

"Oy!" a guard yelled. "Get away from there!"

All of a sudden, several guards ran to the cart, surrounding it. The orc handed the ladle back to Anthanar, who swiveled to face the guards.

"What do you think you're doing, old crust?" one of the geldrins asked.

"They looked as though they needed water," Anthanar replied coolly, lifting the ladle to show them.

"And what gives you the right to give it to them?"

"I was merely—"

"It was my fault," the orc said, lifting himself to his knees. "I summoned the ... the ..." The orc didn't seem to know what to call Anthanar.

Shorlis was standing at the table, unsure what he could do. His stomach felt as though he'd swallowed a heavy brick of lead.

The geldrins surrounding the cart wavered slightly. "What are you, some sort of sorcerer?" one of them asked tentatively.

"No," the orc answered. "I asked him to show us the kindness of water, and he responded. It was my fault."

Emboldened, knowing the orc was not working some unknown spell on them, one of the geldrins laughed. "Oh, that's not good then. Workers aren't supposed to listen to anyone other than us!"

"Doesn't seem like that lesson has sunk in for you, old crust." Another guard sneered.

"No. Wait!" the orc pleaded.

"We've got nothing else to say to you!"

"But plenty to say to you," one of the geldrins said menacingly to Anthanar.

The old chelon looked over to his son. His blue eyes rimmed with a quiet sorrow. Anthanar's face twinged with regret—not regret for helping the strangers, but regret for the pain he knew his son was about to endure. His blue eyes spoke, though his mouth could not. "I love you," they said.

Shorlis's eyes widened, and he bolted around the table as the geldrins began to beat his father. The five guards laughed as they brought down blow upon blow. The orc and the man in the cage beat against the iron bars, yelling helpless pleas at the relentless guards.

As Shorlis rounded the end of the long table, he was tackled to the ground. He cried out in horror as he tried to wrestle away from his assailant. Tenzo pressed hard against him. "Stop. You can't," he whispered hurriedly. "They'll kill you."

"They're killing him!" Shorlis spat back.

Even though Shorlis had grown strong from the hard labor, Tenzo was stronger still.

Shorlis cried as he watched the mob of geldrins pound at his unseen father in their midst.

"What's going on out here?" Commander Chol hollered over the ruckus.

The elf with dark features held a goblet in his hand, sipping at it and watching the commander with what appeared to be amusement. The woman walked ahead of the commander, pulling a wand from her side and flinging it out wide. The geldrin guards flew sideways, rolling over each other in the dirt.

"Hey ..." Chol started, but the woman spun on him, wand at the ready. The commander backed away.

With the arrival of the others, Tenzo had loosened his hold on Shorlis who hefted himself sideways. Tenzo was so stunned by the woman's power that he let his friend go. Shorlis ran past her, not caring who she was, and slid to his father's side.

The old chelon looked up at his son. Anthanar's face was badly beaten, his head bleeding in several places. His blue eyes were bloodshot, and he let out several weak coughs. The whole camp was silent.

"They'll never find what they're looking for," Anthanar croaked.

Shorlis shook his head, tears falling all over his father. "What? Be still."

Anthanar gulped and gripped his son's green arm. "You can't find what's already been found."

"I don't understand," Shorlis whispered through his sobs.

"My staff ..." The old chelon wheezed. "The stone ..."

"Father, don't go." Shorlis hugged his father's bloody head to his own.

"They need your help." Anthanar wheezed, nodding weakly to the cage.

Shorlis didn't answer. He rocked his father in his arms.

"My staff. I ... love you ... my son." Anthanar said no more. His final breath left his body in a quiet gasp.

Deadly silence crossed the camp. Time stopped as everyone processed the scene. A long moment passed, the world unmoving.

Suddenly, padding footfalls broke through the silence. A little being collapsed next to Shorlis and his father. Doran groped at the old chelon's body. "No ..." he whispered, tears pouring off his chin.

"Well ..." A loud voice spoke. "This has been quite the eventful visit." The elf strode to Commander Chol who stood fuming. "I wouldn't say it's been a pleasure, but I'll certainly say you've got quite the lively camp here, Chol. Oh dear. That was poor phrasing." The elf chuckled to himself.

The orc in the caged cart growled in the direction of the elf.

"Well ..." The elf straightened himself again and handed the goblet to Commander Chol. "Let's just stick with eventful, shall we? Chadwa, it seems to me that the good commander has some things he needs to take care of around here. I know you were so looking forward to his gracious hospitality. He is quite the charmer. Wouldn't you agree?" the elf asked, shooting the geldrin a bemused look. "But I'm afraid we've got a delivery to make."

The other riders walked around the building, ready for some grub. Their faces shifted as Chadwa informed them they needed to mount up again.

"I'm so sorry," a voice above Shorlis whispered.

The chelon looked up to see the orc and the man looking down on them with remorse.

"So sorry," the man said.

"Who are you?" Shorlis asked quickly.

"We were captured, attacked in my home," the orc answered.

"Where are you from?" Shorlis pressed.

"Calrok."

"Where is Calrok?" he whispered quickly, seeing the geldrin guards approaching.

"On the eastern coast of Tarrine."

"Tarrine?" Shorlis asked, more to himself.

One of the traveling guards climbed atop the driver's seat and clicked at the horses, lurching the cart into motion. The two prisoners watched the chelon as their cart rolled away.

The infection has spread all the way to Tarrine, Shorlis thought, but the thought was short-lived. The guards surrounded them and roughly dragged the chelon and the dwarf away from the corpse.

Shorlis didn't fight back. He knew there was nothing he could do at that moment. As he was being dragged away, a rage burned inside him. He had wanted to get his father out of this miserable place. This was a horrible place to die.

He heard muffled sobs from other workers around the long table. He realized, all of a sudden, this was not just his loss, but a loss for everyone in the mining camp. He knew then that there would be more losses soon.

CHAPTER TEN

WORKING TOGETHER

Pernden rubbed his temples, exhausted from the long day of meetings and tours. All day, he'd played host to leaders from Calrok and Loralith. Edford had prepared a full day of events for them, and Pernden upheld his obligatory duty to attend most of them. His kingly responsibilities included being present and strengthening both parties' confidence in the fact that Whitestone as a whole stood behind the endeavor to establish a joint city on the Gant Sea.

Much of the prior communication between the parties had been through Edford, so the first interactions between the engineering elves of Loralith and the fisher-orcs of Calrok were thick with tension. Throughout the day, however, Jalko, the Master Fisher-orc, had displayed a great deal of amicability, and the pair of orcs who accompanied him followed his lead well.

The elves were more troublesome. Zilon, a brilliant elf who'd helped build much of Loralith's city over the last few hundred years, had a harder time hiding his emotions. He seemed to view everyone else as less intelligent than him. Occasionally, he sniffed disdainfully at some flaw in the architectural craftsmanship of the men who'd built various buildings around Whitestone. His elven companions often whispered at him to correct his arrogance. Pernden assumed that King Solorin had sent Zilon because of his brilliant work, wanting to show Loralith's support with their best architect, and had chosen the companions specifically to help Zilon play nice with others.

Though most of the day had been tough, Pernden had enjoyed one beam of light. High Commander Mattness had excused herself from the events and sent Nera in her stead. Pernden had to spend the majority of his time with the representatives from Loralith and Calrok, but throughout the day, Nera had been good enough to sneak short moments with him. Short conversations. Quick looks. A comforting grip of his hand.

At the end of the evening, Edford showed the Loralith elves to their rooms, and the king's dining hall fell quiet.

"How are you holding up?" Nera asked.

Pernden was thankful that she'd stayed through dinner and remained after the last few people left. He knew she had to be up early for training the next morning and understood the sacrifice. He sat back in his chair, exhausted, and exhaled a deep sigh. His eyes wandered over the ornate tapestries that clung to the stone walls.

"That was a big sigh." She chuckled, moving to a chair closer to him.

"Was that as awful for you as it was for me?" he asked, his face showing the ache of the long day.

"I thought you did very well," she said. "I was afraid you were going to punch Zilon in the nose, though, when he snorted at Edford's enthusiasm about the intricacies of the Grand Corral."

"Right?" Pernden agreed, still disbelieving the nerve of the stuck-up elf. "When Jalko introduced himself and the other orcs and Zilon could hardly be bothered to look at him, I thought the whole thing was about to come crumbling down."

"Thankfully, Edford has been talking with both parties. He knew what to say to keep things together."

"Yes," Pernden agreed reluctantly. Edford had performed admirably. Though it pained Pernden to admit it, he didn't think he would have been able to hold everything together like the elder man had. "He's put more work into this than most."

"I think it will be a beautiful thing once it's established." Nera nodded thoughtfully, as though she could see the future bustling city by the sea. "Might be a pretty place to live, out there by the sea. High Commander Mattness and I have been discussing the Guard contingent that we'll need to post there."

"Not you," the king blurted. He shifted as the words came out faster than he'd meant them to.

Nera stared at him with a surprised smile. Then she said, "No, not me. It wouldn't make sense to post the Talon Squadron there."

"No. You're right." Though he agreed quickly, his original statement revealed he had more personal stakes in mind.

A blushing smile spread across her face, and her eyes fell to the table.

Pernden slowly stood from his seat. Nera followed his lead and stood. He gazed into her brown eyes. "I—"

"Well done, my King!" Edford entered with a triumphant laugh. "We've made great progress today." The elder man paused, noting the guardian's presence. "Captain Nera, I was about to suggest we go down to the kitchen and have a celebratory cake. I saw them making a cinnamon one earlier. I think it is supposed to be for tomorrow, but today went so well, I thought we might indulge a little early. Why waste a cake on tomorrow when you can enjoy it today?" He shot her a mischievous wink.

Nera turned toward Pernden, disappointment in her eyes, and quickly responded to the elder man. "Unfortunately, Master Edford, I must be up early tomorrow for training."

Pernden touched her elbow, a plea for her to not go.

That smile of hers made him melt. "Another time," she promised.

"Of course," Edford said, straightening. "You won't tell on us if we do, though?"

"No," she laughed. "You two enjoy it. You've earned it today. Good evening."

She turned and walked out of the king's private dining hall. Pernden watched her go, his heart aching.

Edford strode toward Pernden, the look of a giddy boy betraying his grey features. Pernden grinned and shook his head. The man had done great work, and whatever tensions he and the elder man had faced in the past, Pernden agreed that he deserved a little reward. When they arrived in the kitchen, they discovered the little reward was a much larger cake than either of them had anticipated.

Garron grinned as his cousin came around the corner. Dona had just helped him light some candles and collect the wax from long-burned ones. Outside of his cell, she was organizing the mess of books and parchments.

"My triumphant cousin returns?" Garron asked with a smirk.

"Triumphant enough for cinnamon cake." Pernden revealed the small plate from around his back.

"Cinnamon cake?" Dona started. "Enly was saving that for tomorrow!"

Pernden gave her a sheepish look and passed the plate to Garron as though handing it to his cousin quickly would turn her scolding onto him. Garron shook his head and raised a hand innocently.

"I had nothing to do with this," he said as he slowly brought a bite to his mouth. "But it is delicious." His words were muffled by the delicious cake.

Dona put her hands on her hips and glared disapprovingly at Pernden.

"It was Edford's idea." Pernden threw the man into the fire. "Though I probably ate more than he did."

"Well, I'll have to have a conversation with Master Edford tomorrow then," Dona replied. She clicked her tongue and went back to work on the scattered articles. "You boys are always causing trouble."

Pernden shot Garron a glance, and they both felt bad for the scolding Edford was going to receive—but not too bad. He was saving their hides.

"So, did you kiss her?" Garron asked as he took another bite.

"Straight to it with this?" Pernden shook his head. "No, 'How did it go with the representatives from Loralith and Calrok?' Just straight to my love life."

"I told you." Garron gulped the bite down. "It's the highlight of my days." He paused and turned toward Dona. "Aside from seeing Dona, of course."

She gave him a disbelieving side-eye, and he smiled as she turned back toward her organizing.

"Well, the representatives were fine. Thanks for asking," Pernden pressed on. "The elf that King Solorin sent is a bit ..."

"A bit what?"

"High on himself?" Pernden finished the thought, not sure if that was the exact wording he was looking for.

Garron chuckled. "Is that unusual for an elf?"

"Come on, now," Pernden pleaded. "We're supposed to be leaving hardened notions behind us to start something new with this settlement."

"You're right." Garron raised his fork apologetically. "I'm sorry."

"Thank you. Anyway, Jalko and his orcs did surprisingly well, holding it together. I wasn't sure how they'd respond to the elves. This is the first time we've had them all together. They seemed almost solemn."

"Well," Garron started, placing his fork on the clean-scraped plate. "This is a big deal for everyone. No one's been able to establish a city there because of the differences we've had for centuries. They're probably under strict orders to be kind and play nice so everything goes smoothly."

"Yes," Pernden nodded. "It also seems Merrick and Ralowyn have done a good job endearing us to the orcs."

"A huntsman from Tamaria and an elf of Elderwood Forest." Garron shook his head. "Who would have guessed?"

"Ellaria has been proving herself quite the guardian as well."

"She's been telling me of her training. Sounds like Nera is working her hard. Makes me miss the Corral ..." Garron trailed off.

"Cousin," Pernden said softly.

"No, no. It's alright. It sounds like everything is going well and accordingly," Garron said. His innocence faded, and a wry grin crept across his face. "So, did you finally kiss Nera?"

Pernden sighed. "No."

"Foolish boy."

The cousins turned toward the table where Dona had stopped organizing. She looked side to side and straightened her dress.

"That's what I've been telling him," Garron said.

"It's not so easy," Pernden complained. "There are people around me all the time now. Every time we get even a small moment together, something interrupts us. It pains me. Have you ever been in love?"

Garron smirked. "I'm pretty sure Dona and I have a little spark going."

"Well, I never ..." she exclaimed, flustered. "I'm married."

The cousins looked surprised.

"I am," she insisted.

"It's just ..." Pernden chose his words carefully. "You always seem to be here with us."

"Yeah," Garron agreed. "You must spend more time with us than your husband."

"He requires far less babysitting." Dona huffed and gathered some of the tomes and parchments.

Garron shrugged at his cousin. "That's probably fair."

As Dona waddled away with her arms full, she turned and looked over the men. "And that girl has loved you for years. I can't believe it's been this long. How long do you plan to dance around her?"

"Well ..." Pernden seemed to shrink at the scolding. "I—"

"Yes." She didn't let him answer. "You always have people around you, and you hardly get any moments alone with her."

"Right. And—"

Again, Dona didn't let him finish. She clicked her tongue and shook her head sadly. "If you don't do something, you'll watch the world go by you. Nera's a beautiful woman and will make a beautiful wife. And she's probably the only woman I know who can straighten you out."

Garron gave Pernden a goofy grin. *Except maybe Dona*, he thought.

"Don't let time pass you by. *Make* a moment with her. And then make another. And then make another. Don't let stupid things like representatives stand in your way. The only heart you have is yours, until someone you love shares theirs with you."

Pernden didn't dare speak, figuring if he tried, she would cut him off again.

Garron's hands climbed high on the bars as he leaned toward them.

"Dona," he said with a goofy grin. "You're a romantic!"

The little woman stood straighter, cocked her eyebrow as if it were about time the two men recognized her greatness, spun on her feet, and waddled around the corner.

Pernden turned to see Garron leaning on the bars, grinning widely. "You better kiss her before Dona pummels you. You won't be so pretty with two black eyes and a broken nose. Nera will probably have to find someone else."

The king punched his cousin's arm through the bars.

CHAPTER ELEVEN

DANCE UPON THE WAVES

Finally, Orin's crew had found people to help them establish the new city.

For the first time, someone had entertained accepting the venture to form a joint settlement with orcs, and Orin did not let the opportunity slip through his fingers. His words and the fact that he was a member of the fabled Griffin Guard convinced them to hear him out—or at least one of them in particular. Ultimately, Captain Tinothe was well respected by the people of the hovel community, and his word had been the final say on the matter. Their deliberation and debate had taken a full night.

Captain Tinothe was a hard man and probably the reason behind their ability to finally obtain a full-size galleon. He ran a tight ship, and Orin noticed that the man carried himself with a purposeful posture. As Orin watched Tinothe, or Captain Tin, as the people called him, the guardian was impressed by the man's interactions. No one begrudged him for his hard demeanor and the standards to which he held them. The only times he saw the man relax were in the evenings, often taking over the helm because he had a certain affection toward the task. Orin wasn't sure when the man slept.

The community members had spent a day packing what little they had onto their five ships. Another day allowed them to procure everything Captain Tin and Dockmaster Befors had requested. Orin and Coal noted between themselves that the leaders asked for more than necessary for the trip, probably as a test to see how committed Whitestone was to supporting this venture.

With the aid of Aless and Ezel's interactions with merchants, they were able to procure everything without trouble. Befors had been skeptical, but his mood improved dramatically when they'd returned to the docks with everything on the list.

The only problem they'd experienced since the decision was Ezel's involvement. Of course, the grey gnome helped with everything he could, lifting cargo, helping children aboard, tying knots, and rolling barrels. Orin did not miss the fact that the gnome did it all by hand. Not once did his blue magic blaze. The guardian wasn't sure the gnome's reason but avoided asking, recognizing the situation to be delicate.

Since they'd set sail, Ezel had made himself scarce. The deep gnome would appear on the upper deck at night, relishing the fresh air while many of the travelers and crew were down below swaying in hammocks and dreaming of a brighter future. Orin watched his little friend wander toward the bow of the ship. The guardian decided to check on his friend after he spoke with Captain Tin.

The captain of the *Sellena* was exactly where Orin had expected to find him: at the helm. "Good evening, Captain," Orin said as he climbed to the deck of the sterncastle.

"Sir Guardian," Captain Tin replied in his gravelly tone. "You're up late this evening."

"I am," Orin admitted. "I'm a bit nervous about weaving the Narrows."

"We'll make it, or we won't."

Orin started at the macabre and blunt answer. "That's a rather strange way to look at it. What about all these people who trust us to get them to the north safely?"

"Most of them won't know any better. Most of them will be down below when we pass through the Narrows." Captain Tin waved Orin over to the helm. "Take this," he said, pointing to a handle.

Orin hesitated but followed the captain's instructions. "I've never sailed a ship before. I've hardly spent time on the seas before taking this mission."

"Then I think you're going to have to trust someone with a little more experience," Tin said, pulling out his pipe and clearing it. His huge mustache was long enough to blow in the wind. Over the last few days of sailing, the guardian usually saw the captain's bald head covered with a modest brimmed hat to protect it from the sun.

Orin held tensely to the wheel. The handles felt well-polished by much use. He peered over the rest of the ship, doing his best to see in front of them. The moonlight shimmered on the sea, reflecting like a flickering candle on the ever-moving waves.

"You're too tense," Captain Tin said, repacking his pipe.

"What if I run into something and sink us? I don't even know if I'm going straight ... or even if I should be going straight."

Tin chuckled. He lit his pipe and took a couple quick puffs as he leaned on the railing.

"The *Sellena* doesn't really go straight."

"What?" Orin asked, thinking about how tough the Narrows were to navigate.

"Feel the top handle on the wheel," Tin said.

Orin did so.

"Do you feel those notches?"

"Yes," the guardian replied. He felt several grooves that cut around the handle—three in total.

"Those grooves tell you that you're going straight—or as straight as she goes."

Orin did his best to hold the wheel in the straight position.

"You're still too tense," Tin noted again, though the older captain was no longer watching Orin but rather looking out to the sea.

Orin tried to relax, loosening his grip. The wheel turned ever so slightly to the left, but once it had, he was no longer fighting the wheel.

"Did you feel that?"

"I did. What was that?" Orin asked.

"This ship took years of work for us to acquire. And when we did, she was falling apart. We've spent the last two years fixing and righting her. We've patched her. We've replaced masts. We've done many things to make her the beauty she is now."

Orin nodded. The ship was impressive to him, but he was not a sailor. Coal had pointed out several things he didn't like about the *Sellena*—not that the dwarf blamed the crew. He had noted several times how they'd been clever in some repair or another. Coal only seemed sad for them as he noted the more peculiar fixes.

"No matter what we've done, she doesn't like to go straight." Tin shook his head in amusement.

"Is the rudder broken?" Orin asked.

"No. Everything is fine."

Orin stood at the helm feeling it teeter this way and that but never running away from him. His arms moved with the handles, letting the *Sellena* work for him and keeping the ship in a relatively straight position.

"I don't understand," he said.

"I am a regimented man myself," Tin said. "As a guardian, I'm sure you've been well trained on regimen. This was a hard lesson for me to learn, too. Feel the way she moves—never perfectly straight. She is always twisting, always moving with the sea. As long as we nudge her straight, most of the time, she stays on course."

Orin nodded thoughtfully, still not quite sure what the old captain was getting at.

Tin smiled.

"Fate does not always agree with our plans. We have the ability to choose our own, of course. Move in a chosen direction. But sometimes the best course of action is to feel the flow and follow its prompt. We don't always need to fight."

Orin nodded again.

"And sometimes, even when we do fight, we lose."

Orin looked upon the man; the captain's eyes were on Ezel at the bow of the ship.

"What happened?"

"Hmm?" Tin asked, not having heard the guardian as he was lost in his own thoughts.

"What happened with Ezel? Why do Befors and the others avoid him? What history do they have?"

Captain Tinothe's chin dipped to his chest. "It seems to me you should ask your friend. Words have great power to build and destroy. Resentful words from a fool can damage great friendships."

The old captain strode over and took the wheel from Orin. He gripped his pipe in his teeth, looked Orin up and down, nodded, and said, "Thanks for taking a shift so I could light my pipe." He smirked and shot Orin a wink.

Before the guardian reached the steps, he turned around. "Will we stop in Dahrenport before traversing the Narrows?"

137

"No need," Captain Tin replied. "You Whitestone types procured everything we needed for the whole journey. Besides, we might not even make it through the Narrows."

Orin's brows stitched together as the captain's grin widened. Captain Tin gave the guardian another wink, and for some reason, Orin felt better about their chances. He left the captain to his helm and moved toward the front of the ship only to find that Ezel had disappeared.

The guardian felt bad that he'd missed his friend but was exhausted and needed rest. Tomorrow would be a big day.

As the *Sellena* and her four accompanying ships approached the Gant Sea Narrows mid-morning, the ship burst to life with activity. Orin watched several crew members run past him toward pulleys, ropes, and various stations around the galleon. He made his way to the sterncastle where Captain Tin stood near his helmsman, shouting orders Orin didn't understand. The sailors did, however, and they buzzed about, knowing their parts. Even Coal jumped in to help, knowing the captain's nautical language, and better yet, knowing how to accomplish the captain's orders. Orin stepped toward the railing in an attempt to observe without getting in the way.

The ships had stacked up close enough to communicate with signal flags. A young man, no more than fifteen, stood at the back railing waving flags to the smaller ships behind the *Sellena*. Orin watched in wonder as flagmen from the other ships waved their own in an unspoken language.

"They're saying that they're prepared to follow us into the Narrows." A kind voice translated for the guardian.

Orin turned to see Aless, leaning on the railing next to him. "Thank you," he said. "Is it not dangerous for us to go into the Narrows so close to each other?"

"Oh, no, we won't go in this close. They'll spread out in case they need to make quick maneuvers between islands or rocks. If we're too close, they won't be able to make necessary adjustments without running into each other. The waters between islands like the Narrows are savage. They rage in strange directions." She finished pulling her long blond hair into a loose braid that hung over her shoulder. Aless squinted out over the other four ships, reading their signals. "It comes down to a delicate dance upon the waves. Too close and we crash into each other. Too far and we can't help each other. The hope is that the *Sellena*, being our biggest ship, will navigate the safest path and the others can follow through the gaps that were wide enough for the galleon."

"Makes sense to me." Orin shrugged. "But then again, I know almost nothing about sailing."

Aless chuckled and inspected him. "I would have thought a member of the fabled Griffin Guard to be more prideful. You openly share your weaknesses."

Orin laughed in response. "There's not much place for pride in the Guard. Pride usually gets people killed. Knowing your strengths and weaknesses and those of your fellow guardians allows you to work in tandem and produces the greatest results. That's why there are no lone guardians. Everyone is placed in a squadron and knows each other well—well enough to carry one another's weaknesses."

"Sailing in a caravan is similar." Aless nodded thoughtfully. "The smaller vessels behind us will stay as close to us as they safely can."

"But you just said they were going to spread out."

"Oh, they will," Aless assured him. "Because it is flirting with death to stay so close as we are now in such turbulent waters. But they will stay as close as they can because if one of the boats needs help, the only one who can help them will be the nearest ship."

"And what if the *Sellena* is the ship that needs help?"

Her face went grave. "That would be bad for everyone."

Orin turned and searched the waters toward the bow, watching the jutting rocks and islands of the Narrows draw nearer. "So, we find the safest path with the *Sellena*, and the smaller boats follow, and everything should be fine," he said with a twinge of nervousness.

"Hopefully," Aless agreed. "But the *Sellena* is much larger. Some of the smaller vessels may get tossed in between some of the islands where the *Sellena* did not." She paused, her eyes gazing over the smaller ships. "We're in for a very interesting day."

The Gant Sea Narrows were as turbulent as Orin had expected. The craggy islands jutted out of the restless waters all around them. Some of the islands were sheer rock faces; others had small jungles growing wildly on them. Many islands sported a combination of both elements. The sea spray spat up into the air, misting the ships and their crews. Orin would have welcomed the spray that cooled them in the hot sun if Aless had not told him that it was often an indicator of particularly dangerous waters.

As the *Sellena* lurched past another large rocky island, the ship groaned. The crew held a collective breath as though they might need to use it to propel the ship forward in an emergency. So far, though, she'd proven to be a worthy vessel, cutting the sometimes tumultuous waters with apparent ease even as her timbers grumbled. The other ships, however, bounced and jostled erratically behind them. Orin watched as crew members on the smaller vessels buzzed around their boats like bees on flowering bushes.

One part of him relished the fact that he was on the *Sellena*. Another part of him wished he were on one of the other boats so he could help. Though, he was no sailor. Even if he were on one of the other ships, he'd be little help and would more likely be in the way.

Captain Tin calmly called out orders as he saw fit to make adjustments, but for the most part, the crew knew their duties well and adjusted in unison without much prompting. When the moments of silence happened on the *Sellena*, they were almost deafening. The whole crew would collectively hold their breath, hoping they had pulled their riggings just right to avoid a collision with one of the myriad of rocks. Orin hated how little he knew about sailing when everyone went quiet, the only sound the whipping snap of the sails taking the wind. He didn't know if their silence was good or bad. The not knowing was unbearable.

Suddenly, Captain Tin let out a laugh next to the helmsman. The captain gripped his pipe in his teeth and shooed the helmsman aside. "Prepare!" he called to the rest of the crew. Everyone on the ship tensed.

Crashing waves blasted sideways against a rocky outcropping on an elusive island edge. The captain and crew worked their riggings and positions with determined poise. Orin was awestruck. The knot in his stomach made him thankful he'd been too nervous to eat breakfast that morning. As he watched the crew work the ship, he recognized he couldn't be in better hands.

The *Sellena* careened around another of the many islands that dotted the Gant Sea Narrows and wobbled in the wild waves. Eventually, she came into some smooth waves and leveled again.

A whistle from high above in the crow's nest made Captain Tin laugh again and hand the ship's wheel back to his helmsman.

Orin gripped the railing tightly, unsure if he were going to vomit or not.

"The islands get less tight from here," Aless said comfortingly. "That whistle was a signal to the captain that we are through the most difficult parts. Now we just have to make sure the smaller ships make it through that alley."

"Captain!" the flagman hollered. "The *Leslin* is stuck in the whirlpool!"

Captain Tin rushed to the back of the ship to watch.

"What do we do?" Orin asked in a panic.

"Pray, if you're the praying sort," Aless said. "We can't do anything on this side. The other ships will have to help them without getting stuck in the whirlpool themselves. If they can't, the *Leslin* will eventually be spun into the rocks and sunk. It's likely that most of them will be drowned. It's too dangerous for us to try to rescue them from the rocks even if they survive. Captain won't risk another ship."

The guardian watched helplessly as the *Leslin* swayed awkwardly near one of the rocky islands. One of the other ships had already made it through the alley, leaving only two others that could possibly help. The next ship, the *Debbie*, was the smallest and opted to steer far clear of the whirlpool, knowing they could do nothing for the trapped *Leslin*.

Orin saw crew members from the final ship attempt to lob hooked ropes over to the *Leslin,* but the ship turned away from their attempts almost as if she dodged the help.

"The *Leslin* waves their flag in farewell," Aless said somberly.

"What?" The guardian started. "No, there must be something we can do!"

"There isn't." Aless shook her head. "We all knew the risks."

A yelp from a crew member on the main deck below startled them. Orin turned in time to see Ezel's bald head pop above the wooden planks with his eyes ablaze. The helmsman shuddered at the sight, trying to hide himself on the other side of the wheel.

"What do you think you're doing?" Captain Tin asked, pulling the sword from his side.

"Wait!" Orin cried. "Ezel, the *Leslin* is going to be smashed to pieces any moment. Can you help them?"

"That's why I'm here," Ezel signed, his eyes burning bright with blue magic. *"Keep them away from me,"* the little grey gnome signed quickly, nodding toward the crew. Then he clambered to the top of the railing.

Orin stepped behind his friend in an attempt to cover him from anyone who might try to pull the little gnome down from the railing. The flagman had retreated, doing his best to get away from the gnome. Captain Tin glared at Orin.

"You told me that sometimes we have to go with the flow of fate rather than fight it," Orin breathed. "Maybe this is one of those times where you have to let someone else fight fate for you."

Captain Tin's eyes darted to the side, cursing as the guardian used his words against him.

Ezel reached out his hands and swirled them in a rhythmic pattern in front of his little body. The runic tattoos on his arms blazed to life with bright blue light.

Orin looked out toward the *Leslin*. The ship spun toward the rocks at a gut-wrenching speed. Suddenly, the little ship lurched to a halt in the middle of the whirlpool. Ezel's motions turned the other way, as though he were reeling in a giant rope.

On the *Leslin*, crew members that had already given up sprang to life, running about the decks to their riggings and duty positions. Many hopped onto oars and paddled furiously. Slowly, the ship crawled out of the perilous pull of the water trap. Inch by inch it crept away from the rocks that had so nearly claimed them.

Sweat beaded on the deep gnome's bald head and ran down his grimaced face. He pulled with every ounce of strength he could muster.

"Come on," Orin whispered encouragement. "Come on."

The *Leslin* bobbed awkwardly and righted itself in the smooth waters outside the treacherous alley.

Cheers rang across the ship. Orin could even hear celebratory whistles from the other ships.

"You did it, Ezel! You saved them!" The guardian whooped.

The little gnome's lights flickered, and he gave Orin a bleary smile. "*That was ... tough,*" he signed.

"You never cease to amaze me, my little friend." Orin grinned at him and reached an arm out to grab the gnome. Ezel accepted the embrace and rested his bald head on the guardian's shoulder, letting the man carry him.

Aless stared at the two, a look of shocked confusion on her face. Orin nodded to her and turned toward Captain Tin. "I'm taking him below for some rest."

Captain Tin said nothing. He merely nodded his agreement while eyeing the exhausted deep gnome.

Chapter Twelve

Enemy Among the Shadows

Smarlo slammed a tome shut, casting a cloud of dust into the room. He coughed and pushed the volume away from himself. It slid across the small table and halted when it hit a pile of books stacked precariously on the edge. Everything around him morphed into slow motion as the mage jumped up to catch the falling tower of books. He reached out his hand, and the toppling books slowed before they hit the floor.

The orc mage sighed and rubbed the bracer on his wrist. He pondered over the crystals that had been worked into an intricate pattern on the piece of flexible armor that covered his forearm. It baffled him still after years of practice how little he understood of the magics that were housed in the bracer.

"Have some tea," Ralowyn said, coming around the corner with two cups. "You have not slept in days."

Smarlo rubbed his eyes and gratefully took one of the mugs. The steam billowed around his face. He could smell the sweet aroma. He did enjoy having Ralowyn around. He had learned much from the she-elf. She had spent forty years in Elderwood Forest learning of magecraft, and Smarlo was eager to learn what knowledge she offered. In truth, she had taught him more about magic in the last two months than he had garnered in years under Master Tan-Kro—though he would never say as much to the old Master for fear of breaking the elder orc's heart.

"You haven't slept in days either," he said to her after savoring a hot sip.

"But I am an elf. I can stay awake for a week if need be. Though, I do not prefer to do so." She pulled some of her silvery hair behind her pointed ear and took a tentative sip of her tea.

Smarlo slumped into his chair with a sigh. "Seems like it would be a helpful trait."

"It can be." Ralowyn gave him a weary smile.

"We've been at this for days. I've looked through every scroll and tome I can think of that might tell us anything about the rock creature."

"And I have gone through each of them after you," Ralowyn added. "Perhaps there is nothing in the library of Calrok that can reveal the answers to our questions. Calrok is not the only city with a library. In fact, I find it to be the smallest of the ones I have seen. Loralith has scrolls more ancient than this city. Perhaps—"

"No." Smarlo waved a hand at her, setting his tea down on the wooden table. "I spoke to Argus and Lanryn using the Shell of Callencia several days ago. They assured me they'd grab any books they thought might be useful from Galium and Loralith and rush them to Whitestone."

Smarlo thought about the two mages. Argus Azulekor was an old dwarven mage, originally from Kalimandir in the far south of Tarrine. He was the one who imbued the Shells of Callencia with arcane power, an amazing magical feat that allowed the users to speak to each other over vast distances. There were only four, however, for they required great energy and difficult magic to create.

Lanryn was an elf mage and old friend of Ralowyn's. They grew up learning the ways of magic at the wisdom tower in Loralith before each bonded with their magical artifacts. In the tradition of elven mages, they were required at that point to go on their own walks, a type of pilgrimage where they set out to discover their individual magical abilities.

Smarlo was grateful to know the mages, a rather strange sentiment he thought. Friendship between an elf and an orc, up until recently, would never have been accepted—even more so, a friendship between an orc and a dwarf.

In recent years, Smarlo had found himself at the end of Master Tan-Kro's teachings. The old master had much wisdom to share, of course. But Smarlo's magical abilities equaled the old mage's as far as he could tell, and he was hungry to learn more. Conversing with the other mages and Ralowyn had been a treat he never thought he'd have the opportunity to enjoy.

"If only we still had that corpse." Smarlo cursed himself.

"You could not have known," Ralowyn said sternly.

Smarlo let out a frustrated sigh, pushed himself up, and paced the room.

Two guards had been placed in charge of bringing the stony creature's body back to the library while Smarlo and Master Tan-Kro rushed to the beach south of the ports to greet Ralowyn and Belguv. Someone had attacked the guards, killing both of them, and the stony creature's body had been stolen. An enemy among the shadows remained in Calrok.

Smarlo rested his arm on a thick wooden column, placing his forehead on his arm. "If we could have studied him ..."

"What?" Ralowyn asked. "If we could have studied him, what would we have found?"

"I don't know," Smarlo blurted. "Something! Anything! Some clue as to who these people are and why they attacked us. Instead, I've got the entire city watch on alert, looking over their shoulders, knowing there's an enemy out there who killed two of our own. Thankfully, the Scar Squadron is keeping Karnak's absence close to the chest. Imagine what would happen if the rest of the city knew our gar is missing!"

"Do you not think I worry, too?" Ralowyn asked, raising her voice. Smarlo winced. He had never seen the she-elf lose her temper. "I watched as our friend dove headlong into our enemy's ship after we both saw the man I love netted and dragged into the water!"

Silence fell between them. Smarlo had grown fond of the two outsiders. He'd spent considerable time with them, and though he had assumed there was a deep bond between the huntsman and the elf, he had not heard any conversation between them of love.

"I'm sorry," Smarlo said after a long silence. "There's just so much going wrong. Usually, Karnak is here, and we work things out together. He's my best friend."

The sadness of the two mages was palpable and filled the small library.

"I am sorry," Ralowyn said, an awkward squint on her face. "That I am the one with whom you must work this out."

"We are quite the sorry pair," Smarlo replied with a chuckle.

Ralowyn smirked. "We will find them. We must. I have to believe it."

"Yes. We'll figure it out." Smarlo nodded.

"What tome is next?"

Smarlo paused, looking at a closed door behind which sat Master Tan-Kro in his private study. Smarlo knew the old master was pouring over a specific tome, one that the younger orc mage had never been allowed to touch.

It wasn't just him, of course. No orc was allowed to touch it but the master mage. Master Tan-Kro had been in the room as long as Smarlo and Ralowyn had been in the library sifting through all the other works. What would the old mage find in the tome? Smarlo didn't know.

Smarlo banged his fist against the thick wooden column and turned toward another row of shelves.

"I'll grab a few for you to start on," he said. "But I need to check in with Jeslora, the captain of the watch, and Belguv to hear what the Scar Squadron has to report. I'll be back before it gets dark. There's still an enemy in our midst. I don't know who they are or where they're hiding, but we'll find them."

Ralowyn's silvery hair swept across the parchment as she read. She pulled the strands behind her pointed ear where they held for only a short while before they inevitably broke free again. She stood from her chair, needing a quick stretch. She'd found nothing of import in any of the parchments and tomes she'd combed through that night. The sun hadn't risen yet, but she knew it would break the horizon within the hour.

She crossed to Smarlo who lay face down in a book, quietly snoring. She adjusted the blanket she had covered him with several hours ago. He had returned with no news on the lurking enemy within Calrok. Though in truth, they had neither seen nor heard of any disturbance since the killing of the guards who carried the corpse of the stony creature. The elf mage wondered if the assassin was still in Calrok. Perhaps taking the corpse was the last requirement of their job, and the assassin had fled afterward.

Ralowyn smiled as Smarlo let out a snort and his long ear twitched. They were doing everything they could to gather information on Kelvur. She wished they could mount up with the Scar Squadron and fly across the sea. But that could prove to be a fatal error. None knew how far the journey was across the sea. None knew if wyverns had the endurance to fly such a great distance without rest. If the squadron were unable to make it across, they'd have doomed their warriors to death, lost at sea.

The ship that downed Ralowyn had been a mighty vessel—greater than any she'd seen in Calrok. Frankly, it was greater than any she'd seen in all Tarrine. That suggested to her that the distance was vast and required a sturdy ship to traverse it.

She and Smarlo had gone round and round in circles with ideas about how best to venture after their friends. She had even suggested they take a route along the Gant Sea Narrows. They could fly until the wyverns were tired, land on some of the islands to rest, and then start out the next morning. It was good in theory, but Smarlo reminded her that their maps didn't show the Narrows past a certain point. What if they got themselves to the end of the Narrows and then it was still too great a distance for the wyverns? Plus, while wyverns were adept at catching their own fish from the sea near the coast, would they be able to do the same above the open sea? And where would they get fresh water? Too many unknown variables existed.

Ralowyn extinguished the candles and opened the window, letting the morning air refresh the musty room. She nearly knocked over a clay ink pot on the corner of a table strewn with reading materials that had been stacked haphazardly as they'd been deemed unhelpful in the mages' pursuit of knowledge on Kelvur. Thankfully, the clay ink pot swiveled precariously but narrowly stopped before the table's edge.

The sky was lightening, and the she-elf heard birds chirping from a nearby roof. A strange noise caught her pointed ears. *Running!* she thought and leaned out the window to look.

A young orc female dashed down the road.

"Master Tan-Kro!" she yelled. "Master Tan-Kro!"

Ralowyn reached for the Staff of Anvelorian, which flew from the spot where it stood and into her grasp. She did not recognize the young orc woman. The elf's eyes lit up with lavender flame.

The young orc woman skidded to a halt on the stone. She looked warily at the elf. "I-I need to speak to Master Tan-Kro," she said nervously.

"Speak to me," Ralowyn said, her eyes piercing.

"I ..." The she-orc hesitated but decided what she had to say was too important to be held up. "There was someone in the mines!"

"What?" Ralowyn asked, confused.

"There was someone skulking around the mines when we arrived this morning. Scared Kag out of his wits!" she said hurriedly through quick pants.

"What do you mean skulking?"

"Chief Kag said he didn't recognize her. She was acting weird, like she was looking for something!"

"She?" Ralowyn pressed.

"Some orc." She nodded. "Someone he didn't recognize. And then she disappeared into the shadows."

"Did you say Kag?" Smarlo asked, startling Ralowyn as he hurried to the window.

"Yes, Master Smarlo," she affirmed.

"Mining Crew Chief of the Gert section?"

"Yes."

Smarlo's eyes widened.

"What? What is it?" Ralowyn asked.

Smarlo ran to Master Tan-Kro's door and banged on it several times. "Master Tan-Kro," he shouted. "Master, come out."

"What is it?" Ralowyn asked again, the magical flames in her eyes replaced with anxiousness.

"Months ago, I had to go down into the mines to help the miners take care of a disturbance. They had a ranken."

"A ranken?"

"Yes, foul creatures—horrifying beasts taller than either of us. Head like a lizard, covered in slime like that of a salamander. Eight sharp legs like a spider. Hideous monsters. One came up into the mines from deep within the Underrock to nest. If we didn't kill it, others would have come. She'd already killed several miners. Kag and I managed to kill her. Master!" He banged the door a few more times. "While we were climbing back through the caverns toward the mining roads, we stumbled upon an inscription."

"What kind of inscription?" Ralowyn asked, still confused.

Smarlo paused, his eyes widening again in disbelief as he remembered it. "Dark tongue."

"Dark tongue," Ralowyn gasped.

Suddenly, the door flew open next to Smarlo. Master Tan-Kro looked weary, like he was feeling every second of his old age. "Dark tongue?" he hissed.

"Yes, Master," Smarlo started. "Chief Kag and I found a dark tongue inscription in the mines a while back."

"You mean the Underrock?"

"No," Smarlo shook his head. "We weren't in the Underrock when we found them. With everything that happened with the dragon and King Sahr and the sorcerer and the rebellion, we've been so distracted I forgot to tell you. I didn't—"

"The parchment!" Tan-Kro croaked. "Where is the parchment?"

Ralowyn grabbed the small piece of parchment they had spent countless hours examining for what felt like no reason. She handed it to the old master.

"*Colrahanic genorfae,*" he whispered, and suddenly the parchment shifted in his hand. Black ink appeared as though it were soaking through from the other side. The ink formed into wicked curves and sharp bends as it revealed letters in an unfamiliar script to Ralowyn.

"Dark tongue," Smarlo whispered in disbelief as he stared at his master. The younger mage was too shocked to wonder what other secrets Master Tan-Kro might yet hold.

CHAPTER THIRTEEN

A SURPRISE VISIT

The sunset sky painted the damp streets of Whitestone in brilliant oranges as Pernden meandered along them. His nerves were getting the better of him. He'd previously walked with determination toward the Grand Corral, and his goal in heading there was the same as his current one. Perhaps the fact that the Corral was still home to him gave him the advantage of being comfortable in his surroundings. Of course, he'd been to Nera's old home many times in the past, but the impending visit felt different.

He'd had another long day with the representatives, but this time, Nera hadn't been along for the ride. High Commander Mattness decided she couldn't get away with another absence from the delegation and fulfilled her duties in the discussions about the new settlement instead.

Pernden worried that she'd seen his initial disappointment when she arrived instead of Nera. He shook it off quickly and focused on the drudgery of the proceedings Edford had planned for them.

Just before supper, the king took his leave of the representatives under the ruse of needing to speak with High Commander Mattness as she walked across town to the Grand Corral. Of course, he merely wanted to be done with the pomp and circumstance, and he knew Edford would take good care of the delegates in his absence. Mattness understood completely and didn't give him a hard time about it as they walked in silence.

When they arrived at the Grand Corral, they parted ways, and Pernden was disappointed again to not see Nera. Thankfully, Ellaria spotted him and informed him that Nera had gone to visit her mother for dinner.

Pernden kicked a loose stone along the quiet streets. Most of the citizens of Whitestone were already home preparing evening meals with their families. He was glad the people were safe and able to enjoy their families, but he was also jealous. He wondered if he would ever be able to enjoy having a family in any normal sense of the word. Being king came with all sorts of difficulties. How had his uncle Farrin done it?

He thought of his cousin and decided to ask Garron about a king's family issues. He reminisced about growing up with his cousin and wondered how normal that was for a family. *I suppose nothing is normal for a king*, he thought. His steps slowed. What right did he have to pull Nera into that sort of life? How often had she discussed a simple life?

She's her own woman. She'll make her own decision. He comforted himself and smiled when he remembered Dona scolding him and telling him that Nera had loved him for years. His steps quickened again. The reminder gave him courage. He chuckled to himself as he considered whether it was courage or fear of Dona's wrath that fueled him.

As he strode up to the door of the humble home, he took a deep breath. "Make a moment," he quietly encouraged himself.

Then, he knocked.

From inside, he heard someone muttering to the others about who could possibly be there at a time when decent folks should be at home for their own supper. Pernden smiled. He hadn't seen Nera's mother in far too long. Netla was a kind and generous woman. She always looked at him with a twinkle in her eye, as though she knew something about him that he didn't.

The door swung open, and Nera's beautiful smile turned to surprise.

"What are you doing here?" she asked.

"I ..." Pernden stumbled over his words. Viewing Nera in the fading light of sunset, standing in the doorway ... his words stuck and formed a lump in his throat.

"Oh, my!" Netla said from the table. She quickly shooed the children and a middle-aged man out of their seats. "My King," she said, hurrying to greet Pernden at the door.

"Miss Netla," he nodded to her. "I think Pernden will be just fine. You've been calling me that almost all my life."

Netla nodded with enthusiasm and scolded her daughter. "Well, what are you doing leaving the man out in the street?"

"I—"

Netla cut her daughter off. "Have you eaten?"

This time Nera answered. "I don't think Pernden came all the way out here to eat with us, mother!"

"What? A king's got to eat, right? Don't want him wasting away. If you ask me, he's a little too skinny as it is. The castle kitchen staff not feeding you enough, honey?" Netla moved past her daughter and roped Pernden's arm with her own. "Come now, there's plenty of supper for you, too."

Pernden grinned helplessly at Nera as her mother dragged him into the cozy home. Nera raised her eyebrows in amusement and shook her head as though he'd fallen into a trap and she wasn't going to save him.

The dinner was delicious, as was every meal Netla had ever made for him. The small potatoes were cooked and seasoned to perfection, and the round woman had made a special gravy to go with the antelope sausage Bilford had brought. The butcher was almost as round as Netla, and his kindly demeanor made Pernden think the two quite the match. The king was glad to see the woman had found someone to love after her husband had passed away over ten years prior.

Nera's teenage sister, Ada, spoke excitedly to Pernden about some of the books she was reading from the Whitestone Library. Though, she made certain to tell him she was disappointed so many of the scrolls and tomes were missing of late and asked whether it was Mistress Leantz needing them for her new position on the king's council.

"I think Garron has a few," Pernden admitted with a smile.

An awkward silence fell over the table.

"Oh, honey," Netla said from across the table. "How is your cousin?"

"He's well, actually," Pernden assured her. "He's been recovering well. I've been seeing him a lot lately. Dona keeps him fed and healthy and stocked with books. Ellaria continues her visits with him every day."

"Oh, I like her," Netla said. "That child may be the only woman I know with as much spunk as Nera." She gave her eldest daughter a smirk.

Nera rolled her eyes and grinned.

"Yes. That's all fine," Ada cut in. "But I've been reading everything I can find on the Gant Sea. Does he have any tomes on that?"

"I'm not sure," Pernden admitted.

"Well, tell him to return some so the rest of us can read them," she said bluntly.

"Ada!" Her mother scolded her.

The face Ada made suggested she didn't understand the problem.

"You don't boss around the king, no matter how smart you think you are. You apologize!"

"Sorry. Would you *please* tell him to return some so the rest of us can read them?" Ada asked as politely as she could.

Netla covered her face in embarrassment.

"It's alright," Pernden said with a laugh. "Honestly, the smart people boss me around all the time. Who knows, maybe someday you'll be on my council, and then it can be your job to boss me around."

Ada pursed her lips and nodded as though she'd never considered the prospect but liked the idea of it.

Nera's brother, Devohn, piped up, "I'm not going to be on the council. I'm going to be in the Griffin Guard!"

Netla's mouth gaped as though her parenting of these children was a hopeless endeavor. Bilford smiled as he chewed another bite, evidently finding the interactions humorous.

"Oh, is that so? That's a noble call. You must be close to age. You're growing strong. I can tell you'll make a great guardian someday," Pernden encouraged him.

"I'm only ten, but I've already been practicing. I'm going to be a master swordsman, and me and my griffin will be in the Talon Squadron, just like you and Nera!"

"Ah, a swordsman, huh?"

"Yes, I have two wooden ones. They're just for practice, but I engraved them with my own symbol," Devohn said proudly.

"Oh, I'd love to see that," Pernden replied.

Devohn didn't hesitate, jumping out of his seat and dashing off to a room at the back of the home.

"You're as bad as she is," Netla said, nodding at Nera. "Getting him riled up like that."

Pernden shot a sheepish grin toward Nera. When Devohn ran back into the room, Nera was the first to jump up and take one of the wooden swords. The siblings danced around the room swinging the swords and cracking them together in strikes and parries. Pernden wasn't sure how Netla was handling the battle, but when he turned to her with an inquiring look, she gave him a resigned nod toward the two, giving him permission to join them.

He stepped in and requested Nera's practice blade. She gave a deep bow and held the sword out with reverence. Pernden took it in ceremonial fashion as Devohn watched with wide eyes.

The king and the boy danced around each other cracking their wooden swords this way and that. After a while, Devohn looked at Pernden and took a breath. "You're really good!" Devohn exclaimed. "Probably even better than Nera."

His oldest sister gasped and gave him her best offended look.

"Probably," Pernden whispered, giving Devohn a wink.

"Excuse me?" Nera said, turning her feigned offense onto the king.

"Alright," Pernden said to Devohn. "She wins a few of our sparring sessions."

Nera cleared her throat, not taking her eyes away from the king.

"Alright," Pernden twitched under her watchful gaze. "It's pretty close. She wins a lot of them. Maybe half." Pernden turned over his shoulder to see if she was still watching him. When he realized she was, he amended, "Most."

Devohn looked to Nera with amazement, seeing his big sister in a whole new light.

The evening continued with much joy and conversation. Eventually, Bilford realized the hour grew late and decided it was time for him to retire to his home. He'd have to be up early to open the butchery. He gave Netla a squeeze and a quick peck, and she walked him to the door.

Pernden, too, had early morning responsibilities and decided Bilford's exit was probably the cue for his own. Nera quickly stepped up next to him and walked him to the door.

Netla grinned at the king and squeezed him in tight for a hug. She poked at his side and said, "If they aren't feeding you well enough, you come see me anytime, honey."

Pernden laughed and bowed slightly. "Thank you."

Netla released the man and gave her daughter a mischievous glance out of the corner of her eye before she walked toward the kitchen.

Pernden stepped outside under the stars that glinted high in the night sky. Nera closed the door behind him, and to his great delight, she stood outside next to him.

"This has been the best night I've had in a very long time," he said to her. "I haven't felt this normal in ... I don't know how long."

"Since you had to take on the duties of the king?"

"Yes." Pernden shrugged. "That sounds about right."

He pressed his lips together, but Nera's beautiful smile was contagious, and he was soon grinning back at her.

"I don't imagine you just stopped by for supper?" she asked as she drew nearer to him. "Enly feeds you pretty well, whether my mother thinks so or not."

Pernden chuckled. "She does. And I ..." The man's words drifted away from him as he involuntarily took a step closer to her. *This woman*, he thought in disbelief.

"You what?" she asked, placing a hand on his arm.

"I ..." Words no longer worked for Pernden. The starlight sparkled in Nera's brown eyes as she pressed nearer. Heat radiated from her fingertips on his arm. "Nera," was the last thing he said before he pulled the small of her back toward himself, held her face with his other hand, and kissed her.

They sank into their warm embrace and kissed each other tenderly.

A giggle and a swish of a window curtain made them turn, but they saw nothing. A muffled scolding from inside yelled, "Ada, get away from that window!"

Pernden smiled as he looked back at Nera. The two hadn't moved apart; he still held her close. She bit at her bottom lip as she grinned at him.

"I've been meaning to do that for a very long time," he said to her.

"What took you so long?" she asked, not losing her smile.

"I don't know." Pernden laughed sheepishly. "We've been close so many times. We've always been interrupted. I was starting to think we were cursed."

Nera huffed out a laugh and shook her head.

Then she looked deep into his eyes, brushed a lock of his blond hair out of his face, and with a pop of her brow said, "There's no one interrupting us now."

Pernden's grin grew.

Nera pulled him close again and kissed him.

Pernden sauntered toward the castle kitchen, the smell of baking biscuits guiding him. Birds sang sweet melodies in the early morning light that poured through the many castle windows. In a strange twist of fate, he was actually looking forward to gathering with the representatives. Nera would be there.

Apparently, High Commander Mattness felt as though she could take another day away from the delegation to attend to matters at the Grand Corral. Or perhaps she had decided she could only handle the political dealings in one day stints. Either way, a few days earlier Pernden would have begrudged her for it, wallowing in his jealousy at her ability to distance herself from the situation, but not anymore.

The young king spun into the kitchen, humming to himself, and swiped one of Enly's famous biscuits. Enly tried to shoo him away—one of the few people in the castle brave enough to shoo the king—and he gave her a wry wink as he scooted out the other side of the kitchen. He felt so alive. He and Nera had finally kissed. All the years he'd wanted to do it, and finally, he had taken the advice of the foreboding Dona and made the moment. He would have to thank her for her encouragement later.

Upon entering the king's private dining hall, Pernden discovered the sight of Edford and the already gathered orcs couldn't bring down his spirits. Edford eyed the younger man as Pernden swayed to his seat. The elder man squinted and pursed his lips, analyzing the king.

One of the orcs leaned over to whisper to another. They snickered before being quieted by Jalko.

Edford smiled at the orcs and asked, "Something funny? I do love a good joke."

Jalko hesitated, then threw a backhand into the shoulder of the orc on his right. Porg straightened and replied, "The king looks lovesick." Though the orc attempted to speak with a straight face, his tusks parted his lips into a wide grin. Edford continued to eye the king, not hiding his smile very well either.

Pernden tried to adjust his posture in an attempt to mask whatever it was they all saw so clearly. Before the king could reply, Porg explained, "Orcs get lovesick, too. We're a very passionate people. We just thought it a funny thing we have in common." The teasing highlighted another similarity that connected the two people groups.

The elves arrived for breakfast with little fanfare, and the kitchen staff brought the food into the room and served it. Enly and her team had prepared another fine breakfast: fruits and biscuits and eggs and sausage. It wasn't antelope sausage like Bilford had brought to Netla's house the night before, but it was delicious, nonetheless. Though it was a fine spread, Pernden picked at his plate absently while the others ate and engaged in friendly conversation.

Then, the door opened.

In stepped Nera, and Pernden rose from his chair so quickly, he nearly knocked it over. His cheeks flushed as the orcs recognized the connection and laughed.

What is wrong with me? Pernden thought.

Nera flashed him a smile as she walked around the table to an open seat, and his heart melted in his chest. *Oh right,* he remembered. *This woman is going to stop my heart from beating.*

He regained his seat and finally started eating.

When breakfast was over, it took everything within him not to take her hand and run off. They could run to the castle stables, get their griffins, and fly off into the morning. Edford wouldn't be able to stop them. The older man was much better at this stuff anyway. They didn't really need Pernden and Nera there, did they?

As if she knew where his mind was going, Nera stepped close when the others left the room, grabbed his arm gently, and planted a kiss on his cheek. The show of affection grounded him back to the present. Their eyes met, and pure joy radiated through his body.

Porg cleared his throat to let the two know he was still in the room. His toothy grin was wide, and he grabbed a few sausages to take with him. His eyebrows wriggled at the king.

Pernden smirked and sighed. "Alright, let's get to it then." He grabbed an apple from the table and held it up as he walked. "Should I grab anything else in case you get hungry later?"

Porg shook his head and crinkled his nose. "I should have enough," he said patting his satchel. Before he passed the end of the table, he reached out and pocketed two more biscuits.

Nera was distracted much of the day. At one point, Pernden had whispered to her that they should slip away for a picnic dinner near Whitestone Forest. She liked the idea but was pretty sure the king had slipped away from dinner the previous night, if she remembered correctly. And of course, she did. How could she forget?

They walked through the market square, heading toward the keep entrance. The merchants were at their stalls. Edford stopped to show Zilon and Jalko different stalls while Merchant Master Feink explained the wares. Edford would eventually get annoyed by Feink's ramblings and shuffle the group along. The afternoon had continued much the same.

Nera, however, spent much of the day returning Pernden's playful grins with faux scolding leers, attempting to hide her own smiles. She struggled to stay focused. She felt like a dam had burst inside and emotion flooded her. She tried to contain it, but that seemed impossible.

Ellaria had caught up to Nera that morning to tease her about seeing Pernden and had immediately seen something on

Nera's face that gave it all away. Ellaria, of course, thought it was wonderful and wanted to hear all about it, but Nera hadn't had time to share before she left for the castle. She didn't plan on giving a lot of details, just the general story about Pernden showing up unannounced for dinner and the sweetness with which he engaged her whole family.

She caught herself looking at him this time. His long blond hair waved in the wind as he chatted with Porg. It was nice to see him enjoying a conversation with one of the representatives. Pernden was a good and noble man. Most of the time, she felt she believed in him more than he did. Watching him in that moment, she decided she'd been right about him making a good king.

They moved closer to the stairs leading to the keep, leaving the stalls in the square behind. A sudden roll of hushed whispers echoed behind them. Large shadows flitted across the steps, and the group turned toward the sky.

A pegasi unit from Loralith descended into the square, landing at the bottom of the stairs. Porg turned nervously toward Pernden, but the king placed a comforting hand on the orc's shoulder before moving past him to greet the newcomers.

The lead pegasus, a beautiful creature with brown spots, neighed and stamped its hooves as it settled its wings to its side, revealing an elf Pernden recognized.

"Lanryn! What are you doing here?" he asked, hurrying to embrace the elf. "It's good to see you."

The tall elf slid off the back of the pegasus with incredible grace. He smiled and greeted the king. "King Pernden, it brings me joy to see you as well."

"Though we come bearing grave news," a voice from behind the elf said.

Pernden peered around Lanryn and saw Argus Azulekor fumbling off the back of the pegasus. "Argus!" Pernden exclaimed. "What in Finlestia?"

"We'll explain," Lanryn said, gripping the king's shoulder. "Perhaps we can speak somewhere in private, without the delegates present?" He added the last bit in a whisper.

"Sure," Pernden said, furrowing his brow. Though the elf did his best to show a positive face, his lips pressed together in an awkward smile. "Edford, would you see our guests to the dining hall?"

"Yes, my King," Edford responded. "I'm sure Enly has supper almost ready for us anyway."

Garron roiled on his bed, throwing the blanket onto the stone floor of his cell. He uttered a ragged cry and banged his hand against the stone wall. The immediate pain in his knuckles woke him from the night terror. His body was sweaty, and his hair matted against his face. He gasped, trying to catch his breath and slow his pounding heart. He sat up too quickly, and his head filled with fog as darkness pressed on the corners of his eyes.

A tome tumbled from the bed next to him and crashed to the floor. He shook his head. He must have fallen asleep reading. Garron cursed himself. He should have known better than to read on the bed when he was so tired. The trouble was, he was always tired. He avoided sleep like it was a plague. He couldn't escape the things he saw when his mind wandered into the realm of dreams.

The familiar *clank* of the dungeon door sounded through the room, and Garron rose quickly, attempting to tidy the mess he'd made in his sleep. Pernden rounded the corner, watching his feet as he shuffled into the room.

"My triumphant cousin returns?" Garron asked, trying to mask the shake in his voice and wiping the matted hair from his face.

Pernden sighed, his shoulders drooping as he shook his head. Garron could tell something was wrong.

"Is it Nera? Is everything alright?"

"No," Pernden said quickly, and there was an odd mix of emotions on his face. "Nera is fine—great, actually."

"Oh?" Garron piped, though he still didn't understand.

"We've had some friends arrive from Loralith," Pernden continued.

"Not part of the representatives party?" Garron's face scrunched quizzically.

"No. Lanryn and some of the Riders of Loralith."

"The elf that helped you retake the castle," Garron said to himself as he pieced details together.

"Yes, and he brought a dwarf from Galium named Argus Azulekor."

"A dwarf? What in Finlestia?"

"That was my initial reaction as well," Pernden shrugged. "Anyway, they arrived this afternoon. There was an incident in Calrok."

"What kind of incident?" Garron drew closer to the cell bars and his cousin. "Do the representatives from Calrok know of it? Will it cause problems for the settlement?"

"I don't think it will. From what Argus told us, Smarlo, the second-in-command for the Scar Squadron in Calrok—he's a mage, by the way—contacted Argus through the magic Shells of Callencia to let him know what happened. Apparently, it happened before the representatives even left Calrok."

"And they're still playing nice and following through on the commitment. That's good," Garron said, stroking the stubble on his face. "What happened? It can't be that bad if the representatives still came to Whitestone."

"That's what I was thinking, too." Pernden hesitated, and his eyes narrowed as if he were trying to figure something out.

"But ..." Garron nudged him.

"But it was Gar Karnak. Someone came to assassinate him, or at least that's how it appears."

"Wait. Weren't Orin's friends, Merrick and Ralowyn, staying with the gar in Calrok?"

"Yes," Pernden nodded as though he were deep in thought. "Ralowyn is fine. She survived the attack and made it back to Calrok."

"What? They killed the gar and Merrick?"

"Well, no." Pernden hesitated again. "Apparently, Merrick, Karnak, and Ralowyn went after the attackers. Ralowyn lost her mount and dropped into the Gant Sea, and the ship got away."

A sudden flood of dread filled Garron. He already knew where the rest of this conversation was going. He didn't know the fate of the huntsman or the gar, but he knew where they were headed.

"Kelvur," Garron muttered, a quiver in his voice.

Pernden's face tensed. "Yes. How did you know?"

Garron looked up at his cousin in surprise. He tried to get the attention off himself. "What happened to them?"

The king sighed. "That's just it; we don't know. They may have been captured. Ralowyn witnessed Merrick and his astral falcon netted. Strange things are happening in Calrok. They had a prisoner who was like a man of stone, but he was killed by an assassin. The body was stolen, and the guards who were transporting it were killed."

"No, no, no, no!" Garron grew angry, pounding on the bars. "Karnak and Merrick were the ones who helped defeat Jaernok Tur, right?"

Pernden stared at his cousin with concern. "Yes. They both played important roles in it."

"Then you need to go get them!"

"What?"

"I have seen firsthand what that wicked sorcerer can do. If they were able to defeat him the first time, they may be some of the few who can do it in the battles to come."

"Garron, I can't just—"

"Cousin." Garron stopped him. "I am sorry this burden has fallen to you. I truly am. But I can't keep apologizing for it. The burden is yours whether we like it or not. I love you dearly, but you need to heed my words. We are going to need every advantage we can get to make it through what's coming."

"And what is coming?" Pernden asked him.

Garron pulled away from the bars, and the flicker of candles lit him ominously. He locked eyes with Pernden and said, "Death."

CHAPTER FOURTEEN

VALUABLE PRISONERS

Karnak grunted and grabbed at his side as the cart bumped over another rock in the road. The big orc's hands were stained red. He'd gotten the sharp end of a spear for his insolence at the mining camp. Their captors didn't have any problem punishing him, though no one was allowed to touch the huntsman.

Merrick finished ripping away his sleeves and tied them together. "Here," he said, guiding the orc upright so he could wrap the wound. "I'm not as good a healer as my sister." Merrick gave the orc a weak smile. "But this should help."

"Thank you," Karnak said, leaning again into the bars of the rolling cage.

"Try to get some rest," Merrick said.

Karnak didn't reply. He closed his eyes tightly and winced with every bump in the road.

Merrick worried for the orc gar. Seeing Karnak react to every jostle of the cart was hard to watch. He cared deeply for him and fretted about more than the orc's visible wound. Merrick had rarely seen Karnak in such a weakened state.

While their circumstances hadn't changed much from their cage on the ship, Merrick was glad to be on solid ground. The wagon jarred and swayed, but nothing like the ship on the open sea. At least in the wagon he wasn't constantly vomiting. The small victory gave him a hint of hope.

Merrick surveyed the scene. From what he could tell, Kelvur didn't seem much different from Tarrine. Rolling hills dotted with trees surrounded them as they rode along the dirt road. Perhaps all of Finlestia was similar. The familiarities made the world seem smaller to him, though truly, he did not know how big it was. Dozens of other lands they knew nothing about could exist. In a way, the similarities in Kelvur made him feel as though it didn't matter how big Finlestia was.

The huntsman glanced around. They were being escorted by half a dozen Sons of Silence, aside from Hazkul Bern and his witch. Their guards rode horses. There were a few men, a barbarian woman, and one of the stony-skinned creatures. It seemed to Merrick that the Sons of Silence didn't care what race you were, only whether you were deadly. They certainly looked deadly. Each of them sported different weapons and various styles of armor or cloaks. Merrick saw no uniformity among them other than their shared goal to usher him and Karnak to wherever they were taking them.

As the cart hit another rock, Karnak flinched and released a pain-filled grumble. To his credit, he didn't open his eyes and did his best to rest. Merrick thought of Tanessa and Gernot as he looked at the orc. *I promised I would take care of you,* he thought as he watched Karnak's miserable attempt at sleep. *I promised I would bring you home to them.*

He eyed the orc carefully. The spear wound wasn't fatal. He would live through that, but they still had no idea where they were going. The idea that Hazkul Bern and his assassins had been sent to Calrok for Merrick was unsettling, to say the least. That is, if the assassin leader could be taken at his word. Merrick wasn't so sure. He was a huntsman from Tamaria—a nobody. Who would possibly want to assassinate him? It had to be some mistake. He wondered about Valurwind. The stone sculpture of the bird had been taken from him when he was captured and unconscious. Valurwind was probably the most noteworthy thing about him. The astral falcon would be a prize to almost anyone, but she had been essentially unknown to the world outside of the wisdom tower at Loralith when Master Tenlien had gifted the statuette to him.

His thoughts shifted to Ralowyn. He hoped she was alright. She and Henry had been flying into the fray, far behind. He'd thought about her often during their captivity, but Karnak didn't have any answers to his concerns. At best, she'd returned to Calrok for help and was safe. At worst, her body had been swallowed by a great beast of the sea.

Merrick gripped the iron bars and shook the thought from his mind. One of the guards galloped toward the front of the caravan. The arrows in his quiver bounced as he rode.

The arrow!

Merrick sat up with a start. He had been the one to wound the wicked orc sorcerer Jaernok Tur. Had the sorcerer hired the Sons of Silence to assassinate the huntsman for such a thing? He could hardly believe the sorcerer would go to such lengths for something so petty.

"Kelvur is a strange place."

The orc's words surprised the huntsman.

"Save your strength," Merrick said.

Karnak opened his eyes. "It *is* strange."

Merrick sighed and shrugged. "The land seems the same as anywhere else."

"It's not home. I can sense it inside my bones."

"Perhaps," the huntsman allowed, taking a wide look over the landscape again.

"The people are strange. You must admit that." Karnak grunted as he tried to sit more upright. "The one who spoke to us. The one that lost his ..."

Merrick didn't know the relation between the two from the mining camp either.

"The one that looked like a turtle," Karnak said finally. "What are they?"

"I don't know."

"And the stone faces?"

"I don't know," Merrick said again.

"The 'turtles' are called chelons," the cart driver said quietly.

Merrick and Karnak glanced at each other and then toward the driver. He was a human with long matted grey hair. He wore a dark cloak, and as far as either of them could tell, he didn't carry a weapon. Neither of them replied. Their experience with these people had not been good, and they wondered if his conversation were some sort of trick.

After a moment, he continued. "And the 'stone faces' are called geldrins."

Merrick slid closer to Karnak and the man on the cart's raised bench so he could hear better.

"Are they common in Kelvur?" Merrick asked. They had seen many of the geldrins when they were leaving the ship and when they were carted through the mining camp.

The driver grunted. "They didn't used to be. Some years back there were no geldrins. At least none we'd ever seen."

Karnak narrowed his eyes at Merrick. The huntsman was curious, too. "Where did they come from?"

"The north, of course. Well, and east. Northeast." The man finally settled on his answer. "Used to be the people fought against orcs and giants in the old days. But then the orcs disappeared and the geldrins showed up. It's said they killed all the orcs and moved on to pillage the cities of the Eastern Knolls first. At least, that's what I've heard. Never been to the Eastern Knolls."

Karnak attempted a shrug but winced at his wound, and Merrick grimaced in empathy. He said, "I'm sorry. We don't know much of Kelvur's map."

"Well, why did you ask where they came from then?"

"I don't know," Merrick admitted. "I guess I was hoping to learn more about them."

"All you need to know is that geldrins are nasty creatures," the driver murmured.

Merrick gave Karnak a quizzical look. The orc shook his head, also confused by the statement.

"Do you know where they're taking us?" Merrick asked, not sure how much the driver would tell them.

"Ventohl," he said plainly. "Apparently, the sorcerer has come out of the Fell Keep in the Crags to greet you personally all the way at Ventohl. You must be very valuable to him." At that, the driver turned over his shoulder and side-eyed the pair.

Merrick's face turned serious, and Karnak met his gaze. The huntsman's only explanation to their predicament had seemingly been confirmed. He gripped the bars and raised himself to ask the driver another question, but Hazkul Bern rode his horse nearer to the cart.

"I see we're finally in the mood for conversation!" Hazkul said with excitement. "I've been so meaning to ask you some things."

Merrick sank back against the bars, glaring at the elf. Hazkul's dark hair was so fine it blew like dandelion fuzz in the light breeze. He grinned at the prisoners' anger.

"Ah, well, I admit that the tragedy at the Glinso Mining Camp was unfortunate. They do have a barbarous way about them. No offense, Lenda," he called to the barbarian woman.

Her muscles rippled as she turned a confused glare toward Hazkul Bern. Her horse sighed under her immense weight. Hazkul chuckled to himself. "Anyway, we had to stop there. Not because of Commander Chol's notorious hospitality, mind you. But rather that axe of yours."

Karnak flinched, this time not a result of his wound.

"Mighty fine weapon," Hazkul continued. "I imagine you have been the terror of many a foe. A big orc like you, wielding a magic-imbued double-bladed axe. Though it wasn't what the geldrins are looking for in the mine. Turns out, the stone the sorcerer has them searching for is red, and yours is more of an auburn color. Can't say I understand the difference. I don't know why he was so adamant about us getting your axe while we were looking for Merrick. Sorcerers and their trinkets. Admittedly, I have no propensity for such artifacts. I tend to enjoy the simpler things." The elf assassin paused and chewed on his words for a moment before grumbling. "At least I used to ..."

Merrick eyed the assassin. Since their first encounter, any time Hazkul Bern had spoken with them, the elf had never had a shortage of words. But in that moment, he seemed to genuinely be lost in reflection.

"Anyway, I've found magical artifacts to be temperamental; whereas, a good poison-dipped dart or a black dagger is adept at its designed function. Wouldn't you agree?" When they didn't respond, he shrugged and nodded back toward the witch. "Chadwa back there loves the stuff. Can't get enough of it. She's been all sorts of twisted up on that axe of yours. Says it contains a magic she doesn't understand. Apparently, it is connected to you, and it's taking a lot out of her to keep it shielded from you."

Karnak sat up, and a surprise grin crept across his face, his tusks pressing outward, parting his lips. He peered between the cage bars toward the witch near the back of the caravan.

Merrick noticed how Hazkul Bern watched the orc closely. He didn't like the satisfied way the elf studied Karnak. The huntsman interjected, "So, the witch carries our items."

Hazkul Bern didn't immediately look away from Karnak. "Clever," he said, finally turning to Merrick. "You mean to find out whether Chadwa has all your items and attempt to overpower her while she is weary from travel. Can't say I blame you for the idea. If I were in your position, I would also be thinking of ways out. But then again, I would recognize that out on the open road, surrounded by riders, is not the time to try anything. Of course, I would not have been captured in the first place," Hazkul said with a dismissive shrug.

Merrick glared at the elf. "But that was when you were an assassin, of course."

Hazkul laughed. "Dear boy, I am *the* assassin. I have killed kings and would-be conquerors. I am the one that started the Sons of Silence. I am—"

"Right," Merrick interrupted. "The mercenary group that works for a dark sorcerer."

Hazkul paused, and one of his eyes twitched before he adjusted his posture on the back of his horse. "Well, a good leader should always recognize the way of the wind if victory is to be assured. Wouldn't you agree?"

"A plant without root is tossed by the wind as much as a ship without anchor is tossed by the waves," Karnak said, recognizing what Merrick was doing.

"An interesting sentiment," Hazkul replied. "But when an army marches, is it not the flower that gets trampled under the boot?" A wicked grin scrawled across the elf's face. "You see, when the sorcerer's armies finally march from the Crags, there will be no stopping them. They will sweep across the lands like a tidal wave, destroying everything—rooted or otherwise. The only way to survive is to be behind the wave."

"But at what cost?" Merrick asked.

Hazkul snickered. "When you have dealt in life and death as long as I have, the only thing that matters is preserving your own."

This time, Merrick laughed. Hazkul Bern eyed the huntsman curiously. "Oh, I'm sorry," Merrick said. "I just don't believe that someone who has devoted their entire life to becoming as skilled at their craft as you has such lowly motivations."

Karnak grunted a laugh as well.

Hazkul Bern's face shifted a couple of times before returning to a wry grin. "I have enjoyed our rhetoric this time," he nodded to each of them. "But you will be needing your rest. Jaernok Tur is less inclined to dialog than I am."

With that, the elf assassin knocked a fist against the metal cage and pushed his horse to ride at the front of the caravan.

As much as Merrick hated to admit the elf's success, the knock acutely reminded him of their current predicament. They weren't getting out of this cage, and even if they did, they'd be chased down in short order by one of the horsemen. The huntsman glanced back at Chadwa at the rear of the caravan. The witch rode her horse with her eyes closed, as though she were in some sort of trance. Merrick wondered how true Hazkul's words about the witch were. *Is she really tired from traveling and constant shielding? If we could get her distracted, could Karnak call* Dalkeri *back to himself?*

He glanced toward the big orc. Karnak no longer looked as haggard as he had before. A new fire burned in his belly, and his eyes were trained on the witch.

Merrick nodded to himself. *Good,* he thought. *We're going to need his fire.*

A rock in the road jarred the caged cart sideways, and a searing pain flashed through Karnak's side. He clenched his teeth and sat up, noticing that the hour was getting late.

For hours, he had stared at the witch who held his axe under an unseen magical barrier. His eyes shifted countless times from the witch to the sack that held *Dalkeri.* He summoned everything within him to get a sense of the axe, but none came. Admittedly, he hadn't been able to feel *Dalkeri's* magic since their capture. After the assassin mentioned that the witch believed there was some connection between Karnak and the axe, he realized she must be shielding it from him somehow. None of his attempts to connect with it had proven fruitful, so after hours of staring, he had finally given in to sleep.

He glanced toward Merrick who appeared to be resting as well. Karnak hefted himself into an uncomfortable hunched position, attempting to see the caravan's lead. The witch had moved to the front next to Hazkul Bern while the orc had slept. He cursed himself for not being awake when she made the move. *Could I have reached* Dalkeri *as she rode by the cart?* His big hands gripped the bars in rage.

Karnak noticed that the road ahead ran up a rising hill with a thick forest flanking it on either side. As they approached the hill, the barbarian woman forced her horse into a trot, catching up to the group's leader. Karnak could not hear what she said to him, but the elf threw up a hand and signaled a halt. The barbarian woman sniffed the air as though she found some scent on the wind.

The orc squinted, trying to see what was happening.

"You better wake up your friend," the cart driver whispered.

"What?" Karnak asked.

Before the driver could respond, a spear hurtled through the air and pierced the barbarian woman through the back, launching her from her horse.

A moment of confusion lingered before pandemonium broke out. Wild battle cries roared from the forest as armed fighters appeared from behind large trees.

Merrick shook his head and rubbed his bleary eyes. "What's happening?" he shouted as the clangs of metal on metal rang out around them.

"It's an ambush," Karnak shouted back.

"Who are they?" Merrick asked.

"I don't know."

"They are your rescuers," the cart driver shouted back before he drew a sword that was hidden underneath his long cloak. "We're called Javelin. Sit tight!"

"Wait," Karnak shouted. "Where are you going?"

The driver didn't answer. He stepped on top of the cage and launched himself at one of the nearby riders, bringing his sword down upon the rider's head. The battle raged as the caravan riders wheeled about on their horses like a highly skilled cavalry, chopping down the attackers. More continued to appear from the woods.

"Get the cart!" Hazkul Bern barked at one of his men. "Get the cart!"

The man rode over to the cart and dismounted his horse. He climbed atop the driver's box and grabbed the reins. The original driver, however, whirled about and chopped at the horses' harnesses, freeing them from the cart. The creatures stampeded in terror. The man atop the box whipped the useless leather strips at the driver and slashed his throat with a dagger.

Karnak roared and beat at the bars. Hazkul Bern's man leaped from the driver's box back into the saddle of his own horse and rode toward more of the attackers.

"We have to get out of here!" Merrick shouted. He was reaching his arm between the bars and feeling for anything he could find on the driver's box. Unfortunately, he couldn't see anything, and it was difficult to get his hand over the seat.

Suddenly, the trees of the forest crackled and swayed. Karnak watched as a giant rumbled out of the woods and blasted one of the caravan riders clean off his horse. When the rider landed, the other fighters swarmed him.

The giant was easily more than twice Karnak's height. The orc had seen some large trolls, but he'd never seen a giant. The giant kicked another of the caravan riders, sending the horse and rider soaring.

Karnak pulled Merrick back, as though he could somehow protect the huntsman from the approaching giant. Merrick's eyes widened as the giant drew nearer. The giant gripped the cage and peered in at them. He said nothing but grunted as his hardened face scanned them. The giant heaved the caged cart with both hands and set it to the side where his allies surrounded it. Then the giant turned toward the hill and the front of the caravan.

The orc leaned on the bars, trying to view Hazkul Bern around the giant's great mass. The elf assassin grimaced as he threw another dagger, downing another attacker. He paused and narrowed his eyes at Karnak across the battle scene. A wry grin crept across the elf's face, and he gave the orc a quick nod.

"No!" Karnak shouted. Before his cry raised anyone's attention, the elf threw a smoke bomb, covering the road with thick clouds.

By the time the smoke cleared, Hazkul Bern and his witch had vanished, taking *Dalkeri* with them.

Karnak banged his arm against the bars several times and roared.

"An orc and a man in the same cage, and they haven't killed each other. Now I have seen everything," a dark-skinned elf said as he worked his way over to the cart.

Karnak growled unintentionally. Merrick placed a hand on the orc's big shoulder.

The elf looked them over and turned to the giant. "Dak, is the cage too heavy for you?"

"It is heavy." The giant's voice was deep and booming even though he seemed to be speaking quietly. "But it has wheels. I can roll it."

"Good," the elf said. "I think Vorenna will be very curious to see why these two are so important to the sorcerer."

Merrick took a breath as though he were about to say something, but this time, Karnak held him back.

The elf eyed them again and shook his head. "Very curious, indeed."

Chapter Fifteen

Kane Harbor

W aves lapped at the *Sellena* as the crew brought the ship into a good place to anchor. To Orin's relief, several buildings were already in the process of being erected. He knew the plan had been for the elves, orcs, and volunteers from Whitestone to begin housing projects right away and was glad to see things in motion. Captain Tin gave the guardian an approving nod at the sight. The captain licked his chapped lips and exchanged impressed glances with the equally surprised Befors.

The air smelled of the fresh sea, unlike the murky, fog-covered bay south of Stalford. Moreover, the sky was clear, and the waves calm in the bay. People worked noisily at their construction. The whole scene, buzzing with life, exemplified the new day they desired.

As the travelers disembarked and rowed their ship's boats toward land, Orin couldn't help but grin at the awaiting party. He didn't recognize most of the representatives but found Nera's less-than-enthusiastic look rather humorous.

He didn't see his brother. Judging by Nera's face, she had drawn the short stick and Pernden had sent her with the greeting party, though Orin wasn't sure why. He had assumed his brother would be present to personally greet the newcomers on that monumental occasion.

A temporary dock had already been built, and the ship's boats were quickly welcomed by a few workers, unloaded, and sent back to retrieve more travelers.

"Greetings!" Edford called to them as Orin and the others walked toward the greeting party. "I trust your travels have been pleasant?"

"Hello, Edford." Orin pressed together a smile. "Who is it you have here?"

Orin shot a smile to Nera but noticed her gazing past him at the unloading ships.

"This is Zilon from Loralith. He's the chief architect and planner for the new fishing city, which, I am happy to share with you, will be called Kane Harbor."

"Kane Harbor?" Orin asked, giving Edford his full attention.

"Yes." One of the orcs stepped forward. "As your king has explained to us, Danner Kane was a mighty warrior who gave his life in the battle of Whitestone and was instrumental in defeating the sorcerer of Kelvur."

"Danner Kane was a great man," Orin mused.

"We agreed with King Pernden that the honor was appropriate," the orc said, nodding to Orin.

"Yes," Edford agreed. "Kane Harbor will be a symbol of friendship and unity. Let me also introduce Jalko. He's a master fisher-orc of Calrok. He will be leading the ships coming from the orc city to join the efforts here."

The orc placed a finger to his brow and gave a slight bow. Orin returned the gesture of respect.

"This is Befors," Orin began to introduce the man. "He will be the dockmaster for the first docks built here and—"

"How did that ship handle the Narrows?" Nera interrupted. She drew an offended look from Edford, who was playing his role of ambassador perfectly.

"The *Sellena*?" Orin asked, turning to see which ship she was speaking about.

"The large one," she clarified.

"She handled the Narrows masterfully," Orin replied. "Her crew is very capable, and I've never seen a ship her equal."

"That might do," Nera muttered. "Could it sail across the sea?"

"We sailed it all the way from Stalford." Orin paused, looking at his old friend. Her face was stern, and her eyes never left the *Sellena*. He wasn't sure what was going through her mind. "Actually, south of Stalford. Why?"

"Could it make the voyage across the Gant Sea all the way to Kelvur?"

"Kelvur?" Orin asked, thrown by the question. "What in Finlestia would make someone sail across the sea to Kelvur?"

"Can it make the voyage?" she repeated.

Orin was dumbstruck. He turned to Befors who shook his head and shrugged, not knowing the answer.

"I would have to ask Captain Tin," Orin confessed. "Why? What's this all about?"

Nera turned toward Edford. "Edford, can you manage things from here?"

"Yes, my lady," the elder man replied.

She turned to Orin. "Gather your things." She looked past him to Befors. "Have someone send Captain Tin to shore."

"He won't like that, my lady," Befors said, mimicking Edford's address to make sure he didn't offend anyone. He hurried to explain his response. "A captain is always the last off the ship to ensure his men and travelers are cared for."

"Honor is a concept I am familiar with, sir," Nera stated. "But more dire services may yet be needed from the captain."

Befors nodded slowly and glanced at Orin. The guardian looked at the dockmaster with a similarly concerned visage, unsure what they had walked into. Befors hustled back to one of the ship's boats and instructed the rower to hurry back and retrieve Captain Tinothe.

"Nera," Orin said, drawing closer to speak with her privately. "What's this all about?"

Nera's eyes blazed golden yellow and met his. He hadn't noticed before, but she held *Santoralier*, her magic spear, in a firm grasp. He also detected concern in her eyes. "We have much to talk about."

By the time Nera finished explaining what she knew about the disappearance of Merrick and Karnak, Coal, Ezel, and Orin were ready to re-board the *Sellena* and sail across the Gant Sea to find their friends themselves. Coal paced around the room like a hungry lion.

"You must listen," Nera pressed. "We're holding a council tomorrow in Whitestone. Smarlo and Ralowyn are coming from Calrok to discuss the situation."

"Why isn't the king of Drelek coming for the council?" Orin asked.

"King Genjak is in the middle of a campaign across the rest of Drelek to promote the new dawn to all the orc mountain steads," Nera explained. "They still have a lot of shoring up to do. Not everyone understood why King Sahr needed to be taken down."

"Explain to me again how Argus and Lanryn knew what was going on in Calrok," Orin requested, making sure he had the facts right.

"The Shells of Callencia. Smarlo used the one he has to make contact with them," Nera explained.

"Right. Those are the magic shells they use to communicate at vast distances, right?"

"Yes."

"What does that matter?" Coal broke into the conversation. "Merrick is out there somewhere. He could be bloody and bruised. He could be half-dead. He needs us."

"Hold on," Ezel signed. *"I think Orin is on to something."* The grey gnome turned toward Nera. *"Do we know how far they can speak to each other?"*

"I'm sorry, I don't understand," Nera said, with an apologetic smile.

"He wants to know how far away they can use the magic shells," Orin translated. "Can they be used as far as Kelvur?"

"Yes ..." Coal murmured, catching on. "If they can reach across the sea, we'll still be able to talk with folks here."

"I don't know," Nera replied honestly. "I don't know anything about magic."

"But that spear." Coal pointed and furrowed his brow.

"This," Nera said, lifting *Santoralier*. "This is Lightning Rider. I found it in the ruins of a wisdom tower in the Gant Sea Narrows. I know no more about its origin than anyone else. I've only learned how to wield it."

"Magic," Coal grumbled.

"We'll be sending a party to look for Merrick, right?" Orin asked plainly.

Nera hesitated. "I don't know."

"What?" Coal blurted. "Of course, we are!"

"It's not my decision to make," Nera replied. "And if we do, we will need the aid of Captain Tin. No one from Tarrine has crossed the Gant Sea to Kelvur in living memory. We only know of Kelvur from the limited writings of wizards of old and our encounter with the sorcerer."

"Well, bring a scribe for all I care. Our friend needs us, and if he's across the sea, then that's where we'll go." The dwarf huffed and crossed his arms in front of his barrel chest.

Orin placed a hand on Coal's shoulder in an attempt to calm his friend. "We'll be in the meeting tomorrow. And," he said, turning to Coal to make sure the dwarf heard him. "We'll make them see it is a necessary mission."

The guardian looked to Ezel to give him an encouraging nod as well, but the little grey gnome seemed lost in thought. Orin watched him for a moment, wondering what his little friend was thinking.

"I have horses ready for us. We can ride out as soon as this captain of yours arrives," Nera said.

As if on cue, Captain Tinothe entered the room. The captain didn't look pleased at the insistence of his leaving the *Sellena* when so many of his crew remained aboard and so many things needed doing.

The group looked to him, and his expression shifted. "I came in here sour, but it looks as though there's plenty of that to go around." He turned to Orin, looking as if he knew all the promises were too good to be true and he'd expected such a moment since the beginning. "So, what is this then?"

"We may need your help," Orin said plainly. "Can you ride a horse?"

CHAPTER SIXTEEN

THE COUNCIL OF WHITESTONE

Garron breathed deeply, letting the fresh air seep into his lungs and press his ribs outward, stretching his torso. He rolled his shoulders and squinted in the morning light. It was hard to describe the effect open air and sunlight made inside him. He'd been in the dungeons for so long, and the sun touched his skin for the first time in months. Standing on the balcony overlooking Whitestone, Garron let a tear escape.

He heard people arriving inside the council chamber. Representatives from across Tarrine were gathering to discuss the situation. It amazed him what his cousin had done in his short time as king. For a moment, Garron wondered if he could have done the same.

No. You couldn't have, he thought. *You were too busy letting a sorcerer twist your mind. You were weak. Pernden was strong. That's the difference.*

A series of boisterous greetings erupted in the chamber behind him. How people from different races knew each other and shared a bond he had never thought possible before the wicked sorcerer from Kelvur had come fascinated him. In a strange turn of events, something so terrible had brought peace amongst the peoples of Tarrine.

How does such a great threat unite a people so? Garron wondered. *It is a great mystery.*

Suddenly, the curtain wafted wide, and Ellaria strolled out. She didn't say anything but placed her hands on the railing of the balcony and leaned as though it were the only thing holding her up. She blinked several times and bit at her lip, trying to compose herself.

"Are you alright?" Garron asked softly, stepping toward her.

A short huff escaped her lips, and her chin quivered. She shook her head and turned away as the tears conquered her tightly squeezed eyes.

"Ellaria," Garron said, placing a hand on her shoulder.

Before Garron could say anything else, Ellaria turned and melted into his arms.

Garron held her awkwardly in the first embrace he'd experienced in months. He brushed her flying red hair back with his hand and squeezed her tightly.

"I can't imagine how you're feeling right now," he consoled her.

"I'm sorry," she said, pulling herself away and wiping the tears. A pang ran through Garron. He immediately missed the embrace.

"No. It's alright," he said. "It's a strange thing. I remember when I thought Orin was dead. It was an amazing surprise when he returned, and you were one of the ones who brought him back to us."

"But we don't know what's happened to Merrick. He could be dead. He could be hurt. There's no knowing."

Garron nodded. "Here's what we do know: there is a whole room of folks in there right now who are going to figure out a way to get him back. And I have no doubt they will."

Ellaria bobbed her head, sniffed, and wiped her face again. She blew out a determined breath and nodded to Garron as though she believed his words.

Her face shifted into an awkward half-hearted smile. "I came out here to get you. They're ready to start."

Garron winced. Aside from the fact that he'd enjoyed feeling the sun on his face, he'd also been on the balcony to avoid the gathering crowd. Since his imprisonment, he'd only interacted with Pernden, Dona, Ellaria, and Orin. Garron wasn't sure how to face the people in that room. How could he? He'd been the source of so much pain.

As if Ellaria could read his thoughts, she reached out and squeezed Garron's hand. "Come on," she said. "We'll do this together."

Garron took one last glance across the city of Whitestone and followed Ellaria through the curtained doorway.

"There's one last thing," Smarlo said to the gathering.

The orc mage had recounted the events of the attack in Calrok as best he could. Ralowyn filled in the details of the story where she had been directly present. Most listened in silence, nodding here or there. Occasionally, someone gasped in surprise. Overall, the people in the room listened with great interest, trying to wrap their heads around all the details.

Garron could hardly believe all he had heard.

From his robe, Smarlo produced the tiny piece of parchment. The markings on it appeared to be different from the last time he'd looked at the piece. He shook his head and laid it out on the table. "This piece of parchment is the blank one I mentioned before."

Everyone around the table leaned in for a better look. Garron, however, leaned further back. A foreboding feeling made him seek to get as far from the paper as possible—as if the slip of parchment radiated a repelling force.

"It doesn't appear to be blank," Pernden said, a confused look on his face.

Lanryn gasped and turned to Ralowyn, who sat beside him. "Is that what I think it is?"

Ralowyn nodded to the elf mage but said nothing.

"Dark tongue," Argus murmured. The old dwarf stared at the parchment in disbelief.

"Do you know how to read it?" Smarlo asked.

"No," Argus replied. "Not many can. The letters of dark tongue are always shifting. One cannot read it like a normal inscription. One must be in a certain ... state."

Smarlo sat back in his chair, disappointed. He scratched at his long green ear. He had hoped Argus, being a well-traveled mage with great power and knowledge, would be able to translate the note.

"Is there a way to induce this state?" Lanryn asked.

"It is not so simple," Argus sighed. "Only one who has been touched by the dark magics can read it. And even if one of us were, I do not know how it works."

"This parchment is the last clue we have," Smarlo said.

"I wonder if I could read it if we knew how," Ezel signed to Coal.

"Bah," Coal waved the notion away with a grumble. *"We're not even sure the sea witch used dark magic on you."*

"What sea witch?" Garron asked.

All of a sudden, the room went quiet, and all eyes fell on him. Garron shifted nervously under everyone's stares.

"How did you ..." Coal murmured.

"Can you understand me?" Ezel signed.

Garron's eyes darted to each side, avoiding the little gnome's gaze.

After a long silence, Argus Azulekor spoke again. "Was there a sea witch in the story that I missed?"

"No," Coal said. "Ezel was asking if I thought it possible that he was touched by dark magic when the sea witch saved his life all those years ago, but that's a story for another day. We need to figure out a plan to get Merrick and Karnak back."

Garron was thankful for the change in subject. As the conversation continued, he looked across the table at Ezel. The deep gnome stared at the man in bewilderment from his chair, which was piled high with books to elevate him above the table's edge.

"There's more going on here than we understand," Pernden put in. "I agree that we need to find our friends. It appears that our dealings with the sorcerer Jaernok Tur are not yet finished."

"And how do you propose we get across the Gant Sea to save them, my King? We don't even know how far Kelvur is," High Commander Mattness said. "Attempting to fly our griffins, or even the pegasi, could mean certain death."

"What of the mirrors?" Ralowyn asked Argus.

"I dare not attempt anything with them," the old dwarf said.

"We still know very little about them," Lanryn added. "I have been searching the annals at Loralith but have yet to come across even a mention of the Alkhoren Mirrors."

"That's why I've brought Captain Tin," Orin cut in.

Everyone turned toward the captain, except Ezel and Garron, still locked in a staredown. Garron heard none of the discussion around them. The little gnome's look captivated him. Slowly, Ezel signed, *"Can you read the parchment?"*

I don't know, Garron thought with a slight shake of his head. *"Why don't you look at it?"*

"I'm afraid," the man signed back, though he did not realize he'd done so.

Ezel started, surprised by the man's response. *"How ...?"*

Garron looked at his own hands, wondering how his mind had known how to maneuver them in reply. His thoughts raced. What was happening to him? He had no explanation, only that he somehow understood the gnome's language.

Fear gripped him. A great pull urged him to look at the parchment on the table. His body tensed in revulsion as he blinked and twisted to get the parchment further from the corner of his eye.

Ezel's eyes glanced between the parchment and the man. *"You may be the only one of us who can read it. You must. It may be the difference between life and death for our friends,"* the gnome signed.

"I can't," Garron signed, a pleading expression on his face.

Suddenly, Ellaria placed her hand on his arm. Her emerald eyes pierced his own, and the warmth of the woman's hand on his arm strengthened him. Garron swallowed his fear.

He glanced once more at the gnome across the table. Ezel nodded, urging him onward.

Garron turned toward the parchment. His eyes widened as the inked letters appeared to have mirrored shadow letters a couple of inches above the parchment. He stared hard at them as the markings faded in and out of view, shifting and morphing into words.

Pernden rubbed his temples and asked, "Captain Tinothe, can the *Sellena* even make the voyage across the sea?"

The others paused, and the elder man scratched at the stubble on his chin. "There may be no other ship in Tarrine that can."

"Would you take us to Kelvur?" Orin asked frankly.

Pernden watched the captain take stock of his younger brother. The old captain's face lightened, and it seemed to the king that the elder man had taken a liking to Orin.

"I would be willing," Captain Tin said, with a pensive nod. "But my crew are fishermen. Best any of them have done is fight off pirates, and most of them are too young to have experienced even that. The ones who have are too old for much fighting."

"Of course," Pernden said, taking the opportunity to build some rapport with the man. "We will send a squadron of guardians with you."

"The Talon Squadron will accompany you," Nera said.

Pernden felt as though the blood drained from his body. Dread swept over him. "No," he blurted.

"No?" Nera and High Commander Mattness asked at the same time.

"No …" Pernden repeated. But for the life of him, he could not string more words together.

"The Talon Squadron is the best-equipped squadron in the Guard for such a mission," Nera pressed.

"My King, it is the most obvious choice," Mattness added. "Talon is the only squadron to send on a mission with so many unknown variables. As the High Commander, it is my duty to ensure the optimal results for any mission. The only squadron right for this mission *is* the Talon Squadron."

"I ..." Pernden had no argument. They were right, of course. He stared at Nera, not wanting her to go.

She understood his unspoken words, drew her lips together, and nodded solemnly.

"'A beacon in the dark can guide the march.'"

Pernden turned to his cousin. Garron's gaze was glued to the parchment in front of Smarlo as he spoke. The room fell silent for the second time at his cousin's words.

"What did you say?" the king asked.

"'A beacon in the dark can guide the march,'" Garron said in an exasperated tone.

"He reads the parchment," Argus whispered.

"Shh," Garron hushed him. "There's more,"

Everyone in the room held a collective breath and leaned forward. Pernden stared, dumbstruck. *What is this magic?*

"The rest of it doesn't make any sense ..." Garron trailed off.

"What does it say?" Pernden prodded.

"'From the mouth let waters flow. Release the tide to flood below.'"

"Some sort of riddle?" Lanryn's face scrunched as he turned to the other mages.

"Perhaps ..." Argus mumbled.

"Something to do with the mouth of a river?" Ralowyn suggested. "Perhaps they intend to send ships?"

"Sea vessels don't tend to do well on rivers," Coal pointed out.

"Nor do river boats do well on the sea," Orin grumbled, thinking back to their bumpy travels on the *Lady Leila* in the Tandal Sea.

"Aye," Coal nodded.

"'A beacon in the dark' could be the stars. Sailors use the stars to navigate the waters at night," Captain Tin said.

"Maybe an army plans to strike at night," Commander Mattness suggested. "Maybe they plan to march on a certain night when the constellations are aligned?"

"I don't understand the part about flooding below," Coal said. "A wizard was able to save us on the stormy Tandal Sea by using powerful magic to create a tunnel for us to pass through in safety. I doubt the sorcerer has magic as great as a wizard."

"Dark magics are strange magics," Argus pointed out.

The conversation went in circles for a long while as Pernden pondered the words. *A beacon in the dark can guide the march. From the mouth let waters flow. Release the tide to flood below.*

Everyone in the room seemed to have some input on what the riddle could mean, except Smarlo. Pernden stared at the orc mage. The slender orc's long green ears twitched as he sat deep in thought.

Suddenly, Smarlo looked up, and his eyes met the king's. His face blanched, his usual green seeming less bright and more sickly.

"Silence!" Pernden shouted. All talking ceased. "What is it, Master Smarlo?"

The gathering turned toward the orc.

"I didn't consider it at first, but it just dawned on me," he said quietly.

"What is it, Smarlo?" Ralowyn asked in an encouraging tone.

"The stone-faced creature, before he was killed, said something about the tide of war washing us all away." He paused, trying to piece everything together and relay his ideas in a coherent way. "What if the flood is an army?"

"But how does an army cross the sea underwater?" Coal asked incredulously.

"They don't," Smarlo said quickly. "Unless they're *under* the water."

"What?" the dwarf blurted. His face scrunched, and he tugged at the braid in his black beard as though the act might help his brain comprehend what in Finlestia the orc was talking about.

"The Underrock ..." Ralowyn said, her eyes widening.

"Exactly," Smarlo said. "Argus, the magic you used for the Shells of Callencia—can a similar magic be used to set a beacon that someone could sense from far away."

"Well," Argus hemmed. "I don't know. Maybe. I haven't seen such a thing myself, but it's conceivable."

"Smarlo," Pernden cut in. "What am I missing?"

The orc glanced at Ralowyn who nodded a reluctant affirmation that she was reaching a similar conclusion as the orc.

"In ancient writings, magical incantations have been described as flowing waters that come from the mouth," Smarlo explained. "I think the parchment is instructions for someone to utter the words of an incantation to light a beacon. Well, not really light it, but activate it somehow."

"What kind of beacon and where?" Pernden prodded, tired of riddles.

"A beacon that would help an army navigate the maze of the Underrock."

"The Underrock?" Captain Tin asked, his mustache bristling.

"Yes," Smarlo continued. "The Underrock expands far below our feet and is made up of the deepest caverns and tunnels in our world. Grave dangers and wicked creatures lurk there. Most mines do not reach the depths of the Underrock. The cave systems span miles and miles in all directions like a vast web.

No one knows how far they reach. The Underrock could reach every part of Finlestia for all we know."

"Is this even possible?" Pernden asked. "Could an army use the tunnels of the Underrock to come into Tarrine? Even under the Gant Sea?"

"I don't know," Smarlo said. He hesitated for a moment. "I've been reading a tome by the old master miner Kanjor Pukra. I've been fascinated by some of the things they witnessed in the mines of northern Drelek. He mentioned a mine where they dug into a cavern underneath an alpine lake. It's entirely possible that the Underrock has tunnels that traverse underneath the sea."

"And they could lead the army here?"

"Wherever the beacon is, as long as someone started the beacon with the proper words they—" Smarlo jumped to his feet. "The dark tongue in the mines of Calrok! That's why the assassin is still there."

"Master Tan-Kro," Ralowyn said, also leaping to her feet.

"I told him exactly where I'd found the dark tongue. If the assassin hadn't found it yet, she could have followed Master Tan-Kro. I may have sent him to his death."

Debate and deliberation ceased after they realized the implications of the dark tongue on the parchment. They decided to tackle the threat on three fronts: Calrok, Whitestone, and Kelvur.

Nera gathered the team going to Kelvur. She would command the expedition on the trek across the sea with the help of Captain Tin. They decided to separate the holders of the Shells of Callencia in hopes that they would be able to communicate more effectively than the normal pigeon or raven message carriers.

"Do you think the shell will work across the sea?" Nera asked Lanryn.

"Truly, I do not know. We have had no chance to test it," the elf mage confessed.

"Perhaps you can use your wand to strengthen the shell's abilities," Ralowyn suggested.

"Perhaps," Lanryn replied with a contemplative look.

"Boehlen's Beard! Why are we standing here, jawing?" Coal blurted. "We need to get out there."

Nera bit her lip, reminding herself to respond with patience and compassion. She knew the dwarf was worried about his friend. Pernden had assigned her command of the mission, though, and it was her responsibility to make sure the mission was a success. To her, that meant coming home with *everyone* alive, if at all possible.

"Be patient, my friend," Nera said to the dwarf. "We have much to prepare in a short time. Or would you like to get halfway across the sea without provisions and starve the entire crew?"

Coal grumbled to himself but said nothing audible. Orin nudged the dwarf, and he quieted.

"Captain Tinothe," Nera turned to the elder man.

"Tin is fine, ma'am."

"Captain Tin," she said with a nod. "How long will it take to procure the necessary provisions for such a journey?"

"Well," he hemmed. "I don't know how long the journey will be, but Whitestone's market is impressive. I'm sure we could gather everything here, and if you know a good wagoner, we could be off to Kane Harbor to load the ship by morning."

"Good. Go," Nera said. "I'll have the Talon Squadron ready and arriving in Kane Harbor by first light."

Captain Tin gave a slight bow to Nera and whirled for the exit.

"Orin, I need you to hire a wagoner. Ask Master Feink if you don't have someone in mind. He should have a good idea who would be interested in making the trek to Kane Harbor tonight."

"Yes, Captain," Orin replied, his guardian training kicking in. "Anything else I can do to help prepare?"

"Captain Tin will need help in the market. You know where everyone is. Once you solicit the wagoner, help the captain. Ezel, can you help them?"

The little gnome looked from Nera to Orin to Coal. *"I'm not going with you,"* he signed.

"What?" Coal barked.

"I don't understand," Nera said.

"He's not coming with us," Orin explained.

"Not coming with us, my foot," Coal grumbled. *"What do you mean you're not coming?"*

Ezel hesitated then signed, *"The last thing the crew of the* Sellena *needs on such a treacherous mission is me on board. They're going to be scared enough. I'll only make things worse for them."*

"That's just foolishness!" Coal signed back emphatically. *"We're going to need you out there."*

"You'll already have two magic wielders in Ralowyn and Lanryn. You'll be fine. They're both skilled mages."

"What about Merrick?"

"Merrick has a whole squadron of the Griffin Guard coming to rescue him, not to mention Orin and you," Ezel signed.

Coal paused, breathing hard. His signing softened. *"But what about me? What am I going to do without you? We've always done things together. We're a team."*

Ezel stepped closer to the dwarf and patted his oldest friend on the shoulder. *"You'll be fine. There is no one I have more confidence in than you."*

Coal's nose twitched. He sniffed and wiped the tickle away from his nose onto his sleeve. *"And what about you?"*

"I think I can help Garron. I don't know how yet, but I feel I'm supposed to help him," Ezel flourished and nodded toward the man.

"Well, off you go then. And keep yourself safe. I don't want to have to save you after we find Merrick," Coal said aloud with another sniff. He cleared his throat and turned back to Nera. "I can help with the captain. Ezel will be going with the others."

"Alright," Nera said. "Let's get to it then."

"I am going with them to Kelvur," Ellaria growled.

"You can't," Pernden said with a deep sigh. "I need you to go to Calrok with Garron."

Ellaria let out an incredulous laugh. "Me brother is out there somewhere, and he needs me help!"

"I'm sending the best people I can to find him."

"And that's why I'm going," she sneered.

"Do you think I like any of this?" Pernden snapped. "Do you think I want to send Nera across the sea to where that monster lives?"

Ellaria took an unintentional step backward toward the railing.

"I'm sorry," Pernden said. "Sometimes we have to do things we don't want to do so we can do the right thing."

Ellaria slammed a fist on the balcony railing. Tears streamed down her face.

"Nera is the best of the best. You know how much Orin and Coal and Ezel love Merrick. And tell me you don't feel better knowing that Ralowyn will stop at nothing to find him," Pernden implored. "But I need *you* with Garron. I can't go with him to Calrok. Dona has no fighting ability. No one else has spent any time with him except you. No one has helped him heal as much as you have."

"He's me brother," Ellaria choked out.

"Let me take care of your brother. You take care of my cousin."

Pernden's eyes softened as he stepped next to the young woman.

"Just yesterday you had him in prison. What changed?" Ellaria asked.

"It's hard to explain." Pernden stretched, massaging the sides of his head, and ran his hands through his hair with a deep sigh. "His first thought when I told him what was going on was that we needed to rescue Merrick and Karnak—two people he's never met. After that, he said we were going to need all the help we could get. It's like he knows something we don't, or at least senses something we don't. I thought he might be able to add something to the meeting. Did you know he could read dark tongue?"

Ellaria shook her head. She thumbed the green stone hanging around her neck. "Every time I've visited him, I start by grabbing his hand and reaching within using the magic of this stone. At first, everything felt thick and heavy, like wading through the mud in a bog. Over time it got easier, as though the fog was lifting and the air was getting lighter. It's hard to explain."

"Sounds like we both have a lot of inexplicable feelings." Pernden huffed as he leaned onto the railing. "Ellaria, I don't know if I'm doing the right thing with my cousin. I know I'm sending the best people to find your brother. But the only way I can send the best people to Calrok is if you go with Garron. He's the only one we know who can read dark tongue. So, he has to go. But what if he isn't completely free of the sorcerer's grasp? You're the only one who can help him."

Ellaria exhaled a deep sigh and leaned down on her elbows next to the king. She said nothing for a long while. Pernden wondered what she might be thinking. He was asking a lot from her, but what choice did he have? The whole situation had come crashing into his lap.

"They are the best, aren't they?" Ellaria asked softly.

Pernden turned toward her. "They really are."

Ellaria gnawed at the inside of her lip and nodded as though she were trying to keep herself from breaking into sobs. A single tear slipped out and rolled off her chin. She quickly wiped it away, stood up straight, brushed her red hair out of her face, and said, "I'll go."

Garron listened intently as Argus and Smarlo discussed some nuance of the Shells of Callencia that he did not understand. Argus was going to stay in Whitestone so that those in the city would have a way to communicate quickly with the others. It had been a critical factor in their victory against Jaernok Tur when they'd run him off before.

How did I get here? Garron wondered to himself.

Just that morning, Pernden had released him from his cell. He wondered if he wouldn't rather be back in it. He hated that he could read dark tongue. He didn't even know how he was able to do so. Though he still didn't understand how he could read the Nari inscription in Kel Joran's lost notes, that ability was much less menacing than the evil dark tongue.

Little fingers nudged his hand. Startled out of his own thoughts, Garron turned to see Ezel standing next to him, half the man's height.

"Are you alright?" Ezel asked, narrowing his eyes.

"I'm fine," Garron lied. He caught himself quickly and signed, *"It's just a lot."*

The deep gnome smiled at the man. *"It always seems that way."*

Garron smiled back at the gnome. That was another thing he didn't understand. *How am I able to understand his language?*

Ellaria abruptly popped up on his other side. "We about ready to go?" she asked.

"We?" Garron asked, stunned.

"Aye," Ellaria nodded. She grabbed Garron's arm and squeezed. "Who's going to babysit you if Dona stays here? I'm pretty sure she'd miss Len far too much."

"Who's Len?" Garron asked.

"Her husband, you dolt."

"You knew Dona had a husband?"

"Aye. Don't tell me you never asked her about Len," Ellaria scolded.

"Well ... I ..." Garron stumbled over his words and looked to Ezel for help.

"I don't even know who Dona is," the gnome signed and shrugged.

"Wow," Ellaria said with a disbelieving nod at Garron. "Looks like you need more hand-holding than I thought."

Garron gave her a sheepish grin.

Having finished his conversation with Smarlo, Argus turned to the grey gnome. "Ezel, what are you doing over here?"

"I'll be going to Calrok with Garron," he signed.

"With me?" Garron repeated aloud.

"What was that?" Argus asked.

"He says he's going to Calrok with me," the man shifted quickly. "With us."

Smarlo and Ezel exchanged looks for a moment. Then, the orc mage grinned and said, "How far we've come."

The gnome's hand flipped quickly.

"How far, indeed," Ellaria translated for the orc.

Garron gave Smarlo a curious look.

"I threw a concussive potion at him when we first met," Smarlo confessed with an awkward shrug. "And her, actually. Sorry about that," he said to Ellaria.

"We didn't know we were on the same side yet." She waved it off.

Smarlo nodded his thanks for her forgiveness.

"Well, I'd better head to the Whitestone Library and see Mistress Leantz before she heads home for the evening," Argus said. "I'd like to take a look at some of the scrolls there. Swift flight to you all."

And with that, the dwarf mage hurried off, his blue cloak fluttering behind him.

"Oh," Garron started. "That reminds me. I'm going to need a ride."

CHAPTER SEVENTEEN

AN OLD FOE

To become an assassin as renowned as Hazkul Bern—which is to say everyone knows about him and wants to hire him, but nobody knows who he is—requires a significant level of cunning. It also requires a healthy regard for self-preservation.

Hazkul Bern was no fool, and he did not idly approach the city of Ventohl, empty-handed. He and Chadwa had ridden hard all the way to the edge of the Eastern Knolls before they slowed. Their horses were frothed with sweat and perturbed at the elongated pressure to gallop.

Riding the road over and around hills toward the city, Hazkul Bern grimaced at the sight of the tall spires of Ventohl. In its prime, Ventohl was a gleaming beacon on a hill, an elven city of great architecture, art, and culture. Years ago, his ancestral cousins had built the city high on the hill, overlooking the surrounding knolls, with views of the Crags in the north.

As Hazkul gazed upon the castle with several of the surrounding walls in disrepair, it seemed far less splendid. Though the city had long been his, the area seemed much darker of late. Of course, the sun was going down, but that wasn't the kind of darkness he saw. Riding toward it, Hazkul decided the city seemed lifeless as great storm clouds swirled above, adding an ominous backdrop to the silhouetted castle.

Might be time to plant that garden, he thought as he thumbed a bag of seeds in one of his pockets. *Brighten things up a bit.*

He chuckled at the notion. He'd never been afraid of the dark. As Kelvur's best assassin—well, he'd venture to say Finlestia's best assassin—he'd spent a majority of his time in the dark. As he rode toward the gates of Ventohl, his city—the home base for the Sons of Silence all these years—a growing frustration swept over him. The sorcerer was waiting.

That blasted sorcerer always sat in his chair. Hazkul knew it was a power play, but he found it quite rude. He knew, too, that the sorcerer wasn't going to be happy about the huntsman's escape.

The assassin glanced over to Chadwa, riding nearby. The witch had been an associate of his for years. In fact, Hazkul almost considered her a friend, though assassins usually don't have friends. He was reluctant to use the word unless he was trying to seal a deal. She wasn't the greatest of conversationalists, but after years of working together, he'd come to trust the witch.

They'd first met years earlier when Hazkul was wrapping up an assassination on a rich noble from Zor Togis. It was an easy mark, but Hazkul had taken it himself; one must always keep up his skills.

Hilariously, a group of thieves had planned a heist that very night. The man wasn't a very well-liked nobleman.

They were a clunky group, loud for thieves. Hazkul was fairly certain it was their first heist—probably a desperate lot turning to thieving to feed themselves. Turned out to also be their last heist. The entirety of the nobleman's guard swarmed the thieves. Hazkul had watched with amusement from a high parapet as the guards tore the group to pieces—all except one.

Chadwa, Hazkul came to learn later, had been exiled from her own people for some crime she never explained to him. He was convinced it was a crime of passion. *You can just tell these things about some people,* he thought.

Regardless, he'd watched her whip her wand with deadly precision and escape the horde of guards. She impressed the elf, and he followed her to her camp in the woods.

It was a solemn camp, not much but a few bed rolls around a cold firepit. When Hazkul approached the camp, he walked in silence, but somehow, she'd sensed him. That's when he knew he wanted to work with her. She had senses enhanced by magic that could even detect his highly practiced stealth.

They'd been through a lot over the years. Since the sorcerer emerged from the Crags of the Fell Keep, things had changed. The cities in the south avoided the north like a plague. The Sons of Silence no longer had folks seeking them out for assassination jobs. Instead, the sorcerer had adopted them as a mercenary army. Hazkul spit at the thought of the word "mercenary."

The orcs of the Crags had all but disappeared, and the sorcerer's army of geldrins seemed to be popping up everywhere. The city of Ventohl teemed with the brutes. A fine line of tension existed between them and the Sons of Silence, everyone playing nice as best they could. Having seen the sheer number of geldrins the sorcerer commanded, Hazkul had no doubts they could have squashed his group at Ventohl in a proper battle.

The sorcerer let Hazkul continue his rule over the decaying city only because the assassin's group would dissipate without the elf. The sorcerer evidently needed them enough to keep them around.

Hazkul let out a deep sigh as the portcullis at the entrance of Ventohl creaked to life. He knew the sorcerer was watching them from a high window. Trying to sneak into the castle would have been useless, so through the front gate they rode. This was his castle after all. No one was going to make him slink in through the back entrance. He was Hazkul Bern, master assassin and leader of the Sons of Silence.

Of course, the elf was not looking forward to facing the sorcerer. He didn't know how the orc would react to the news of their captives' escape, but he knew it wouldn't be good.

"My chair is rather comfortable, isn't it?" Hazkul said coolly as the geldrin guards allowed him entrance to his own throne room. "Took it from a noble creep in Zor Yelnis who didn't want to pay for services rendered. Awfully unprofessional."

Jaernok Tur sat seething on the throne. The sorcerer orc was large in the chair even as he leaned back. His glare was dark and menacing with eyes black as obsidian. Hazkul didn't like looking into those eyes. The elf was an assassin, with questionable intentions on the best of days, but the eyes of the sorcerer exuded pure evil. Jaernok Tur's stone hand gripped the magical staff standing upright next to him. Hazkul had always wondered about that arm. *Must have a good story behind it.* The elf thought he felt the vibrations of the staff on the stone floor under his feet.

The sorcerer's cloak was black as well, probably the only part of the sorcerer Hazkul did like; the orc had style. The strangest thing about the orc, though, was the eerie raven-like hue that always surrounded him. It was as if his magic made it difficult to see him clearly.

Chadwa sidled over to a nearby pillar and leaned on it. Hazkul gripped the bag in his hand and took a few steps closer. He stopped when a man with his arms crossed in front of him appeared from behind his throne and stood next to the sorcerer. Hazkul grimaced. Jaernok Tur's new pet human, a mountain of a man from Tarrine, named Jolan had emerged.

"Where's the huntsman?" Jolan sneered.

"You know, Trent's apprentice is pretty good with armor. He could probably shine yours up, maybe even fix that crest on the front," Hazkul said nodding at the man's disheveled armor.

Jolan's entire countenance changed as he rubbed at the fading crest of a blue shield flanked by white wings with a silver griffin. Hazkul smiled at the man's discomfort. He loved getting under his skin.

"Where is the huntsman?"

Hazkul's skin crawled at the second voice. Every time the sorcerer spoke, reverberating whispers echoed his words.

Maybe that's the strangest thing about him, Hazkul thought. *It's certainly creepy.*

A wicked grin grew across Jolan's face. Hazkul shifted quickly, attempting to appear his usual nonchalant self.

"We ran into a little trouble," Hazkul began.

Jaernok Tur sat up, and black smoke billowed and wafted from the edges of his cloak. The tall staff's pinnacle buzzed with black arcs of pure energy, and the room darkened. The orc's tusks shifted as he snarled.

"But we didn't come back empty-handed," Hazkul said, raising the bag.

"Silence," Jaernok Tur said, his words bouncing eerily off the stone walls. "Where is the huntsman?"

"Javelin ambushed us along the road near the Duskwood," the elf said. "Didn't know they had a giant with them. I thought you had extinguished the giants with your great might and power."

Jaernok Tur ground his teeth in annoyance.

Another point for me, Hazkul thought with satisfaction.

"That doesn't answer the question," Jolan spat.

"You Tarrinians have no patience. Honestly." Hazkul let out an incredulous laugh and jutted a thumb toward the man. Chadwa said nothing to aid him in the awkward moment. Her eyes were locked on the man. Hazkul shuddered. He wasn't sure whether he'd rather be under the terrifying glare of the witch or the sorcerer. "Anyway, we had the huntsman in our custody until the ambush."

"Does he live?" the sorcerer asked.

"He does. Javelin seemed to think they were liberating some fellow freedom fighters."

Jaernok Tur growled.

Right, Hazkul remembered. *He does so hate that they call themselves freedom fighters.*

"However," the elf continued. "The mission to Calrok wasn't a complete loss. Though our geldrin pal, Jilgor, is most likely dead—not as tough as the rest of your army seemed to think he was. A big orc knocked him flying. If he did survive, Gilk likely finished him off before he could reveal any of your plans."

Jaernok Tur stood to his feet, his cloak flowing with smoky tendrils. To Hazkul Bern's surprise, the orc strode to the side of the throne in thought.

"It's good you tapped both of them for the task," Jolan said.

Jaernok Tur raised a hand to silence the man.

Hazkul turned to Chadwa with a curious look. She returned his gaze, her face slightly scrunched. She wasn't sure what they were talking about either. "What task might that be?" the elf inquired.

The sorcerer orc wheeled and glared at Jolan. The massive man withered under the orc's hard stare.

I think you may have said too much, Jolan, Hazkul mused. *A pet should never forget his place, especially if he has a hard master.*

Suddenly, Jaernok Tur turned on the elf. "What is it you brought?" he asked, eyeing the heavy sack in Hazkul's hand.

"Well," the elf said, thinking he may need to temper the sorcerer's expectations. "Chadwa had to shield it the whole way because it appeared the orc had some connection to the axe."

He nodded to Chadwa who clearly experienced great relief at discontinuing the shield she'd used to cover the axe. The orc's eyes widened with hunger.

Hazkul took an involuntary step back. The elf held the bag out as far as he could, not wanting the orc to draw nearer than necessary, especially with that wild look in his eyes. Jaernok Tur took the sack. The sorcerer's staff stood upright next to him, seemingly of its own volition. Hazkul eyed it nervously.

Slowly, the orc opened the bag and pulled out the axe. A wide grin crept across his visage. Everyone watched the sorcerer in silence. The orc threw the bag to the side, sending it sliding toward Chadwa.

"You managed to retrieve the young gar's axe," Jaernok Tur whispered. "How did you separate him from it?"

"Well, we had the orc gar too," Hazkul said carefully, not sure if the statement would make the sorcerer angry or not.

"Was he taken by Javelin, too?"

"He was ..."

The sorcerer didn't seem to care one way or the other. His dark eyes lingered on the battle axe, drinking it in with reverie.

After a moment, Hazkul couldn't take the silence anymore and dared to speak again. "We stopped by Glinso Mining Camp since I remembered Commander Chol mentioning they were looking for a powerful magic stone. This one wasn't red, but I thought it couldn't hurt to see if it was the right one."

"You've done well," Jaernok Tur said, holding the axe in one hand and running his other hand over the glinting orange stone embedded in the weapon.

"I do have a professional prowess unequaled by most," Hazkul replied, shooting a smug smirk at Jolan.

"Still need to get the huntsman back from Javelin," the man said.

The comment snapped the sorcerer from his trance. Hazkul glowered at the smirking man.

"You will send a band of assassins to acquire him. And this time you will bring him to me at the Fell Keep," Jaernok Tur hissed. "He is the only man to ever make me bleed. I plan to finish him myself."

"Well," Hazkul hemmed. The Crags were notoriously nasty terrain, and the elf had no desire to visit the Fell Keep. He'd never been there, and he didn't want to go. *Not the sort of place I'd like to holiday,* he thought. "That's quite unnecessary. I can send some scouts to find their camp and have a group ready to seize him within a few days. No sense in going all the way back there when I can have him here by week's end."

"No." The single word resounded menacingly as trailing whispers echoed it. "I must take this back to the Fell Keep and consult Lord Kilretheon."

The elf shuddered, remembering the real reason he was afraid of the sorcerer. The sorcerer orc was in league with a monolith dragon, Kilretheon the Red. Hazkul had never seen the monster, of course, but he'd heard legends about the mythical monolith dragons. He was pretty sure most of the tales were highly exaggerated, but the elf's interactions with the eerie sorcerer gave him pause.

"I need to get back right aw—"

Suddenly, the orc's eyes went pitch, and his gaze seemed far off. Jolan stepped to the sorcerer's side, shaking his head at Hazkul to warn the elf not to try anything. Hazkul stared at the odd display as the sorcerer had a mumbled conversation with someone unseen.

For a fraction of a moment, Hazkul Bern's assassin instincts imagined a scenario where the elf leaped forward, slicing the man's and orc's throats, ending their unrest in a flash of blackened steel. But as quickly as Jaernok Tur had gone into the state, he snapped back to the present.

When Hazkul turned to Chadwa that time, her face was filled with fear. He found that fact disconcerting.

Jaernok Tur looked at Hazkul and said, "Get the huntsman." Then he turned to Jolan. "The beacon has been set."

Chapter Eighteen

Across the Sea

The *Sellena's* crew had proven to be quite capable, and Nera was pleased with how quickly they'd gotten underway. She and Captain Tin met frequently as they sailed. She asked the old captain questions about sailing, and he answered her in his noncommittal way. His manner bothered her at first, but as the days passed and she got to know him more, she found him a competent leader—hard-nosed when it came to action but gentle when it came to encouragement.

Nera walked over to the railing of the main deck and patted Tam on the back. The guardian was having difficulty keeping his lunch down. She hadn't initially intended on bringing him, but Commander Mattness reminded her she was a guardian down with Ellaria headed to Calrok. Tam was young but ardent. She'd been watching him for a while for possible inclusion in Talon Squadron, and he'd been her first choice should the need to fill a spot arise.

Tam looked up to her, his face a little green.

"How you holding up?" Nera asked with a sympathetic smile.

"Fine," Tam burbled as he wiped his face with his sleeve. "I'm fine."

Nera nodded to him. "Hopefully, we won't be out here long. We could make landfall tomorrow for all we know."

"Or it could be another week." Captain Tin smirked a few feet away.

Nera shot him a scolding look to relay that he wasn't helping. "How are the griffins?" she asked Tam. Nera had assigned him to organize the flight schedule. Guardians would bring their griffins to the main deck to take to the fresh air. The first couple of days, the creatures were miserable being cooped up belowdecks. They seemed much happier with their regular exercise.

"They're doing better," Tam said, swaying slightly. "If only I can do a bit better."

"You're doing great," Nera reassured him.

She patted the guardian on the back once more and stepped toward Captain Tinothe.

"The sea doesn't care whether you have a strong or weak stomach," he said with a chuckle. "Takes some time to get your sea legs. I once knew a sailor who couldn't keep his lunch for months. Eventually, he shook the sick and turned into a fine sailor."

"Yeah?" Tam asked, looking miserable.

"Yeah. You're looking at him." The captain winked.

The guardian stared in disbelief, gulped, and stood straighter.

"That's a lad," the captain said as he turned and led Nera toward the sterncastle.

They climbed the steps, and Nera nodded with an impressed look toward Orin who was taking a shift at the helm. He smiled back and puffed with pride.

"Quite the crew we have here," Nera said to the captain.

"Aye," he nodded, pulling his pipe out and cleaning it. "Charting new waters."

"Really?" Nera asked, surprised, though she didn't know why. Of course they were off the maps. She'd never seen a map past the Gant Sea, nor had anyone else in Tarrine.

"Been off the map for a couple of days now."

"Straight east then?" she asked.

"The *Sellena* doesn't really go straight," Orin said.

Captain Tin smirked as he loaded his pipe. Nera gave him a questioning look, but he didn't explain. "Only question is what might be out here."

"What do you mean?" she asked nervously.

"Going to tell her of the perils of the sea?" Coal asked as he climbed the steps to the deck. "Going to tell her of krakens and sea serpents? Great worms that rise from the depths and bind your vessels, squeezing a ship like a snake crushes its meal?"

"Could be," the captain said with a shrug. He lit his pipe and puffed a couple of times. "Could not."

"My sister, Ada, told me such tales. She's quite the bookworm, and she went through a season of reading everything she could find about the sea. Of course, she was dazzled by the wilder tales—as any youngster would be."

"I remember that," Orin said with a chuckle, not taking his eyes off the sea in front of the ship.

Coal examined the man and laughed. "Would have been nice if you had known how to sail when we were stuck on the Tandal."

"You don't know what you don't know until you know it," Orin replied.

"I like that," Captain Tin said. "I think I'll use that the next time I talk to young Tam."

Nera rolled her eyes at their banter. She was pleased with the level of camaraderie they shared. It made her think how similarly the ship of the sea and the guard of the air operated.

Though their situation was brought on by an irrefutable urgency, they could only travel as fast as the sea would carry them. When they'd embarked, everyone's nerves had been on edge. A few days into the trip, however, they had felt a shift in the mood and settled into a routine. The crew and guardians had fallen into a rhythm together.

Nera knew tensions would surge again once they reached Kelvur, but she was thankful for smooth sailing.

The *Sellena* sang to the sleeping crew with an ambient orchestra of wooden creaks and groans. Hammocks swayed as the vessel bobbed along, cutting toward the east. The night was quiet, and the moon was high, shining a bright reflection off the waves. A perfect night for sailing.

Coal leaned on the railing at the fore of the ship, staring over the rolling waves. The stars were bright, and he identified the constellations that weren't washed out by the great light of the moon. He'd done that same exercise thirty times already because he was unable to sleep. His heart ached. He knew Ezel was doing the right thing by going to Calrok with Garron and Ellaria, but it didn't mean the dwarf liked it.

And then there was Merrick. Over the last couple of years, Coal and Ezel had enjoyed Merrick's company on many occasions, and the man was another of the dwarf's best friends. Their fun times at the *Flagkeep Tavern* in Tamaria felt so long ago. He shuddered at the reminder that Merrick was in danger. He couldn't bring himself to think the huntsman could already be dead, though he wondered if that wouldn't be a better fate. If the sorcerer had gotten his hands on the huntsman, who knows what vile things he would do to the man. If Merrick were dead, though, this whole mission was a lost cause.

"Why did Ezel stay behind?"

Captain Tin's gravelly voice surprised Coal in the otherwise quiet night. The dwarf's barrel chest leaked a heavy sigh that floated away on the sea breeze. "He needed to help someone."

The man nodded solemnly, not saying anything.

"Hard to believe we're sailing all the way to Kelvur," Coal said, staring ahead.

"There was a time I would have believed we would do such a thing."

Coal huffed a chuckle. "We were much younger then."

"Dumber too." Tin smirked.

"There can be no doubt of that," the dwarf said, stroking his black beard. After a long silence between them, Coal turned and looked up at the man. "I'm sorry about the way we left all those years ago."

"How could you not?" the man replied.

"We abandoned you all in a horrible predicament, and now we find ourselves in a dire situation, and you don't even hesitate to help."

Tin eyed the dwarf and nodded thoughtfully. "I know you were down below with the night shift when we went through the Narrows," Tin said as he puffed his pipe. "But I'm sure you heard what Ezel did to save the *Leslin.*"

"Hardly squares us up," the dwarf said mournfully.

The captain shrugged slightly. "You know how we originally got the *Sellena?*"

"No, actually."

"It was supposed to be the flagship for a Stalford merchant's fleet. Of course, he hired some rich man's son to captain it for him. I will never understand the 'favors' rich men do for each other. Needless to say, the rich man's son was a bub and had no sense. He wrecked the ship on some rocks off the coast of Vandor. The merchant's 'friends' at the shipyard deemed it 'unsalvageable,' and that's when we got it."

Coal smiled at the story. "Not so unsalvageable, it seems to me."

"Right," Captain Tin said. "It took us years to get her to the state she's in now. And here she is. Might be the first Tarrinian vessel to sail to Kelvur."

"That's pretty amazing," the dwarf said quietly.

"Aye," the man nodded. "Even more amazing are the truths that a ship can teach a man." His eyebrows popped, and he side-eyed Coal as he added, "Or a dwarf."

Coal turned to him and asked, "What has the *Sellena* taught you?"

The captain smirked. "Not all lost causes are truly lost."

Coal stared at the old captain as the man watched the waves and puffed on his pipe. The dwarf was overwhelmed with an immense gratitude. *Could he really forgive me just like that?* he wondered.

Suddenly, he was filled with hope. Merrick was out there. Just like Tin hadn't given up on Coal, the dwarf wouldn't give up on the huntsman.

A resonating sound from the depths shook the night as the *Sellena* bucked awkwardly to the side. Coal and the captain locked eyes.

Captain Tin bolted toward the aft of the ship and yelled back at the dwarf, "Ring the bell!"

Nera tumbled out of her hammock and hit the deck hard. After taking a second to gather herself, she locked eyes with Ralowyn, who was also on the floor. The alarm bell rang from the main deck as sailors and guardians scrambled throughout the bowels of the ship. Nera jumped to her feet to don her armor. "What is it?"

"I do not know," Ralowyn replied.

The elf mage brushed her silver hair behind her pointed ears as she dressed and grabbed her staff. When she did, lavender magic burst to life around the staff, and her eyes blazed with a similarly hued light. The sight surprised Nera. She had seen Ralowyn do magic before, but she had never seen it in such a dark place. The elf exuded a lavender aura, brightening the whole deck around them.

Is that what I look like when I use Santoralier? Nera wondered.

Incoherent shouts rang out with the ship's warning bell.

"We need to hurry," Ralowyn said, helping the guardian with the last pieces of her armor.

"Go ahead." Nera nodded toward the ladder. "I'm right behind you."

Ralowyn's eyes narrowed with determination as she nodded, spun, and hurried up the steps to the next deck.

Nera strapped her last bracer on, grabbed her spear, and ran to where the rest of guardians and sailors slept. The hammocks were all empty and the sailors gone. A few of the guardians were lashing their last pieces of armor to themselves.

"Tam," Nera shouted.

"Yes, ma'am?" he yelled back over the noise, cinching his last bracer.

"Post up at the stairs for relay," she commanded. "I'll assess the situation and issue instructions. Talon Squadron." The rest of the guardians huffed out the usual grunting reply to let her know they were listening. "Prepare your griffins and wait for my mark."

Again, they grunted their affirmation.

Nera whirled about and ambled up the ladder toward the upper deck. Griffin Guard armor was lightweight and allowed for a wide range of motion. As she climbed the ladder and the ship bucked, she was grateful for the artistry of her armor.

Water splashed heavily into the opening as she pulled herself to the main deck. Nera coughed and sputtered, trying to catch her breath. She slipped awkwardly onto the deck. As she did, her eyes widened in shock.

A giant serpentine creature wailed and writhed as sailors threw harpoons and Lanryn whipped his wand, shooting magic bolts at its thick hide. The beast rose from the waters, higher than the mainmast of the *Sellena*, dwarfing the ship and her crew. Great volumes of water splashed over the sides as the ship was tipped and battered from underneath.

Captain Tin shouted at sailors, organizing them to defend their vessel. Coal had moved on from the warning bell to pass out harpoons and bows.

The scene was unlike anything Nera had ever witnessed.

Suddenly, Ralowyn grabbed the woman's arm, an attempt to help the guardian gain her feet. "What in Finlestia?" Nera asked.

"Sea serpent," the elf shouted over the commotion.

Nera rolled herself over and hollered down to Tam, "Fly! Fly! Fly!"

Coal grabbed a bow and quiver for himself and ran to a spot at the bow of the ship where he could lob arrows at the great sea serpent without hitting any of the crew. The sailors did everything they could to fight the beast.

Some jabbed at the serpent as it drew near enough to the ship. Some hurled well-thrown harpoons, most of which bounced off the thick hide of the monster. Others loosed arrow after arrow, only a few able to find some crack in the creature's scales and stick. Coal shook his head. *We're in trouble.*

The monster's head lowered toward the surface of the water, and for a moment, the sailors stared on in confusion. The dwarf watched, waiting for the beast's next move. One of the young sailors who was bailing the water with which the great serpent was drowning the *Sellena* screamed from the portside.

Just as the massive tail of the sea serpent came slamming down on top of them, the entire crew turned to watch it smash the ship's foremast. Some of the more fortunate sailors dove out of the way, while others were crushed under the immense weight of the serpent's body. The creature coiled around the ship, its tail slipping over the starboard side and back into the Gant Sea.

The serpent elevated its head once more, eyeing its prey. A sudden flash of lightning crackled through the air and blasted into the beast. It wailed sonorously, writhing and bucking the ship and its crew. Several sailors screamed, but if they survived, none would hold their cries against them.

Coal gathered himself and threw his broken bow to the side. He'd almost been crushed when the creature's tail came down on the *Sellena*.

"Boehlen's Beard," he grumbled to himself. He scrambled to another sailor who had also narrowly escaped the serpent's destruction.

Coal cursed himself for not having his battle hammer. It lay belowdecks, surely tossed around in all the ship's wild bucking. He had not brought it with him to the main deck earlier when he was identifying constellations. *Fool, you should always be ready.*

The sailor next to him whimpered, and the dwarf became keenly aware that they were alone on that side of the beast's squeezing body. He looked at the sailor and realized the young man held a harpoon in his weak grasp.

"Hand it over now, lad," Coal said as gently as he could muster. "We're not out of this fight just yet."

Ralowyn held the Staff of Anvelorian high as she willed every ounce of magical power she could to hold the structural integrity of the *Sellena* together under the pressure of the squeezing sea serpent. Nera let *Santoralier* fly, and the spear turned to a streak of lightning smashing into the monster again. The sea serpent squeezed harder as it let out a bloodcurdling wail.

"Wait!" Ralowyn yelled to Nera.

The woman turned to the elf, as several strands of hair escaped her big black braid, giving her a wild appearance. A group of sailors wrenched half of the hold hatchway open, and griffins and their guardians spilled out, flying high into the night sky. Shadowpaw gripped the frame of the wooden hatchway as she approached Nera, ready to join the fight.

"Wait!" Ralowyn yelled again as the guardians began their swooping attacks on the great serpent. The recovering sailors were also rejoining the fray.

"What do you need?" Nera called over the noise.

"I ..." Ralowyn grunted from the effort of keeping the *Sellena* from being crushed.

"Ralowyn!" Nera shouted incredulously. "We're going to be ripped apart."

As the guardians swarmed the head of the serpent, the great monster lashed this way and that, snapping its horrible fangs. Griffins dipped and flapped just out of reach. The sea serpent didn't enjoy the new game and slithered its head over the *Sellena* and into the sea on the other side, wrapping the ship even tighter.

The elf's eyes widened in horror. She wouldn't be able to hold out forever. If she couldn't find a way out of this, they may never find Merrick and Karnak. A wave of helplessness washed over her. She felt like she was adrift again, barely afloat and hopeless.

An idea tickled the back of her mind.

"Tell everyone to stop," she said to Nera.

"What?" the woman yelled back. "Are you crazy? You can't hold us together forever."

"Command them to stop! Now!"

Nera shook her head, not understanding.

"You have to trust me," Ralowyn said through gritted teeth as she grunted under the strain.

Nera growled and mounted Shadowpaw. They launched into the air, and the captain of the Talon Squadron swooped low to speak hurriedly to the captain of the *Sellena*. Captain

Tin looked wide-eyed at the elf, but whatever the guardian was saying to him was delivered with enough urgency and confidence that he ran about commanding his sailors to stop their attempts to pierce the great serpent's hide.

The guardian flew higher and waved off the Talon Squadron, many of whom looked at the captain as though she were going mad.

Maker, let this work, Ralowyn prayed.

The elf released her magical barrier between the ship and the sea serpent. She ran toward the body of the great monster. The *Sellena* moaned under the strain, and the sailors braced themselves as they glanced around at the deck as though it would shatter underneath them at any second.

Nera and Shadowpaw swooped to the deck next to Ralowyn as she ran. The elf slid to a halt, her hand resting on the slowly expanding and contracting serpentine body. A magical light blazed to life, enveloping the mage. Many of the crew shielded their eyes from the brightness, but none could bring themselves to look away.

Ralowyn reached with everything she had. She could sense the great serpent, could feel inside him. She could tell he was frightened. *Did we sail through your territory?* Ralowyn thought to the creature. The monster twitched, and its muscles tightened, shaking the entire ship.

Please, Ralowyn pressed with her thoughts and emotions. *Please stop. You are going to kill us.*

The sea serpent tightened once more. The *Sellena* let out an unnerving *crack!*

No! Please. We will leave. We will get out of your territory. We mean you no harm, my friend.

Ralowyn began to cry. Trying to connect with such a beast was something she had never done. Her emotions were raw and heavy. More than that, the desperation in her had no way to release itself from her body. She couldn't do it. The sea serpent was going to snap their vessel, and the entire crew would be lost at sea. The only ones with a chance at surviving would be the already flying griffin guardians, and she wasn't sure they were close enough to land for them to make it either.

Suddenly, the elf felt a surge of energy charge her body. The tingling sensation rolled through her, as though it permeated the very blood in her veins. She could see the sea serpent's heart in her mind and reached out again. *Stop.*

The monster loosened its grip slightly.

Ralowyn's lavender eyes widened, and she pressed her hand against the body of the creature. She noticed strange ribbons of yellow light weaving and dancing around her normal purple magic.

Release us and leave.

The coiled body of the sea serpent slithered in one direction, the tail appearing over the edge of the hull, following the rest of its massive length. As the tail slid and dripped off the portside of the *Sellena,* it revealed a surprised dwarf and a rather green-gilled sailor.

Coal stared at the elf, dumbfounded. "Well, I didn't expect that," he said, the tip of the harpoon in his hand clunking heavily to the deck.

Ralowyn shifted uncomfortably under his stare and felt a hand leave her shoulder. She turned to see Nera, curling her fingers and studying her hand in bewilderment.

All around the ship, sailors cheered. The Talon Squadron above roared their customary grunts.

"How did you do that?" the elf asked.

Nera shook her head, stunned.

"Nera," Ralowyn said, stepping toward her. The guardian pulled away.

Realizing that she'd done so, Nera shook away her confusion. "Sorry," she said. "I'm not even sure what I just did."

Ralowyn took a slow step toward the guardian and placed a comforting hand on her shoulder. Nothing happened. At least, nothing magical happened. Nera exhaled and nodded as though she had been worried that the elf's touch would trigger more unexpected magic.

"I am not sure either," Ralowyn said. "But I think you just saved us all."

CHAPTER NINETEEN

A BRAVE LITTLE DWARF

Shorlis slipped on loose gravel, tearing his knee as it landed hard on a jagged stone. The chelon grabbed at his injured knee, blood mixing with the dirt caking his hand. He gritted his teeth and lifted the pick that lay next to him, using it to heft himself to his feet. He stepped a few times to test it. His knee would be fine, just another bloody scrape. One of the many he'd gotten in the rough Mines of Glinso.

"Hey! Get back to work," a geldrin guard barked at the chelon.

Shorlis didn't acknowledge the guard. He wiped a green hand across his brow, coagulating more dirt into mud with his sweat. He lifted his pick and went back to work. He only swung it down once before the geldrin shouted at him again.

"Hey! You hear me?" the geldrin hollered. "You deaf or something?"

Shorlis looked up to the geldrin at the top of the trench. The chelon's whole body ached. He felt as though he had nothing left to give. Frankly, he didn't have the energy to deal with the moronic geldrin today. Shorlis stared indignantly.

Obviously not liking the way Shorlis looked at him, the guard shifted uneasily. The chelon couldn't say why, but for some reason the geldrin's discomfort was humorous to him, and a smirk crept across Shorlis's face as he shook his head.

The geldrin's eyes widened with rage. "Come here. Now!" he barked.

"Shorlis," Tenzo hissed from farther down the trench. "What are you doing? You're going to get yourself killed."

Shorlis rolled his eyes and reached for his pick.

"Hey! I'm talking to you," the guard shouted, sliding down the trench toward the chelon.

Out of nowhere, Doran stepped in front of the geldrin. The young dwarf held his water bucket in one hand and his ladle in the other.

"Get out of here," the geldrin swatted at the dwarf as he shuffled past him. "This chelon doesn't get any water. I'm about to teach him a lesson in respect."

"Like the respect you showed his father?"

The geldrin turned on the little dwarf. Doran's face was menacing, and his eyes poured tears freely. The guard spit as he exhaled a cackle. "I'll deal with you in a minute."

Shorlis glared at the geldrin as he approached, ready to take whatever beating the guard meant to dole out on him, but something happened he did not expect. Doran ran at the geldrin and whacked at the guard with his ladle, screaming, "You killed him!" over and over again.

The geldrin spun on the dwarf and blasted him in the head with the pommel of his sword. Doran grunted as he tumbled away.

"You little wretch," the geldrin spat.

"No!" Shorlis yelled as the guard swung his sword down on the dazed dwarf.

An unbridled rage boiled over within Shorlis, filling the innermost parts of his shell. He wrenched his pick from the dirt and ran full speed at the geldrin guard. The chelon brought the pick down into the geldrin's shoulder with a sickening *Cthunk!*

The geldrin spun and grabbed at the chelon's linen shirt, the stony face sculpted into a look of astonishment.

Shorlis pushed the guard away and dove to his knees, scooping the little dwarf into his arms. But Doran would cry no more.

Grief erupted as Shorlis roared his agony and other miners poked around the corners to see what the commotion was all about. Tenzo appeared next to Shorlis, his own face bearing a look of shock. The muscled chelon kicked at the corpse of the geldrin that lay nearby. "Shorlis," he said, patting his friend on the shoulder and eyeing the little dwarf clutched in the chelon's grasp. "Shorlis, he's gone."

"What more can they take from us?" Shorlis spat back. He looked around to all the miners in the section. Several of them had tears streaming down their faces. "What more?" he asked. He rose to his feet, holding Doran out, begging someone to answer him.

"They've already taken everything," Tenzo said.

"No more," Shorlis growled. "This ends today!"

He laid Doran's body on the ground with as much reverence as he could muster through his rage. He closed the little dwarf's eyes. He turned and looked at the geldrin, his pick stuck in the dead guard's shoulder. The geldrin's sword lay on the ground next to him.

A tool of slavery or a weapon for freedom? Shorlis thought.

He grabbed the sword and lifted it before him. He glanced around at the others and then to Tenzo. The big chelon's chin quivered, and he gave Shorlis a nod. Before anything was spoken between them, Shorlis and Tenzo rushed up the side of the trench with a mighty battle cry.

The geldrin guards at the Glinso Mining Camp had long grown complacent in their duties. They had experienced little resistance from the workers the entire time the camp had operated, and never had a miner openly defied their commands. Any that had misbehaved had been dealt with quickly.

When the miners poured out of the trenches yelling things like, "For Doran!" or "For Freedom!" the guards were ill-prepared.

The miners fought with a ferocity and energy the guards did not think the workers possessed. As the miners brandished the tools of their slavery as weapons to bring about their freedom, the geldrins were overwhelmed by the swarming mobs. As each fell, their weapons were passed about, arming the miners for their continued march through the camp.

Shorlis brought his sword down, finishing off another geldrin guard that Tenzo had bowled over. Tenzo kept that guard's sword for himself. Shorlis nodded to him; the big chelon would need it. No doubt Commander Chol was bunkered in the building ahead with several geldrin guards.

As the mob of miners approached the building where the commander spent the majority of his days, several mounted guards barreled around the corner. Commander Chol sneered as he locked eyes with Shorlis. The horses stamped at the ground nervously in the presence of the raging mob. No one moved.

"You're all dead now!" Commander Chol spat. "Your freedom is not what you think. It's really your doom."

Miners swayed and shifted their makeshift weapons in their hands. Many of them turned to Shorlis as though they were waiting for him to lead them. Shorlis's beak clicked together as he clenched his jaw.

Commander Chol's stony face twisted into a wicked grin. "What do you have left to fight for?" He shifted his gaze to the rest of the mob. "What do any of you have left to fight for?"

The mob grew uneasy. Shorlis glanced around, and Tenzo growled quietly next to him, "Everything."

Shorlis nodded and narrowed his eyes at the commander. "Everything!" he shouted, as he burst into a sprint.

Without hesitation, the rest of the mob sprang into action and ran alongside the young chelon.

Commander Chol and the riders turned and rode off. The frantic horses kicked up dirt as they carried the captors away. Several geldrins hurried around the building and skidded to a halt before running directly into the mob.

Shorlis shook his head and spat. *Coward,* he thought of Chol. *Leaving your own men to cover your retreat.*

The guards that were left behind stood no chance against the swarm of miners. Several miners were cut down by the desperate swings of the guards' swords, but the geldrins were quickly overpowered.

As Shorlis and Tenzo entered the building, a geldrin leaped from his hiding place and cracked the muscled chelon over the head, sending him sprawling down the entry hallway. Shorlis swung his sword at the attacker, who dodged and batted it away with his own. The weapons clanged together, and they sounded strange to Shorlis in the enclosed hallway.

The geldrin jumped forward, jabbing his sword straight at the chelon's chest. Shorlis lifted his sword and spun away, barely deflecting the strike wide. The geldrin brought his sword around again so quickly, the only thing the chelon could do was duck. He slammed into the wall and stumbled down the hallway.

Shorlis's eyes widened, but he tried to hide the fact that he was terrified. One-on-one with a geldrin guard who had much more sword training than himself was not good odds for his survival. *Think, think*, he chanted internally. His hard shell bumped against the wall with a *Clunk!* The geldrin grinned wickedly at him, knowing the chelon had nowhere to go. Shorlis bumped against the wall with his shell a couple of times, firing himself up, when suddenly, he had an idea.

The chelon let out a primal war cry as he rushed the geldrin. The move obviously caught the geldrin off guard as he batted Shorlis's sword away and unsuccessfully tried to swing at the chelon himself. The sword glanced off Shorlis's thick shell as he turned his shoulder into the geldrin's stomach, tackling the guard. The geldrin whacked at the chelon's hard shell with his sword while Shorlis pounded away with his free hand.

They jostled for position, each taking and landing blows on the other. Eventually though, the geldrin's superior strength earned him the top position.

The guard raised his sword high, preparing to plunge the blade into Shorlis's throat, when suddenly, the geldrin froze. His manic eyes squinted in confusion, and he fell forward. Tenzo ripped his sword from the geldrin's back as the guard hunched over, lifeless.

Shorlis rolled the limp geldrin off of himself and sat with his shell against the wall. He felt with his fingers at the shredded section of his linen shirt. He touched some rough spots on his shell and grimaced. The geldrin hadn't broken through, but he'd definitely left Shorlis with a chipped shell.

The two friends sat together, breathing heavily.

After a while, Tenzo hefted himself up and extended his hand to Shorlis. "Let's check the rest of the building together."

"I think that might be wise," Shorlis nodded as he took his friend's hand.

In one day, the slave miners at Glinso Mining Camp had done something none of them had dared to do since its inception. They had overthrown their oppressors and freed themselves. Many of them had been at the camp for well over a year and hardly knew what to do with their newfound freedom.

The miners killed all the geldrins, including the ones that oversaw the dock workers on the edge of the sea. Getting information out of any geldrins they could take alive would likely prove fruitless, and moreover, the spurned miners would stop at nothing to vanquish the stony creatures. It would have been folly for Shorlis or Tenzo to get in between the mob and their captors.

Eventually, the liberated prisoners gathered, exhausted and aimless. Shorlis had gathered several of the others to help him distribute the food stores among the gathered people. It was strange for them to be handed so much food, and many of them ate more than their malnourished stomachs could handle.

As Shorlis stepped onto the front porch of the command building, Tenzo handed him a piece of bread. He took the torn piece of bread with gratitude. Shorlis took a bite and looked out over the gathered people.

"Look at what we've done," he said quietly.

"We've freed ourselves from the clutches of evil tyrants," Tenzo said stoically.

Tears filled Shorlis's eyes again, and he wondered how he still had any left. "But my father. And Doran ..."

"Were killed by those very same tyrants."

"But if we could have done this before, they would be free with us now," Shorlis gulped his sadness.

Tenzo shook his head with a frown. "Many died today. It's impossible to guess whether Anthanar or Doran would have survived."

"I would have defended them. We would have kept them safe."

"No," Tenzo shook his head again. "We may never have stood and fought. Even though we whispered of the possibility, we were always too afraid of losing them."

Shorlis didn't know what to say. He knew Tenzo was right, but his friend's words didn't make the losses hurt any less.

"Besides," Tenzo said. "There is a right time for everything."

Shorlis spun to look at his muscled friend. As he did, he saw a strange look in his eyes that reminded the chelon of his father.

There is a right time for everything, Shorlis repeated the words internally. *How many times did you say those words to me, Father?* Shorlis realized how much of an impact his father and Doran had made with their sacrifices.

He stepped to the front of the porch, and as he did, the people in the gathered crowd hushed and faced him. He glanced around, looking at as many of them as he could. All these people were free because of the sacrifice of those two.

Tenzo nudged Shorlis's arm. "They're waiting for you to say something."

"What?" he asked, not knowing how long he'd been standing there, staring. "What am I supposed to say?"

"Anthanar always told them stories." Tenzo shrugged and took another bite of bread.

Shorlis shook his head as though the notion was silly. But as the others looked on in anticipation, he could think of nothing better to say.

"My father," he began, projecting his voice so those farther away could hear him. "He told us stories in the dark of night. He told us stories of hope when darkness surrounded us and we felt as though there was nothing left to hope for."

People shifted, drawing nearer and getting comfortable to listen to what the young chelon had to say.

"He told us stories about heroes of old," he continued. "Heroes that never gave up, even in the direst of circumstances. Heroes that would stop at nothing to defeat the evil that threatened the world and those they loved.

"But today I'll tell you a new story. A story of a people with no homes to return to. A story about two heroes who sparked a flame of freedom in the hearts of those people. One hero showed great kindness to strangers. The other ..." Shorlis choked a gulp and smiled through his tears.

"The other was a brave little dwarf. Their names were Anthanar and Doran."

CHAPTER TWENTY

FROM ONE PRISON TO THE NEXT

D uskwood was an overgrown and gnarled forest. The giant, Dak, rolled the cage as long as he could before it was deemed too cumbersome to continue. The dark-skinned elf, who seemed to be leading the group of Javelin warriors, suggested that dragging the cage through the underbrush any farther would leave an obvious trail for people to find. It was hard enough for his crew to hide the giant's tracks. They removed Merrick and Karnak from the cage and discarded it. The giant made a joking remark about the cage being much lighter with the orc out of it.

The members of the Javelin squad had bound Merrick and Karnak's hands before pulling them out of the cage. Their situation didn't appear much better than when they were captives to Hazkul Bern. At least they were able to walk on their own two feet—a strangely invigorating relief.

After another hour, Merrick found himself staring at the giant, tall above him, for probably the thirtieth time as they walked through the thick wood.

"You stare like a tiny puppy," the giant said, his voice as large as him. "But not as cute. You're kind of creeping me out."

"Sorry," Merrick said, looking away. "I've never seen a giant."

"There are not many of us left," Dak said with a hint of sadness.

"Really?" Merrick asked, curious and attentive to an opportunity to gather information.

"Used to be lots of us, back before the Crags were filled with lakes of fire."

The giant shook his head mournfully.

"And what are the Crags? Was that your home? Is that where you come from?"

"Well, don't you have a lot of questions now," the dark-skinned elf butted in.

"He was only making conversation, Feliketh," Dak said.

Feliketh's eyes narrowed at the huntsman as Merrick smiled at the knowledge of the elf's name.

"You answer his questions too freely, my friend," the elf said. "Vorenna is going to have many questions to ask before they get any answers of their own. You must remember the types of deceivers we fight against. For all we know, the sorcerer wanted us to take these two, and they have come to spy on us, find our camp, and slit our throats as we sleep."

Karnak grunted, his shoulders rolling with stifled laughter.

"Whoa," Merrick said. "We're not spies. We were prisoners."

"See," Dak reasoned. "Prisoners. Not spies."

Feliketh smacked his bald forehead. "You believe his words too easily. Of course a spy isn't going to say he's a spy."

"You discredit his words too easily," the giant mumbled, but the words still sounded loud.

"It's true. We're not even from here," Merrick said, but Karnak gave him a warning look and a slight shake of his head.

"Well, that's obvious," Feliketh laughed. "I haven't seen an orc in ... probably as long as it has been since you've seen a giant."

The people in Kelvur seemed to have some notion about orcs that Merrick and Karnak weren't privy to.

"Where have you and your kin been hiding?" the elf asked Karnak directly.

Karnak glared at the elf.

"Boy," Feliketh continued, turning toward Dak. "Your new friend over here is very companionable."

The giant sighed and rolled his eyes.

They walked in relative silence for a number of hours before the group came upon a meadow with a stream where they took a break. Birds flitted to and fro, as Merrick breathed in the familiar scent of sun-warmed grass and flowers—the smell of home. He imagined that if the group hadn't invaded the space, there would be a falcon hunting from the edge of the meadow. The place made him miss Rora.

How did I end up here? he wondered to himself.

As he thought about it, their story was going to seem outlandish to this Vorenna they were being dragged to meet. He was a humble huntsman from Tamaria in Tarrine. How would he explain that he got mixed up in a war that seemingly had nothing to do with him and ended up fighting off a wicked sorcerer before befriending an orc gar?

Maybe his common ground with these people was the sorcerer. If they were fighting him too, maybe he and Karnak could convince them they were on the same side.

But even if they did convince this Javelin group, how would they get home? Karnak had lost his axe, Fire Storm, and their captors had taken the magical statuette of Valurwind. He missed Valurwind, too. Their bond had grown, and the astral falcon had filled some of the holes in his heart he'd been left with when Rora died.

He looked at Karnak. The two of them were sitting in the shade of a tree at the edge of the meadow. The gar's hands were bound in front of him, but he seemed not to care. The orc's eyes scanned the area as though he were calculating something.

"Karnak," Merrick whispered.

The sound of his name startled the orc, and he flinched. "What? I'm counting the group. They've got a large number here. If we're going to their camp and they have more warriors there, it may be harder to escape."

"Escaping is all good and well," Merrick said. "But what then? We have no ride. We have no idea where we are. We have no way to get back across the Gant Sea. There's something bigger going on here that we don't know about. Even if we do escape, we may end up captured by the Sons of Silence again."

"We'll find a way. We have to."

"Listen," Merrick urged. "I want to get back to them, too—"

"No!" Karnak growled under his breath. "Tanessa and Gernot are back there with one of those geldrins. They have no idea what they're dealing with. They attacked my family."

"You don't think I know that?" Merrick growled back through clenched teeth. "And what of Ralowyn? What happened to her? She was right behind us on Henry. I can only hope she saw us go down and retreated to Calrok. But what if she didn't? What if she's hurt, or ..." His words trailed off. He couldn't speak them.

Karnak's large muscles tensed as his fists squeezed tighter, a physical attempt to suppress his frustration. "This whole thing is ..."

"I know," Merrick said, softening. They sat quietly for a moment. "I'm sure Tanessa got Smarlo, and he and the Scar Squadron took care of the geldrin."

The big orc exhaled, and his tension eased. "I'm sure you're right." He hit his leg a few times with his bound hands and turned toward the man. "I'm sorry."

"I am, too," Merrick gave the orc a weak smile.

Karnak stared at the forest grass between his feet. "I thought I could get us out." Merrick looked at the orc quizzically. "I thought if I could just get *Dalkeri* to come to me, then I could break us out of that cage, and we would be halfway home by now. But the witch ... I don't know. I just feel powerless."

Merrick nodded thoughtfully. "I know the feeling."

The orc looked to the man again, and his shoulders bobbed in a slight chuckle. "I suppose you do."

Merrick smiled, and his chin popped as he reminisced. "I remember a surprise journey, not so long ago, that started off horribly for me."

Karnak deflated. "Another thing I'm sorry about."

The huntsman shook his head. "I have forgiven you for that."

"Doesn't mean I'm not still sorry about it."

"Regardless," Merrick pressed on. "I felt so small. I was thrust into a war that was so much bigger than me. A war I had no part in. And yet, the surprise journey led me to places I never expected and required from me things I did not know I had within me to give. It challenged me and forced me to become more than what I was before. I was able to accomplish that with the help of some amazing friends. And in the end, I came out of all of it with a new brother."

A tear escaped the orc's eye, and he twitched his face awkwardly, trying to whisk it away. He nodded to the man and pressed his lips around his tusks in a grateful smile.

Merrick continued. "Whatever *this* surprise journey throws at us, we'll handle it. After everything we've been through ..."

Karnak grunted a laugh. "We'll figure this out."

"We will." The man smiled. "Plus, I promised Tanessa I'd get you home."

The orc's eyes widened, and he gave the huntsman an awkward look. "You're going to be in so much trouble."

"Yeah ..."

"She probably didn't expect us to be gone so long. She probably meant that day."

"She didn't say that ..." Merrick said with a slow shrug. "I'm hoping I get some grace on that front."

The two shared a laugh, and for a moment they forgot their circumstances. The sun was shining, and though they were bound as prisoners, at least they were together.

Though they'd been let out of the cage, when the Javelin group threw burlap sacks over their heads and hoisted them on the shoulders of the giant, Karnak couldn't help but feel like they were headed from one prison to the next. Admittedly, Dak carried them over his shoulder with a remarkable gentleness the orc didn't expect from a giant. Karnak found himself resting in short spurts, feeling an odd sense of safety as they bobbed along.

They knew the camp was close when they heard the noise of groups of people milling about, speaking to one another. Karnak was relieved to think they might actually get a chance to make some headway with the Kelvurians. He hoped Feliketh wouldn't be in their interrogations with this Vorenna. The elf was far too skeptical, and the orc didn't want him to poison the leader's mind before they could explain themselves.

After his discussion with Merrick earlier, Karnak's mood had improved dramatically. He decided he needed to approach this with the mindset of a gar. How many times had he needed to negotiate something with a gar from another city in Drelek? He could reason with people. *As long as this Vorenna is a reasonable Kelvurian,* he thought. He had yet to have the opportunity to reason with any Kelvurian in all his encounters with them.

When Dak lowered them gently to the ground, a couple of soldiers led them by the arms through the camp. Karnak noted the difference of the ground they walked on. It felt like patches of wild grass interspersed with dirt rather than the crunching detritus of the forest floor. Clearly, they were in a great meadow or had left the forest altogether.

He heard the flaps of a tent opening, and suddenly the late afternoon sun no longer licked at his shoulders. The soldiers tied his bonds to some sort of pole and ripped the bag off his head. Karnak blinked several times as he refocused on his surroundings. He stood in the middle of a well-furnished battle tent. It had a couple of bed pallets and chests. There were two rugs, one next to each bed. A couple of lanterns flickered on what looked to be a desk crafted from wood.

Karnak's face scrunched in confusion. The soldiers took the sack off Merrick's head. The huntsman's shoulder-length brown hair was a ratty mess. He was also tied to the tent's center pole. When the soldiers exited the tent, leaving the two prisoners alone, the man and the orc gawked at their surroundings, eventually meeting each other with blank stares.

"Well, this is not what I was expecting," Merrick said.

"No," the orc agreed.

He grabbed the pole between them and gave it a testing shake. He found it to be movable with his great strength as the canopy above them waved. For a moment, the orc thought this to be the perfect time to attempt an escape. However, he remembered his friend's wise words and dismissed the idea.

"They may be just as confused by us," Karnak finally spoke again.

"What do you mean?"

"You heard the elf."

"Feliketh?"

"Yes," the orc said with a nod. "When they first took us from the sorcerer's men, he sounded as though he couldn't believe we were in the cage together."

"Right," Merrick remembered. "Did you catch the part about them not having seen an orc in a long time?"

"I did," Karnak said, his brow furrowing and his tusks shifting as he thought about it. "Did the geldrins kill all the orcs of Kelvur?"

"I don't know. But we've seen a lot of strange people here. Chelons, geldrins, giants." Merrick emphasized the last one.

The tent flaps whipped open, and a woman in heavy armor strode in. She was tall for a woman and quite muscular. With the fur that lined her armor and the myriad of braids in her blond hair, she had a savage beauty to her. Karnak wondered if she was a barbarian like the one from the Sons of Silence. She made Merrick look small, and the orc took a step closer to the pole, as though he might be able to protect the man.

"So, you're not from Kelvur," she said. It was a statement, not a question.

The orc and the man glanced at each other, then Karnak said, "We're from Tarrine."

"Tarrinian," she seemed to chew on the answer. Her eyes flitted to Merrick and back to Karnak. She looked at him intently. "Why are you here?"

The big orc suppressed a laugh. Then, with a sideways tip of his head, he answered, "That is a long story."

CHAPTER TWENTY-ONE

LANDFALL

Nera watched in awe as Tam scribbled away on a piece of parchment. "Did you get that one there? And over there?" She asked, excitedly pointing out islands as they sailed by.

"Yes, ma'am," Tam answered, exasperated. "But I need to get higher to get a better view."

"Well, up the mast you go then, lad!" Captain Tinothe ordered.

Tam hurried to the mast ladder and clambered his way to the fighting top.

Captain Tinothe smirked.

"What?" Nera asked with a smile of her own. Though they knew they'd be engaging the enemy soon, they were all excited about seeing land.

The *Sellena's* captain held out a finger to her and turned. "Aless, bring a bucket to young mister Tam in the top, would you?"

"Oh dear," Aless said as she hustled away from her excited conversation with Orin.

"What is it?" Nera asked.

"If he thought the sway of the sea was bad down here ..." Tin trailed off, his smirk twisting his mustache. "Let's just hope his excitement keeps him distracted."

When they left Kane Harbor in Tarrine, the crew was in such a rush, they hadn't considered the need for someone with the ability to draw. Tam had the gift, so when Nera spotted Kelvurian land for the first time, she summoned the young man so he could start drawing. He was a guardian, of course, but being the only one who could draw at all, he was the closest thing to a cartographer the *Sellena* had.

Orin stepped close to Nera as they watched the islands drift by. "Hard to believe," he said.

"It is," she agreed, as one of the Talon Squadron scouts flew by. She'd sent two of them to the air right after getting Tam started on drawing the islands. They could scout ahead and get a good look to see what dangers might be awaiting them.

"Pernden would love this," Orin said.

Nera laughed. "He'd rather be doing just about anything over his kingly responsibilities."

Orin laughed, too. "That's true."

"But yes, he would love this," she affirmed, her voice sounding far off. She missed him.

Orin interpreted her look and placed a comforting hand on her back before saying, "We'll find Merrick and figure this whole thing out. We'll be headed back to Tarrine and my brother in no time."

Nera smiled appreciatively at him. "I can't imagine what Ellaria's feeling right now."

"She's tough. One of the toughest women I've ever met," Orin mused. "Which is saying something since that puts her in league with women like you."

Nera grinned. "She is. While she's still got training to do, it was an easy choice to bring her into the Guard. Just because she's tough doesn't mean she isn't also worried about her brother."

"Of course," Orin agreed. "But that's why we're here."

"Yes," Nera said, nodding thoughtfully. "Let's not let her down."

While the rest of the crew eagerly anticipated making landfall, Ralowyn battled tension in her stomach. She was worried. None of them had seen the Kelvurian ship. As amazing a feat as it was that the *Sellena* had gotten them across the Gant Sea, the elf didn't think the ship could survive a fight with the Kelvurian ship.

Ralowyn made her way to a lower deck, looking for quiet. She wanted to meditate before they got themselves into another encounter. She would need to be at full strength if she was going to be of any use in whatever trouble they found themselves, especially if they ran into that witch.

When she reached the belowdecks, she found Coal packing his bag. The dwarf was double-checking the items he had packed.

"Coal," she said softly.

The dwarf started and turned to her with wide eyes. He grabbed at his chest as though he were trying to keep his heart from leaping out. "Boehlen's Beard ... you scared me."

"I am sorry," she replied. She eyed the bag. "What are you doing?"

Coal looked at the bag in front of him and shook his head. "Preparing."

"Preparing for what?" she asked, drawing closer.

Coal grabbed at his battle hammer and squeezed it tight in his hand. "I wasn't ready when the sea serpent came."

"What do you mean?"

"I wasn't ready. I didn't have my hammer, and we almost didn't make it. Then what would have happened to Merrick? Who would have saved him?"

The dwarf sniffed and lowered his head even more.

Ralowyn knelt next to him. "I was afraid, too. I am still afraid."

Coal met her gaze. He wiped his tears away with the cloth wrapping that covered his thick dwarf hands. "He's out there somewhere. I know it. Since Ezel's not here, I've got to find him. It's up to me."

A smile of compassion swept across the fair face of the elf. "The great thing about love is that it is bigger than one person. You have a big heart, Coal, and you love your friends with great ferocity. But you are not the only one who loves Merrick. Orin has sailed across the sea with us to find him. And I love Merrick in a way neither of you do."

Coal nodded and pulled at his black beard. "I just don't want to let him down."

"You will not. Because we will find him together."

As they sailed away from the multitude of islands and turned north to follow the coast of Kelvur, Orin watched one of the guardians land a griffin on the main deck to discuss something with Nera. Watching the guardians fly around over the sea gave Orin a strange feeling. He hadn't flown on griffin-back in a long time. With everything that had happened and the difficulty in pairing griffins and guardians, he likely never would again.

It seemed as though he'd traded life in the sky for life on the sea with all the ships he'd been on recently. As Orin smelled the saltwater spray that misted from the bow of the *Sellena*, he wasn't disappointed by the prospect.

Suddenly, a sailor raced to the bell and rang it. *Here we go*, Orin thought. He rolled his shoulders and twisted his neck, releasing tension. He ran to Nera as the other guardian flew off.

"What's happening?" he asked.

"There's some sort of town up the coast a little way," she said quickly, moving toward the stairs. "Captain Tin has ordered all hands on deck for readiness."

"Did they see the ship?"

Nera paused, revealing her hesitation to admit the answer. "No," she said with a hint of disappointment. Not seeing the Kelvurian ship meant they might have to continue to other ports up the coast in their search.

When Nera disappeared belowdecks, Orin returned to the bow of the ship and gazed up the coast, hoping for a glimpse of the town. Coal and Ralowyn soon appeared by his side.

"What do you see?" Coal asked.

"Nothing yet," Orin replied, unconsciously gripping the hilt of his sheathed sword. His other hand rested on the wooden railing, slick with sea spray.

"There is some sort of dock ahead," Ralowyn said plainly.

The man and the dwarf looked at her, remembering her elf eyes were much keener than their own.

"And the ship?" Coal prodded.

"No ship," she replied. "But there are people gathering on the dock."

"A defense guard," the dwarf growled.

Orin tensed.

"I do not think so," the elf said as she brushed her silvery hair out of her face.

When the *Sellena* finally anchored out of range of potential land projectiles, the entire Talon Squadron, save for Tam, took flight. Orin watched as Nera and her group flew to the awaiting crowd, then as Nera and Shadowpaw flew lower and eventually landed. Orin couldn't make out what the Kelvurians looked like from that distance.

Every nerve in Orin's body tingled. A warm feeling bubbled inside him, and his skin prickled. He didn't like seeing Nera land alone among the crowd, but the rest of Talon floated just above her. If they saw any danger, they'd swoop down to protect her in a heartbeat.

One of the other guardians dropped to the ground. Orin squinted as he strained to see what was going on. As quickly as the guardian had landed, he took to the sky again and flew directly toward the *Sellena.*

After a quick conversation with Captain Tinothe, a couple of sailors prepared the ship's boat, and Orin, Coal, Ellaria, and Tam were loaded onto the boat. Tam appeared to be uncomfortable on the boat, but he sketched away, like he was trying to finish what he had been drawing before he was called down from the top.

Orin stared at the dock as the sailors rowed them toward the watching crowd. As they drew nearer, he caught a glimpse of a tall muscular person that looked to him like a turtle. He turned to Coal whose face revealed his own confusion. "Have you ever come across someone like that?" the man asked the dwarf.

"I have not," Coal said slowly.

"What in Finlestia?"

As the sailors oared the water to bring them into the dock, Nera appeared through the crowd with another one of the turtle-like creatures.

"Orin, Coal, Ralowyn," Nera said quickly. "This is Shorlis. He may be able to help us on our quest."

The chelon recounted his tale about how he and his people were dragged into slavery for the geldrins and set to work in the mine for over a year. He told how his father gave them hope at night by telling the prisoners stories, how his father was killed for helping an orc and a man in a caged cart. He told how a dwarf child spurred their revolt into action, and how just a day prior they had taken over the camp and run off the geldrins. Many of the camp's residents crowded around the room and in the doorway to listen to its retelling. The story had become an instant favorite of the people, everyone especially liking it because of their involvement.

When Shorlis finished, the group from Tarrine sat around the crowded command room in silence. He wasn't sure what they were thinking. *Do they believe all of my story?* he wondered. *Or are they dumbfounded?*

Finally, after a long silence, Nera stepped forward. She hadn't sat down during the entire retelling, and she'd paced the little space in the corner while she chewed on the information. "That had to be Merrick and Karnak."

"Aye," Coal said eagerly. "Which way did they go, lad?"

Shorlis adjusted himself in his seat and met the dwarf's gaze. "They took the road northeast. I imagine they were taking the prisoners to Ventohl."

"Ventohl?" Nera asked. "Where's that?"

"It's an old elvish city on the southern edge of the Crags. My father told me stories of what the city was like before the Crags erupted into flame. It was once a beautiful place. Now it's a den of thieves and murderers."

"The sorcerer is probably there too," Coal exclaimed. "Let's get on the road."

The dwarf jumped up, taking his hammer in his hand and swinging his bag to his back.

"Coal," Ralowyn said gently. "We must know more. This is a strange land to us."

"But—"

"There's a map in the other room," Tenzo cut in. "It shows much more of Kelvur than the old ones we had in the Shoals."

"I'd like to see that, Captain," Tam said quickly, though it sounded as though he were asking her permission.

Nera nodded her consent.

"The path you travel is a dangerous one. Not only will you be going into one of the sorcerer's dens, but the geldrins will likely be riding back here soon to retake this place," Shorlis said gravely.

"Do your people need help to evacuate?" Nera asked.

"No. Most have no home to go back to. The geldrins didn't leave much during their raids on our homes. But here, we could build a new home, together. The dock is just the start, but we could build a fishing community here."

"So, you plan to fight the geldrins when they return?"

"We fought them before," he said plainly.

He watched the woman as her face shifted. She seemed deep in thought when the dwarf jumped back into the conversation.

"Did he seem alright?" Coal asked quietly.

Shorlis looked to the dwarf. Coal seemed tough, maybe even a warrior. But for some reason, this dwarf was adamant about finding the man. "He seemed thin and dry." He wasn't sure if they were the proper descriptions, but they were the ones chelons used when suggesting one of their own looked unwell.

"Then we need to go now," the dwarf said with finality.

Seeing the dwarf's compassion and love for his friend, Shorlis remembered what his father had said, "They need your help." The chelon balled his fists and squeezed as tightly as he could. The others argued about the best course of action, but the chelon heard none of it. *The staff.*

"I intend to go with you."

The chelon's words made the room go silent.

"But what about your people?" Nera asked. "What if the geldrins come back?"

"If the geldrins do come back, Tenzo will take care of the people here. No one knows this place better than us. The people know every crack and crevice—most of them we dug ourselves. They will defend it." Shorlis hesitated for a moment. "And besides, I have a strange feeling that if I help you, the geldrins won't come back."

The woman eyed him. "What do you mean?"

"My father was the wisest chelon I've ever known, and I'm not saying that out of mere sonly devotion. He often knew things that seemed impossible for anyone to know. With his dying breath, he told me that your friends needed my help—or you do. I don't know which. Either way, I know in my shell that I'm supposed to go with you."

"Well, we'll take all the help we can get," the dwarf said. "You know Kelvur better than any of us."

"That's all well and good," Orin said from the corner. "But what about the *Sellena*?"

"I was thinking the same thing," Nera agreed. "When we do find Merrick and Karnak, we're going to need a way home."

"Right," Orin said. "We need a port, and we can't leave these people to die."

Coal let out a sigh that sounded more like a disappointed growl.

Ralowyn placed a comforting hand on the dwarf's shoulder and asked, "Shorlis, are there a lot of griffins in Kelvur?"

The chelon's face scrunched at the seemingly random question. "Not here in the north. Most of them live far south of the Palisade."

"Perhaps Coal and I can scout ahead. If the caged cart was as Shorlis described, it would have been heavy and should be easy to track. We can go quickly without being noticed. We wouldn't draw attention like the guardians flying through the air on griffins," the elf suggested to Nera.

The woman didn't seem to like the idea, but before she could respond, Orin said, "I'll go with them. I can protect them."

Nera closed her eyes and let out her own frustrated sigh. Shorlis watched the woman. He did not envy her position. He wasn't sure how someone could lead a group of warriors across the sea into unknown circumstances.

"Fine," she agreed. "I'll talk to Captain Tin. Perhaps some of his crew can help your people build a proper dock. And Talon Squadron will teach them how to fortify the town."

"Very well," Shorlis nodded his appreciation. "And I will go with you. But first, I need to go to the Shoals. There's something there that we're going to need."

CHAPTER TWENTY-TWO

DARK TONGUE

As soon as they landed in the gar's paddock in Calrok, Smarlo slipped from his wyvern, Klovur, and rushed to check on Tanessa and Gernot. He bounded through the door and surprised them at the dinner table. Tanessa looked at him with hopeful eyes, but Smarlo had no news about Karnak. He quickly relayed what they'd decided at the Council of Whitestone, emphasizing the part about them sending the Griffin Guard's best across the sea in search of Karnak and Merrick. It wasn't much, but it was all he had to offer her in his haste.

He ran back outside, Tanessa in his wake, just as Garron was helping Ezel off the back of the pegasus Lanryn had given them. Ellaria held Silverwing close and brushed at the griffin's neck feathers. Somehow, Tanessa knew exactly who Ellaria was and ran to hug her. Smarlo led Garron to the stable where Benley the pegasus would be safe.

Their stay at the house of Karnak was short, however, as the group rushed toward Calrok's deep mines.

Smarlo led the others along a dirt road on the edge of the city that wound around and skirted the cliffs. The sun was setting, and much of the city by the sea seemed to be quiet as the inhabitants settled into their evening routines. The orc mage glanced back every once in a while to make sure he wasn't leaving the others in his dust—most importantly, Garron.

The mage's mind raced. It was strange to think how only a few months prior it would have been unheard of for a man to be in the orc city, yet a man may be the only one who could help them solve the mysteries they faced.

Part of Smarlo was jealous. He had always been underwhelmed with Calrok's access to magical resources. Their modest library was one of the smaller mage libraries in Drelek's already limited magic community. He wondered whether he would have been able to read the dark tongue if he'd had more tomes or ancient scrolls at his disposal. The notion was silly, of course, because Argus Azulekor had explained that dark tongue wasn't something a mage could learn.

Regardless, Smarlo found himself at the mercy of a man, and if the orc hadn't enjoyed so much time with Merrick recently, he wasn't sure whether he would have had the humility to accept the help. He'd always been one to find the answers himself. His world was changing. If he was honest with himself, he was glad. He had long wished for more magical knowledge than Master Tan-Kro had to offer.

Master Tan-Kro! He thought of the old orc in danger and picked up the pace.

He glanced back as they rounded a bend, noting that Ezel was keeping up, and nodded with appreciation at the little gnome's effort as he kept in stride. The entry cavern to the mines lay just ahead. Several orcs, part of Calrok's city watch, stood guard at the entrance.

Smarlo's heart felt as though it dropped into his stomach.

"Hold!" one of the guards called as he readied his pike.

"Put that away," the other one barked at him. "Are you blind? Master Smarlo, good to see you back, sir." The guard lifted a finger to his brow and gave a slight nod in the orcs' customary greeting of honor.

"What's happened here?" Smarlo panted.

The guards' eyes widened, and they tensed as the others ran up behind the mage.

"There was a ..." The orc guard started but hesitated as though he wasn't sure whether he should say anything with the outsiders present.

Smarlo waved him on. "Never mind them."

"Well, there was a disturbance in the mines. They've been closed for two days. Commander Belguv talked to Captain Jeslora, and she's been posting city watch guards here since."

Belguv. Smarlo nodded. He was thankful for the commander. Belguv had taken care of the Scar Squadron and many of Smarlo's own duties while the orc mage tried to figure out the mess in which they'd found themselves. Belguv was as sturdy an orc as any could ask for.

"What happened in the mine?"

"Don't know," the guard said. "They don't really tell us anything."

"No," the hasty guard agreed. "But the master goblin has been blubbering all night back there in his office."

"Oh, so your ears work just fine then?" the other guard scolded. "Shouldn't be eavesdropping on the Master Miner."

"I wasn't eavesdropping. I was just—"

"I must talk to Master Miner Forg," Smarlo cut in.

"I'm sorry, sir. But our orders are not to let anyone in."

"And who gave you those orders?" Smarlo asked, quickly.

"The captain of the watch, herself."

"And who gave the captain those orders?"

"Well, I suppose it was Commander Belguv."

"And who gives Commander Belguv orders?" Smarlo asked, impatiently.

"Well, that would be you, sir," the hasty orc said, happy he got to answer one of the questions.

They stood there for a moment until it dawned on the smarter of the two guards. "Oh, right. Please, sir," he said as he stood to the side and ushered the mage in. He looked warily at the others.

"They're coming with me," Smarlo said, and into the entrance cavern they stepped.

While it was getting dark outside, it was pitch black in the cavern. Garron, suddenly blind and helpless, slowed down and held his hands out in front of him.

"Oh, sorry." Smarlo's voice came from the darkness in front of the man.

The orc mage whispered something Garron didn't hear, and the man's eyes started to water. He blinked them several times, and as he did, it was as if a fog lifted. The dark cavern grew lighter in his vision—not bright like daylight, but light enough for him to see clearly enough. The closer objects were, the easier they were to see. The farther away, the darker they became. Garron wiggled his fingers in front of himself, hardly understanding what his brain told him.

"That should help your human eyes see in the dark. I—"

The orc mage stopped as he watched the gnome and the woman behind Garron. The man turned to watch as well.

A tattooed rune on Ezel's forehead blazed in blue faery fire. His eyes glowed with the same magic. The little gnome grabbed

Ellaria's hand, and suddenly, her eyes erupted with a green glow. Ezel stepped away and let his magic extinguish. Deep gnomes thrive in the deepest of caverns and see well in the dark. He nodded to the orc mage, as if to say they were ready to continue.

Garron turned back to Smarlo, who stood motionless with a curious look on his face. The man marveled again at how the magic let him see so well in the pitch.

"That was interesting," Smarlo said. "I'd love for you to explain that magic to me sometime."

Ezel's hand flourished a quick response.

"Soon," Ellaria and Garron both translated. They paused awkwardly. Garron cursed himself internally and let Ellaria finish the translation for Smarlo.

"He says when we get the chance," she finished, her eyes still glowing green.

"Right," the orc mage said and spun on the spot.

They hurried to a side section of the entrance cavern where several openings lined the wall. Smarlo dipped into one and immediately started questioning a goblin inside.

"Forg, I need to know what happened," the orc pressed.

"You mages," Forg wailed. "You think you can do whatever you like, and no one else can do a thing. I'm ruined! I'm the first Master Miner in centuries to have the mine closed for two whole days. Do you know how much coin we've already lost?"

"Forg," Smarlo barked at him. "This has nothing to do with coin. Lives are at stake."

"Always life or death with you mages." The goblin waved a dismissive hand. "What about livelihoods?"

"Forg!" Smarlo hollered as a fireball erupted in his hand. "Start talking. What happened here?"

The fireball clearly got the goblin's attention since the master miner shrank away from the mage.

"Master Tan-Kro came into the mine saying he needed to inspect some dark tongue. Saying something about the Gert section. That section has been nothing but trouble, I tell you."

"Get to it," Smarlo growled.

"Anyway," the goblin continued. "The master mage brought two of the city watch with him, and I couldn't say anything to dissuade him. I tried to tell him that the crew in the Gert section was finally starting to do well after the whole ranken mess."

"Ranken?" Garron asked.

The goblin eyed the man suspiciously.

"You looking for trade secrets? Trying to slander my operation? Trying to put me out of business?" The goblin leaned into an aggressive posture as he scowled at the tall man.

"I'll explain later," Smarlo told Garron. "What happened, Forg?"

Forg leered at Garron then said, "Anyway, the master mage asked if anyone would show him the way, and of course, Kag was eager to show him. I'm starting to think you mages planted Kag in my operation to spy on me. Or maybe so you could use him to gain access to my mines without me knowing what you're doing," he accused. "What did you find down there? Some kind of magic crystals? You know, anything in the mine is proprietary. I'll go to the gar and tell him how I've been mistreated."

Smarlo stepped closer to the goblin and loomed high over him as a second fireball blazed into his other hand. The orc mage looked menacing enough to Garron, and it appeared Master Miner Forg felt the same as he cowered behind a chair.

"Anyway," Forg said shakily. "They went down to the Gert section of the mine and haven't returned. Commander Belguv shut me down for 'further investigation.' I had to send all the other miners home—even the ones in the Lando section, and that's not even close to the Gert section."

The flames in Smarlo's hands dissipated, and he began to pace. Garron watched the mage and wondered what he was thinking. The goblin started to creep out from behind the chair, believing the immediate threat of his demise to be over.

"Why are you still here if everyone was evacuated?" Garron asked.

The goblin's face screwed up as if the man had asked him some terribly offensive question. "Where else would I be?" he snarled.

Garron looked sideways to Ezel. The gnome shrugged and signed, "*Goblins.*"

"We have to get down there," Smarlo said finally, stopping his pacing and facing the others.

"Where do we go?" Ellaria asked.

"I've only been down there once," the orc mage admitted.

"Do you remember the way?" Garron asked, realizing the orc wasn't confident.

"Maybe," Smarlo said. He quickly waved off the doubt. "But we're not going to risk getting lost. He's going to lead us."

The master miner's eyes went wide, and his whole body began to tremble.

A few hours later, the group took a quick break next to a cave water spring. Smarlo gazed down the cut corridor before them. He wasn't sure, but he had a vague memory of the spot. He supposed he and Kag had stopped for water at this same trickling spring.

The trek to the Gert section this time around was much less pleasant. Forg was a miserable companion. The short goblin complained about how the mages had been tricking him into doing their bidding. At one point, he accused them of bewitching Kag. It was the only explanation the goblin could think of because he was far too keen an employer to have hired a mage spy.

After several attempts at shutting him up with reasoned arguments to discount the goblin's paranoia, Smarlo had resorted to threats. Those, however, only kept the goblin quiet for short stints before he continued to ramble about how if the mage killed him, the whole mining operation would go down in flames. He was the master miner, of course, and what could a mine do without a master miner?

The only thing that quieted the goblin, eventually, was the very real threat that he would give away their location to the assassin that might be in the caves. That scared him into silence.

Smarlo had grown more on edge each time they passed a marker that jogged his memory of the place. The farther they went into the mines, the closer they were to the open cavern section. Kag had explained to him the last time he was down there that there were dozens—maybe hundreds—of passageways and tunnels that led straight to the Underrock. They didn't know at the time. It was a section they had only recently opened through a mining tunnel.

The orc mage remembered the scribblings on the wall, the strange symbols he couldn't read. He and Kag had come across them on their way out of the rough Gert section. *I hope Garron can read them,* Smarlo thought.

"How are we looking?" the man asked as he stepped away from the spring and closer to the orc.

"We're getting closer. My guess is we'll move into the Gert section within an hour or so."

"Right," Garron nodded, though they both stared down the corridor into the dark. "That's where the dark tongue is?"

"Yes." Smarlo paused and glanced at the man. "But I'm not exactly sure where it was."

"Well, that's what we brought the whiner for, right?" Garron rolled his eyes at the goblin still guzzling water from the spring.

"He wasn't there when Kag and I found the inscription. He can get us to the Gert section, but from there we'll have to find it." The orc's face shifted, and he added, "And hopefully, we find Master Tan-Kro and the others."

"I'm sure we'll find them," Garron said, giving the orc an encouraging pat.

Smarlo appreciated the notion but wasn't as optimistic. "Are you going to be able to read the dark tongue?"

Garron fidgeted. He didn't answer right away. His eyes looked far off for a moment. "I hope so."

Neither of them said anything for a minute. They stared down the corridor while the others waited their turn to drink from the spring. Eventually, Forg came up for air and let out a loud belch that echoed off the tunnel walls.

"Sorry," the goblin whispered.

"At least he's trying to be quiet now," Smarlo said to Garron and shook his head.

"I don't really understand what's happening to me," the man blurted.

Smarlo turned toward him. "What do you mean?"

"The dark tongue. I don't know why I was able to read it at the council."

"Argus said only people who have touched the dark magics of the world can read it."

"I know, but ..." The man chewed the inside of his cheek, trying to formulate his thoughts. "I was able to read an ancient inscription of the Nari in a book as well. It was a language that even the man who transcribed it didn't understand. How could I?"

"Language and magic are connected in rather interesting ways. I can't say exactly how deep their connection goes, but the word and magic enjoy great fellowship. It's why magics vary so fascinatingly from race to race when they don't use the common tongue. Even when we do magic without audible words, you'll notice that mages use hand gestures. I imagine it is much like the magic Ezel wields."

The man's eyes intently watched the orc as he spoke.

"Could that be why I can understand his sign language?"

"Perhaps," Smarlo said, itching his long, pointed ear. "But I have to admit, I don't know much about his magic. He's ... unique."

Ezel padded over to the pair, looking to each of them and signing.

"We'll get some," Garron assured him.

Smarlo stared at the man.

"Oh, sorry," Garron apologized. "He wants to make sure we get some water before we continue."

Smarlo nodded. "Let's do it then and be on our way."

When they entered the rough caverns of the Gert section, Garron's mouth dropped as he marveled at the wild angles of the walls and dramatic stalactites that dotted the ceilings. He'd never seen anything like it in his entire life, and he probably would not have if not for Smarlo's magic cantrip helping his vision. He looked all about, trying to take in the scene. He felt dizzy as he thought about the millions of tons of rock that sat as a roof overhead, but even that thought did little to detract from his awe.

He spun and saw that Ellaria was also dazzled by the grand view. Ezel smirked at both of the humans, finding their amazement humorous.

"Have you ever seen anything like this?" the woman asked quietly.

"Never," Garron admitted. "It's something else."

"Aye, that it is. Oops! Sorry," she said to Garron as she tumbled against him.

She held onto him, as she caught herself. Suddenly, the view of the cavern no longer held his attention.

"It's alright," he said.

"Right," Ellaria said sheepishly. "Wasn't looking where I was going."

Garron watched her as she straightened and looked to see where Smarlo was.

"Ellaria," the man said. "How are you holding up?"

"Bah," she grunted, waving him off.

"No. Really," Garron pressed. "You've cared for me so much. I can care how you're doing, too."

She nodded in surrender, and Garron thought it odd how her glowing green eyes bobbed in his dark vision.

"I'm alright. Really," she assured him. "Merrick will be fine. He was before, and I wasn't there to save him last time. Others were. Those same people are on their way to find him right now. In me time with the guard, I've come to learn there are none more capable than the Talon Squadron."

"Good," he said. "I'm glad you have some sort of peace on it."

They walked together behind the rest of the group as Smarlo looked for some marker that would remind him of the location of the inscription.

"How in Finlestia did you understand Ezel's sign language?" Ellaria suddenly asked.

Garron repressed a laugh and shook his head. "I have no idea. Smarlo seems to think it might have something to do with language and magic, but he says he doesn't really understand Ezel's magic."

Ellaria smirked. "Neither does Argus. Apparently, he was bombarding Ezel and Coal with questions for the couple of weeks leading up to the coronation—" She stopped. "Sorry."

"No need," Garron said. "Pernden is a much better king than I ever could have been."

"I don't think you give yourself enough credit. I've come to know you as a good man."

"A good man in the dungeons of Whitestone," he replied, his words dripping with sarcasm.

The woman gave him an unamused look.

He shook his head and let out a sigh. "How do you and Ezel do that magic?" he asked, changing the subject.

"I don't know," Ellaria admitted. "He does most of it. I didn't even know I could do magic until we traveled to the Palori Ruins. Let me tell you, it was a surprise. Ezel and I figured out that our magic is connected somehow. I don't understand it, and I'm not sure he does either. But it works."

"What does it feel like when—"

"Master Smarlo?" A hushed voice called from a side passage. "Master Smarlo, is that you?"

"Kag?" Smarlo started. "What in Finlestia happened?"

"We were attacked," Kag said as he crawled out from underneath an overhanging layered rock. "Someone in the darkness. It was like a ghost."

"The assassin's still here?" Forg wailed.

"No, Master Forg," the orc miner said. His eyes rimmed with tears. "Got Master Tan-Kro and his guards. Killed them so fast. We didn't stand a chance."

"It's alright, Kag," Smarlo said, stepping closer to the orc and placing a comforting hand on his shoulder. "Where did the assassin go?"

"Disappeared. Like a ghost," Kag said again. "When the others were killed, I ran and hid. A coward, I am."

"You're no coward, my friend," Smarlo reassured him. "I've seen what you're capable of. If you hadn't hid, you would have been killed as well."

"The ghost was looking for me, but no one knows these caverns like me. That's why Master Forg made me the Gert section crew chief," he said, nodding toward the goblin.

Forg didn't like the attention, it seemed, and pressed himself behind Smarlo's cloak.

"Then what happened?" the orc mage prompted the miner.

"Well, then it disappeared. It looked for me for a long time, but every time it came near, I held my breath."

Ezel's hands flourished quickly, and several of his runes on his arms blazed to life as he looked from side to side.

"Could the assassin still be here? Hiding somewhere?" Garron translated for the others.

Everyone tensed and looked about.

"Kag." Smarlo turned back to his friend. "I can't remember where we found that dark tongue etched into the cave wall. I need you to show us where it is. Can you do that?"

The emotional orc's chin and tusks quivered, but he stood straighter and pressed his lips together as he nodded.

It didn't take long for the miner to lead the group directly to where the inscription was hidden in the dark. When they arrived, Smarlo ran to inspect the body of an orc that lay motionless on the ground. The orc mage growled and sniffed at his tears, while he covered the face of his fallen master.

Garron watched uneasily. He didn't like this. Not at all. A strange sensation washed over him. It was the same pull he'd felt when the parchment lay bare on the table in Whitestone. His body tensed and twisted away from the inscription of its own volition.

"Garron, the inscription is below. We need to climb down over the ledge here—"

"No," Kag said quickly. "We built a ramp and a platform. I thought you would need it when you came back. I was leading Master Tan-Kro there ..." He trailed off.

"Very well," Smarlo said.

The group walked down the wooden ramp that Kag showed them. Forg wanted nothing to do with the entire endeavor and stayed at the top with the miner.

As the others moved toward the platform, revulsion welled within Garron. His legs fought against his mind, and his eyes blinked erratically as they tried to avoid looking at the dark tongue inscription. His body was caught in a battle of push and pull. He almost couldn't bear it anymore, when Ellaria grabbed his hand and helped him along.

He looked to her, her emerald eyes kind and familiar. She nodded encouragingly as she walked with him, step for step. As they drew nearer, Garron's eyes widened in fear. His body ached and prickled uncomfortably.

"I can't do this," he mumbled. "I can't. I just can't."

"You can," the woman said. "I'm here with you. We'll do it together."

"No, no, no, no ..." he murmured, starting to pull away.

Ezel clapped, and Garron met the little gnome's gaze. *"I know this is hard for you,"* Ezel signed. *"But you're the only one who can do this."*

"I can't, though. I'm too weak. I've failed so much."

"You read the dark tongue on the parchment in Whitestone. You were strong enough then, and you're strong enough now. It doesn't matter how you've failed in the past. The only thing that matters is what you choose to do right now."

Though Garron wasn't sure it was possible, it seemed like a storm swelled in the cavern. It could have been in his head, but reality bent around him. The noise that blew in his ears and the pull that drew at things deep within him, reeling him ever closer to the inscription, played tricks with his mind.

"I can never make up for what I've done," Garron cried over the maelstrom.

"Neither can I," Ezel signed. His eyes welled with tears, and his candid response silenced everything. The little gnome appeared as the singular focus in Garron's vision. *"Years ago, when a sea witch saved my life, I didn't know how to control this new magic. There was ... an accident. I know you didn't mean to betray your people. You didn't have control of yourself. You were tricked.*

"I didn't have control either. I blew up three of the finest sea ships I've ever seen. I killed people. People I knew. People I loved. My friends. I didn't mean to. But I did."

"How can we ever atone?" Garron whimpered, tears pouring from his face.

"I saved a ship while we were sailing through the Narrows. Many of the people on that ship were descendants or survivors

themselves from the ships I destroyed. I don't think saving that one ship can pay for what I've done. Honestly, I don't know that we can do anything to make up for it." Ezel signed the last part slowly, tears streaking his little grey face. *"But that won't keep me from trying."*

The little gnome reached out his hand. As Garron reached for it, the storm inside him roared again, as though it didn't want the man to grab the deep gnome's hand. As soon as their hands connected, the storm ceased. Garron blinked in confusion, and Ezel gave the man a motivating nod.

The man forced his body to turn as he looked up at the inscription. The etched letters danced to life as shadowy mirrored letters faded in and out, forming into words.

CHAPTER TWENTY-THREE

A QUIET CASTLE

The castle at Whitestone was strangely cold in the morning as Pernden walked down the corridor toward the kitchen. He knew Enly would bring food to him in the king's private dining hall, but he didn't want to sit in the empty room by himself. There had been so much commotion lately: preparing for the setup of Kane Harbor, meeting with the delegates, receiving Argus and the contingent from Loralith, and overseeing the Council of Whitestone. With it all, he'd been constantly surrounded by people.

It felt odd, the quiet—almost unnerving, as though the emptiness were a reflection of his life. The only noises he heard were those of the occasional bird outside the high windows of the castle. As he rounded another corner, he heard the banging of pans in the kitchen as they clanged together or a member of the kitchen staff tossed one to the side.

Pernden smiled.

The aroma seeping from the room informed him Enly was making biscuits with her special gravy. The smell attached itself to a memory in Pernden's mind. He and his brothers and cousins used to run about the castle with stick swords. Dona would shoo them out of the hallway, so the kitchen staff could bring breakfast to the king's private dining hall where they'd all eat. Simpler times.

At least for him. He was sure King Farrin and his father had plenty of complicated matters to discuss during those breakfast meetings, but he never paid attention. Now that he was king, he wished he had.

A pang of heartache hit him as Pernden stood outside the kitchen. So much life and love had filled the king's dining hall before. Now it sat empty, and he didn't want to be there.

Before he headed to Kane Harbor, Edford might have annoyed the king, but at least he kept the hall from such haunting silence.

Pernden wondered if the place would ever be filled with such life again. He thought of Nera standing beside him, their children running and playing with those of his cousin and his brother. They had lost so much over the years, but maybe, if they survived the new threat, they could bring life back to the quiet castle.

Dona rounded out of the kitchen and jumped in surprise, nearly dropping the plate she carried. "My King! You scared me."

"Sorry, Dona," Pernden said sheepishly.

"What's the matter?"

How does she always know? he wondered.

"Nothing," he said.

Dona gave him an appraising look, not believing him. "I was just bringing you some breakfast. With your cousin gone, it seemed best to get back to my old tasks."

"Oh," Pernden said, his eyes and the emptiness in his stomach growing at the sight of biscuits covered in mouthwatering hot gravy. "I was hoping to take my breakfast with me. I'm headed to the stables to see Rocktail."

"I see," the short woman said. "You miss Nera. And Garron. And maybe even Edford?" She smiled wryly.

How in Finlestia? he thought.

"It is rather quiet around here with everyone off gallivanting across Finlestia, isn't it?" she continued. "It's a mite lonely, actually."

The woman seemed to shrink a little. *She must miss Garron, too. Must have made her feel like the old days when she took care of us.*

"It's a little too quiet, I think," Pernden agreed.

"Well," she said, her body ruffling as she stood taller. "Why don't you take this with you then, and I'll have someone collect it from the stable later, so you don't have to worry about bringing it back."

She gave him a wink and pushed the plate into his hands.

"Thanks, Dona."

"Shoo. Shoo, now. And you'd better clean that plate. There are already enough bugs in that stable. George will have a fit if you leave food in there."

"Yes, Dona," Pernden said, as he hurried off with a smile.

The wind whipped Pernden's long blond hair as he and Rocktail raced through the sky. Flying with his griffin had been limited recently, and for the first time in a long while, he felt free. Free of the burden of the kingship and the duties that weighed him down. It was funny to think that, just that morning, he had felt so alone.

From Pernden's vantage point, Whitestone looked stunning. The great city was built from the same white granite that jutted out of the rolling green hills and vibrant forest like stone giants.

When he was younger, Pernden wondered if they had once been giants turned to stone by a wizard.

Of course, he didn't think that anymore but, instead, saw them as great gifts from the Maker. He hadn't given much thought to the Maker for many years, especially with all the heartache he'd endured growing up. After everything that had happened recently and everything he and his brother and his cousin and Nera had been through, he couldn't help but wonder if the Maker had some grander plans they could not yet see.

He patted Rocktail on the neck, and the griffin clicked happily at him. Rocktail was obviously thrilled with the exercise as well. *Perhaps we'll go to the Corral and run some drills*, the king thought.

Rocktail adjusted his wings into a steep angle, bringing them about when Pernden turned him. As the two glided along, Pernden gazed far below at the Grand Corral. Guardians ran about, carrying on as usual. Some sparred. Some ran diving drills with their griffins. Some practiced acrobatic aerial maneuvers. There was a simplicity to the place that he missed.

Pernden had loved the Griffin Guard from his first day. He'd trained hard and took to it like a griffin to the sky. He liked the regimen of it all. It didn't feel constricting to him. The Guard let him fly around on griffin-back. He didn't know anything that made him feel freer and more alive.

Beyond that, the unique camaraderie among the Guard resulted in a bond among them that couldn't be broken or shaken—for most of them, at least.

The king shook his head at the thought of Jolan. He and the commander had never really gotten along. The mountain of a guardian was abrasive and hard to get along with, but Pernden never expected him to betray the Guard like he did.

Part of him wished he were in Kelvur with the others. If he were honest, most parts of him felt that way. There was a part that wanted to find Jolan and bring justice upon the man's head.

The wind of the high altitude at which they flew ruffled Rocktail's feathers as he adjusted them into a slow descent. Suddenly, the griffin turned his head, looking at something behind them. Pernden looked over his shoulder, allowing Rocktail to maneuver them into a position to see whatever tailed them. Commander Mattness waved a hand at him, signaling she needed to convene with him.

As they flew near to each other, she shouted, "My King I've been looking for you. The dwarf mage seeks your presence!"

What in Finlestia? Pernden thought. "I'll meet him at once. Where is he?"

"In the dungeons, my King."

Pernden's face shifted to seriousness, and he pressed forward on Rocktail, urging them into a swift dive.

CHAPTER TWENTY-FOUR

REMEMBER

Merrick was surprised at how quickly the Javelin leader believed what they told her. Vorenna nodded thoughtfully as they spoke and asked short, direct questions, but never questioned the authenticity of their words. Once they recounted everything they could remember, they stood in silence for a long time while Vorenna mulled over the information.

"Go back to the part where you injured the sorcerer," she said.

"Well," Merrick hemmed. "We were in the king's chamber in Whitestone."

"The city where the griffins are?"

"Right. The Griffin Guard."

"Continue."

"Pernden, Ralowyn, and I flew in through the window. Goblins poured into the room through the chamber doors. I got two arrows off: one when I first entered the room, before the goblins came in, and one in the midst of the chaos. Only my first arrow struck the sorcerer orc. A traitor dove in front of the other."

"Where did the arrow hit the sorcerer?" Vorenna asked carefully.

"It struck him in the side," Merrick replied. As the scene reformed in his memory, he changed his answer. "Well, actually, it was headed straight for him, but he raised his stone arm and spun to avoid it. It scraped off his arm and struck him in the side."

"Was his arm bleeding?"

"What?"

"Where the arrow scraped his arm, was it bleeding?" she asked again.

"Well, no ... at least, I don't think so. There was so much chaos, I didn't notice if his arm was bleeding or not. Maybe it was," Merrick admitted.

Vorenna's eyes narrowed. The woman seemed disappointed as she pressed her fingers until they popped, rippling the muscles in her forearms. She strode toward the two prisoners tied to the center pole of the tent. She pulled out her dagger and leaned closer to the man.

"We told you everything," Karnak growled at the barbarian woman.

"I know. And I believe you," she said plainly.

Vorenna cut the bonds holding Merrick's hands to the pole. Then she turned and cut Karnak's.

Merrick rubbed his wrists as he pulled the bonds away. "But why?"

"Because such an outlandish tale told as truth could only be told by two people: one who is mad and likely poses no threat to my people or one who is, in fact, telling the truth." She gave him a sidelong smirk. "It seems to me we share a common enemy. Though I admit I'm jealous; I have yet to make the sorcerer bleed, myself."

She reached out a large hand, and Merrick gripped her forearm. She stared at him strangely, but then gripped his forearm as well, her fingers wrapping all the way around. "Is this how you shake hands in Tarrine?"

Merrick suppressed a laugh. "Well, if you had any doubts that we weren't telling the truth about where we're from, I guess I just proved it."

"Come with me," she said.

The two followed her out of the tent. The sun was lowering, and the people of the camp milled about. Tents and stalls were scattered in no apparent order or configuration that Merrick could tell. The only distinguishable feature of the place was the ruins of an old castle. The stonework looked as though it had originally been well crafted with artful designs on the outside. But the stones were charred and, in some places, appeared to be melted.

Merrick wondered about dragons. He hadn't even thought of the dragon that the sorcerer had brought into Tarrine from Kelvur. *Do they have more dragons here?*

People glanced at them, and some gawked at the big green orc as they made their way to the ruins. Merrick thought it strange. So many of the people were from different races. He saw dwarves, elves, halflings, gnomes, muscled barbarians, a couple of centaurs, and even a giant.

"Vorenna, what happened to the orcs? Why does everyone look at us like we're some sort of oddity?" Merrick asked.

"There will be time for all of that over supper," she said as they fell into the stream of people flowing into the ruins.

The old castle had no roof, and the walls opened into a large courtyard. Tall grass was trampled underfoot as people filled the space. Several of the towers around the battlement remained intact, but only a portion of the keep still stood. Merrick wondered what the place might have looked like when it was first built.

Vorenna led them to an area toward the front of the gathered crowd. There she met Feliketh, conversing with an old dwarf. The elf grimaced at the sight of Merrick and Karnak. Vorenna whispered something to the bald elf, and he reacted with a huge sigh. Merrick couldn't hear what she said to him, but Feliketh ushered them to the side out of the way.

Merrick watched as a group of children set up small pyres of wood.

"What is this?" the huntsman quietly asked the orc.

"I'm not sure," Karnak admitted.

"It's the pyre lighting," Feliketh said with a sigh. "One for each of our fallen comrades. Sixteen in all this time, including the driver of your cart."

"Do you have more spies with the sorcerer's people?" Karnak asked.

The elf smirked and rolled his eyes. "You really aren't from Kelvur. The sorcerer doesn't really have 'people.' His armies are filled with geldrins and ghouls."

"That didn't answer my question," Karnak said.

Feliketh let out another annoyed sigh. "He was the first of our spies. We found and executed a spy from Ventohl two weeks ago, and Vorenna thought it would be wise to have our own. Of course, your driver was excited to see a couple of prisoners from the sea for transport and sent a courier running."

"So, two spies then," the orc noted.

Feliketh eyed the orc with an impressed look. "There may be more. There may not."

Karnak shot Merrick a satisfied look. The huntsman smirked at the orc's amusement in ruffling the elf.

"Do you think they have another spy in your camp?" Merrick asked.

"There may be more. There may not," Feliketh replied with a smirk of his own.

Children lined up next to Vorenna at the front of the gathering. Two of them rubbed their noses as they sniffled. Several people at the front of the crowd suppressed their own sobs. A soldier walked up to Javelin's commander and handed her a torch. A woman leaned down and handed each of the eight children a small bundle of sticks as she made her way down the line.

Vorenna stepped forward, and what little whispering was left among the crowd ceased. Merrick watched the scene settle under the colorful evening sky. The barbarian woman stood tall above most of the crowd.

She raised the torch high and said, "The past lays the path for the future, and the future remembers the past."

"Remember," the people said together, as though they were saying it over the children at the front. Several of the voices cracked and choked, but none fell into full sobs.

The huntsman found it hard to hold back his own tears as Vorenna lit each bundle of sticks held by the children. The little ones made their way around the small pyres, lighting each one before adding their flaming bundle to an all-new pile.

"That is the pyre of the path," Feliketh whispered to them. "A reminder that there have been so many others before, not to be forgotten."

For a long time, everyone gathered stood in silence as the small pyres burned. The sky shifted into the deep blue before the night, and Vorenna stepped forward to speak again.

"Take memory and take heart. For the ones that sleep tonight have found rest."

"Remember," the people said again.

"Remember," Vorenna repeated. "Now eat with your families. Eat with your friends. If you've lost both, come see me, and I will find you new ones."

With that, the gathering began to disperse. No one spoke above a whisper as they left. Many wrapped arms around others, embracing them. Vorenna stood at the front, but no one came to see her. One of the children at the front melted into a heap on the ground, sobbing. An elderly woman from the crowd walked over to the boy and bent down to hug him. A younger woman, holding a baby, joined her. They wrapped the little boy in their arms and hugged him together.

"You're alright, now," the old woman cooed to him. "We'll be your family now."

Vorenna nodded to them as they padded by. When everyone had left, she strode over to Merrick and Karnak. Tears streaked her face, and Merrick noticed the ice blue of her glossy eyes. She said nothing but nodded.

"How many come to see you after these?" Karnak asked, hardly holding himself together.

"None," she croaked.

"Never?" Merrick asked.

"Never."

The huntsman processed the implication of her answer. *Who are these people? How long have they been out here? What have they been through to forge them all like family?*

He had so many questions, but he couldn't bring himself to break the quiet of the place again.

As they sat around a fire, eating vegetable soup and bread, Karnak couldn't help but glance at the other fires of the camp. On one hand, he thought it a sad way to live—all these people in tents scattered around the ruins of a castle. On the other hand, he was deeply moved by the somber memorial he had witnessed earlier, and more so, the way the people embraced each other and left no one behind. No one was left alone; everyone had a place.

"How long have you been here?" the orc asked Vorenna.

The barbarian woman took a big swig of her soup and ripped a bite of bread from the loaf she held in the other hand. She chewed quickly and began to answer, even though she hadn't finished the generous bite. "We've been here for a couple of weeks. There are several castle ruins hidden in fields and meadows that dot the overgrown Duskwood."

Nelan, a balding dwarf and one of Vorenna's commanders, smiled, set his bowl to the side, and cut into the conversation. The white wisps of hair on his head matched the equally white beard that hung to his belt. "We pack camp and move to a different ruin whenever we fear our location may be compromised."

"I see," Karnak said solemnly. "So, you have no home."

"Not many do, this far north of the Palisade." The dwarf shrugged.

"What's the Palisade?" Merrick asked.

Karnak leaned in, holding his bowl to the side. He was curious about that as well.

"It's a great wall," the dwarf said as he raised his hands above his head and spread them wide. "It spans the entire land of Kelvur, from the Gant Sea to the Lerian Sea."

"I don't understand," the orc admitted. "We don't know much of Kelvur in Tarrine."

Nelan wiggled his nose, his beard waggling along. "The Palisade is a mighty work of architecture."

"It's a cage," Vorenna cut in as she dropped her empty bowl.

"Posh," the dwarf scolded.

"A cage for what?" Merrick asked.

"For us," she said, lifting her hands and turning side to side as if to implicate the whole camp. "The castaways."

"Bah," Nelan scoffed at her again. "It wasn't built for us."

"It might not have been built for us originally, but in the centuries since ...?"

"Well," Nelan ruffled, but he didn't disagree with her.

"The 'civilized' people of the Zors south of the Palisade have been banishing people to the north for as long as anyone can remember," the barbarian woman said, taking a long draw from her wine skin.

"Banishing people?" Karnak asked in surprise.

"That's where all these people came from," Vorenna said.

"Come now," the dwarf stopped her. "Most of these people were born north of the Palisade. We're not the only group north of the Palisade. There are others. There used to be many, especially in the Eastern Knolls. But the sorcerer's reach has grown far, and there seem to be fewer and fewer people since his arrival."

Vorenna spat at the mention of Jaernok Tur.

"Do the other groups fight as well?" Karnak asked.

"Some did," the dwarf replied with a solemn shake of his head. "But we're the only ones left that we know of, aside from the cowards of Ventohl."

Vorenna spat again. "Cowards," she echoed.

"The Sons of Silence were never the best of neighbors. At least before the sorcerer came, they worked with people. When Jaernok Tur arrived from the Crags, everything changed. The Sons of Silence closed off Ventohl. They no longer traded with the wild folk. There was a time when many a young wild folk would dream of becoming an assassin and joining their ranks to travel south to the Zors."

"What are the Zors?" Merrick asked.

"They're the cities and towns where people south of the Palisade live. Well, the islanders anyway."

"Do they even know what's happening north of the wall?"

"I doubt it," Vorenna growled.

Karnak observed the commander of Javelin. She was a fierce woman, brooding in her own way. He thought she might be a boiling pot, the bubbles only just staying below the rim.

"This is a lot," Merrick admitted.

"You have traveled a long way—and not comfortably," Nelan sympathized.

"It's everything," Karnak said, shaking his head. "First Jaernok Tur's forces spread from the Crags, taking out the orcs and giants. Why didn't he continue south?"

"The Palisade is quite the wall—" Nelan started to say, but Vorenna hushed him with an outstretched arm.

"Continue," she said to Karnak, leaning forward and staring intently at him.

"I just mean, why did he not continue to conquer Kelvur? Why did he come to Tarrine instead?"

"Now that is the question, isn't it?" Vorenna whispered.

"Perhaps he thought Tarrine an easier target. If he conquered it, then he could sail legions of captured people south of the wall to attack the Zors," Nelan reasoned.

"All the way across the sea?" Karnak questioned the logic. "Doesn't make sense. I've only ever seen one ship that has crossed the Gant Sea, and that was the one on which we were brought here. Tarrine doesn't have such vessels."

Karnak replayed events in his mind, trying to recall anything he could that might give him a clue.

"Jaernok Tur originally coming to Tarrine had nothing to do with me," Merrick said. "I was a nobody. A huntsman."

"No one is nobody," Vorenna said to the man.

"No, but Merrick is right. Jaernok Tur didn't have any idea Merrick existed until he shot the sorcerer with an arrow," Karnak said. "It must be something else."

Vorenna stared hard at Karnak, waiting for him to work something out. The orc gar searched his memory. *What could it possibly be?* he wondered.

"Maybe he was looking for something he needs."

A smile spread across Vorenna's face. "Exactly."

"What could he be looking for?" Merrick asked. "What could he possibly need in Tarrine? Could it have been your axe?"

"I don't know," Karnak mused. "If that was his original purpose, he could have had me killed the first time we met in Ruk. It must have been something else."

"Well, if he was looking for something, and you stopped him ..." Nelan trailed off.

"It means he doesn't have it." Vorenna laughed. "It means the 'all-powerful' sorcerer isn't all powerful. He still needs things, and he's not invincible."

Karnak wasn't sure he liked the vicious grin on the barbarian woman's face, but he couldn't help but return it with one of his own. Somehow, they'd been thrust into the middle of this war. Karnak realized they may yet have the opportunity to end the sorcerer's tyranny once and for all. And though he'd rather be with Tanessa and Gernot, he was glad they were in Tarrine, far away from the wicked sorcerer. The orc planned to keep it that way.

Sorry Tanessa, he thought. *Looks like I won't be coming home just yet.*

CHAPTER TWENTY-FIVE

STRANGER IN THE SHOALS

Approaching the Shoals for the first time since his capture was a surreal experience for Shorlis. It was even stranger when he considered his odd set of companions in the rowboat.

Aside from the two sailors who rowed the boat, there was the captain of the Talon Squadron, Nera, who pondered everything. One of her guardians, Tam, scribbled drawings of maps and people on parchment. Shorlis felt a kinship with the young man. Finally, an elf mage named Lanryn fiddled with a shell, whispering to it like a madman.

If someone would have told the chelon that the first time he'd be heading home in over a year would be under such conditions, he would have scoffed. As they rowed between sandy islands toward his home, he had a sneaking suspicion his future might hold more similar circumstances.

Shorlis's sea green eyes glossed the moment he caught sight of his island. Even with half the village lying in charred heaps, he knew his home. He felt it in his shell. An unfamiliar sensation pulsed inside of him like a beacon.

"There," Shorlis pointed. "That's it over there."

The sailors oared the ship's boat toward the island, bringing them to rest on the soft sand. The chelon's feet hit the sand, and his knees followed. The mere act of setting foot on his island broke Shorlis. His shell bobbed as he doubled over in tears.

Father, he thought. *You should be here with me. Why aren't you here?*

To his great surprise, the woman knelt next to him and wrapped an arm around him. She hugged him close and rubbed his arms, telling him it was all going to be alright. He stayed in her embrace for a long time, not having the strength to continue.

Finally, Nera asked him, "Are you ready to find what we came for?"

Shorlis nodded and wiped the tears that dripped off the bottom of his beak. "We're going to need it," he said. "I don't know why, and I don't know how it's going to help us. But my father told me it was important for helping your friends."

Nera helped the chelon to his feet, and he thanked her for her kindness. He wasn't embarrassed. He knew sorrow would hit him sooner or later, and he was grateful that someone he hardly knew from a land across the sea would have such great compassion for him, like the woman did when his grief overcame him.

He stepped through the sand leading them toward the village. Seeing the charred remains of many of the huts he'd grown up running around was painful. The geldrins had made hasty work, and it seemed they'd rushed out of the place after Shorlis had struck Commander Chol. A satisfied grin crept across his face at the memory, but it was short-lived as he caught sight of Tellen's skeletal remains. Nera commanded the sailors to bury the decomposed chelon with every respect.

Shorlis turned away, taking in all the destruction. The island must have received a great rainstorm from the sea shortly after the chelons were dragged away because several of the huts were only half-burned and remained standing at odd decrepit angles.

When Shorlis saw his own home still standing—or at least most of it—the sight stopped him in his tracks. Emotional thoughts flooded through him. *Maybe we could come back. Maybe we could rebuild.* The notion faded almost instantly, replaced by, *The geldrins would come back stronger and finish the task. They would only steal us back. The only way to fight them is to work with the other miners.*

"Shorlis," Nera said softly. "Are you alright?"

"Yes," he replied. "I'm sorry. This is just ... harder than I expected."

"I can't imagine."

Shorlis drew a deep breath, puffing himself up, and strode forward, straight into his hut. Though the roof and half the structure had been burned, it was familiar. It was home. He turned away from the disheveled and weather-damaged section. A whole year's worth of sea storms had left that half a complete disaster, filled with palm leaves and debris. Parchments and scrolls, many half-charred, were strewn about. A crab skittered away as the chelon pushed through the door to his father's room.

The bamboo floor creaked and groaned under his weight. The rods had taken quite the beating, and the new strain of his weight wasn't helping.

"Help me move this?" he asked Tam.

The two pushed the bed pallet over and leaned it against the wall. The hut's wood moaned in protest. For a moment Shorlis and Tam held their hands out above the pallet, wondering if it was going to take the wall down. When that didn't appear to be imminent, they moved to the center of the room, and Shorlis felt the pulsing sensation inside his shell again.

He knelt and felt the wooden rods of the floor, finding a previously undetected seam. *How did I never know of this before?*

His scolding was unfounded, of course. He knew there was no possible way he would have found it by accident. His father had hidden it with care when the grand hut was built.

As Shorlis pried the floor open, the sensation within him swelled. An outstretched compartment was hidden beneath the floor, and inside lay a long artifact wrapped in linen cloth.

"Perhaps I should retrieve it?" Lanryn asked with mild concern.

"No," Shorlis shook his head. "It'll be alright."

The chelon reached into the compartment and gingerly lifted the staff out of the hole. The linen fell away from the staff, and the room glowed in its red light. Shorlis held the staff in front of him, inspecting it with wide eyes. The staff was made of some hardened wood that he could not identify. The grains whirled and spiraled in brilliant irregular patterns all the way to the swirling mount at the top where a red stone was encased.

Ribbons of red magic danced about, filling the room and wheeling around them. The chelon could feel the power emanating from the staff. *What in Finlestia?* he wondered. When he turned to Lanryn to hear the mage's estimation of the artifact, the elf's face contorted with shock, and he took an involuntary step backward.

"What is it?" Shorlis asked, worry edging into his mind.

"Your eyes," Tam said. "They're red like the magic."

"Like this," Nera said. She showed Shorlis her brown eyes, then gripped *Santoralier* tightly. The spear burst to life, and her eyes blazed golden.

Suddenly, the magic yellow arcs twisted into beautiful streaks, joining the red ribbons of light. Lanryn watched intently.

"Your father did not teach you to wield such a thing, did he?" the elf asked.

"No," Shorlis said.

"This is old magic," Lanryn said, shaking his head, mystified. "Just like the Staff of Anvelorian that Ralowyn wields. I cannot help but think they are all connected somehow."

Shorlis stood and marveled at the staff for a long time. He didn't know how it was going to help them or how he would use it. Somehow, deep inside, he knew this final gift from his father would change his fate forever.

Thank you, Father.

Tam helped Shorlis gather the scrolls and tomes that had survived the fires and weather. Even if parts of them were destroyed, Shorlis hoped that one day he'd be able to remember their tales and recreate or fix them. He probably wouldn't get the chance to do so until the wicked sorcerer Jaernok Tur was defeated. But somehow, his new staff filled him with courage, and he had hope that they could accomplish the feat.

The chelon brought out another bundle of parchments and handed them to Lanryn. "I don't think there are many more to be saved," Shorlis said.

"At least we can save some," the elf nodded with admiration. "Your father had a treasure trove of writings here."

"And he shared them with everyone." The chelon gave a somber smile. "He told stories from all these writings to everyone he met. He even told some that aren't written here. I hope to one day put them down on parchment."

"That is a worthy goal," a voice said, as a stranger stepped through the sand.

Lanryn dropped the bundle and raised his wand as Shorlis gripped the magical staff tightly, not sure what he intended to do with it.

The two watched the stranger with wary eyes. He was tall and looked like an elderly man with a long white beard. He wore a burgundy cloak with golden accents that glinted in the sunlight as the fabric blew in the sea breeze. He held a staff of his own, and as they inspected him, he leaned on it, sporting a pressed smile.

"I see you have *Menthrora,*" he said, with an approving nod.

Shorlis looked awkwardly at the staff in his hand.

"Though admittedly," the stranger continued. "I had hoped to see your father." The stranger paused for a moment, seeming to collect himself. "He was a dear friend."

Lanryn glanced at Shorlis, but the chelon did not have an answer for his unspoken question. He had no idea who the stranger was. *Where did he even come from?*

Nera strode slowly to their sides, having noticed the unknown individual's approach. Shorlis's mind spun.

"I suppose you have no idea who I am," the stranger said, his words rimmed with a hint of surprise. "Your father was such a storyteller. He never mentioned me?"

The stranger released his staff, and the thing stood upright in the sand. He took both hands, slowly raising them so the companions could see what he was doing, and lifted back the burgundy hood of his cloak, revealing more white hair.

"My name," he said, "is Enkeli."

"The wizard," Lanryn said quietly, in utter shock.

The elf mage lowered his wand absently to his side, and his action made Shorlis and Nera uncertain and hesitant.

"Why are you here?" Nera asked, not entirely lowering her spear.

"I came to see an old friend," Enkeli said. "But it seems as though I am too late. Anthanar is gone, isn't he?"

At the sound of his father's name, Shorlis completely let his guard down. "How did you know my father?" the chelon asked, tears welling in his eyes.

"Your father was an amazing chelon," the wizard said. "Let's make a fire and some dinner. It seems I have much to tell you."

The group mostly ate in silence, none of them knowing what to say or ask. The fish Enkeli cooked was quite tasty. Shorlis wasn't sure he'd ever had anything that tasted so good. Then again, he had been a slave in a mining camp for over a year, so he couldn't be sure it wasn't a trick of his mind.

Finally, when the chelon could take the quiet no longer, he poked at the fire with a stick, stoking the burning embers, and asked, "How did you know my father?"

Enkeli smiled, his warm face wrinkling kindly. "Your father and I traveled together a long time ago. I knew him long before he met your mother."

Shorlis's eyes lit up at the mention of his mother. "I don't understand," he said, bewildered.

"Where do you think your father got all those stories?" the wizard asked with a laugh. "I imagine he told you many?"

"Me and everyone else." Shorlis laughed.

Enkeli smirked and nodded thoughtfully. "He always had a flair for it."

"Master Enkeli," Lanryn cut in, tentatively.

"Speak, young Lanryn," he said to the 250-year-old elf.

"You said '*Menthrora*' earlier. Though I've studied dozens of old languages, I could not think what it means," the elf said, sounding embarrassed.

"Ah, the staff," the wizard said. "*Menthrora*, or Magic of the Heart. It's from an ancient language, from which the elven tongue borrowed the root *rora*."

Lanryn nodded in excitement at the revelation.

"*Menthrora*," Shorlis whispered to himself, searing the name into his mind.

"Your father did not tell you this," Enkeli said, more of a statement than a question.

"No," the chelon replied. "At least not until the attack. But we couldn't get to the staff until now."

Enkeli eyed him and then the staff. The wizard seemed to be pondering something about the chelon that Shorlis himself didn't know. If Enkeli knew both of the chelon's parents, what else might he know?

"Where did my father get the sta—" Shorlis corrected himself. "*Menthrora?*"

"While we were in Candara, far south of Kelvur."

"Candara?" Lanryn asked, shaking his head. "I've never heard of the place."

Enkeli smiled at the group. "Finlestia is a much wider world than you know."

Shorlis glanced around at the others. None of them seemed to know where the wizard spoke of. The fact that the Tarrinians also didn't know about lands beyond Kelvur and Tarrine made the chelon feel better about his ignorance.

"Did your father ever tell you the story of the monolith dragons?" the wizard asked Shorlis.

"He told me many stories about dragons, but I recall none about monolith dragons, as you say," the chelon admitted.

"Ah. Well, then," Enkeli said, with a twinkle in his eye. "Seems like the perfect story for this evening."

The wizard rolled his sleeves and wiggled his fingers. The group watched as he moved his hands in deliberate patterns over the firepit. The embers roared to new life, and the wizard sat back in satisfaction.

"Wonderful," he said. "Now to it. Long ago, at the creation of the world, the Maker gathered the creatures of Finlestia around the First Tree. The Tree stood as a monument to the life the Maker spread far and wide throughout the world."

As Enkeli spoke, shapes and images appeared in the roaring fire. Shorlis watched, transfixed, hardly believing his eyes.

"While the creatures were gathered, the Maker brought into being twelve monolith dragons, one for each of the great lands of Finlestia."

Tam leaned closer to the fire, inspecting the morphing flames as they revealed map-like images.

"The monolith dragons were to rule over the rest of the creatures and protect them, helping creation abound. But the dragons saw the special care with which they were made and dared to pride themselves above the rest of creation.

"They tapped into the magic of creation and, from the dirt, drew up lesser dragons in their own likeness. They spread their spawn throughout the lands, and that is why every land of Finlestia has their own knowledge of dragons," the wizard pointed out.

"The monolith dragons, however, could not create dragons of their same size and might. Because of this, the monolith dragons held a council. Many of them wanted the power to create as great as the Maker. Some of them disagreed, reminding the others that it was not their purpose to replace the world's need for the Maker but rather to foster the continued growth of the world."

As the wizard continued, the fire burst into several flitting scenes.

"Battles broke out amongst the monolith dragons. They raged against one another, leaving devastation in their wake. Lines were drawn, and eight of the dragons banded together to create a new magic, one they could wield to recreate the world in their own vision. Before their work could be completed, the others stormed the meeting."

An image of the First Tree blazed high in the fire.

"The others had met back at the First Tree and decided to take a branch from the tree. They deemed it their only option. Perhaps they could harness the power of the magic in the First Tree and defeat their siblings' wicked plan before they started.

"When they used the branch and struck the mountain on which the eight were working their combined magic, the earth rumbled and cracked. The mountain exploded, scattering pieces to all the lands of Finlestia. The monolith dragons themselves were nearly destroyed. In fact, several of them were. The remaining monolith dragons flew back to their own lands, and they never came together again."

The images in the fire dissipated, and the flames slowly simmered down to smoldering coals.

"What happened to the monolith dragons after that?" Lanryn asked.

"No one knows for sure what happened to all of them. Some of the survivors may have eventually succumbed to their injuries, but most have been lying dormant for centuries," Enkeli said, producing a long pipe from under his cloak.

"They're still out there?" The elf mage started.

"Some of them," the wizard said with a nonchalant shrug. "But they have been quiet for a very long time—or at least most of them have." He grumbled the last part.

"It's sad," Shorlis said quietly.

"Sure," Lanryn shrugged. "But it sounds like it was for the better. Can you imagine if those monolith dragons were still trampling the world right now?"

"No," the chelon said softly. "I mean, it's sad that they were given the job of caring for the world—probably including each other—and instead, they destroyed themselves."

"Reminds me of what happened in Tarrine," Tam said.

Nera nodded thoughtfully. "We were fighting a battle no one would win—the Griffin Guard fighting the wyvern riders of Drelek. We lost so many and fought with such anger and vengeance. If another threat hadn't united us, we likely would have destroyed ourselves."

Enkeli smiled. "It seems to me the fight isn't over."

Nera shrugged sideways, acknowledging the truth of his words.

"You play a greater part in this than you yet know," he said to the woman.

A couple of tears slid down her cheeks, and Shorlis was surprised to see them. He wasn't sure why. The woman had great compassion. At the same time, he found her to be a strong, determined warrior. Her sudden tears wrenched him.

The chelon turned toward the wizard, eyeing him curiously. Enkeli's face was that of an approving father, and for some reason, his gaze gave Shorlis an indescribable peace.

"And your story," the wizard said to the chelon. "Has only just begun."

CHAPTER TWENTY-SIX

SPIES AND THEIR GAMES

Hazkul Bern cracked his neck and rolled his shoulders as he looked out the high tower window in Ventohl castle. He watched as riders approached, their horses ragged and sluggish. He smirked to himself.

"Chadwa," he said to the witch who'd just entered the room. "Isn't it funny how things can change so quickly?"

The witch said nothing. She strode to his side and looked out the window. Apparently satisfied that he'd seen the approaching riders, she didn't feel the need to report it. It bothered Hazkul sometimes that the witch was so quiet. But then again, their group of assassins was called the Sons of Silence.

Maybe she takes that a little too literally, he thought with an amused grin.

"Geldrins riding from the west," he said aloud. "Can only be coming from the Glinso Mining Camp."

He narrowed his elven eyes and made out Commander Chol, himself.

"Oh," he said with another smirk. "This should be good. Seems like our dear friend Commander Chol is visiting us."

Chadwa pursed her lips. The witch didn't like Chol. In fairness, Hazkul wasn't terribly fond of geldrins himself. But as far as geldrins went, the commander had always been hospitable to them when they'd had to interact.

"Come, Chadwa," Hazkul said, turning a roguish smile to the witch. "He's not that bad. At least he's better than that dog Jolan. Wouldn't you agree?"

Hazkul shuddered at the thought of the man.

"The man has no personality," the elf said. "Well, at least no personality besides grumpy, angry man."

Chadwa's eyebrow raised, and she stared at the elf.

"Oh, alright. I know you're right. I am way more handsome and could kill him in seconds," Hazkul waved her off, bashfully. "You do know how to butter me up. Come on. Let's see what tidings our dear friend Commander Chol brings."

It didn't take Commander Chol long to vent his frustration at the situation. Hazkul Bern listened carefully, smirking occasionally at whatever slight or grievance the geldrin believed was his right to complain about. It struck Hazkul as comical that the commander would think he had any right to complain about his treatment by his former slaves.

Though Hazkul was the leader of an assassin organization, he did have moral lines he was unwilling to cross. One of those was slavery. Many of the members of the Sons of Silence were descendants of escaped slaves. Over the years, assassins had killed many of the slaving nobles and had essentially eradicated the practice in Kelvur. That is, until Jaernok Tur came out of the Crags.

"We have to storm the camp and retake the mine!" Chol spat as he refilled his wine.

"Oh, see," Hazkul said with a shake of his head. "That's where I think we misunderstand one another. You have always been hospitable to me when I've needed to pass through your neck of the woods, and I plan to return that courtesy. But *we* will not be 'storming the camp' to reclaim it. *I* have no purpose there."

"But Jaernok Tur—" Chol began to argue.

"The sorcerer gave you responsibility for the camp. I have my own tasks."

"But they killed all my geldrins," the commander said, fuming. He itched at the scar on his face. Hazkul thought it funny how the geldrin resorted to that tick whenever he was overwhelmed.

"Then you will have to ask your master for more," the elf said with a nonchalant shrug. "What business is it of mine?"

The geldrin commander squirmed. Hazkul knew the last thing the commander wanted to do was speak to Jaernok Tur about his failure. The elf watched the geldrin hem and haw for a moment, weighing his options.

"You know how badly he wants the treasure," Chol said finally, fighting hard to avoid the elf's stare.

"He did seem to like the axe I brought," the elf mused. Another grin tugged at the edge of his mouth as he shifted to another topic with which to twist the geldrin. "You're sure it wasn't the artifact you were looking for?"

"No. The stone was supposed to be red. The scroll described it like a blood stone. The one in your axe didn't seem red enough," Chol explained, not looking entirely convinced of his own words. "The scroll also said it was in the west. It said nothing of Tarrine. That's where you got the axe, right?"

Hazkul smiled. The elf knew, of course, that the sorcerer had them retrieving two different artifacts, but Chol's hesitation told him the geldrin was not so certain. "It is. You do realize Tarrine is in the west, right?"

The geldrin grumbled to himself, considering the possibility.

"Whether the weapon was or wasn't the one the sorcerer was searching for matters little. He seemed to like it, nonetheless. Would you agree, Chadwa?" he said airily.

"You have to help me," Chol blurted. "We must retake the mining camp."

"There you go, throwing that 'we' around again." Hazkul clicked his tongue as he shook his head at the geldrin. "I've already told you, I've got my own tasks."

"What tasks?" the geldrin asked, getting louder. When Chadwa took a few steps closer from the corner, the commander forced himself to calm down under her disconcerting stare.

I do like when she does that, Hazkul thought in amusement.

"What could be so important that it would take precedence over this?" Chol asked, quieter this time.

"You haven't been maintaining the roads between Glinso and Ventohl very well."

The geldrin commander's stony face twisted. "I, what?"

"Well, as I see it, the sorcerer gave you command of the western region. Everything west of Ventohl is under your purview. Sadly, several of my own men ... and ladies," Hazkul added, nodding to Chadwa. "Well, they were killed when a ragtag militia ambushed us on your road. Your master wasn't very pleased with that. Probably figured you had already defeated any resistance in the west. Boy, wasn't that a surprise?"

Chol's jaw slackened. He huffed a few times, unable to find words for the elf's insinuation.

"Not to mention," Hazkul said as he walked to a side table and poured himself a glass of wine. "The driver we used for the cage cart was from your little town. You wouldn't believe how quickly he turned on us. I would hate to find out you had anything to do with the ambush. Especially because the sorcerer wanted the huntsman so badly."

Chol was flabbergasted. The geldrin stared at the elf with his one good eye. Hazkul smirked as he took a sip, letting the geldrin stew. *I do love when they squirm.*

He had never liked the geldrins. There was something ... off about them. Hazkul had never even seen one until Jaernok Tur marched them out of the Crags.

"Look," the elf finally said. "I'm not saying you had anything to do with the ambush. Of course not. But you must admit, it doesn't look good when you set it next to the fact that you lost the Glinso Mining Camp. Wouldn't you agree? Now, I've never seen a geldrin do anything against the sorcerer. You all serve your master well. But who knows what he'd think."

The geldrin's head drooped. He muttered to himself as he kicked at the floor.

"Look, Chol," Hazkul said, more sympathetically. "I understand what it's like when you feel you have no options left. Let's face it, I've been there myself. Most of the Sons of Silence came here originally because they had nowhere else to go. How about this," he said, stepping closer to the geldrin. "I'll let you and your crew stay here a few days so you can work this out. Then, when you're ready, we can discuss your options."

Hazkul led the geldrin to the door and ushered him out, instructing one of Ventohl's attendants to show the geldrin to some quarters. He closed the door behind the commander.

The elf turned and found himself square in the sights of a disapproving Chadwa.

"What?" he said, shrugging as though he'd done nothing wrong. "I know what you're thinking. Geldrins are bad. They're dumb, and they're bad. I don't disagree. But," he said, raising a finger and an eyebrow. "We've never encountered a geldrin in such a dire situation. We've never had a geldrin in our ranks. And I definitely never wanted one, let alone expected the possibility. But think what he might be able to do for us that we can't do because we don't have stone skin."

The witch stared at him through her messy black bangs, unconvinced.

"I know, I know," he said, raising his hands in mock surrender. "Geldrins just do what the sorcerer tells them to do. It's actually kind of weird how they follow him so blindly."

She rolled her eyes.

"Right. Dumb. But seriously," he said, pouring another glass of wine. "There's something not right about them. I mean, they're just ... off. Wouldn't you agree?"

Chadwa didn't reply as she turned and headed for the door.

"Good talk, Chadwa," Hazkul said, making sure she could hear him as she left. "Maybe next time we can go for a walk and hold hands."

The door slammed, and the elf smirked.

CHAPTER TWENTY-SEVEN

MUSTER THE GUARD

Pernden rounded the corner into the dungeons under Whitestone like he'd done countless times in recent months. As he did, he slowed and observed Argus Azulekor riffling through the pages of one of the tomes Dona had brought to Garron a few weeks back. Pernden wasn't sure his cousin had gotten around to that one yet.

"Master Argus," the king said, sweeping into the cell next to the dwarf.

"Argus is fine, lad," the dwarf said, not looking up from the book. It dawned on the mage that he addressed the king of Whitestone. "I mean, Argus will do, my King."

The man rolled his eyes. He strode to the desk where Garron did most of his late-night reading. Pernden flipped the open book and read the title. *The Lost Notes on Nari* by Kel Joran. His face scrunched. *He was telling me about this book weeks ago,* Pernden thought. *Why is he so hung up on this one? I guess a good mystery helps to pass the time.*

He turned to the dwarf, who held up a finger without a word. He finished reading whatever he had been studying and looked up. "Sorry about that," he said, laying the book on the bed next to him. "Wanted to finish that page."

"What is it you'd like to see me about?" Pernden asked.

"Yes. Right," Argus said, hoisting himself off the bed and producing a Shell of Callencia from one of his robe pockets. "Watch this."

An orb of magical light blinked in and out of existence, floating just above the shell and sending erratic reflections of light dancing around the cell. It blinked a few times before disappearing altogether.

"What does it mean?" Pernden asked.

"Well, Lanryn has been keeping us updated on the *Sellena's* progress across the sea. Eventually though, we could no longer hear him, and this started happening. My guess is that it's Lanryn attempting to use the shell, even though he's too far for the magic to be effective."

"So, we have no idea how they're doing out there?"

"Well." The dwarf hesitated. "I wouldn't exactly say that. I think the blinking means that they're still alive, trying to reach us. Or at least, Lanryn is alive."

Pernden's brow furrowed.

"I mean," the old dwarf retracted. "They are most likely all alive, but it's not conclusive because, if Lanryn survived and no one else had, he would still be able to—"

Pernden raised a hand to halt the mage mid-sentence. "Is this all you needed to see me for?" the king asked.

"Oh! Smarlo reached out to tell us of the dark tongue in the mines in Calrok."

"Why didn't you start with that?"

"Well," the dwarf began sheepishly. "I was looking for any books that might have some magic in them that could help me increase the range of the shells. Then I got sidetracked on this fascinating tome about Last Lake. Your cousin has some interesting manuscripts down here."

"The dark tongue, Argus," Pernden pressed.

"Right. Calrok's master mage was dead when they arrived. It appears he went down into the mines with two guards and a miner—all dead except the miner. They were attacked by an assassin."

"How did the miner survive?"

"No one knows a mine like the miners that work it. He hid until Smarlo and the rest of them arrived."

"Did they find the dark tongue? Was Garron able to read it?" Pernden asked.

"Yes," Argus said. "Now I really wish I'd led with this. The beacon is started."

"What?"

"They were too late," the dwarf said with a shrug. "Whoever the assassin was, they must have known how to start it."

"What does that mean?" the king asked, concerned for his cousin.

"Well," Argus said. "Garron read it. And apparently, it's a call."

"A call for what?"

"Not for what, for whom," the mage corrected. His visage grew grave. "An army is headed for Calrok."

Pernden and Rocktail raced through the sky. The griffin beat his wings and ducked his head, propelling them forward. Pernden's long, blond hair whipped his face as the griffin soared through the air. The king breathed rapidly, his worry and frustration getting the better of him.

On the back of his griffin he could let his emotions roam. But as soon as he landed in the Corral, his cool command presence would have to be on full display.

Rocktail dove toward the Grand Corral. It was late afternoon, and the Guard was winding down their training and shifting to their evening responsibilities. Several guardians still practiced diving techniques off the high side of the Corral as Pernden approached. High Commander Mattness was among them.

The king was happy to see as he landed that the High Commander noticed his approach and glided her own griffin into the training field to meet him.

"My King," she said.

"High Commander Mattness. We've got a problem," Pernden said quickly.

"What is it?"

The woman slid off her griffin and landed gracefully, as though she had done so all her life.

"Let's talk in the war room."

They strode quickly across the field, the High Commander giving a couple of guardians instruction to board her and the king's griffins in the stables. They promptly responded and dashed across the field.

The leaders entered the main front structure of the Corral and wound their way up the stairs to the war room, situated above the gates. Mattness closed the doors behind them.

"Would you like some tea?" she asked as she moved toward a side table and started to prepare some.

"No," Pernden said. He took a deep breath and slowed down. "Thank you."

High Commander Mattness nodded. Pernden had great respect for the woman. Nera had learned much from her over the years and had grown to be one of the Griffin Guard's elite warriors. Not only was Mattness as tough as they came; she was also a compassionate leader. A trait Pernden had seen in his own mentors.

The king walked over to the woodpile and tossed another log on the fire in the hearth. The guardians on fire duty had already gotten the fires going. Soon the building would be filled with guardians ready for dinner and much-deserved rest.

As he poked the log into place, Pernden experienced an odd nostalgia. How many times had he come to this room with High Commander Danner Kane? How many times with Melkis? How many times had he stoked the fire while they discussed important business for the Guard? He'd been privileged to work so closely with the men. Back then he was only a captain. Now he stood in the room as king.

"There's an army coming," Pernden said shortly.

"Coming here?" Mattness asked, her face hardening with concern.

"No. To Calrok."

"I see," Mattness said, taking the kettle from the fire and pouring it into her cup. "When?"

"We don't know exactly," Pernden shook his head. "But the beacon is lit. Well, not lit. It's in the dark, in the mines of Calrok. Regardless, it's been started. Whoever is following the beacon is coming."

"Will they come from the Underrock?" she asked, stirring the tea.

"We don't know." The king paused and mulled the question over some more. "Why would they have put the beacon in the mines if they couldn't get to it? They've already sailed across the sea once."

"Can they close the tunnels that lead to the Underrock?"

She stepped forward and motioned for Pernden to take a seat at the table. He obliged. She set the tea in front of him, and before he could say anything, turned to make another one for herself.

"Not likely. The way I hear it, there are possibly hundreds of tunnels weaving around down there."

The guardian poured hot water into her own cup and crossed to sit next to Pernden. She pursed her lips in a pensive manner. He envisioned her mind working things out.

"Wyverns will be of little help in the mines," she said. She blew the steam off her cup and tested a sip. "As would griffins."

Pernden grunted. It wasn't the reaction he was hoping for.

"That's true," he grumbled, taking a sip of his own.

"Regardless," she said, dipping her head to the side. "Our new allies are in trouble. It seems the best way we can solidify that alliance is by coming to their aid."

"Yes," the king said, excited, though he paused.

Of course he wanted to stand and unite to defend their allies. Obviously, it would be a great way to show their dedication to a long-term alliance. However, if he were honest, his motivations were more personal. His cousin was there, and he would do anything to protect Garron. They'd already lost far too many family members. But there was something deeper.

Pernden was a warrior. Too long, he'd been stuck in the rut of kingly duties. His blood boiled within him. He couldn't remember when this had happened, but at some point, he had found himself longing for battle. In a strange way, he missed it.

"I would like to lead the squadrons myself," Mattness said, not looking up from her tea.

"What? Why?" the king asked in surprise.

"Since I've become High Commander, the Griffin Guard has been operating under an unprecedented time of peace. Every

High Commander in the Chronicles of the Griffin Guard has led the Guard through tumultuous times ..." Her words trailed off.

Pernden watched the woman, wondering what she was thinking. He would allow her the honor, of course. It was hers to command. But he sensed she had more personal motivations as well.

"What is it?" he asked.

"I was bewitched by the sorcerer, like so many others. If I had been stronger ..."

"You came through at a crucial time. If you hadn't rallied the Guard, we may not have won Whitestone back."

She shook her head slightly. "I have much left to prove as High Commander, and I will not sit idly by while guardians are out there fighting. I already sent the Talon Squadron across the sea."

There it was. *She feels guilty,* Pernden thought. He set his cup down and slid it away. He reached toward Commander Mattness, placing a hand on her shoulder.

"I have a lot to prove, myself," he said. "This seems to me the perfect time for us to prove our worth. If all goes well, the scribes will add us to the Chronicles, and years from now young guardians will read of the deeds we accomplished, riding to the aid of our allies."

He took a deep swig of the warm tea as though there was nothing left to discuss.

High Commander Mattness's face was stern, but she only asked, "Your order, my King?"

Pernden stood and leaned over, placing his hands on the table. He chewed at the inside of his mouth for a second as he thought about how this moment would be remembered in the Chronicles of the Griffin Guard.

"High Commander Mattness," he said, standing up straight. "Muster the Guard."

CHAPTER TWENTY-EIGHT

SEARCH IN A STRANGE LAND

O rin emerged from the brush slowly, proceeding down the dirt road with stealth. It seemed odd to him that some sort of battle had taken place in the middle of the road and no parties had returned to clean up the remains. He figured someone would have at least come back for the weapons and equipment. He couldn't quite see the carnage, but when Ralowyn mentioned the devastation ahead, the small group had skirted into the cover of the forest.

Nearing the remains, he saw it had been a bloody battle. While there seemed to only be half a dozen bodies, the stains on the road suggested there were plenty of others. *Perhaps a party did come back,* he thought.

"Orin, over here," Coal called in a hushed tone.

He and Ralowyn hurried to the dwarf.

"What is it?" the man asked.

The dwarf didn't say anything. He pointed one of his thick fingers and traced a shape through the air, indicating a massive footprint in the dirt. Orin's eyes widened, and he looked to the dwarf for an explanation.

"Giant," Coal said nervously. "I thought them mostly to be myth nowadays."

"He must be huge," Orin said. "Taller than a troll."

"Very likely," Ralowyn agreed.

"What do you think happened here?" Orin asked.

"Looks like an ambush," Coal reasoned. "There were likely more casualties. Seems many of them were dragged away."

"They are buried on the edge of the forest over there," the elf said.

Orin and Coal glanced in the direction she indicated. Several mounds of fresh dirt ran along the edge of the forest.

"If they were going to bury their dead, why wouldn't they take them home?" the man asked.

"I don't know," Coal grumbled.

"Perhaps they could not do so," Ralowyn said. "Perhaps they have no home."

Orin turned to the giant footprint. "Maybe they had to leave quickly."

"I am not convinced the giant was not with them," the elf mentioned. "His tracks seem to coincide with the rest of the tracks coming out of the wood and going back in."

She walked away from the other two, following something in the dirt. Orin and Coal investigated the area some more.

"Horse prints," the dwarf pointed out. "Only two sets continuing on the road."

"Maybe a prisoner cart?" Orin asked.

"No." Coal shook his head. "No wheel tracks. Most likely some cowards fleeing from the battle."

"Could be," Orin said, turning about. "But those look like wheel tracks over there."

"Aye," the dwarf agreed, hurrying to inspect them.

They followed the wheel tracks that came to a wild pattern in the road that looked like the cart had danced in circles for a while. They didn't appear to go any farther, but the pair saw no cart.

"Do you think the giant could carry a cart?" Orin asked.

Coal's face scrunched. "I don't know …" He looked around and then exclaimed, "Boehlen's Beard. Where's the elf?"

Orin turned side to side, looking for any sign of Ralowyn. *Where did she get off to?* the man wondered. *It's bad enough we have to find Merrick, but now we have to find her, too?*

A noise in the brush startled them. Orin drew his sword so quickly, it took his mind a second to realize he'd done so. Coal stood ready beside him, war hammer in hand. The two glanced back and forth between each other and the bushes. Coal took a couple of slow strides closer to the bush.

"Whoever's in there better come out, or you'll take a Galium battle hammer to the face!" he threatened.

Suddenly, a red and white fox jumped out of the bush. The head of Coal's hammer fell to the ground. He groaned and slapped his forehead. Orin slid his sword back into its sheath.

"Well, that's not what I was expecting," the man said, embarrassed.

"Aye," the dwarf agreed. "Let's not tell anyone about this."

Suddenly, Ralowyn popped out from behind a tree and asked, "Tell anyone about what?"

The other two nearly jumped out of their skins. Coal unsuccessfully tried to mask a yelp. Orin shook his head at her in disapproval.

"That's not right," he said. "You can't scare people like that."

"Come on," she said. "The tracks lead this way."

Orin was sure he saw a smirk on the elf's fair face.

For a while, they meandered through the overgrown woods. Ralowyn could spot signs of the travelers here and there, but mostly, she saw the gouging tracks of the cart's wheels. They followed the tracks until they came to a beautiful meadow. Flowers of many colors grew, and butterflies floated to and fro, happily going about their business.

One butterfly landed on Coal's shoulder, and the dwarf did a furious jig before attempting to smash the insect. Ralowyn stepped in, however, and lightly lifted the butterfly away from the dwarf and sent it on its way.

Coal didn't look pleased, and Orin shifted around nervously.

"Are you two alright?" she asked.

"Don't like butterflies," Coal grumbled. "Dumb faeries."

"We had ..." Orin paused, trying to think of a way to explain without sounding ridiculous to the elf. "An incident."

"How many of them are faeries, you think?" Coal asked, seemingly counting the butterflies while he gripped his hammer.

Ralowyn resisted the urge to laugh. "I assure you, these are just butterflies."

"Oh? And how do you know that?" The dwarf questioned her, still not taking his eyes off a butterfly that floated closer than he liked.

"I have a connection with creatures," she reminded him.

"Oh. Oh, yeah," he said. He relaxed his stance and lowered his hammer. "Well, fair enough."

Ralowyn studied a couple of butterflies on the edge of the meadow. She knew they were faeries in disguise. As long as they didn't bother their group, she saw no reason to worry her companions.

She examined the meadow. There were plenty of footprints. They must have stopped for a break. The wheel tracks had stopped a ways back. She assumed the giant had lifted and carried it somewhere they could hide it. The only reason the elf brought them to the meadow was it appeared the only notable feature remotely near the end of the tracks.

Thank the Maker, she thought when they found some footprints in the meadow. Whoever was hiding their tracks was skilled at doing so.

The tracks in the meadow didn't lead in a single direction back into the thick woods, and Ralowyn started to worry they might not be able to pick up the trail again.

"Where to next?" Coal asked, ready to keep moving.

"I do not know," she said.

"What do you mean you don't know?"

"I need some time to figure out which way they went. They clearly spent some time here. There are footprints going in every direction."

The three of them wandered around the meadow looking for any sign that could point them in the right direction. Coal swatted at butterflies, occasionally getting nervous when they flitted near him.

Orin realized he was only adding to the footprints and took a seat out of the way. A few minutes later, Coal was planted next to the man. Ralowyn searched onward. Nothing seemed to be an obvious path.

Merrick, where are you? she wondered.

She looked over the prints for hours and came up with nothing. Eventually, even she was losing hope.

"Ralowyn," Orin called to her. "Come take a rest. Your eyes must be tired. Maybe we can get another look at it with fresh eyes."

"No," she said stubbornly. *I must find him.*

Her tired eyes landed on a fox that sat on the edge of the meadow, watching her curiously.

I do not suppose you know where they went, do you?

She rolled her eyes and kept moving, but the fox moved closer. She eyed the fox out of the corner of her eye. She moved to the left, and the fox moved closer. She moved to the right, and the fox stayed planted. When she moved to the left again, the fox inched even closer.

You do know something.

Lavender light burst from the pinnacle of her magic staff. Her eyes blazed with purple faery fire.

What do you know? Please, will you help me? I am looking for someone very dear to me.

The fox's green eyes flickered purple, and he rose to his feet. He moved to another edge of the meadow and waited for her.

"Orin, Coal," she called. "I may have found us some help."

They loped after the fox who led them through the woods. Orin marveled at Ralowyn's ability to connect with the woodland creature. *How does she do that?* he wondered. He didn't understand it, but every once in a while, as they climbed over a fallen tree or pressed through some brush to follow the creature, Ralowyn would make a comment to assure them they were going the right way.

Coal also watched with fascination but grumbled more than the man. He protested when Orin offered to help him over particularly large logs and made all sorts of fuss about the fox whenever it disappeared and reappeared.

"Boehlen's Beard. Why doesn't the creature pick a smarter route?" he asked.

"He shares his own path with us," Ralowyn replied. "It is a great honor that he allows us to walk his path."

Coal grumbled and waved Orin's outstretched hand away. And so, on they went.

As evening began to descend on them, the shadows of the branches bathed the forest in an eerie verdant dim. The group stepped more cautiously, knowing Orin couldn't see as well as the other two in the dark. The man appreciated the gesture and did his best to keep pace. Eventually, Orin broke their silent trudging and asked, "Should we stop for the evening? Make camp?"

Coal sighed and mumbled to himself. The impatient dwarf was bullheaded sometimes, but Orin knew it was because he cared so much and worried about their friend.

"No," Ralowyn said, whispering to them. "Do you hear that?"

The man and the dwarf perked up, trying to hear whatever the elf referenced.

"I don't hear anything," Coal whispered.

"Me neither," Orin confirmed.

Ralowyn shushed them with an outstretched hand. Orin assumed she heard something with her pointed elven ears that he and Coal could not. The two waited for some clue as to what she sensed.

"We are close," she said, finally. "We must go on."

They pressed farther through the forest, and as they did, Orin thought he heard talking in the distance. His eyes widened, and his pace quickened. Coal noticed it, too, and they hurried to catch up to the elf. She turned and halted them.

"You must be quiet," she whispered. "They cannot know we approach. There are far more of them than there are of us."

Orin looked at Coal and nodded. She wasn't wrong. Even he could hear it was some sort of camp. There were only three of them. Ralowyn was a powerful mage, but the man wasn't convinced she could take on a camp full of warriors.

"What do we need to do?" Orin asked.

"Follow my steps exactly," she told them.

She knelt on one knee and beckoned the fox toward her. The creature loped to her without hesitation and relished her pets. "Thank you," she said to him. "You have been kind to my friends and me. I cannot thank you enough for what you have done this day. You may very well have saved lives. And for that, I am forever grateful."

The fox bobbed its head, and Orin's face scrunched. *Did it just bow to her?*

Ralowyn stood, and the lavender flames in her eyes vanished. The fox's purple eyes flickered and returned to their wild green. He looked at Orin and Coal, and for a moment, the man thought the fox was regarding them as well. But the fox didn't linger and scampered silently into the brush.

How in Finlestia? he wondered.

"Now," Ralowyn whispered to them. "Draw close to me as quietly as you can. You must follow my steps exactly. We will find a place from which we can observe the camp. We need to know what stands before us."

They followed the elf as she wove through the forest, striding nimbly and in near silence. Orin did his best to be quiet but noted a couple of quiet crunches that made the elf flinch. At first, Coal crunched away, unable to mimic the long stride of the slender elf. It didn't take long for her to shorten her gait. Once she had, the three moved along much more quietly.

Ralowyn led them to a small hill, covered in a copse of trees and underbrush, at the edge of the forest. She halted them and crept to a spot where she thought she might be able to get a good view of the camp. Once confident about their ability to stay hidden in the spot she had chosen, she waved them over.

As Orin moved into position next to her, the camp came into his view. Tents sprawled around the ruins of what looked to be an old castle. Fires glowed throughout the camp as people gathered around for their evening meals. In an odd way, Orin was relieved to see people doing something normal. When a giant shuffled around the stone ruins of the castle, the man's jaw dropped.

"Giant," the dwarf whispered next to him.

"Yes," Orin replied. "I see that." He was glad he wasn't the only one stunned by the appearance of the giant.

"Centaurs, too," Coal said.

Orin's gaze drifted to a group of centaurs huddled around a campfire. With the upper body of a man and the lower body of a horse, they were unlike anything the man had seen. They stamped their hooves and bellowed at two centaurs who cracked wooden swords in a sparring match. Orin couldn't take his eyes off the creatures.

"How are we going to tell if they have Merrick and Karnak?" Coal asked.

"They are here," Ralowyn said with certainty.

"How do you know?" asked the dwarf.

The elf pondered the question for a moment. "I do not know how to explain that," she admitted. "But our fox friend assured me."

"He spoke to you?" Orin asked.

"Not in words. But he assured me."

Orin wasn't sure what she meant, but he knew that Merrick trusted Ralowyn implicitly, and he didn't have much choice but to do so as well.

"So, where are they?" he finally asked.

"That is what we must find out," she replied.

They watched the camp for a long time, looking for any sign of their friends. Orin ran through scenario after scenario. They still hadn't spotted Merrick or Karnak, and Orin started to imagine the worst.

"Maybe they're tied up in one of the tents," he suggested.

"Perhaps," Ralowyn answered.

"Maybe they're in a cage somewhere in the castle," Coal added.

"Perhaps," she answered again.

"Well, we have to do something," Coal grumbled. "We have to find them."

The dwarf shifted as though he planned to get up and march directly into the middle of the camp. Orin grabbed at him and held him down. "What are you doing?"

"I can't take it anymore," the dwarf said. "I just can't take the worry."

"I'm worried, too," Orin growled at him. "But getting yourself killed or captured isn't going to help anything. Then we'll have you to worry about, too."

"That doesn't matter," Coal growled back.

"It matters to me," the man said. "I want to find Merrick, too. So does Ralowyn. Of course, she wants to find him."

"I do," she whispered kindly.

"But you're my friend, too," he said to the dwarf. "I would go to all these lengths to find you, as well. But I want to do this in the safest way possible."

Coal's face creased as the truth of Orin's words hit him. He sagged, and his words turned soft. "What if there is no safe way?"

"If there's no safe way, I will charge beside you like we did from the gates of Galium to meet the goblin force of Drelek."

Coal nodded to him, and Orin breathed out a relieved sigh.

"Let us watch until night falls," the elf said. "We will learn much from watching. If we do not see any sign of them by then, we will take a more direct approach."

Orin nodded his agreement and turned to view the sprawling camp. As he did so, he saw a large woman in great armor emerge from the castle ruins with a big green orc and a man who looked like Merrick.

"Merrick," Ralowyn whispered.

Orin knew the elf could see them better, and a wave of elation washed over him.

CHAPTER TWENTY-NINE

A COOL BREEZE

Merrick walked behind Vorenna and Karnak. The two were leaders of their people, and that connection bonded them in a way only they could understand. The huntsman listened, but his mind wandered in and out of their conversation.

"What is your home like?" Feliketh asked him.

"Not much different than here, actually," Merrick said, raising his hands and indicating the area. "Where I come from, we have a large city called Tamaria. It's the center for trade and merchants from around Tarrine. But there is good forest and plains land outside the city for hunting."

"Is there a city guard that protects the people? I've heard of such things in the Zors in the south, but obviously," he motioned around, "we do not have that here."

"Tamaria is strange among the cities of Tarrine. There are guard towers built all over the city. When the original builders formed the city, they didn't anticipate how it would grow over the years. And grow it did. The strange part is, though, they never tore the old towers down. They left them standing, and every day and night there is a man posted at the top of each. I'm not sure why they never tore them down, honestly."

The elf listened carefully and nodded along. "What about this Griffin Squad?"

"Griffin Guard," Merrick corrected him. "They're in a city called Whitestone."

"Ah, yes," Feliketh said. "And they are the warriors of Tarrine."

"Well, yes," the man said, hesitantly. "But there are warriors in many cities. Men are not the only ones with warriors in Tarrine."

The elf's lips pursed, and Merrick took note of the odd expression on his face.

"Merrick," Karnak said, suddenly turning to him. "Tell Vorenna of the beauty of Calrok."

The huntsman smiled. "It's a sight to behold," he said with fervor.

"The Scar Cliffs glow majestically in the sunset," Karnak continued to explain to the barbarian woman.

"Is the Griffin Guard a large force?" Feliketh asked, drawing Merrick's attention back to the elf.

"I suppose," Merrick answered thoughtfully. "They have quite a few squadrons, and their prowess is known far and wide throughout Tarrine."

"What other places have armies?"

Merrick looked at the elf, curiously.

"I am a warrior," the elf said quickly. "And I may be fighting a losing war. I have heard little of triumph and the glorious deeds of warriors far away. It is inspiring."

"Right," Merrick said. "Sorry. The Scar Squadron in Calrok is amazing. They are the toughest wyvern riders in all of Drelek. Their training on the Scar Cliffs forges them into the most skilled warriors among the orcs."

"They sound impressive."

The group walked to the tent where Merrick and Karnak were staying. The guards that followed stood patiently to the side, ready to guard the tent when their leader was done with the prisoners.

Vorenna bid them good night and turned to Feliketh. The elf took one last look at Merrick and nodded to him before following the barbarian woman who spoke quickly to the elf.

Merrick entered the tent behind Karnak, and the two sat on the pallet beds.

"What do you think?" Karnak asked him.

"What do you mean?"

"About all of this," the big orc said.

"Well, after seeing what the sorcerer did to us in Tarrine, I'm not sure Javelin stands much of a chance. He wasn't even at full power when he nearly destroyed both Drelek and Whitestone."

Karnak shifted his tusks as he thought. "I don't like it either. But they've survived out here as long as Jaernok Tur has been around. Maybe they can deal a blow to his forces."

"I've seen flies survive on the back of a boar. It doesn't mean the flies can take him down," Merrick said, shaking his head.

"But the flies eat the boar in the end."

"When something else kills the boar first," the man pointed out.

The orc stood and paced. He stretched his shoulders and tightened the knot of black hair on the back of his head. "It seems to me we fight the same fight."

Merrick stood and faced the orc. "But what can we do here?"

Karnak's tusks wavered as a snarl slipped out of his mouth. The big orc lay down on the pallet. "We can't do nothing."

"You're right. Of course, you're right," Merrick agreed, lying down on his pallet again.

They lay for a long time in silence before sleep descended in their midst.

Karnak tossed and turned through the night. The orc didn't like the fact that he felt stuck. As gar of Calrok, he'd been called upon to come up with solutions for many things over the years, and he liked to believe there was an answer for everything. He grunted as he rolled to his back. *I wish Smarlo were here,* he thought. *How many times have we figured things out? Or, Tanessa, you would know what to do.*

He scolded himself silently. It wasn't Merrick's fault. He wasn't giving the man enough credit. It was Merrick who had calmed him when the orc felt he might burst. It was Merrick who'd experienced this whole thing with him. The stinging reality of the huntsman's thoughts on the whole thing pricked Karnak, like a thorn in his side. *What could two people do in a war far bigger than them?*

The guards outside shifted quietly. Karnak imagined they were bored out of their minds, moving around to keep themselves awake. He rolled to his side, looking at the man lying on the pallet nearby. Karnak sighed. They were doing the best they could with the situation they'd been handed.

He squeezed his eyes shut, trying to fall back asleep. A sudden breeze blew in through the tent flap, chilling the orc with the cool night air. He peeked one eye open but didn't notice anything out of the ordinary. He shut his eyes again, hoping to find rest. In the morning, he and Merrick would work things out, and maybe Vorenna would aid them in finding a way home.

Karnak wasn't sure what caused him to open his eyes again, but something inside the orc prompted him to do so. When he did, he saw a shadowy figure standing over the huntsman. The orc shot up out of his bed, and the black-clad figure ripped the huntsman from his bed and pressed a dagger to his throat.

"Make a noise, and I'll kill the huntsman here and now."

Merrick gulped, his eyes bleary and confused.

"Let him go," the orc whispered.

"I said no noise," the hooded figure said, putting pressure on the dagger.

Merrick winced.

A million thoughts raced through Karnak's mind. He'd been in the same predicament before. The pair stared at each other as Merrick tried to control his breathing to save his neck.

Suddenly, the tent flap whipped open, and Karnak glanced to the entryway. He saw the two bodies of the guards sprawled outside as Feliketh strode into the tent.

"Wait," Karnak said, shooting out a hand to stay the elf.

Feliketh looked from the intruder to the orc and back to the intruder. "I see," he said.

They stood in silence, and Karnak scowled at the intruder. *Nowhere to go now,* he thought dangerously.

"Seems we have a predicament," Feliketh said.

"I came in here, and the orc was already awake," the hooded figure said.

"You can hardly blame him," the bald elf replied. "You are holding his friend at daggerpoint."

Karnak didn't understand the tactic but figured Feliketh had more experience with the Sons of Silence than he did.

"What do we do now?" the intruder asked.

What a strange question, the orc thought. *How about I rip your limbs off, and we go our separate ways?*

"Seems to me we have a few choices," Feliketh said, taking a few steps closer to the orc's side. "You can release the man and disappear. Though, I doubt your master would appreciate that."

The intruder's eyes narrowed.

"Or you can turn this tent into a bloody mess and take the chance the orc won't rip you, limb from limb," the elf said with a shrug.

A wicked grin grew across the orc's face.

"Or," the elf said, pulling his sword from its sheath. "I can kill the orc while you escape with the prisoner."

Karnak turned toward the elf in shock. The elf's sword hovered near his own throat.

"Oh, don't look at me like that," Feliketh scoffed. "It hurts my feelings that you would think so little of me that you'd believe I would throw my life away in a losing battle. Honestly, it's sad."

The orc growled, a primal resonance rising from the fire in his belly.

"So beastly," Feliketh said, clicking his tongue. "I thought you would understand. After all, you led your people in a rebellion against a tyrant. You must have sensed the way the tide was moving here?"

"But Javelin fights against the tyrant," Karnak said slowly.

The elf laughed. "A hopeless cause. I have been here for so long. They don't suspect a thing. Do you know how hard it is to hold a disguise while everyone around you is so idiotic? Of course, I threw off the scent by blaming others for the times we were attacked and had to move. Vorenna was so easy to convince when I came up with a way to send out our own spy."

"And what will you tell her about this? How will you explain this away," Karnak growled.

"I won't need to," Feliketh said, with a wicked grin. Karnak didn't like the look in the elf's eyes. "I'll kill you. Nihel will take the huntsman outside of camp while everyone sleeps. Then, I'll kill Vorenna, leaving these helpless sods without any leadership. Nelan is hardly the same stature as Vorenna in battle. They'll be lost.

"Plus, the huntsman has given me so much information about the military strength of the cities in your precious Tarrine." The elf paused and dipped his head in an appreciative nod to Merrick. The man winced again, gritting his teeth. "I'll singlehandedly present to the sorcerer his greatest victory in this war, and no doubt, he will reward me. Best of all, I won't have to listen to dumb and pointless orders anymore."

"Jaernok Tur infiltrated some of Tarrine's greatest societies while he was there. What do you think you've gleaned that would put you in his good graces?" Karnak grunted as the sword tip drew nearer.

"See, you're not thinking with that entrepreneurial spirit. Does he know the current state of your forces in the aftermath? There's always something to learn." The elf paused, looking at him with disbelief. "This is why the orcs are all gone. They don't have the capacity to think. All bravado and heart. Not a single ounce of brain to the lot of them."

"It's the heart that makes friends fight for each other," a voice said from the tent opening.

"What?" Feliketh asked as he turned to see a stout dwarf with a bushy black beard and menacing war hammer.

Karnak didn't waste any time and dove on the elf, tackling him to the ground.

Ralowyn lifted the Staff of Anvelorian high, and purple ribbons of magic swirled around the tent, sending everyone flying. The assassin recovered quickly and ran. Merrick grabbed at the assassin as he tried to find his footing.

"No!" Merrick hollered. "Don't let him escape."

Orin stepped out from behind a nearby tent as the assassin fled. He flourished his sword as the assassin dove at him, daggers first.

Karnak rolled over and found that Feliketh had run off.

He growled as he pushed himself up. "I have to get to Vorenna's tent before the elf does," he yelled as he bolted between a pair of tents.

"Great!" Coal called after him sarcastically.

Merrick took off and was right on the orc's heels.

As they ran toward the Javelin leader's tent, they caught a glimpse of the elf saying something to the guards before slipping in the tent flap.

Karnak slowed as Merrick caught up. He looked at the man and shook his head.

"They're not going to let us in there," Merrick said, not slowing down.

Karnak sighed and pumped his legs faster. The guards adjusted into a ready stance, drawing their weapons. The orc cursed silently. They didn't have a choice. They needed to get in that tent, so they weren't slowing down.

Suddenly, the two guards split and sprawled to the ground on either side. Magic wisps of purple light swirled around them as their armor clamored, and they grunted in two heaps.

Karnak didn't need to look back to know Ralowyn was close behind. The orc and the huntsman sprinted through the opening of the leader's tent and skidded to a halt.

"Now we have a party," Feliketh said.

The elf stood next to the leader's bed. His sword tip rested on Vorenna's chest. The barbarian woman breathed through gritted teeth.

"I was just telling Vorenna how I wish things could have been different. Of course, that's mostly your fault," he said, nodding toward Karnak. The orc bared his tusks, and his fists clenched tighter, sending ripples up his muscular arms. "So tough, and so dumb." The elf laughed and looked at Vorenna. "Something you two have in common."

Karnak took a step forward while the elf's eyes were on his waiting victim.

"Oh, please," Feliketh said. "Please take another step. I wanted her to know it was me who ended her and her precious Javelin. But I'll tell you what. How about we make a deal? I'll take the huntsman with me, and I'll let Vorenna—"

Without warning, the Javelin leader swung her thick legs out and blasted the elf in the knees. His legs buckled underneath him, and the woman was on him in a flash. He swung his sword hitting her with little strength as she beat down on his face. She ripped the sword away from his grasp and ran it through the elf's chest.

"I want you to know that you didn't beat us," Vorenna said, spitting with her venomous words. "You didn't end us. Now that I know what lengths the sorcerer will go to in his attempt to destroy us, we will end this whole thing. But hear me as you die." She shook him, making sure his eyes saw her. "You are a traitor to your people. And you will receive no pyre among the Javelin."

The barbarian woman stood, taking the sword and finishing the elf. She looked toward Karnak and Merrick with a ferocious glare of her icy blue eyes. The orc raised his hands to make sure she knew they weren't enemies.

"Are you alright?" he asked her.

Vorenna's body heaved with her breath as she worked herself out of her rage.

The tent flap opened, and Coal walked in. Vorenna's eyes widened in confusion, and Karnak stepped in front of the dwarf to cover him from view. "He's a friend."

"You two sure are a lot of trouble," Coal grumbled to Merrick.

Karnak rolled his eyes and sighed.

CHAPTER THIRTY

DORANTOWN

Enkeli the wizard stepped close to Nera as the guardian breathed in the smell of the sea. She twisted her boot in the sand, feeling it give way underneath her. There was something about the wizard's look that made her feel like a child again. Enkeli stood next to her, not saying anything. He puffed at his long pipe and smiled, taking in the sight and sound of the morning's rolling waves.

Nera wondered about Pernden. She imagined he was at home in Whitestone, going stir-crazy. A glowing grin swept across her countenance. They hadn't been able to contact Whitestone in several days, and she hoped he was getting some rest. He had been so exhausted by all the duties that had fallen to him. *Hopefully, he's getting out to the training grounds,* she thought.

"You are here, but your heart is across the sea," the old wizard said with a smirk.

Nera turned her brown eyes on him. "You perceive more than most, wizard," she said, trying to sound tough.

Enkeli chuckled to himself. "He will need you when all this is over."

"Pernden?" she asked, but somehow, she knew the wizard meant the king.

"There are many more things to come," the wizard said, ominously.

"What? Can you tell us? Prepare us?"

"It does not work that way, my dear."

Nera looked over the crystal blue water. She wondered what Enkeli knew, but for some reason, she did not question his response. Strangely, she knew he would tell her what she needed to hear.

"You are a brave leader, a mighty warrior, and a strong woman," he said matter-of-factly. "You will face every challenge with wisdom and grace."

The fatherly tone with which the wizard spoke pricked at something deep within her heart. Her eyes began to well, and she didn't know why.

"When all is said and done, he will need you. But," he turned to her, his old eyes gazing deep into her being. "Others will need you first."

"Others?" Nera asked, confused.

Enkeli nodded to Shorlis who carried a bundle of scrolls in his arms toward the boat. "You have found your strength. He will find his. Though right now, he's not sure where to find it."

Nera watched the chelon. She didn't know exactly what the wizard meant. Two days earlier, she had no idea what a chelon was or that they even existed.

"How can I help him?" she asked.

"You'll know, when the time is right."

"You don't give very detailed answers, do you?" she asked, eyeing the wizard with a smirk of her own.

Enkeli grinned, his face wrinkling with well-worn smile lines, and looked back to the waves. "No," he mused. "The art of encouragement is not always saying what people want to hear but telling them what they need to hear so they can rise to greater things."

Nera nodded thoughtfully. She'd have to keep that pearl of wisdom for younger guardians in the future.

"How can you be so certain we'll survive this journey?"

"Is that what I said?" The wizard puffed at his pipe, not looking at her.

She thought about it. *He said Pernden would need me after all this is over. Doesn't that mean he knows what will happen? Can he know that?* She inhaled, ready to ask another question, but hesitated. The wizard's ways were strange. They were foreign to her. She couldn't possibly comprehend all his riddles.

Enkeli chuckled again. "It brings this old wizard great joy to see fierce love," he said. "And that is what I see in you."

Nera could feel the tears gathering again. *What is it with this wizard?* She fought them back, setting her jaw tight.

He gave her a kindly smile and walked away through the sand, leaving her alone beside the rising tide of crystal water.

"I think that's the last of the ones we can salvage," Shorlis said to Tam. "Thank you for helping me with them."

"Of course," Tam assured the chelon. "Would you mind me looking at some of the scrolls when we get back to the camp? I'd love to see everything that's drawn in them to help me continue my maps."

"Sure," Shorlis said. "Though my father was a better storyteller than artist. Any of the scrolls he transcribed will likely be unhelpful." A weak smile touched the chelon's soft beak.

"Thank you," Tam said. "Are you alright?"

"I'll be fine."

Tam eyed the chelon. "That didn't answer my question."

Shorlis sighed and looked at the man. He was a little shorter than the chelon and leanly built. Men were always so insistent. That fact didn't seem to change whether they were men of Kelvur or Tarrine, but he didn't begrudge the man for his compassion.

"The last week has been something out of the old stories—wild and unexpected. Warriors and people rising to fight for right, many dying as heroes." He choked on his words. "And my father is gone. He was always there for me. No matter what. I spent my whole life with him by my side. It's only been a few days, and I still look for him when I turn around. I don't even know where they buried him—or if they did. I know burial is the usual way of the geldrins. For all I know, they could have returned his body to the sea or burned him."

Tam looked up at the chelon. "I'm sorry that happened to you."

Shorlis shook away the man's condolences. "Everything has been like a sea storm rolling over the Shoals. The winds whip every which way and the rains pour and trees get uprooted and palms fly. It's chaos. Everything has been so crazy; I've hardly had time to grieve. And now, I'm not sure I want to."

Tam's brows furrowed. "I'm not sure I understand."

"It's nothing," the chelon said quickly. "I'll be fine. We need to find your friends, and that's what we'll do."

Tam gave Shorlis a hesitant nod but didn't press the issue further. The chelon was relieved. If he was honest, he didn't understand either. His emotions had been raw and on overload for several days, and he wasn't sure he'd be able to explain what was going on inside him.

He shook the doubts away and waded to the boat, laying *Menthrora* into the back. He held the boat steady, taking one last look at the half-burned village, his home.

Far on the other side of the village, Enkeli the wizard stood, granting the chelon a tight smile. Shorlis didn't know why the wizard couldn't come with them. When he'd asked, Enkeli simply replied, "This is your story to tell." For some reason he could not explain, the chelon had been content with the vague reply.

He waved to the wizard, and Enkeli shooed him with an entirely different wave. The gesture sent the chelon into motion as he hopped into the boat beside Nera.

When the boat paddled into the dock at the Glinso Mining Camp, Tenzo and some of the guardians met them. Nera and the others had paddled most of the day between the sandy isles of the Shoals, making their way back. Meanwhile, the guardians had taught the former miners to use the skills they'd developed to dig defensive trenches and stack stones for walls they could hide behind for cover.

"Welcome back to Dorantown," Tenzo said to the group, as a sailor from the *Sellena* roped them to the dock.

"Dorantown?" Shorlis asked.

"Felt right when we discussed it last night. No one wanted to call it Glinso anymore. Trying to put that terrible part behind us, you know?"

Nera watched as the chelon nodded his silent approval.

"Did you get what you were searching for?" the muscular chelon asked.

In response, Shorlis lifted *Menthrora* into the sky. Magic bands and ribbons of red light danced away from the staff as the chelon quickly lowered it.

"Are you alright?" Nera asked.

"I'll be fine," Shorlis said, seeming embarrassed. "I just don't understand how to use this thing yet."

"It's like any weapon, I suppose," Nera encouraged. "Might take some practice, but I'm sure you'll master it in no time."

Shorlis shook his head as they walked up the dock. "If my father were here, he could teach me how to wield it."

"Maybe," the woman tentatively agreed. "I don't know much about magic. I'm no mage."

"You wield your spear with such skill, though."

The guardian laughed. "I knew how to wield a spear long before this one came into my possession. *Santoralier* is still a spear, but with powerful magic. I have only learned how to use it because I first learned how to use a spear. I am still learning the magical side of the thing," she said, shrugging the spear in her hand.

She smiled at the chelon, who seemed to be deep in thought.

"I suppose," he said slowly. "My father taught me how to use a staff, but those were made of rod wood. There was no magic in them."

"See. Just like me. You'll figure out the magic as we go. Besides, Lanryn knows stuff about magic, and Ralowyn's staff seems similar enough. I'm sure she'll be able to help you grow in your abilities."

When they arrived at the camp's main building, they found it filled with elders from the large group of inhabitants. The guardian Nera left in charge, Jensen, was patiently trying to explain something to an older dwarf.

The Talon Squadron captain smiled at Jensen's forced patience. She was glad she'd gone searching for the staff and had left the man to handle preparations in the newly dubbed Dorantown.

Jensen caught Nera out of the corner of his eye and hurriedly excused himself from the dwarf.

"Captain," he said, stepping through the crowd. "How did the mission go?"

Nera liked Jensen. He was a sturdy guardian and had been in the Talon Squadron for a number of years. He was always one to jump in whenever there was work to be done.

"Good. We found the staff," she said, looking around at the crowd. "How are things going here?"

"We've got several guardians out helping workers fortify Dorantown. Several more are helping Captain Tinothe and his crew plan and build a proper sea dock, and I have others on foot patrol. We've kept the griffins grounded, as you ordered. Though, I'm not sure how long we can keep them in the makeshift stable. We may need to build a more suitable stable for them."

"Oh?" Nera asked. "Is there a problem?"

"Well," Jensen hemmed. He looked around before he lowered his voice. "The people of Dorantown seem to really like the griffins. They've never seen creatures like them."

"Sure," she said, eyeing him curiously. "Isn't that a good thing, though?"

"The problem, Captain, is that the children keep feeding the griffins. They think it some sort of game."

Nera huffed a chuckle. "Griffins have to eat, Jensen."

"Ma'am," Jensen said, concern etching his face. "They won't stop feeding them. If the griffins stay grounded and eat all day, they will be out of fighting shape in no time."

Nera nodded her surrender. "You're right," she said. "Why don't you have a guardian help guide some builders to create a proper stable for them. It is a good skill for them to know."

"Yes, Captain," he said. "Right away."

"No word from Orin?"

"No, ma'am."

"Alright," she said. "Lanryn and I will scout ahead and look for any sign of them. I'm leaving you in charge of the guard here. Work with Captain Tinothe and Shorlis to ensure they have everything they need."

Shorlis withdrew from a nearby conversation he was having with an elf.

"Captain," the chelon spoke. "I'll be joining you."

Nera nodded. "Right. Then Tenzo?"

"Yes, Captain," Shorlis affirmed. "He is more than capable."

"Actually," Lanryn cut in. "If it's alright with you, Captain, I could stay here and help. Also, staying by the coast may be my best chance of making the Shell of Callencia work. I'm not sure I can get it to work, but I'd like to try."

"Sure," Nera agreed. "It would be good for us to be able to touch base with home."

"I'll go in Lanryn's stead," Tam piped. He attempted to bury his eagerness. "I can continue to chart our journey through Kelvur."

Nera smiled at the young guardian. He'd taken to his role as the voyage's cartographer. She had to admit, his drawings were quite good.

"Alright then," she said. "We'll leave at first light."

CHAPTER THIRTY-ONE

NOISES IN THE DARK

G arron was brushing Benley's flanks when Ezel strode into the stable in the meadow of Gar Karnak's home overlooking the orc city of Calrok.

The man glanced at the deep gnome then back to the handsome pegasus. Benley was mostly white with brown spotting all over his body. He was a strong pegasus and had been good to his passengers on the way to Calrok. Lanryn had loaned them the grand beast, and though spending time with the creature made him miss his old griffin, Garron thought he might get used to working with a pegasus instead.

Ezel climbed to the top of a railing a few feet away and perched himself comfortably. Garron felt the gnome's eyes on him. After holding out as long as he could, he finally turned to Ezel and asked, "What can I do for you, Ezel?"

Since their time in the caves, Garron had fallen asleep each night against all the willpower he could muster. The experience in the caves had drained him to the point of exhaustion. Unfortunately for him, that meant falling asleep, and worse, falling prey to the ever-present night terrors.

He'd woken up screaming several times over the previous nights, and Ezel and Ellaria had run to his side. Each time, he was not only terrified but also mortified to have woken his companions. Ezel didn't have much chance at full rest, bunking in the main room of the cottage with the man. Though Ellaria was in the next room, Garron's outcries were loud enough to rouse her every time.

Ellaria would hold Garron's hand, and his dread would melt away. The trio had taken to sleeping in the same room where Ellaria held Garron's hand from the bed, while the man slept on the floor. Ezel stayed close by in his makeshift nest of blankets. For some reason, it worked. The night before, Garron had gotten his first full night's sleep in months.

"You slept," Ezel signed, with a nod of approval.

"Yes," the man signed back.

"Ellaria's magic helped?"

"It's the only answer I can think of, myself."

He didn't understand Ellaria's magic. He knew she'd been a learned healer for her family in Tamaria and had healed his cousin Orin from his injuries in a battle close to the plains city. He also knew they'd discovered Ellaria had some ability to wield magic through the emerald stone tied around her neck. Somehow, she'd tapped into the magical source and was able to help Garron recover from the bewitching he'd experienced at the wicked hands of Jaernok Tur.

"There is something special about her magic," the gnome signed.

Garron nodded his agreement, his eyes far off. *"She's ... something else."*

He was grateful for the woman. His recovery had been hard, and most of the time, he felt as though he were far from full health. He knew her healing touch had helped him through many unseen things—terrible things that haunted him from within.

Ezel grinned at the man, the little gnome's face looking rather silly.

"What?" the man asked aloud.

Ezel's eyebrows wiggled at the man. *"She's also quite beautiful,"* he signed.

"What?" Garron scoffed.

"For a human woman, that is," Ezel flourished.

"You forget that I was in prison in the dungeons," Garron signed back, rolling his eyes.

"I seem to recall Ellaria visited you every day," the gnome pointed out.

The man blew out a disbelieving breath. *"On the order of the king."*

"Oh. Right," Ezel signed with sarcastic flair. *"And in all that time together, you didn't grow closer at all. My mistake. I thought her to be an attractive woman."*

"She is," Garron emphasized with his voice. He shook his head. *"You don't get it. Even if she were to be interested in courting, she could never be with a man like me."*

"Why?"

"Because of what I've done!" Garron glared at the gnome, his chest heaving. He tried to calm himself down.

"What about me?" the gnome asked.

"That's different."

"Is it?"

Suddenly, Ellaria stepped through the opening into the stable. The man and the gnome regarded her and let the heat between them cool.

"Hey, you two," she said, eyeing them suspiciously. "Tanessa has breakfast for us. We'll need to have our strength up. The Guard should be coming in tonight."

"Thank you," Garron said, trying not to meet the woman's emerald eyes. "Let me clean this up and give Benley a little treat, and I'll be right over."

"Aye." She turned to the gnome. "Ezel?"

The deep gnome stared hard at the man for a second longer before signing to her, *"Lead the way."*

Garron placed his forehead against the pegasus's face, relishing in the fact that the creature wasn't going to give him guff like the others. Benley, however, neighed and stamped at the ground, as if to scold the man.

"Not you, too," Garron said. "Ezel doesn't understand. Things for men and gnomes are different."

Benley lifted his chin several times and stamped some more.

"Fine, take his side," Garron said. "But just remember who brushed you so nicely and brought you a treat."

The man produced an apple from a small pouch tied to his belt. The pegasus excitedly took it from the man and nibbled at the fruit. Garron raised an eyebrow at him as the creature crunched happily. The man chuckled and shook his head. "Let's call it a draw for now."

Smarlo banged the desk in Master Tan-Kro's office—well, his office. It was still hard to believe the master mage was gone. Unfortunately, that meant Smarlo now sat as Calrok's master mage. He had been Tan-Kro's ward and in line to take up the mantle. Even so, he wished the old master were still there.

He pounded the desk again before laying his face flat on an open tome. It was the first time Smarlo had stopped in days. Since Garron read the dark tongue and they'd discovered the beacon was already set, the orc mage had been running about putting different things into motion.

First, he met with the city watch and set up a force to protect the miners that were going to start closing off all the tunnels they deemed likely to lead into the Underrock. Several heated discussions about how to allocate the guards followed, as the Gert section of the mines opened into vast caverns with a myriad of scattering tunnels. Plus, Jeslora, the captain of the city watch, wasn't keen on sending a majority of her orcs to the mines. With the last attack having come from a ship of the sea, she didn't like the idea of minimal units manning the towers by the docks. Smarlo assured her that the Scar Squadron would be on the lookout for intruders from the sea.

Meanwhile, Belguv was almost single-handedly running the Scar Squadron and preparing them for battle. There wasn't much they'd be able to do with their wyverns in the caves. The beasts were too large to fight effectively in the confined and sharply adorned caverns. Belguv had a rotation of orcs perched on the Scar Cliffs in pairs, watching over the sea, while the others readied and familiarized themselves with the mines.

Smarlo had reached out to Argus Azulekor shortly after they deciphered the dark tongue, and the Griffin Guard was on its way to the city as the orc mage sat face down in the little office of the Calrok mage library.

Karnak, you should be here doing all this, Smarlo cursed his friend silently, though he knew it wasn't fair to do so. Wherever Karnak was, Smarlo knew the gar wasn't away willingly. If he had even a sliver of a chance to return home, the gar would take it.

Smarlo was merely upset. He hated that all the responsibility had fallen into his lap. He wasn't the gar. A few days ago, he wasn't even Calrok's master mage. Suddenly, he was organizing preparations for the city to defend itself against attackers. *How did this happen?*

Thinking about it made him tired. His brain felt so numb he couldn't even think anymore. His head and his eyelids grew heavier, and before he knew it, Smarlo drifted off to sleep.

Pernden flew near High Commander Mattness at the front of the Griffin Guard formation. The 4th and the 7th Squadrons were mustered to fly to Calrok in order to aid their allies against the unknown incoming force.

The High Commander raised an arm and signaled to the captains leading their individual squadrons. The squadrons shifted and spread, giving the griffins more space between them. High Commander Mattness had ordered the last two squadrons to stay in Whitestone and placed one of the remaining commanders in charge.

Pernden had to tell Mistress Leantz to stand in as Steward of Whitestone in a similar conversation. She had argued against the king going but eventually relented when he seemed set to go whether she liked it or not. Pernden was grateful for the woman. She had been kind to him and understanding. He explained to her that the mixture of her wisdom and compassion was the exact reason she needed to stand in as steward.

With things under good guidance in Whitestone, Pernden felt completely comfortable flying north with the Guard. Perhaps comfortable wasn't the right word. His jaw was set, though, and he flew with a determination unmatched by anyone.

The wind whipped his blond hair, and his eyes glossed with tears as he squinted. Rocktail flew at a steady pace. They couldn't fly at full speed and arrive in Calrok exhausted. They had no idea how soon the incoming force would appear. The leaders planned to meet when the Guard flew into Calrok, and they hoped they had enough time to organize their forces.

Rocktail's feathers riffled as his wings adjusted. Pernden patted the griffin, and Rocktail clicked happily. It seemed the griffin was thankful for the extended flying. *Me too,* Pernden thought, also thankful. They had not been getting such flights in recent times.

Pernden shook his head as his thoughts shifted to his cousin. In a peculiar way, he missed Garron being in the dungeons. He'd come to rely on him for support and liked the fact that his cousin was always available to him. Of course, that was no reason to keep someone in the dungeons, but he was also worried about losing Garron. He knew his cousin to be a noble man, whether Garron believed it of himself or not. And he knew that Garron would not leave the orc city to their own fate if he believed he could do something to help.

Onward they flew. Two complete Griffin Guard squadrons headed to defend an orc city that, only a year ago, would have defended itself against them.

Belguv shook Smarlo's shoulder, stirring the mage from his slumber. Smarlo wiped at his face and stared blearily at the big orc.

"What?" he mumbled. "Was I asleep?"

"Yes," Belguv said quietly.

Smarlo glanced toward the window and realized evening was drawing the world into a cool night. His eyes widened in panic as he jumped to his feet.

"It's alright," the Scar Squadron commander said. "The Guard was spotted just a moment ago. They crested the south ridge and will draw to the edge of the city, shortly. I have already sent a few riders out to greet them and help them set up camp. The few I could spare."

"Thank you, Belguv," Smarlo said. "We should get out there."

Belguv held out a big hand to stay him. "Take a moment," he said pointing to the edge of his lip by one of his tusks.

Smarlo nodded, again thanking the orc, and wiped the drool off his face. "I'll be out there shortly," Smarlo said.

Belguv left him, and Smarlo looked down at himself to make sure he wasn't as disheveled as he felt. *How does Karnak always appear as a strong leader?* he wondered. Then again, Karnak was the son of Plak, Calrok's previous gar, and had been raised to do so.

The mage dragged his hand across the desk and the open book. It dawned on him that it was the tome Master Tan-Kro had never let him read. It was the same one the Master Mage was scouring for information while Smarlo and Ralowyn were sifting through the rest of the library.

Smarlo supposed he would have to read the book when things settled down in the city. It was his now, after all. He noted the topic title at the top of the open page: "Dark Tongue and the Underrock."

The orc mage scanned the page quickly, his eyes widening. As soon as he finished the page, he dashed from the room.

Garron helped the Guard orient their camp on the southern edge of the city. The man felt awkward seeing so many familiar faces. Men and women—warriors with whom he'd charged into battle, but that was before he'd betrayed them and their city while he was their sworn protector and king.

One of the guardians glanced at Garron as she walked by with bundles of tent cloth. The split second felt like an eternity. He wondered if other guardians were looking at him. Wondered if they were judging him, disgusted by the traitor.

Suddenly, Ezel nudged him. Garron glanced around quickly, wondering how long he'd been frozen there.

"Come," the gnome gestured. *"You can help me with the poles."* He paused for a moment when Garron didn't immediately follow. *"Are you alright?"*

"I betrayed them all," Garron signed. *"I was supposed to protect them. I was supposed to lead them. Our friends ... their friends and brothers and sisters died because of me."*

Ezel's face scrunched, and he stepped closer to the man as guardians passed behind the little gnome, standing twice his height.

"I would remind you that you were under the control of a wicked sorcerer, but I doubt that will ease the guilt. Instead, I'll suggest that you would be abandoning them now if you decided you couldn't be here among them. You can't do anything about what happened in the past, but you can give them everything you have with a choice right now."

Garron sighed. Ezel was right, he knew. The man peered around, and though he expected many to be standing around gawking at him, none were. Guardians walked about, accomplishing their tasks, each one lending a hand. Slowly, he looked back at the deep gnome.

Ezel smiled at him and turned to lead the man toward some equipment with which they could provide aid.

The Guardian camp was set up quickly, and several of the Calrok locals helped erect makeshift stables for the griffins. No one was quite sure how the wyverns of the Scar Cliffs would react to so many griffins coming into the area, so setting the camp on the south side of the city had the least chance of forcing a potential issue.

When Garron saw his cousin, looking regal in his kingly armor, he smiled. When Pernden noticed him, he quickly wrapped up orders to a captain of one of the squadrons and swiveled to greet Garron with a hug.

"Are you alright?" Pernden asked in his ear.

"I am," Garron said. "I doubt anyone will find the Guard's presence here an easy transition, but the orcs have treated Ellaria, Ezel, and I well. No doubt, Merrick and Ralowyn made a good impression on the people and made it easy for them to accept outsiders in small quantities.

Pernden asked, "Has Smarlo been handling the preparations well?"

"The orcs listen to him well. No one questions his authority. He has been Gar Karnak's right hand for many years."

Pernden scratched his cheek. "How is the gar's wife handling everything?"

Garron looked at his cousin with admiration. *Even on the eve of battle, you worry about the family of a missing orc gar.* "She is strong," he told him. "She has been a gracious host, and I've come to be fond of her company."

"Good," Pernden said. "I would like to express my gratitude for her hospitality to my kin and my condolences for her difficulties. First, we have to meet with the leaders to figure out where the Guard can best reinforce the city. Where is Smarlo?"

Garron shook his head with a slight shrug. "He left us hours ago, saying he needed to go to Calrok's mage library for something. I don't know what."

Ezel stepped up to the two men, signing to Garron and then pointing to the sky.

"Oh," Garron said, spinning. "They approach now."

"Good," Pernden said. "Ezel, would you mind grabbing High Commander Mattness? She needs to be in the meeting with us."

"Of course," the gnome flourished and hustled away.

"King Pernden," Ellaria said, oddly tentative for the normally direct woman. Garron watched her as she asked, "Any news of me brother?"

Pernden pressed his lips together and shook his head. "No. I'm sorry. Argus thinks the *Sellena* and her crew are still alive, but we have not been able to get word from them in a few days. He thinks they moved out of the magical range of the shells. He's still in Whitestone searching the tomes and scrolls in the dungeons."

Garron made an odd face. "Sorry about that."

"Not at all." Pernden waved away his worry. "Apparently, working in the dim light reminds the dwarf of Kalimandir."

"I suppose so," Garron said with the hint of a smile.

Something caught the king's eye, and he stepped sideways to see around Garron. "They're coming in for a landing. I'll go and greet them. Join us in the command tent?"

"We will," Garron affirmed, as Pernden hurried away.

Garron turned toward Ellaria, unable to imagine the worry the woman must be working through. Her green eyes passively watched the king greeting the orc mage. Garron guessed that, though her eyes were pointed in that direction, they were really far off in her own thoughts.

"Are you alright?" he asked, touching her elbow gently. He didn't want to startle her, but the slight touch jarred her back to the present. He looked deep into her emerald eyes and asked again. "Are you alright?"

The woman pushed her wild red hair out of her face, and her nose twitched as she held back forming tears. "He'll be alright," she said, seemingly trying to convince herself. "Orin and Coal and Nera and Ralowyn. They're all out there looking for him."

Garron flinched at the mention of his cousin. He knew Orin and Ellaria had been through much on their journey from Tamaria to Whitestone. Journeys like that can bond people in deep ways. Garron caught his jealous line of thought and cursed himself for thinking such a stupid thing. Orin was out there somewhere, possibly in danger. And Ellaria was here in pain, on the eve of battle.

Ezel, he thought. *Why did you have to put such an idea in my head?* He would have to have another, more heated, conversation with the gnome later. Until then, he turned his attention to Ellaria.

"Let's get into the command tent," he said, ushering her in that direction. "The meeting will take your mind off those worries, and we can focus on what we *can* help with."

She nodded her assent, and the two moved through the bustling camp toward the command tent.

Smarlo explained all the measures he'd put into motion. Discussion followed about how the Guard could best serve the city's needs.

"Men cannot see in the dark like orcs can," Smarlo said, bluntly. "We need every orc in the mines, fighting. If one of your squadrons watches over the sea to ensure we aren't attacked from there, the other can watch the mine entrance, should the enemy force prove too difficult to stop down below."

"Why don't we close the mines? Surely, you could collapse the entrance, and then the force would have no way into the city," Commander Mattness said.

"Unfortunately, that is not an option," Smarlo said.

"Certainly, the mine can't be worth more than your people's lives," Pernden said. "Whitestone can help rebuild your markets through trade."

"It's not that," Smarlo rejected the notion. "I just read in a book that Master Tan-Kro left open on his desk that dark tongue inscriptions have been found in areas of the Underrock all over Drelek for centuries. We don't know how many there are or what all of them say. If we close up the mine, the enemy force could end up surfacing ... well, anywhere!"

"So, we must engage them here," Garron said. "This is the only beacon we know about. This is our best chance at fighting them off. Anywhere else we'd be reacting. At least here, we can prepare to defend."

Ezel signed something to Garron.

"Right," the man said, turning to Smarlo. "What about the magic we used to allow me to see in the mines?"

"I can cast the enchantment on as many guardians as possible—maybe even a whole squadron. But it will only last for a day at most. Then their regular vision would return, and they'd be blind in the dark."

"Then we protect you, so that if the battle wages longer than that, you can revitalize the spell," Pernden said.

"Perhaps," Smarlo hemmed. "But the other squadron will need to watch the sea."

"Absolutely," Commander Mattness said. "They will guard it as if it were their own home."

"I appreciate that," Smarlo nodded to the woman. "The miners have been working day and night to close the most likely routes to the Underrock, but there are so many, it will be hard to tell which ones they'll be coming from."

Pernden asked, "Is there a way we can force them into a tunnel of our choosing? Set a trap for them?"

"Gert Section Chief Kag is doing his best to make sure they enter into a chamber that he and I have been in before. Large, troll-sized mounds cover the cavern floor. They should provide us with some cover," Smarlo explained.

"High Commander," Pernden said. "I'll lead the 4th Squadron down into the mines with our allies while you lead the 7th here above."

"That is not going to happen," Mattness said firmly, stepping toward him. "I will be leading the 4th into the mines, and you will stay above with the 7th. I cannot allow you to put yourself into such danger."

Smarlo's eyes widened as the king stepped uncomfortably close to the woman.

"High Commander," the king said. "I am the king of Whitestone—"

"Exactly why I can't allow it," she said. "You are too important to the future of our people."

"Every guardian is important!" Pernden shouted.

"That!" Garron butted in. "That is why you need to be protected. You sometimes seem more like my father than I am. He was a king who cared about everyone. It did not matter their station. That is the kind of king Whitestone needs to lead it into the future."

"You think I would leave my cousin to go into the depths of the mines to fight by himself?" Pernden turned his anger onto the man.

"I won't be by myself," Garron retorted.

"I will protect him," the High Commander said.

"As will I," Ellaria added.

The deep gnome also waved his hands.

"No one needs to protect me. I will fight alongside our allies, and we will be victorious," Garron spat.

The king was fuming, and Smarlo wasn't sure whether to step in or let the men sort it out themselves. *Men can be so impetuous sometimes,* the orc mage thought.

"I won't let you go in there to die!" Pernden shouted back.

"You don't always have to be the hero," Garron said. "You need to be a king."

The tent fell silent, and Pernden looked to Ellaria for help. The woman hesitated, and Smarlo stepped in before the argument could get any uglier. "I must agree," the orc mage said. "It will be important for you and the other leaders of Tarrine to unite against the Kelvur forces if we are overcome."

"And if we all die down there, you'll have plenty of chances to be a hero in the battles to come," Garron chided.

Smarlo flinched. He didn't think that statement would help calm the situation. To his surprise, the young king straightened and addressed those gathered, in a more even tone.

"I will ride with the 7th to the Scar Cliffs. I will not sit here in camp," the king said with some finality.

"We can all agree with that, I think," Smarlo said, glancing around at the others to make sure none of them rekindled their argument. When no one said anything, the orc mage continued, "I'll cast the cantrip on each of the guardians as they enter the mines. That way we can get the most out of it before the spell wears off. We can do that at first light, once everyone has had time to rest. When we're done here, I need to use the Shell of Callencia to reach out to Deklahn, King Genjak's mage adviser. The king has been traveling around Drelek, but he needs to know about the possibility of the army using the Underrock to reach other Drelek cities. They will need to send orcs and goblins out to search for the other beacons. I'll get—"

Suddenly, the Scar Squadron's youngest orc, Targ, burst through the tent entrance.

"Something's coming!" he said between heaving breaths.

"What?" Belguv asked, grabbing at the young orc. "What do you mean?"

"Noises." Targ huffed out. "Lots of them." He gulped another breath and added, "Coming from the Underrock!"

Chapter Thirty-Two

No More Hiding

O nce Vorenna came out of her rage, she seemed exhausted, as though she had used up some deep reserve inside her. Karnak introduced the Javelin leader to their friends from Tarrine.

"This is Coal, a son of Kalimandir. I don't remember how the dwarf clans are separated, but he is a true friend."

Coal stepped forward and bowed his head slightly. "Pleasure, ma'am."

Vorenna looked the dwarf up and down, her hazel eyes glinting with something Karnak hadn't seen from the barbarian woman before. Coal's eyebrows popped in surprise, and he blushed.

"This is Ralowyn." The orc continued the introductions. "Daughter of Elderwood Forest, elf mage of Loralith."

The barbarian woman tore her eyes away from the dwarf to look upon the elf woman. She nodded a greeting.

"This is Orin, a son of Whitestone. Member of the famed Griffin Guard," the orc said, gesturing to the man.

"Karnak—" Orin said, dabbing at his soaked shirt. When the orc realized it was blood, he checked the man for wounds. Orin winced but pushed away. "It's fine. I'll be alright. Mostly a flesh wound."

"We can get someone to bandage you up, right away," Vorenna said, poking her head out the tent door and ushering instructions to the guards.

"Thank you," Orin said. "But I was trying to say that the assassin got away."

"Right," Coal said. "Sneaky little snake disappeared between some tents, and we couldn't find him."

"Is he still here?" Ralowyn asked, worried.

"No," Vorenna comforted them. "The snake will slither back to his master." She stole a glance at the body of her former second-in-command lying on the ground.

"Was he from the Sons of Silence?" Karnak asked.

"We can only assume. I imagine the assassin is running back to Ventohl, as we speak," the Javelin leader spat.

"What are we going to do?" Karnak asked.

"We'll march on Ventohl at first light. I mean to end this," Vorenna growled. "They're a relentless foe. They will not stop until they've gotten into the very heart of our group and torn us apart from within. They know where we are, and they will never leave us alone. There can be no more hiding."

Karnak said, "We'll need weapons."

"We will go with you to meet the sorcerer's forces," Merrick affirmed.

"I'll go too. I'll stand right by your side, lad," Coal butted in.

Vorenna studied the group curiously. "You would all stand with us and fight?"

"Jaernok Tur seeks to conquer us all," Karnak explained. "He attacked us in Tarrine already. We were able to repel him then, but he's searching for something powerful. Whatever it is, our best chance to finish him for good is to take him down now, before he finds it. He won't relent. He won't stop until he's conquered Kelvur and Tarrine. Your war is our war. We face an enemy we can't defeat on our own."

Without a word, Vorenna walked over to Feliketh's body. She ripped the sword out of the elf and turned back toward the group.

"This is a fine sword. Though," she glanced down to the elf and then at the orc. "I think the armor might be too small for you. But the huntsman can wear it."

"I prefer to be light and agile," Merrick said. "Perhaps there is an extra spear I can use? And a bow?"

Karnak smirked at the man. Merrick knew his strengths. The huntsman had made the right requests. "And I prefer an axe," the orc said, though a pang of longing hit him. No axe was like *Dalkeri*. "But I'll take the sword, too."

Vorenna took a few steps and handed Karnak the sword. She glanced over to Coal and asked, "Do you need anything, Master Coal?"

The dwarf looked side to side as he blushed. "I've got my hammer, ma'am. Thank you."

"Well, if you do," Vorenna said, leaning down to get closer to him. "You do let me know."

"Yes, ma'am," the dwarf said, awkwardly.

"Handsome dwarf like you deserves nothing but the best."

Coal flushed.

Karnak and Merrick glanced at one another, each sporting an amused grin. Neither of them had expected to see such a side to the barbarian woman.

Vorenna straightened and addressed them all. "It is late, and you should get some rest. Tomorrow, we march on Ventohl. Welcome to Javelin."

Outside the tent under the calm night sky, old friends reunited with relieved greetings and hugs. Merrick was happy to see Orin and Coal as they slapped him on the back and shook his hand. The huntsman laughed as the great orc lifted and squeezed Ralowyn in a mighty hug. She looked so beautiful when she smiled and her silvery hair went flying.

Merrick excused himself from the other two and tapped Karnak's shoulder. "May I?"

"Of course," Karnak said with a wide grin. The orc turned to greet the others.

Ralowyn's head tilted to the side, making her pointed ear slice between the silvery strands of her hair. Merrick stepped close to her and used a finger to draw the hair behind her ear like she always did.

"I was worried about you," he said quietly.

"I was worried about you," she said, scrunching her face. Her nose crinkled when she made that face. Merrick always loved that. "You look thin."

"Let's just say, they didn't feed us very well while we were caged. Javelin has been feeding us much better, though." He grinned.

A smile flashed across her face. Her teeth were brilliantly white in the moonlight. Merrick wondered if she looked bad in any light. He couldn't imagine it. He was sure the moon and stars existed to bathe her in their dazzling light.

"I am glad to find you alright," she said.

"Yeah." Merrick shrugged sideways. "Much better now. What took you so long?"

Ralowyn's eyebrow shot up in mock surprise, but her smile was undeniable.

Merrick pressed closer to her. On their journey, he'd thought over and over about the moment he'd see Ralowyn again. He had always been too nervous to share his feelings for her before. He was only a huntsman from Tamaria—a nobody. She was an elf mage from the woodland realm of Loralith. But after everything he'd endured, the huntsman didn't care anymore. He wasn't going to waste the moment.

He reached his hand up and cupped the side of her lovely face with tenderness. The elf's skin was soft as silk on his fingers. Ralowyn's eyes met his, and she pressed her cheek into his hand as though she'd missed his touch. That was the only indication he needed. He wrapped his other hand around her waist and drew her close enough to kiss. And kiss her, he did.

"Nice ..." The approving voice of the dwarf said.

Not drawing away from Ralowyn quite yet, Merrick turned to see Coal, Orin, and Karnak, nudging each other and watching the man and the elf with grins on their faces.

"Oh, don't let us interrupt you," Orin said with a smirk.

"No," Coal agreed. "Though I knew it all along."

"You did not," Orin rolled his eyes at the dwarf.

"I did," he emphasized.

"Tanessa has been telling me this was going to happen," Karnak added. "She made me bet when they would finally kiss. Does it count if we're all the way in Kelvur, or will it only count when we get back to Tarrine. You know how wild journeys can play with emotions."

"Oh, it counts," Orin said.

"It definitely counts," Coal agreed.

"I guess she wins then," the orc grumbled.

"Alright, alright," Merrick said.

He looked at Ralowyn, still smiling at the others.

In that moment, Merrick decided these people really were his family, just like Karnak said. The huntsman thought it odd how, even on the eve of battle, they could have so much joy and fellowship.

Ralowyn turned back to him with a twinkle in her eye.

"I suppose," Merrick said to her. "We should kiss again—to make sure it counts."

The elf smiled and leaned in again.

Later that night, Orin sat up, unable to sleep. He stretched his arms and dabbed at the bandaging wrapped around him. It reminded him of when Ellaria had bandaged him so long ago. He smiled at the memory. *Boy,* he thought. *I could go for her magic healing right about now. This would be nothing for her.*

Orin hadn't gotten to talk to her in a while. With him traveling with Coal and Ezel to the south of Tarrine in search of folks to establish Kane Harbor and her training with Silverwing at the Grand Corral, they hadn't spent much time together. He'd have to enjoy a meal with her at the Corral when he returned to Whitestone. Ellaria was like a sister to him, and he missed her company.

The moonlight soaked through the tent's cloth, allowing Orin to see quite well as he surveyed the tent. Ralowyn lay on the other pallet bed, snoring softly. Coal and Karnak looked like breathing mounds of blankets on the ground. Merrick was rolled in a blanket on the ground between the two pallets.

Merrick, Orin thought. *He never would have been in this place if it weren't for me. None of them would have.*

Suddenly, the huntsman stirred on the ground. His eyes opened slowly as he inspected Orin's looming figure. "Sorry," Orin whispered hastily, realizing he might look menacing sitting high on the pallet above the man. "Did I wake you?"

"No," Merrick whispered back. "Bad dream."

Orin nodded. He'd had his fair share of bad dreams over the years. War has a peculiar way of coming back at night. Orin had been trained as a warrior, though. He couldn't imagine what the huntsman was going through.

"I'm sorry," he said to Merrick.

Merrick didn't sit up. "It's fine. You didn't wake me."

"No." Orin shook his head. "Not for that."

Merrick squinted through the dark, trying to see Orin through his bleary eyes. "What do you mean?"

Orin sighed. "I mean for everything. For everything I've put your family through. Especially you and Ellaria."

"What are you talking about?" Merrick asked quietly. He sat up and rubbed his eyes, leaning his back against the pallet bed that Ralowyn slept in. He smirked as he heard the familiar snoring he'd gotten used to hearing from the other room in Karnak's cottage.

"Think about it," Orin said. "You never would have gotten into this whole mess if it weren't for me."

Merrick stifled a chuckle. "You can't honestly think that."

"If your sister never found me, you never would have helped me get home. We never would have gotten separated and nearly killed. You never would have shot the sorcerer with an arrow, and you wouldn't be here now. Neither would the rest of them," Orin said, stretching out his hand to indicate everyone in the tent.

The huntsman nodded with a smile. "I also never would have learned to fly. I never would have been the first man in generations to enter the halls of Loralith or meet with their king and queen. I never would have met her." Merrick paused and gazed at the beautiful elf woman, snoring away. He smirked and turned back to Orin. "I never would have gone to see the city by the sea and live with the orcs. I never would have learned how fierce and loyal and loving and stubborn they can be. I never would have learned how much we are alike. Where you see blame, I see a whole new life."

"But everything you've been through …" Orin said.

"I've gone through with friends and people who love me." The huntsman shrugged. "And we'll go through more. Though I wouldn't have minded if you guys got here a little sooner."

Orin opened his mouth to reply but saw the grin growing across the huntsman's face.

"Look," Merrick continued. "Everyone goes through difficult times in life. Granted, some are more difficult than others. But that doesn't matter. What matters is how we look at it and how we tackle the challenges as they come. And frankly, I'm glad my friends are here with me. I wouldn't trade that for anything."

Orin dipped his chin and shook his head. "You are something else. When I first met you, I didn't know what to make of you."

"I was going through some stuff," Merrick admitted.

"But look at you now."

"It's funny how people can make each other better," the huntsman said.

"Yes. It is," Orin agreed.

After a moment of silence between them, Merrick lay back down and pulled the blanket around himself.

"We better get some rest," he said. "Tomorrow brings another new challenge for us to overcome."

"Yes. Sleep well, brother," Orin replied.

Merrick rolled over, tightening the blanket even more. Suddenly, his head popped up, and he looked back at Orin. "Oh, by the way," he said. "Coal says you're quite the sailor now?"

Orin grinned. High praise from the dwarf. "I may be getting the hang of it. There is a simplicity and a peace to it that I enjoy."

"Good," Merrick said with a yawn. "That's good."

Orin lay back on the pallet bed. He stared at the canvas above him, blue in the moon's glow. The soft rippling of the fabric at the beckon of the wind made it appear as rolling waves. He smiled to himself. *Coal thinks I'm turning into quite the sailor?* he mused. *Maybe I'll have to do some more sailing when all this is over.*

After a while, the man drifted off to sleep, sailing the seas to distant and undiscovered lands, if only in his dreams.

CHAPTER THIRTY-THREE

SHIFTING TIDES

The assassin cried as his body wrenched in pain. Hazkul Bern rubbed his eyes and temples. The elf was beyond frustrated. The huntsman was proving to be rather annoying, though Hazkul was more perturbed by the orc. Gar Karnak was becoming a thorn in the elf's side. This was the third time the huntsman had been within their grasp and, somehow, had slipped through their fingers yet again.

Fingers ... Hazkul thought. *Ah yes.*

He flicked his fingers out, and Chadwa drew her wand closer to herself, relieving the assassin from the agonizing hex.

"Tell me again what happened," Hazkul said. "And this time, let's hope I enjoy your story better."

The assassin, a human, gulped. He'd already told the elf the story, but Hazkul Bern hadn't liked it. The elf smirked, wondering how or if the man would change the story. He waited patiently, enjoying the man's internal torment.

"I had the huntsman in my grasp, with my dagger pressed to his throat."

"Good so far," Hazkul said, flippantly. The assassin was sticking to his story. *Brave.*

"But the orc was awake. He was growling at me when an elf walked into the tent."

"Right. And what did the elf look like again?"

"He had dark skin. He was bald. Medium armor," the man listed.

Hazkul knew who it was—Feliketh, a Son of Silence in disguise to keep Ventohl apprised of the group's movements. Hazkul Bern hadn't shared that information with the sorcerer, and if this all played out the way he thought it might, he would have to spin a tale of his own.

"Go on," the elf said, his dark brows shifting as he glared at the man.

"Well, the elf turned on the orc." The man obviously didn't know that Feliketh was a plant. Hazkul was so very good at secrets. "But a dwarf came into the tent. And then another elf, but she was different. She had magic. Knocked me clear away. I sliced another man in my escape."

The elf pressed his lips together in disappointment. "And why did you not stay and make another attempt on the huntsman?"

"Well, as I said already ..." the man grumbled.

Chadwa raised her wand, and the man wrenched to the side.

"Oh dear," Hazkul said. "Chadwa really didn't like that tone. Would you like to try again?"

The elf raised his hand, and the witch lowered her wand once more. The man heaved forward in a coughing fit. He pressed himself to his knees again and rolled his shoulders, straightening and protruding his jaw.

Very brave, Hazkul mused.

"I waited and watched for them to return, but I heard their conversations as I stayed hidden. They were flanked by four guards, too." Chadwa started to raise her wand, but the man lifted his hands in surrender, continuing, "But ... but I thought the fact that they are marching on Ventohl this day was of more importance than the huntsman."

Hazkul stroked his smooth chin thoughtfully. The elf was glad the man had returned with such news. It proved his loyalty to the Sons of Silence. Frankly, Hazkul Bern cared little for Jaernok Tur's wants and desires. The elf saw the orc mage as a means to an end. The orc was riding a wave of destruction, and Hazkul didn't want to get caught in it. The only way to survive it was to go with the wave.

"You've done well, Nihel," he said to the man. The assassin eyed his leader, suspiciously. "Come now, Nihel. Think about it. You've proven yourself loyal to the Sons of Silence, which is the only right thing to do. You brought us critical information about an imminent attack. Plus, if the huntsman is with them, you might as well take the credit for forcing them to hand deliver him to us."

Hazkul pursed his lips at the notion. *That wouldn't do.*

He whipped his hand toward Chadwa. The witch lifted her wand again, and the man screamed in agony. He writhed on the floor for a few seconds before the sickening snap of crunching bones sounded and his body stopped moving altogether.

Hazkul sighed as he walked to the window. Below, geldrin forces gathered and organized themselves. He missed the good old days when he didn't have geldrins crawling all over Ventohl. To be honest, he was getting a little tired of everyone depending on him. *Remember when I just got paid to kill people?* he thought. *Things were simpler then. Nobody ever bothered me. They just said, 'Hey, we'll give you coin if you'll kill this noble for me.'*

A couple of geldrins punched at each other in the courtyard. The sorcerer's insistence on keeping a group of them at Ventohl annoyed the elf. Almost as much as that orc from Tarrine.

Chadwa stepped next to him and gazed out the window. Her dark eyes looked creepy in the morning light.

"Chadwa, my dear," Hazkul said. "What have we found ourselves in the middle of?"

The witch didn't answer.

"Yes," the elf continued. "Every which way we look, a storm is brewing. The waves are tossing and turning. It's hard to see which way the tides are shifting."

Hazkul sighed again and turned to leave the room. He needed to find Commander Chol. The commander was going to lead the geldrins in defending Ventohl, an honor the commander begged for, and which Hazkul was happy to give him. *Any possible way to earn favors,* he thought. Meanwhile, Hazkul, himself, would lead the Sons of Silence. It was going to be a long day.

He stumbled but caught himself as he tripped over the limp hand of the dead assassin, still lying on the floor.

"Would you have someone clean this up?"

Chadwa shot him a look.

"What?" Hazkul shrugged. "It's better than talking to our resident geldrin commander."

The witch did not seem to think so, but Hazkul knew the face she made was her way of saying the task would get done. He swiveled on his heels and strode from the room.

CHAPTER THIRTY-FOUR

GUARDIANS OF CALROK

G riffins landed hastily, dropping off their riders near the entrance to Calrok's deep mines. Each guardian received the charm that would aid their vision in the vast darkness of the caverns below. Smarlo waved them on as soon as each was ready. Garron, Ezel, and Ellaria, with the help of a miner, led them down the twisting mine corridors and into the darkness.

Smarlo continued to cast the charm on each guardian as they landed and approached. High Commander Mattness assured him there were only a few more and then the two of them could join the group sprinting to the caverns below. With any luck, they would make it to the designated cavern before the enemy arrived. Unfortunately, sound carried and bounced around the Underrock caverns, and it would be impossible to tell how far away the army was or how long it would take them to get to the ambush cavern.

When the last guardian was done and sent in to chase the others, Smarlo turned to Mattness, who was already bowing her head and waiting for his touch. He quickly murmured the words, placing his long green fingers on her head.

"Alright," he said. "We need to get in there."

"Right," she replied. The two disappeared into the entrance cavern.

371

Along the way, Smarlo quickly checked in with each relay orc. They'd set up a relay system in order to get messages from the caverns below to the surface in a hurry. It worked brilliantly, but they'd had to call half the orcs down to the fight, leaving extra space between the ones left.

"There are guardians at the entrance. They're our last line of defense," he hurriedly explained to each of them. "If the forces from below break through, stop at nothing to warn them."

Every time he said it to another of the relay orcs, a pit grew in his stomach. The thought of an enemy force overwhelming them in the caverns was terrifying. It would be far worse if the force flooded onto the city of Calrok. Civilians and orclings would be in danger, and Smarlo couldn't bear the thought of Tanessa and Gernot having to fight off more of the gravel-faced creatures, though he wasn't sure the force would be made up of the creatures. Perhaps the army was made up of worse monsters. The thought spurred the orc mage to sprint faster.

Pernden barked orders at the guardians flying toward the edge of the Scar Cliffs by the sea. He'd split the 7th Squadron into two, taking command over the half flying to the designated perch for them to watch over the harbor. He let their captain command the other half that was sprawled around the entrance to the mine.

The king nudged Rocktail into a descent toward the cliff edge where two wyvern riders watched. *They don't know the battle is on,* Pernden thought as he glided toward them. The wyverns bucked and wriggled their long necks at the approaching griffins. Their orcish riders attempted to calm them.

Rocktail clicked and roiled his shoulder blades, anxiously. "Easy there," the king said, patting the griffin's neck. "They're our allies this time, remember?"

The two wyvern riders did their best to settle their mounts, but Pernden chose not to land, thinking it better not to force the beasts into close proximity.

He shouted to the orcs, "The battle is on! We've been sent to take watch over the city. We do not see in the dark as well as you and your kin. They need every available orc warrior in the mines."

The orcs looked at each other and discussed something too quietly for Pernden to hear.

"I assure you; we will give our very lives for the city if the sacrifice is required to save them," he shouted. "Your kin need you."

The orcs accepted the notion, and their wyverns rolled over the edge of the cliff into dives.

Pernden exhaled a sigh of relief. The last thing they needed was infighting. As he guided Rocktail to the foremost point of the perch, the sincerity with which he'd promised the orcs protection struck him. He had not made it loosely or without conviction. No. He meant it. The guardians would give their own lives to defend the people of Calrok. It was a rather strange notion that he was the first king of Whitestone to offer such a promise to an orc city.

He thought back to what he had said to Edford. *Shared battle forges a bond between people that is not easily broken. This will likely only solidify that, assuming we win.*

Pernden glanced around at the guardians with him, each a stalwart member of their order. He would gladly fight alongside any of them.

A young guardian, the newest addition to the 7th Squadron, rode her griffin toward the edge near Pernden. From that angle, she'd be able to see the other side of the ridge. The king expected she was on one of her first missions.

"Don't be afraid," Pernden said. "Remember your training, and it will guide you."

"I'm not afraid, my King," she said. "We will see victory here."

Her confident reply wasn't arrogant but rather convinced. "What is your name, guardian?"

"Wendi," she said, but quickly added, "my King."

Pernden shook his head with a chuckle. "Well, Wendi, you remind me of the toughest guardian I know."

"Who's that?" she asked, sitting taller in her saddle.

"Captain Nera," he replied.

The young guardian beamed. "I hope to live up to your high praise, my King. She is fierce."

"Fiercest woman I know," the king agreed. "And I have no doubt you will perform admirably this night." Pernden turned to the rest of the guardians, ten in total. "Guardians, we must keep a wary eye on the city. Look for anything out of place. The enemy could also come from the sea. We will not let this city fall."

The guardians lifted grunts in affirmative reply.

Good, Pernden thought. *Now, let us find this enemy that would sneak around in darkness.*

When Garron finally entered the designated cavern where they intended to ambush the incoming forces, he slid to a halt.

The entire area was silent, and he shuddered to think what that might mean. He narrowed his eyes, searching for signs of anyone, but saw nothing, even with his enchantment-enhanced vision. He strained his ears, wondering if perhaps the battle had been forced into another cavern, but he heard nothing. Ezel and Ellaria crept into the cavern behind him, also keenly aware of the silence.

Ezel motioned toward a large stone stalagmite. A troll of similar size hugged the massive stone trying to blend into it. Garron nodded to the gnome. It was one of the few trolls that lived in Calrok.

Suddenly, a silent motion on the left caught their attention; they hustled toward the waving orc. It was Belguv.

"Why is it so quiet?" Garron whispered as low as he could.

"We don't know," the orc exhaled back. "The noise grew louder and louder. We think they are coming from that direction," he said, pointing across the cavern.

"Well, where are they?"

"The noise was getting louder, and right when we thought they were about to enter the cavern, everything went silent."

"Have you sent anyone to scout the tunnels?" Garron asked.

"No. We didn't want them to hear us and realize we're waiting for them." The orc shook his head.

"I'll go," the man said.

Ezel grabbed him by the arm. *"You're not going without me,"* he signed.

"Or me," Ellaria signed as well.

Garron nodded. *Actually, this might work,* he thought.

"Belguv, the three of us can scout it. We can sign to each other, so we don't have to make any noise," the man insisted.

The grizzled orc looked at the man, unsure. "We don't even know what's coming for us."

375

"That's why we need to scout it out."

Belguv hesitated until several guardians entered the chamber and halted, looking confused. "Fine," the orc said. He slapped a large green hand on the man's shoulder. "Don't get yourself killed before the battle even starts."

"We won't," Garron assured him.

"I need to organize these grunts," he said, indicating the growing gaggle of guardians.

Garron, Ezel, and Ellaria crept through the silent cavern, weaving around the troll-sized stalagmites. They received bewildered glances from orcs hidden behind stalagmites, but Garron nodded to each as they passed in silence. They rounded another stalagmite, where a particularly nervous goblin hid, and found themselves standing before a wide tunnel opening. It looked more like a large crack in the vast stone wall, running all the way up to the shadows of the stalactite-pocked ceiling.

"This must have been one of the tunnels that proved too difficult for the miners to close in time," Ezel signed.

Garron's heart beat like a drum inside his chest. Though his eyes were enhanced with enchantment, it was hard to see down the tunnel without wading into its darkness. The dark vision only allowed him to see a certain range before obscurity took over again. Ezel nudged him, taking the lead position and starting down the tunnel. As Ellaria tried to pass, Garron stepped ahead, hoping to shield her from whatever might be waiting for them down the tunnel.

The little gnome walked slowly but evenly, looking all around as they continued. The tunnel widened and narrowed and widened again. The ceiling was blackness above, too high to see in the dark. Offshoot tunnels and corridors stretched out to who knows where, and the occasional alcove caused them to slow for inspection.

Finally, they reached a widened part of the tunnel and were surprised to find rope ladders hanging on the walls. There were at least a dozen of them. Garron grabbed at one of the ladders. It was sturdy. *"Is it possible they climbed to another tunnel from here that would lead them to the surface?"* he signed.

"Maybe," Ellaria signed back.

"I don't know," Ezel added, seeming unconvinced.

A sudden cracking noise down the tunnel from whence they came grabbed their attention.

Ezel strode several steps back down the tunnel and illuminated his magic. The gnome glowed like a blue lantern in the darkness, bathing everything in a moonish hue. Something skittered between stalactites on the ceiling.

Garron ran to meet the gnome, and Ezel pointed up as they hurried down the tunnel. They slowed to a jog, so as not to trip on anything, then they saw another. They only saw feet disappearing among the stone teeth which hung above. Ellaria drew a shimmering emerald arrow and let it fly toward the ceiling. It struck something with the sound of an arrow hitting flesh rather than stone, and a horrifying screech rang out through the tunnel.

Three creatures, almost like men, dropped from the dark recesses above. One landed awkwardly and screeched at them again, an arrow protruding from its leg. Garron's eyes widened. He'd read about such creatures with their grey sickly skin. As they stumbled toward the trio with their shambling gait, evil intent was locked in their dead eyes.

"Ghouls!" he shouted. He raised his sword and rushed forward.

When Smarlo entered the designated ambush cavern and heard the quietly echoed yell of a man from somewhere deeper in the tunnels, he ran to greet Belguv.

"What's happening?" the orc mage asked.

"The man and the gnome and the woman went to scout the tunnel on the far end of the cavern."

"What? You let them go alone?"

Belguv glowered at the orc mage but bit back his rage. "They insisted, and I needed to organize the guardians that you sent muddling down here."

"What do we know?" Smarlo asked quickly, shifting the subject. The last thing they needed in the already tense situation was to vent their charged emotions on each other.

"The noises were growing louder, echoing through the tunnels, and suddenly they stopped. No warning. No sign of them since. That noise you just heard was the first one since everything went silent.

Smarlo took a few steps, High Commander Mattness shadowing him. "That tunnel?" he asked, pointing across the cavern.

"Yes," Belguv affirmed. "That's where they went."

Smarlo sighed and ran as quietly as he could toward the tunnel.

"What is it?" Mattness asked behind him.

"I don't know," he admitted.

He slid to a halt, standing before the great crack in the stone. Another echoed holler bounced through the tunnel, tickling Smarlo's long green ears. He couldn't quite make it out, but it almost sounded like a word. He waited, staring into the shadows. *Come on,* he thought. *Say it again. What are you trying to relay?*

The shout reverberated off the stone walls again, slightly closer this time. This time he caught "ing." *What "ing?"*

Another cry rang out, and he understood it. His heart dropped into his stomach, and his legs felt as though they were filling with sand. *Ceiling?* He looked up and conjured a great fireball in his hand. He spun and lobbed it into the ceiling, not hitting one of the myriad stalactites but instead scorching the flesh of a creature which screamed in horror and fell to the stone floor far below.

"They're above!" Smarlo hollered over through the cavern. "They're on the ceiling!"

Suddenly, the ceiling teemed with life, like a kicked-over anthill. Swarms of creatures climbed down the walls. Giant bat-like creatures dove straight from the stalactites, crashing onto the warriors below.

"Death wings!" Mattness cried.

"Fight! Fight!" Smarlo yelled.

The cavern erupted into mayhem.

Rocktail fidgeted, ruffling his feathers and laying them flat again. The griffin could always tell when Pernden was tense. One of the stable trainers at the Grand Corral tried to explain it to the man once, but he didn't understand. All he could remember was that griffins have higher senses than men. Somehow, the creatures were able to sense things in men before they even felt them.

The king blinked his eyes several times. He'd been straining to spot anything out of the ordinary on the Gant Sea around the city harbor. They'd been sitting there for a few hours, and nothing appeared to be concerning. In fact, it was so quiet that one would be tempted to believe there was no battle raging far below in the city's underbelly.

Every fiber of Pernden's being wished he were in the mines with his men. He couldn't explain the tug in his heart that drew him to them. The king strained hard to find attackers approaching from the sea in the hopes that he wouldn't have to endure the entire battle waiting on a cliffside. He didn't want the people of Calrok to be in danger, of course. He just hated the feeling of uselessness.

He threw his head back with a great sigh, gazing toward the stars and the moon above. The king drew in a deep breath through his nose, smelling the salty sea in the air. It was an oddly beautiful night, considering the circumstances. The land didn't care about the wars of its peoples.

Pernden strained his eyes, scanning the water and the docks far below. He saw nothing at first, but as he continued to look, he caught an ominous shadow on the waters in the pale moonlight. The calm waves that lapped into the docks creased around the shadow.

What in Finlestia? he thought, as he leaned forward to get a better view. He clicked at Rocktail and shouted back to the others as he dove off the cliff. "Be wary, guardians."

Rocktail glided easily from the cliff toward the harbor. The winds weren't particularly strong, and the pair covered the distance without any difficulty. As Rocktail flapped them toward the docks, the shadow on the water faded and wavered, but still it remained. It wasn't until Pernden and Rocktail were almost directly above it when a ship came into view.

Magnificent painted sails zipped on intricate pulleys, drawing them back and revealing the largest ship the king had ever seen.

Rocktail flapped wildly, climbing higher to get away from the surprise ship. "To arms! To arms!" Pernden shouted.

Several bells rang out from the guard towers. He knew there were only enough city watchmen to man the towers. They would, of course, leave the towers to join the fight. But the king also knew the bells were a warning to the people. At the very least, the people could defend themselves.

Pernden waved his arms at the guardians on the cliffside. They weren't able to hear him from this distance, so he hoped they got the message from his signaling. The Guard had developed many signals over the years as it was often hard to hear over the wind while flying through the air. The king held Rocktail high as the ship careened into the docks, snapping great wooden beams in half. *Their ship is either so strong that such a thing won't harm it, or they have no intention of retreat,* he thought. *Either way, they're here.*

The stone-faced creatures he'd heard about streamed off the ship and ran in all directions to meet the city watch.

"We've got to get down there," the king said to Rocktail. As he leaned in for the dive, he glanced toward the ship and noticed several of the brutes pulling frantically at the hold cover. The cover itself was bumping and seemed on the verge of exploding. As soon as there was the slightest opening, man-sized bat-like creatures burst from the hold. Dozens poured into the night sky.

"Death wings!" Pernden shouted, as he and Rocktail soared higher.

The king turned toward the cliffs, thankful to see the guardians already halfway to him. He looked to the sky. The stars shimmered, and the moon was bright. No sign of a storm. He cursed under his breath. The last time he and the Talon

Squadron faced off against death wings, the lightning from a sea storm had proven useful in fending off the savage monsters.

Pernden breathed hard and thought, *This is going to be a long night.*

Garron swung his sword, lopping the head off another ghoul that shambled viciously toward him. He cursed himself for being so dumb. Why would he think he was better equipped to scout ahead than any number of the orcs that worked in the mines or had natural dark vision? Perhaps he was trying too hard to prove to himself that he could be a hero again. Or maybe he was becoming reckless now that he didn't have anything to lose—though that wasn't entirely true. He didn't have time to think of such things, though. The only thing that mattered at that exact moment was fighting their way back to the ambush cavern to join the others.

A blue orb made of pure light blasted through the body of another ghoul next to him.

"Thank you, Ezel." He growled as he charged another—the growl more to himself than anyone else. *Can't get distracted in battle,* he thought. *Distractions get you killed. You know that. You can't be that rusty. How long has it been since you've been in a battle? No. Stop. Focus.*

He slashed through another of the dark monsters, but a death wing dropped from above with a screech. The monster landed heavily on the man, and Garron held his sword up with both hands, the blade digging through his glove and squeezing blood out of his palm. The creature snapped its wicked teeth hungrily, cutting its own neck on the outstretched blade in an attempt to eat the man's face.

An emerald arrow burst into green flame as it struck the death wing between the eyes, dropping the beast immediately. Garron heaved the heavy form of the dead monster and pushed the leathery wings off himself.

"I think we're fighting the stragglers," Ellaria shouted, hoisting the man up from the ground.

"We have to push through," Garron said quickly.

Ellaria nodded at him and ran to meet Ezel. "Hold them off for us. We only need a second."

Garron charged forward to a narrower section of the tunnel. He didn't love the limited motion it allowed him to move and chop with his sword, but it also kept his enemies coming at him in limited numbers.

A ghoul reached out its grotesque clawed hand and grabbed Garron's cloak while he stabbed his sword into another. This was bad. Really bad. He wasn't sure how they were going to get out of this one.

"Garron, duck!" Ellaria shouted from behind him.

The man swiveled to see a radiating light. Blue and green ribbons of magic swirled around each other in a mystical dance.

"Duck!" she repeated.

Garron grabbed the ghoul that held him by the cloak and dragged the monster to the floor. Before any of the other ghouls could pile on, a searing arrow of magnificent light sizzled through the air above him. He could feel the energy as it flew by, prickling the hairs on his body. The arrow barreled through ghoul after ghoul, forcing many of them to pop sickeningly. The smell of searing rotten flesh permeated the tunnel.

The ghoul on top of Garron bit his shoulder hard. The man hollered and elbowed the creature several times in the head before it released its jaws. He slammed the ghoul's head into a rock, rolled on top of it, and finished it with his sword. Thankfully, the monster had bitten his non-sword-wielding arm.

He looked up to the woman and the gnome, smiling at them weakly. Ezel extended a little hand to the man, but Garron hefted his own weight up. He turned toward the direction they needed to go and was surprised to see the ghouls clumped together, staggering over each other.

Garron smirked.

Suddenly, several of the ghouls were pushed aside as a large stone-like creature stepped out from behind them.

Garron's smirk faded.

Smarlo conjured and threw fireball after fireball. The smell of burning meat filled the cavern, and the smoky air became stifling. The orc mage downed another death wing with a magic missile and stepped around a large stalagmite. He breathed for a split second before a ghoul dove at him. High Commander Mattness sliced the creature in two as quickly as it had appeared.

Mattness had been covering Smarlo from the ground forces, while he did what he could to down the death wings. Several of the orcs and goblins toward the top side of the cavern had bows and arrows and were doing a fair job at downing the flying beasts as well.

The clanging of metal on metal rang out in high pitches over the growls, grunts, and roars that accompanied the battle. The echoes off the stone walls made the noise dizzying to listen to. The sheer number of enemies was staggering. It was hard to believe that the force was able to climb among the stalactites unnoticed.

But these are creatures of the dark. They thrive in such villainy, the orc mage thought morosely.

"Are you ready to go again?" Mattness asked, nearly out of breath and landing her shoulder hard on the stone next to him.

"Yes," Smarlo said. He was exhausted, but there was no choice. They were fighting, not only for their own lives, but for the lives of everyone in Calrok and all of Tarrine. If the enemy gained a foothold in Calrok, it would only be the beginning of their conquest.

Smarlo hoisted himself away from the stalagmite and blasted a nearby ghoul with a fireball. A terrified orc miner gave the orc mage a thankful nod. Admittedly, Smarlo was impressed the miner was still alive. The orc mage returned an approving nod of his own, and the gesture encouraged the miner. He growled and ran off to meet another lumpish ghoul.

As Smarlo examined the situation, his eyes widened. It seemed as though there were even more death wings than before. *How many are still clinging tight to the ceiling?* He didn't know. But he knew he was going to need help.

"Mattness!" he shouted as he heaved another magic missile that pierced the heart of a death wing, dropping it thirty feet to the stone floor below. "We need to get to Ezel and Ellaria. They can help me down the death wings, and then we only have to worry about the ground troops."

A stone-faced monster swung his axe at the orc mage, and Smarlo ducked, although not fast enough. A searing pain shot from his ear, throbbing through his head. Mattness drove her sword into the creature's ribs and twisted. The monster's gravelly face contorted, and he dropped to the ground.

Smarlo grabbed at his ear, blood covering his hand and dripping down his arm. Half his ear was missing!

"Are you alright?" Mattness asked.

"I-I think so," Smarlo replied, in shock.

"Then let's get to them," she said, wrenching her sword free from the dead monster.

They fought their way to the tunnel where the others had gone scouting. Waves of enemies poured out but didn't attack them directly. The ghouls and stone men scattered as though they were running from some hideous monster that rose from the Underrock.

A bright blast of energy roared from the tunnel, searing the creatures as they ran. The green and blue light exploded, sending even more of the monsters flying. A strange rumbling made the stone floor feel as though it were moving. Mattness turned to Smarlo, worry etching her face. The orc mage's eyes narrowed as Garron, Ezel, and Ellaria burst from the tunnel, stepping over dead ghouls and fighting their hearts out.

Smarlo turned to the High Commander and said quickly, "I have an idea."

Rocktail slashed at a death wing with his talons and ripped at the creature's chest with his razor-sharp beak. Pernden chopped down with his sword, Wintertide, crippling the monster's wing. The pair made short work of the monster, and Pernden was pleased to see the other guardians seemed to be handling the death wings with ease.

The ground forces were another story altogether. The city watch, or what was left of them, fought valiantly, but they were taking heavy losses. Orcs streamed from buildings all around the docks wielding whatever weapons or tools they could find to fight against the invasion force.

Pernden grunted and leaned Rocktail into a dive. They landed hard in the middle of a group of the stony monsters. Rocktail ripped several of them with his talons and beak. Pernden slid from his saddle and slashed at a nearby monster. The creature looked much bigger up close. Pernden remembered how big Karnak was. The stone creature before him seemed to be just as big.

The monster twirled his axe in his hands. A crooked sneer crossed his gravel face, and Pernden furrowed his brow. "Is that supposed to be a smile?" he quipped.

"I'll show you my real smile while I stand over your dying body, man-kin," the creature said.

Pernden's eyes widened. Smarlo had mentioned that the one they captured spoke to them, but for some reason, seeing the creatures, the king hadn't expected them to talk.

The brute dashed at the king with more agility than Pernden expected. He dodged this way and that, avoiding the axe as he parried quickly. The monster raised his axe high and swung down, aiming for Pernden's head. The king rolled to the side, slicing backward.

A blade of ice flew back at the brute's knee, separating his lower leg from the rest of his body. The stony creature looked at the king with surprise. Pernden smirked. He charged the monster whose stone face crinkled as the king ran him through with *Wintertide*.

More of the brutes surrounded the king, having seen the power of his mystic weapon and not wanting to face him alone. "Plenty to go around, fellas," Pernden said. "Who's first?"

The monsters charged, swinging their weapons and stumbling over each other in their chaotic attack. Their uncoordinated effort forced Pernden on the defensive immediately, but he pressed all his willpower into every swing of his sword, shooting blades of ice in every direction. Every parry released a splintering shard of ice that flew through the air, and several of the brutes had soon fallen to the shards.

He swiped *Wintertide* wide, sending a blade of ice cutting through the air and cleaving the midsection of one of the unfortunate creatures. Only two remained near him, and a wicked grin grew across his face. *Is that worry on their faces?* the king wondered. It was hard to tell.

Suddenly, a spear streaked through the air and crashed into Pernden's side, piercing his armor. The impact launched him from his feet and into the dirt. He clambered to one knee, quickly lifting his sword to dissuade any of the brutes from taking advantage of the surprise strike. He wrenched the spear from his side, gritting his teeth as the sharp spearhead grated against the jagged metal of his armor.

The king stood, taking a quick glance at the blood-covered spear. He blinked a few times, focusing on the wound to feel how deep it went. It was hard to tell with all the adrenaline coursing through him, but the fact that he was still standing gave him some relief. The relief drained from his face as a mountain of a man stepped between the two stony monsters.

"You fools," he said. "*Wintertide* is a weapon set apart."

"Jolan," Pernden grunted. "What are you doing here?"

The grizzled man stepped forward, and the king saw the faint remains of the crest of Whitestone on his armor. "I could ask you the same thing, Captain. The Guard in an orc city? Have you forgotten what they've taken from us?"

"Have I forgotten?" Pernden asked. "Are you serious? Have you forgotten what the sorcerer did to Whitestone?"

"You don't know the wave of destruction that comes to swallow Tarrine."

"And why would you be the herald for that destruction?" Pernden growled. "You were always a bitter and selfish man."

"Selfish? Selfish!" Jolan screamed wildly. "Everything I have done was for our people."

"Killing Danner Kane, the High Commander of our order, was for our people?"

"He was a traitor!" Jolan spat.

"You were the one who betrayed us."

"I was following the lead of my king."

"Garron?" Pernden asked in disbelief. "The sorcerer twisted my cousin's mind. You must know that. He was deceived. But we've been able to clear his mind. He's here in Calrok, defending Tarrine."

"No!" Jolan roared, stepping forward and raising his sword.

"The sorcerer has twisted your mind," Pernden yelled. "We have people who have figured out how to clear that wicked fog. They can clear your mind, too!"

"No! You can't help me," he yelled again as he repeatedly swung his sword in rage. Pernden deftly parried the swings and stepped away.

"You can help us stop all of this," the king said, waving his hand toward the mayhem. "What does the sorcerer offer you that keeps you under his power?"

"You know nothing of his power," Jolan shot back. "There are powers far greater than you know. You were always so pompous. Melkis and Kane favored you—their little protégé. But you're nothing but a young fool. Jaernok Tur knows of magics that make *Wintertide* look like a toy sword. He's learning how to bring the dead back to life."

"What?" Pernden shot the man a quizzical look. "This is about Anlon?"

Jolan charged forward with a frenzy of strikes. "You don't ever say his name!"

His furious swipes were powerful, and it took great effort on Pernden's part to avoid the large man's blade. The slashes were also wild, leaving space for the king to throw a counterstrike, slicing under Jolan's arm plates. The big man stumbled backward in surprise.

"Your son is dead," Pernden shouted. "Orin saw it with his own eyes."

"Orin is dead, too," Jolan sneered, though his face betrayed a hint of confusion.

"No," the king said. "He survived. He returned to us. He was heartbroken to hear that the commander over his squadron had betrayed the Guard."

Jolan shook his head in disbelief. "No. No, that can't be true."

"It is," Pernden said. "Do you really think the sorcerer can bring your son back? Look at his wicked magic. Even if he did manage to bring Anlon back, would you really have your son ripped from the halls of Kerathane to live under the tyranny of an evil sorcerer from Kelvur?"

"Silence!" Jolan shouted. "Just silence ..."

The man's eyes darted wildly, as though he were trying to think. Pernden didn't relent.

"Jolan, we were able to help Garron. We can help you too."

The hulking man glared at Pernden, his eyes filled with unbridled rage. He let out a sick snarl and launched himself toward the king.

Ellaria loosed another glowing emerald arrow as Garron leaned in to hear Smarlo.

"We need to get everyone back toward the entrance of the cavern. *Everyone* needs to get there. Can you help me?" the orc mage asked.

"We can certainly try," the man replied.

"Retreat!" Smarlo hollered over the din of the battle.

Echoes of the command bounced around the cavern, spurring orcs and goblins and guardians into motion. Garron dashed between massive stalagmites, slashing and cutting down ghouls as he went.

"Run back to the entrance tunnel. We need to back out of the cavern," he said to an orc. The orc didn't hesitate but hustled toward the entrance, using his axe to cut down a ghoul in his way.

Garron ran to the aid of a guardian who was engaged in a fight with one of the stony brutes. Garron didn't slow down as he wrapped the monster in a tackle. They hit the floor hard, sending the stone brute's jagged sword spiraling away on the cool stone. The guardian stabbed their enemy with her sword.

"Thanks," she said, helping Garron to his feet.

"Don't mention it," he said. "We've got to get back to the entrance."

And on it went, until Garron could not see any more of their allies among the massive stalagmites. The place still swarmed. More of their enemies had crawled down from the ceiling.

"Smarlo!" Garron yelled as he kicked a ghoul to the side. "Whatever you're going to do, you better do it now."

"You need to get over here," Smarlo shouted back.

Several more ghouls rounded nearby stalagmites and faced the man. "I'm not sure that's possible," Garron hollered, cutting one of the ghouls down.

Smarlo looked at Ellaria as Mattness and a group of guardians held the monsters at bay. "I need your help. How fast can you shoot those arrows?"

"Fast." Ellaria nodded, determined to help.

"I'm going to throw as many fireballs as I can at the ceiling, and I need you to shoot as many of those magic arrows as you can. I want to drop the ceiling on these monsters," the orc mage said.

"But what about Garron?" Ellaria shot back.

Suddenly, Ezel pushed past the woman and signed quickly to her as he dashed into the stalagmites and ghouls.

"Never mind," she said. "Let's do this."

When the blasts began exploding high above him, Garron realized he was in trouble. A stone spike cracked off the ceiling and fell, impaling a ghoul and pinning him awkwardly to the floor. The monsters all around pushed and shoved each other as splintered stalactites showered them with deadly shards. Garron found himself no longer fighting the horde but rather trying not to be trampled by their stampede. Explosion after explosion erupted on the ceiling. Fiery blasts and green bursts sent stalactites spiraling through the air and unfortunate creatures, still attempting to cling to the ceiling, plummeting to their deaths.

Garron pushed and shoved, slicing a ghoul here and there when he could maneuver his sword enough to down one of the monsters. They pressed against each other, jamming tightly between stalagmites. Others clambered to the tops of the troll-size stones. Garron was starting to feel like he couldn't breathe as they jammed together.

Suddenly, a blast of blue magic sent several of the ghouls sprawling. The man shoved a ghoul off of himself and rolled to finish the creature with his sword. Ezel appeared from around a stalagmite, his eyes and several of the runes on his arms blazing with blue faery fire.

"Let's go! They're going to bring down the ceiling!" the little gnome signed.

"Right behind you," Garron said, stumbling to his feet.

The ground shook, and the mountain above them rumbled in an ominous tone. Stalactites shook themselves loose, dropping from high above. Stone javelins pierced scattering ghouls, while bigger stalactites smashed others completely.

"Faster! Faster!" Garron shouted, scooping Ezel up and throwing the gnome on his back.

A stone-faced brute stepped in front of them, looking as scared as they felt. He hesitated, lifting his jagged sword in front of him. A stalactite blasted him through the shoulder, killing him instantly. Ezel slapped Garron wildly to get the stunned man moving again as the stone roof above them collapsed.

Pernden batted away Jolan's sword for the thirtieth time. The king was getting tired, and the wound in his side wasn't doing him any favors. Pernden had taken to evading the strikes as best he could because the large man's swings rocked the younger man's arms every time their swords clanged together. He tried to get clever a few times, using *Wintertide's* magic to aid him, but Jolan had sparred many times with the late Master Melkis in the Grand Corral and knew the sword well.

The king stumbled briefly and stood upright. He blinked a few times, wondering how much blood he'd lost. *This isn't good,* he thought. He glanced around. The other guardians had disposed of most of the death wings, and only a few chased the remaining bat-like monsters. The others were engaging the enemy on the ground. Pernden had no idea how things were going in the mines, but it looked like they might just win the battle aboveground.

"Jolan," he rasped. "It's not too late. The Guard is going to finish these troops, and this battle is over."

The big man looked around. "No," he hemmed. "No. We must win. I have to win."

"You really think you can take the sorcerer at his word? His words are poison, Jolan!"

"You don't know what he can do!"

"He twists everything. He is evil. Nothing good can come of the wicked things he does," Pernden shouted, almost pleading.

Jolan's eyes went black, and he appeared to be looking far off. The man muttered, and his face contorted as though he were having an argument with someone else. Pernden crept closer to the man, who seemed frozen in place. The king felt a wave of pity wash over him as he drew nearer to the man. The heartache on the man's face was so real.

A tear rose in Pernden's eye. He knew Jolan. He'd been a commander of the Griffin Guard. Surely, there was a way to save him.

Jolan's face reddened with anger. The rage on the man's face was proof to Pernden that the king had been wrong, so he lifted *Wintertide* and prepared to strike. Suddenly, the black drained from Jolan's eyes, and the fierce man glared at Pernden.

The king's eyes widened as he felt the stabbing pain of Jolan's sword. Pernden gulped and ran *Wintertide* into the man's side. The large man's chin quivered as he stumbled a few steps backward, pulling his sword free from the king. Pernden cried out as he fell to the ground.

He saw Rocktail swoop in and savagely attack Jolan before both faded from his field of vision. Someone screamed, but the sound seemed far off in his ears. Wendi dove to her knees next to him. His mind reeled. Wendi ripped away his armor, pressing against his wound, frantically repeating, "No."

CHAPTER THIRTY-FIVE

ALL HASTE

Nera knelt for a better look at the tracks on the dirt road. The wheel tracks ran over each other in crisscrossing angles, and footprints covered the place. "It seems there was some sort of skirmish here," she called to the others.

Shorlis checked the edge of the road where it met the forest while Tam sketched an image of a dead geldrin. "That seems fair to say," the young guardian shouted back.

Nera could say little else with certainty. She hoped none of their people had been involved in the skirmish, but there was no way to tell. She followed the wheel tracks that went off the road. Several tracks led into the woods.

"I might have something here," Nera shouted.

"Me too," Tam said.

The captain of the Talon Squadron turned to see the young guardian staring wide-eyed at the ground. "What is it?"

"Uh," he stammered. "This is hard to explain."

Nera walked over when Shorlis said, "It's a giant footprint."

"What?" she asked.

"There must be a giant with one of the groups," Shorlis explained, as if the idea of a giant among them were not out of the ordinary.

Nera gawked at the enormous print. "I thought giants an old myth."

"Me too," Tam agreed.

"Giants have been living in Kelvur for centuries. There was a lively community of them in the Eastern Knolls before the Crags erupted," Shorlis said. "Are there no giants in Tarrine?"

"No," Nera responded. "Haven't been for a long time. So long that most of us believed them to be only tales."

The chelon paused and lifted his head toward the sky as though he were trying to hear something. The guardians watched him, wondering what he sensed.

"We must get off the road," he said quietly.

They ran to the woods on the north side of the road, diving behind the trees and brush. Nera watched the road and waited for something to happen. She heard nothing and saw nothing for a long time. Eventually, the noise of someone traipsing through the forest on the other side of the road caught her ear. Whoever it was, they were not being stealthy.

Nera gripped her spear and shot a pointed look toward Tam. He pulled his sword from its sheath and held it near his body with both hands. Then, Nera looked to Shorlis and gave the chelon a deterring shake of her head. Their best chance against whatever was coming out of the woods was the two trained guardians. They didn't yet know what the chelon could do with the magic staff he carried.

The noise grew closer to the road. Sticks broke and cracked as the runner barreled through the undergrowth. Finally, a man burst from the forest and into view.

Orin spun from side to side, getting his bearings. He turned left while he took a few deep breaths.

"What in Finlestia?" Nera called out as she appeared from behind the tree.

The man's eyes widened, and he grabbed his chest. "You scared the air out of me," he gulped.

"Sorry," Nera said, approaching him with the others in tow. "What are you doing here? Where are Coal and Ralowyn?"

"Marching," Orin said taking another deep breath to slow his heart. "They're marching with Javelin to Ventohl. They mean to take the city."

"Wait. What?" Nera asked.

"Ventohl is where the Sons of Silence live," Shorlis explained.

Orin nodded, thankful the chelon could fill in a little information while he caught his breath.

"And why are Coal and Ralowyn marching with this Javelin?" she pressed.

"We found Merrick and Karnak—both alive. They were rescued from the Sons of Silence right here," Orin explained quickly, as he indicated the battle remnants. "Long story short, there was another attempt at stealing Merrick and an assassination attempt on the leader of Javelin. Karnak decided the best thing to do was march with them to end this."

Nera tried to grasp everything as Orin spoke. "I don't understand," she said. "We came all the way across the sea to save them."

"And that's exactly what we need to do," Orin replied. "But not just them. The people of Kelvur are fighting against the same sorcerer that tried to destroy us. He is looking for something that will make him stronger. If we don't help these people fight him now, he will come back to Tarrine, and we may not be able to stop him next time."

"How can we help?" Shorlis asked, stepping forward with his staff glowing red.

"Ah, right," the winded man continued. "I'm the runner. I was sent to deliver the news to you and the squadron. We figured I'd better go since I was injured and they needed all their warriors to fight. Plus, you would be more likely to rally the Talon Squadron at my word than that of a stranger."

Nera nodded. That was true. She wasn't sure what she would have done for a Kelvurian stranger claiming to know her people. She didn't like any of this. As the captain of the squadron and the commander of the entire mission, she felt she didn't have enough information to make the best decision. It frustrated her. She had to trust the decisions of an orc gar she barely knew. She did know Orin though, and she trusted him. If he believed it was the right decision, she would have to follow his lead.

"Alright," she said, standing straight. "Let's get you back to Dorantown and—"

"No," he said. "You need to keep going. They're going to need you. I can keep running back to the town and rally Talon."

"I'll go ahead with Shorlis, Captain," Tam offered.

Nera looked at the young man and then the chelon. She wouldn't risk Tam's life by sending him with someone who wielded so much unknown power. "No," she said. "Shorlis and I will go ahead."

"It should be easy for us to find. If I remember, this road should lead us straight to Ventohl," the chelon explained.

"That's what this map they gave me says," Orin affirmed. "Tam and I will run back as fast as we can and send the squadron to meet you in Ventohl."

"Do it with all haste," Nera ordered.

With that, the two men ran down the road and around a bend. Nera looked at Shorlis and turned to the northeast. The chelon began to jog, and she matched his pace. She hadn't been particularly fond of many of the things they'd experienced on this mission to Kelvur, and she didn't feel entirely comfortable with this decision either. Regardless, she knew leaders often had to make decisions whether they were comfortable with them or not.

As she jogged alongside the chelon, she thought it was going to be a long day. If they were lucky, the squadron would catch up to them quickly, and they'd be able to fly the rest of the way. *One can only hope.*

After a few hours, running as fast as they could, Shorlis called out to Nera, asking her to slow down. It was hard work running at such a pace, and he was starting to worry that he'd be exhausted by the time they arrived at Ventohl. He didn't want to get there and be so tired he was unable to help with the battle. That thought, coupled with the fact that he didn't have any real experience with his new staff, *Menthrora,* made him feel inadequate.

"Let's take a break," Nera said, pointing to a small creek that burbled nearby. "We can freshen up and then be on our way."

Shorlis nodded his agreement. He marveled at the woman. She was a force to be reckoned with. If she were as tired as he was, she surely didn't show it. Nera scooped water from the creek and sipped at it. Shorlis knelt next to her and did the same.

"What is the name of your spear?" he asked. He couldn't remember what she'd told him before.

"*Santoralier,*" she replied. "It means Lightning Rider."

"And how did you come to possess it?"

"Well, that's a bit of a story," the woman said, dipping her head to the side.

"I could use a longer break," Shorlis admitted.

The woman sat back and said, "I could, too."

"I thought I was the only one," the chelon said with a weak grin. "You don't look tired at all."

"That comes from training. One of the things that happens during battle is pure exhaustion overwhelms you. But you don't want your enemy to know you're tired, do you?"

"No. I suppose not," Shorlis answered.

"Right. So, as we train, we practice the art of drawing from the deep wells inside. That's why Griffin Guard training is so rigorous. We're trained to the point of exhaustion, and then we train more. It teaches us that we always have more in us. We just have to push forward and draw on it."

"Is that how you learned to use *Santoralier?*" the chelon asked.

Nera smiled. "This spear is strange—much like your staff, I imagine. I found it in an abandoned wisdom tower on an island in the Gant Sea Narrows. The moment I held it ..." She paused, trying to think of how to describe the feeling. "It was as if the spear were meant for me. I don't quite know how to describe it, but it felt right in my hands."

Shorlis nodded solemnly. "This was my father's staff. I don't feel like it's supposed to be mine. If he didn't die at Dorantown, wouldn't he be the one wielding it now, running with you toward a battle at Ventohl?"

"And yet, here you are." Nera gave him an approving nod. "You run with me to the aid of people you don't know. To fight for them. To help them. To protect them. I know no more noble cause."

The chelon's gaze fell to the ground. "I don't understand why he wouldn't tell me of these things. Why didn't he tell me about *Menthrora?* Did he not think I could handle it? There are many things I don't understand."

"Welcome to what we all experience," Nera said with a sympathetic smile.

The chelon half rolled his sea green eyes.

"I know you feel lost right now," she continued. "I lost my father when I was young. I was so angry. I was frustrated with everything. My father was a member of the Griffin Guard. In my mind, he was a hero of the age. Of course, I was too young to understand the reality that he was in danger every time he left on mission. I just saw him as leaving to destroy the bad orcs that wanted to take my siblings and me away in the middle of the night. But when he died, I felt like I didn't know anything anymore."

Shorlis's eyes glossed as she spoke. Nera knew exactly what he was feeling. Anthanar had always been the chelon's guiding light. Shorlis never had the chance to know his mother, but losing his father was different. His father had been there every day of his life. Until now.

Nera stood and extended her hand to aid the chelon to his feet. "It took me a long time to recognize some of the things my father taught me. In fact, many of them were things I didn't realize I'd learned from him. It was only when my mother would say things like, 'You got that from your father,' that I'd see it. What I'm saying is, just because he's gone doesn't mean you don't still have him. You had many years with your father, and I know for sure you learned things from him you haven't yet realized."

Shorlis didn't try to hide the tears that streamed down his face as he took Nera's hand and hopped to his feet. "Thank you," he said.

"Of course," she replied with a quick nod. "Remember when you picked up the staff?"

"Yes," Shorlis said, remembering how the power emanated from the artifact and he felt it reverberate through his body. "I could feel it in my shell."

Nera smiled. "If I had a shell, I'm sure I would have felt *Santoralier* in it as well. No one is meant to wield that staff but you."

Shorlis lifted *Menthrora* before himself, marveling at the grains and polish of the wood. His eyes traced the artifact all the way to the top where the red stone glinted and glowed. He felt the magical staff hum in his hand, and he knew Nera was right.

CHAPTER THIRTY-SIX

SMOKE AND SHADOWS

When he first laid eyes on the castle at Ventohl, Merrick thought it impressive and ominous. Though, as his group approached, he realized some of the walls were not actually walls but lines of stone-faced geldrins. This made the structure itself appear less impressive, while the scene looked no less ominous. The sight gave him a shiver.

He still struggled on many nights with the terrible nightmares that haunted him. The impending battle probably wouldn't help. Regardless of how he'd walk away from the engagement, they needed to end this war. The sorcerer was relentless, and if it wasn't now, the huntsman had no doubt he would have to march against him again soon enough.

Merrick glanced over to Vorenna. The barbarian woman signaled at several captains in her army. Several units planned to skirt a hill south of the castle that gave them cover. From there they were supposed to lob arrows and draw the geldrins out of the castle. This would allow more Javelin units to flank them and get through the open walls. Merrick wondered if any of the castles north of the Palisade were still completely intact. The two he'd seen were a far cry from Whitestone's or Tamaria's castles.

Coal grumbled something next to the huntsman as they hid behind trees on the forest's edge.

404

"What was that?" Merrick whispered.

"Oh," the dwarf started, but then he suppressed a laugh and shook his head. "I was just thinking, so much for the quiet life. Ezel and I thought running a river boat on the Palori River was going to be our way to peace and relaxation. The simple life, you know?"

The huntsman smirked. "I hate to tell you this, but you two are far too interesting to fall into obscurity. History forgets the quiet lives of most. But tales are told of those with great passion or compassion. And you've always been one for a good tale."

Coal smiled back at the man. "You know this is the second time in recent memory I'm running into battle alongside a man-kin? Sort of breaks the mold of the dwarven stories of Kalimandir."

"You are not cast from that same mold, my friend."

"That's true," the dwarf mused. He rubbed the ever-present wrappings on his arm. Merrick knew the clan tattoo that adorned his friend's hand. He also knew it was something the dwarf rarely talked about. Despite the many stories Coal had told him over the years, he held many secrets from his past.

Karnak sidled over to the pair.

"I've just spoken to Vorenna. The archers are moving into place. We'll wait for her signal to move on the castle," the orc explained. "Are you all ready?"

Merrick and Coal nodded without a word.

"I thought the castle was full of assassins," Ralowyn said, not looking at them but scanning Ventohl's defenses.

"The assassins run the place," Karnak affirmed. "But apparently, there is always a geldrin unit present these days."

"Assassins and geldrins," Coal said eagerly. "Plenty of heads to knock for the both of us, lass."

Ralowyn gave the dwarf a weak smile, but her gaze dropped to the brush. Merrick couldn't tell whether she was avoiding looking at him, but he noticed worry rimming her gentle face. He stepped away from Coal and Karnak, drawing close to the elf.

"We've been in bad spots before and made it through," he said softly, grabbing her hand tenderly. "We'll make it through this one, too."

She nodded quietly, then turned to him. Her eyes melted his heart. "There is also a witch."

"We'll fight her together—you and me. Who's strong enough to beat us together?"

A smile tugged at the edge of her mouth. "How you are so confident always surprises me. You take everything in stride."

Merrick muffled a laugh. "We don't live as long as you elves. If you spend too much time worrying about tomorrow, you'll get to the end of your life and realize you spent more time worrying than living."

"That is very wise," Ralowyn mused. "Perhaps a little reckless," she side-eyed him, "but wise."

"Besides," Merrick said. "I've got plans for you and me. We're going to—"

"Silence," Karnak hushed them all. "It's starting."

Arrows flew in great volleys, raining down on the geldrins lined up to fill the gaps in the castle's walls. Several geldrins dropped, falling instantly as multiple arrows found their marks. Another volley felled several more, as geldrin archers moved forward to lob arrows of their own over the hill. When a third volley struck down several of the geldrin archers, a commander barked orders and moved a unit of geldrins out of the castle.

Merrick took a deep breath. He squeezed Ralowyn's hand one more time, giving her a comforting nod, and braced for Vorenna's signal.

Karnak charged out of the forest, followed by dozens of Javelin warriors. The orc was impressed at their ability to run into battle in utter silence. Orcs are a passionate people, and a good battle cry is almost always warranted. Of course, silence made sense for their purposes.

A large group of geldrins was already halfway over the hill, going for the Javelin archers on the other side. The last thing the flanking group wanted was to turn those geldrins back on themselves before they were able to engage the enemies still in the castle. If they did draw their attention, however, one of the archer spotters would tell their group, and they would charge the geldrins' backs. That group of geldrins was in a bad position, regardless of whether they noticed the flankers or not.

Karnak hurtled over a large rock as he barreled across the field, several paces ahead of most of the Javelin warriors. The elves of the group out-sprinted the orc, but his muscular legs carried him at a blistering pace. His tusks moved side to side as he sported a wicked grin.

The castle defenders saw the attackers, and the battle was on.

Several arrows zipped by Karnak's head, forcing him to duck and dodge. The close calls enraged him even more, and he eagerly gripped the axe Vorenna had given him. Another arrow hurled toward him but deflected several feet above his head. A shimmering purple hue rippled at the impact.

Ralowyn, he thought with a grin.

Geldrins poured out of the castle's dilapidated walls to meet the Javelin warriors.

Karnak let out a primal roar, and many of the warriors behind him joined the battle cry.

The first geldrin Karnak met looked stunned at the sight of the big orc. So shocked, he nearly dropped his spear. Unfortunately for the geldrin, that was too much of a delay, and Karnak cut him down with one slice of his giant axe. Another geldrin swung his sword at the orc, but Karnak easily deflected the attack and overpowered the stone warrior. He shoved in close, hitting the geldrin hard with his big shoulder, forcing the monster to stumble enough for Karnak to swing his axe and separate the geldrin's head from the rest of his body.

Merrick drove his spear into a nearby geldrin, while Coal blasted his heavy war hammer through the chin of another. Ralowyn kept them covered from arrows with a magical shield, while she lobbed her own magic missiles from the Staff of Anvelorian.

Suddenly, a giant stone-faced creature lumbered out of the castle, swinging a huge axe.

"Geldranos!" someone yelled.

The sight of the enormous geldrin stopped Karnak in his tracks. He'd fought trolls double his size but never anything this big. And it was looking directly at him.

Nera and Shorlis paced themselves. They would be no help in the battle if they arrived exhausted. Nera continually checked over her shoulder, hoping the Talon Squadron would appear over a ridge of trees. It was the best they could hope for. At least then, they could fly the rest of the way.

Shorlis might not be particularly fond of the transportation, but Nera would instruct Shadowpaw to carry the chelon with care. It was a tactic they'd practiced many times at the Grand Corral. It was the only way to bring guardians back home should their griffin perish and the guardian survive.

Nera thought about the others. She was in command of this rescue mission and felt as though she were failing miserably. She was supposed to bring them home safe, not rush them headlong into battle. Regardless, she wasn't even there to protect them and was powerless to get there any faster.

Shorlis veered to the side, stepping off the road and leading them to a small creek. The water rippled smoothly over rounded river stones, and the shadows of the forest colored the verdant scene. The area reminded Nera of the Talon Squadron's secret base of operations in Whitestone Forest. Clawstone was a place she'd always loved. If the situation they had found themselves in were less dire, she might enjoy exploring Duskwood.

The guardian was baffled at how the chelon sensed where they could find water at all times. As Shorlis knelt next to the water, his shell seemed larger, and Nera thought he looked like a giant tortoise—until he turned and smiled at her.

"I thought we should drink some water," he said, gulping the refreshing liquid.

"Yes, good idea," she replied, kneeling next to him.

He scooped more into his mouth and stood to look around.

"Any idea how much farther?" Nera asked.

"No," he responded with a shake of his head. "I've never been to Ventohl. I only know the direction from the maps. The road from the camp only goes to Ventohl."

"If you had told me that, I could have come by myself or with Tam and sent you back with Orin," she said, eyeing him.

"Exactly why I didn't tell you. I didn't want you to leave me behind."

The guardian watched as the chelon tested his staff. He swung *Menthrora*, not as she'd seen any mage do, but as someone who had skill with a non-magical staff, twirling and swiping in controlled movements. It seemed a dance to her eyes. Shorlis released a sudden burst of red magical energy that launched toward the road, exploding as it landed.

"Oops," the chelon said, running to inspect the site.

Nera ran up behind him and found the road to be completely intact, if not a bit scorched. "Interesting. Do you think you can reproduce the action that created that fireball?"

"Definitely," he said with a smile.

A noise from high above tickled their ears. Nera looked up to see that the Talon Squadron had caught up with them.

Ralowyn tensed her hands to strengthen the shimmering purple shield hovering over Merrick. She could no longer cover Karnak as the orc ran ahead to engage more enemies. Her only hope to protect him from arrows was to finish the geldrins and assassins that lined the tops of the walls. She lobbed magical fireballs at the archers, landing hit after hit. The magical orbs exploded into lavender flames, splattering on her targets and those nearby.

The elf continued to make her way systematically along the wall until all the archers abandoned their perch. It was an effective technique she'd never used before but thought worth noting. She may yet need to use it again.

She turned to find Merrick twirling his spear to parry the chops of a geldrin that attacked him with ferocity. Ralowyn pushed her staff out in front of herself, and the geldrin went flying to the side. Merrick turned to see her. Their eyes met for a second, but his widened almost immediately. He hurled his spear through the air, the weapon barely missing the elf as it zipped past and struck a geldrin who was charging her from behind.

Merrick ran over and pulled the spear from the dead geldrin. "Watch your back," he said quickly, turning to find his next foe.

They stood back-to-back for a moment while the mayhem unfolded around them. The chaos of the battle reminded her of Ruk and what they'd walked into during the orc resistance's attack on Drelek's capitol city. Ralowyn opened her mouth to respond, but the word that escaped was, "Karnak!"

"Geldranos!" someone screamed. Several others echoed the word.

Ralowyn's eyes widened at the massive geldrin that stared down the fierce orc gar. The elf dashed from her position next to Merrick, trusting the huntsman could handle his own battle for the moment. She lifted the Staff of Anvelorian high as she ran, muttering an incantation she had never used but had read about in a scroll at the wisdom tower of Loralith.

The geldranos lumbered at the orc with a menacing sneer on his stony face. *Why does Karnak not move?* the elf thought. *No. Focus.* If she was going to get this spell to work, it was going to take serious focus.

As the geldranos ran into range where he could bring his large axe down on the orc, Ralowyn skidded to a halt, throwing her empty hand forward and pointing the staff in the direction of the monster. She felt as if time slowed around her. Great ribbons of purple light wrapped and flourished around each other in whipping tendrils, shooting straight for the geldranos.

The ribbons of light seized the large beast and lifted him into the air. He swung his axe in an arc toward the orc but hit nothing. The geldranos let out an odd croak, and his jagged face showed surprise. His legs wobbled as though he were trying to stomp down on the orc, but his feet wouldn't reach the ground. The huge monster suddenly looked panicked as he waved his arms, trying to regain some balance.

Thundering steps to her right caught Ralowyn's attention. Dak the giant barreled toward the geldranos and didn't slow down as he plowed into the giant geldrin. The elf couldn't hold the spell as the giant added his weight, and the two toppled to the ground, beating and tearing at one another.

The first several Javelin warriors that burst through the open wall into Ventohl were struck down by hidden assassins, awaiting their opportunity to ambush the unwary soldiers. Karnak, having been distracted by the enormous geldranos, was one of the warriors that entered after the assassins had revealed themselves. He would not have called them unskilled in a fight, but he mused that they were probably much better at killing when they hunted their prey from the shadows. Fighting one-on-one with the big orc warrior, who had spent his entire life training for battle, was not going well for them.

Karnak's axe crashed hard on an assassin's shoulder, killing him instantly. The orc was a storm of fury, channeling his anger over their attack on his home and unleashing it upon all those associated with the Sons of Silence.

The orc gar caught a glimpse of Merrick to his side. The huntsman had come a long way. His skill with a spear was impressive, and the man fought with infinite courage. An assassin tiptoed behind the man, raising a dagger to strike. Karnak hurled his massive axe end over end. The axe blasted the assassin in the chest, sending her flying.

Merrick turned with a wary nod to Karnak before he rushed an assassin ready to strike at the orc. Karnak hurried to his axe and yanked it free. He rejoined Merrick, striking down another assassin.

"This one doesn't fly back," Karnak managed to say through heaving breaths.

"What?" Merrick asked.

The orc lifted the axe and shook it. The blades were stained red, but the orc laughed. "I miss *Dalkeri*."

Merrick let out a nervous laugh. "Where is Hazkul Bern?" Merrick huffed.

"The elf has to be here somewhere," Karnak growled.

He scanned the scene. Individual battles waged all over the castle grounds. The broken walls did little to keep Javelin out but had given the assassins plenty of places to jump out of and catch them off guard. The area was littered with the slain from both sides. Karnak's eyes traced the keep, thinking the elf might be cowardly enough to hide there while all his assassins died. If he was, Karnak would not stop until he tore the entire keep down to get at the elf.

"We have to get to the—" The orc's words stopped suddenly.

Hazkul Bern. The leader of the Sons of Silence twisted in a deadly dance as he sliced an unfortunate Javelin warrior with his black dagger and stabbed another with his sword. *There is an assassin who can fight,* the orc thought.

Karnak charged ahead, batting assassins away on either side as he ran.

"Boehlen's Beard!" Coal heaved as he ran up next to Merrick. "That orc doesn't stop."

"No, he doesn't," Merrick said, shaking his head. "Come on. We have to catch up to him."

"Good luck with that," Coal muttered but hurried along next to the huntsman, nonetheless.

Merrick grimaced at all the death they passed. This would likely add fuel to the night terrors he already experienced. But he couldn't worry about such things. An assassin turned toward him. Coal rammed his hammer head into the assassin's knees, dropping him with a sickening crack of bones. Merrick finished the assassin off with one quick jab of his spear.

The huntsman spun and dodged as another assassin let loose several whirring objects, glinting wickedly as they spun by. Merrick brought his spear around, forcing the assassin to jump over the low strike. She was a nimble opponent, and she pulled two long daggers from her cloak. Her eyes narrowed appraisingly.

Great, Merrick thought. *She's probably deciding what killing technique she wants to use on me. I've got to keep her at a distance.* He knew from training with the Scar Squadron in Calrok that his spear was cumbersome if his opponent got in too close. He couldn't afford that to happen in an actual battle.

The assassin took two quick steps toward him, brandishing her daggers. Merrick met her steps with warding waves of his spear, keeping the tip aimed directly at her. She slowly stepped to the side, forcing him to turn to keep her in his sights.

Suddenly, she stopped. She replaced one of her daggers in her cloak, and her eyes softened. Slowly, showing her hand, she pulled her black cloth mask away, revealing the face of a young, rather beautiful woman. Merrick hesitated, his spear wavering. She pulled back the hood that cover her red hair, letting it fly freely in the wind that blew over the grounds.

The fierce, yet soft beauty of the woman reminded him of his sister. It was as though Merrick had been frozen in place. For some reason, goblins and orcs and geldrins had been more like bedtime story monsters that needed to be vanquished. In a strange way, the cloaked and masked assassins had seemed much the same. But now, he saw a young woman standing before him. A woman who likely had little choice in her life, one who had run out of options and found the only place that would take her in.

Before Merrick realized it, she'd taken several steps closer to him—close enough for his spear to be more of a hindrance than a help. The woman's eyes narrowed again, but this time they were accompanied by a macabre grin.

Suddenly, she flew into the air, screaming as she flailed wildly. She slammed hard to the ground, flew up a few feet, and crashed down again. Ralowyn stepped past the huntsman and bludgeoned the assassin with her staff.

"What are you doing?" the elf asked, frantically. "She could have killed you."

"I ... I don't know," Merrick said, feeling oddly stupid. "She reminded me of Ellaria."

"Ellaria would never wish you harm. Everyone on this battlefield is a potential threat to your life."

"No, I know," he replied. He paused for a moment, glancing at the limp form of the woman, her messy red hair covering the carnage Ralowyn's attack had done to the assassin. Ralowyn stepped into his line of sight, concern edging her fair features. "Thank you," he said.

"Boehlen's Beard," Coal grumbled, as he lifted his hammer from another defeated foe. "Is that the witch you told me about?"

Merrick and Ralowyn looked up and saw Hazkul Bern's witch, whipping her wand around and striking down Javelin warriors with flaming orbs of magic.

"We've got to get over there," Merrick said quickly to the elf. "They won't stand a chance against her without you. I'll be right behind you."

Karnak deliberately ascended the stairs that led to a row of stone pillars. Hazkul Bern had seen him coming and made quite the show of walking nonchalantly toward the courtyard. The orc gar knew he was likely walking into a trap where the elf could ambush him, but he didn't care. He wanted to finish this.

The elf eyed him and disappeared behind a pillar that no longer held the weight of a roof. The open-air courtyard may have had a covering when the original builders designed it, but like much of the rest of Ventohl, it was incomplete. As Karnak stepped between two of the pillars, he found himself facing the elf, who stood on the other side of the rectangular courtyard.

"You know," Hazkul Bern said. "I was planning to plant a garden here. Can you imagine how beautiful these pillars would look with vines growing around them?"

Karnak didn't say anything. He glanced quickly around the area, scanning for booby traps or anything the elf might be hiding.

Hazkul Bern smirked. "I assure you, there are no traps here. Like I said, I wanted to grow a garden here. There is a fountain on the other side of this ornate wall. It would make for such a lovely place to walk and think and read. Wouldn't you agree?" His words were airy as though he spoke of a dream. "Unfortunately, with all the filth pouring out of the Crags these days, I've had no time to nurture it."

"Nurture," the orc scoffed.

"Oh, come now," the elf reprimanded. "You aren't so blind to the world to think me a mere killing machine. Like all people, I have dreams, too. Admittedly, I have accomplished so many already. None have been able to best me, even to this—"

"Because you have no loyalty," Karnak growled. "You shift your sights as soon as you think you might lose."

"Thank you," Hazkul Bern said, as though Karnak understood him. "Finally, someone else who sees the wisdom of it."

Karnak gritted his teeth. Of course, the elf knew the orc wasn't complimenting him. Hazkul was just trying to rile him up.

"You know," the elf continued. "You're really taking this eye for an eye thing way too far. I came to your home with no intention to destroy it. And yet, you run an army through my walls. Several of which are on fire now, by the way. Sure, I left soot all over your house, but that's easily swept up. And maybe, if I'm honest, I accidentally emotionally scarred your wife and the little tyke, but—"

Karnak lunged at the elf with a mighty roar. Hazkul Bern nimbly dodged the orc's brutish attack, stepping away from him with a wide grin.

"You won't speak of them ever again," Karnak growled viciously, readying his stance.

Hazkul Bern stepped lightly, circling the orc. "Karnak," the elf said, clicking his tongue and shaking his head. "Don't you see? It's your loyalty that landed you here. And your loyalty to what? Some stray huntsman? What do you owe him?"

"More than you know."

The elf guffawed. "You really believe that? You know, if it weren't for him and the sorcerer wanting him, your family would never have gotten involved in this."

"If it wasn't for him, the sorcerer might have killed everyone in my city, including my family," Karnak spat.

Hazkul stopped his stalking and pursed his lips. "You may have a fair point there. Then again, Jaernok Tur is not one to share details, especially when it has to do with a failure."

The nonchalant comment about the sorcerer took Karnak by surprise. He expected Hazkul Bern to be enamored or bewitched by the sorcerer. He hadn't expected such blatant indifference. "Have you never considered fighting back?" the orc asked, taking advantage of the elf's momentary pause and stepping to the side.

Hazkul smirked. "You see," he said, raising his black dagger and pointing it at Karnak. "That's the difference between us. Where you see a tyrant to fight at all costs, I see inevitability. After all, who can stand against a monolith dragon?"

"A what?" Karnak asked. He stopped pacing and stood dumbfounded.

"Oh," the elf mocked. "You don't know about the monolith dragon?"

Karnak racked his brain. He had no memory of hearing anything about a "monolith dragon." He was frustrated by the elf's tone and unsure he could trust a word out of the assassin's mouth. "Enlighten me," Karnak growled.

"You know," Hazkul said. "Seeing the way you've treated my home, I don't think I will. I had every intention of killing you here, but now I think a slight maiming is in order. I'll keep you alive in the dungeons so you can see for yourself. Admittedly, I haven't seen the creature myself, but as odd as that sorcerer is, it's easy to see he's in league with some old magic."

"You follow blindly," Karnak scoffed.

"Follow is the wrong word," Hazkul said. "I stay ahead of the tide."

"Your foolish pride will be your downfall."

"Strange," the elf said. "I was just thinking it was your foolishness that would be yours."

Without warning, the elf assassin lunged forward with a flurry of strikes from his dagger and his sword.

Ralowyn swung the Staff of Anvelorian wide as she deflected another magic bolt that streaked from the witch's wand. The magical energy sizzled away, striking the ground nearby and charring some grass. Merrick and Coal fought wildly, working their way through the assassins that surrounded the witch. Chadwa's dark eyes glinted with a maniacal fever as she lobbed curse after curse at the she-elf.

It took everything Ralowyn had to keep herself protected as she pressed forward. She held the staff in front of her body with both hands, creating a lavender-hued barrier of light that acted as a shield. The witch's attacks buffeted the barrier with constant blows, the force of which sprayed off the edges of the shield sending Ralowyn's silvery hair flying in a frenzy.

When the witch's onslaught ceased, Ralowyn was almost too afraid to look up, expecting it to continue the moment she did. The elf peered through the shield and saw that the witch stood ahead, beckoning her with pale fingers. Strangely, Ralowyn took several steps toward the witch, reacting to an odd tug from within.

What is this hex? the elf wondered, as she stepped evenly.

The witch shot her wand forward with a sudden jab, and a magical force tightly wrapped Ralowyn. It felt as though she were being gripped in the fist of a giant. The elf tried to lift the Staff of Anvelorian and use one of her own spells, but the invisible hand clenched tighter, pressing the staff hard against Ralowyn's body.

"Ralowyn!" Merrick shouted from behind her. The huntsman could do little for her while he and Coal were engaged with the assassins.

The witch's grin faded, and her face took on a disappointed disposition. Perhaps she expected the elf to show her some form of magic to excite her. The witch eyed Ralowyn.

No, the elf thought. *She eyes the Staff of Anvelorian.*

The invisible force ripped the magical staff from the elf's grasp. Ralowyn cried out in pain as her fingers cracked, the force prying them away from the staff. The lavender fire in the elf's eyes flickered but didn't go out, as the invisible hand squeezed her so tightly, she had to fight for breath.

Meanwhile, the Staff of Anvelorian floated the twelve feet to the witch's waiting hand. Chadwa smiled wickedly, feeling the hum of the artifact as she inspected it. But her smile was short-lived. She shook the staff as though the action would make the artifact work for her. The staff *verved* as she did. The lavender glow at the spiraled pinnacle leaked ribbons of light, but still nothing happened.

The witch's eyes narrowed as she looked back to the elf, still immobilized in the hex. Ralowyn smirked. But so did the witch as she lifted her wand and aimed it directly at the elf's head. Ralowyn's eyes widened in horror. The elf didn't know what would happen to the staff if she perished. *Would it choose to work for the one who slays me? Is that what happened when Anvelorian died all those centuries ago?* She racked her brain, attempting to remember the tales of Anvelorian. Try as she might, she could not remember how the old master mage had died.

A rogue tear escaped her eye. She wasn't afraid of dying. She was afraid of what the witch could do with the power of the staff. What she could do to the invading Javelin warriors. What she could do to Merrick.

The witch lifted her wand as though she were winding up for a powerful strike to end the elf, when a sudden bolt of lightning struck her.

Ralowyn fell to the ground, gasping for breath as she was released from the clutches of the invisible hand. The witch slowly pressed her seared body up from the ground. Smoke wafted from her in spirals.

Merrick hoisted Ralowyn to her feet, having finally reached the elf. She extended her hand, and the Staff of Anvelorian rose from the ground in an attempt to fly back to the elf. The witch, however, grabbed at it in a last-ditch effort to wield the magical staff. A sudden blow from Coal's war hammer put that effort to rest.

The dwarf shuddered as he said, "Witches."

"Are you alright?" Merrick asked, glancing around to make sure no one would attack them as they recovered.

"I will be fine," she replied. "It appears our friends have arrived."

All around the grounds of Ventohl, the Talon Squadron swooped in from the sky. Each griffin had its rider and also carried a miner from Dorantown in its great talons. The griffins glided low to release the miners, who didn't hesitate to join the fight.

Nera gave Ralowyn a wink as she flew by on Shadowpaw, who carried their new friend Shorlis in her talons. The elf nodded her thanks, realizing a strike from *Santoralier* had saved her. Shorlis pointed to a rough area of the battle where a number of geldrins fought with Javelin warriors, and they soared in that direction.

"Coal," Merrick said. "Take care of her. I need to get to Karnak."

"Seems more likely she can take care of me, but ..." the dwarf grumbled.

"Take care of each other then," the huntsman said quickly. "Can you open a path for me?"

"Aye." The dwarf grinned, gripping his battle hammer in both hands. "We can do that."

Ralowyn shook the ache out of her muscles and readied herself. *Yes, we can do that.*

The Talon Squadron's arrival quickly turned the tide in favor of Javelin. Shorlis watched from above as griffins and guardians slammed down hard on geldrins and assassins, instantly ending them. It was methodical and devastating. The chelon marveled at their strength. With the Griffin Guard on their side, he dared to hope they might end the scourge of the Crags once and for all.

Shorlis blinked at the bright streak of lightning that crashed down on a geldrin and rippled into several wicked arcs, downing others nearby. Nera was a fierce warrior, and the chelon thought he might learn much more from her than she'd initially insisted, even if she didn't know the arcane arts like a well-studied mage.

The chelon surveyed the castle grounds of Ventohl, watching everything unfold.

"There!" he shouted, making Shadowpaw click her beak in surprise. "Down there!" he shouted again, hoping Nera could hear him and see where he pointed.

"Where?" Nera asked, leaning over and around the griffin's neck.

"That geldrin over there—that's Commander Chol," he said, almost in a panic.

"Well, let's go visit an old friend, shall we?" Nera shouted back over the wind that whipped by their ears.

Shorlis grinned and gripped *Menthrora* tightly with both hands. He wasn't entirely comfortable being carried in the griffin's embrace at first, but seeing Chol on the ground below made every other thought evaporate. His entire being was focused on a singular purpose: get to the geldrin and end him.

A shudder ran through the chelon's body, releasing several pops inside his shell. A strange sensation flushed him as he considered what he planned to do to the geldrin commander. He had dreamed so many scenarios while back in the Glinso Mining Camp. But even in his wildest imaginings, he could not have come up with the scene he found before him.

How could he? He had never seen or held the magical staff, *Menthrora*. That alone was hardly possible to imagine. But further, how could he have imagined flying over a battle at Ventohl in the grasp of a griffin.

The young chelon was overwhelmed. Tears formed in his eyes and fell from his face in heavy drops. He blinked them away, narrowing his eyes to focus on the geldrin as they swooped low.

Shadowpaw released Shorlis smoothly, landing him on his feet with ease. The chelon sprinted forward, catching Commander Chol's attention as the griffin crashed down hard on a pair of nearby geldrins. Nera hurled *Santoralier*, which blasted into a group of assassins, killing several of them instantly.

The look on Chol's face revealed utter confusion at the sight of the chelon. "You little crust," he babbled. "How ..."

Shorlis raised *Menthrora*, and the stone at the pinnacle of the wooden staff burst into blazing red light. Shorlis's sea green eyes mirrored the light, flickering red. He looked savage, even primal, as he glared at the geldrin commander.

"Where did you get that, Crust?" Chol asked.

The chelon didn't answer. He only stared.

"So, we're doing this again," Chol jeered. He held his sword to the side and scratched at the scar over his eye. "You know how badly this itches?"

Shorlis's shoulders heaved with the intensity of his breathing. He stood there, saying nothing to the geldrin, still trying to formulate some way to use the magic staff to destroy the commander.

Chol's one good eye flicked to either side. He sighed heavily, seemingly realizing that all the geldrins under his command were currently occupied and he would have to deal with the chelon himself.

"You do know that I wasn't the one that killed the old crust?" the geldrin asked. "Or the little dwarf. I actually kind of liked that little spit."

Shorlis launched into a sprint directly at the geldrin commander, like he'd done so long ago in the Shoals. Chol wasn't smiling this time. The fires that blazed in the chelon's eyes burned like the very essence of fury itself.

He raised *Menthrora* and whipped it forward at the geldrin. A blast of pure magical energy exploded from the end of the staff, enveloping Chol in its light. The geldrin screamed. Shorlis dug his feet into the ground, gripping *Menthrora* with both hands, doing everything he could to hold onto the staff as it expelled greater power than the chelon ever anticipated. In truth, he had not known what to expect. As he held the staff, roaring in his hands, he was filled with a mix of emotions.

Chol's scream was quickly overpowered by *Menthrora's* raging hum which grew louder until it finally exploded. Everyone nearby was knocked to the ground. Several guardians were blown off the backs of their griffins. Those griffins shook out their feathers as they awkwardly regained their footing.

Shorlis pressed himself up to a seated position, looking for Chol. Where the geldrin had stood, only charred earth remained. The chelon's eyes widened as he looked in horror at the staff that lay beside him on the ground.

Maker, what power is this?

"Shorlis," Nera called from nearby. She was brushing Shadowpaw's feathers after finishing a quick check on the griffin. "Shorlis, what was that?"

"I don't know," the chelon said, his whole body shaking.

The explosion caught both the orc gar and the elf assassin by surprise. They slid away from the deadly dance they'd been locked in and glared at each other, each one perking his ears to hear what was happening outside the courtyard.

Karnak smirked at Hazkul Bern when the battle didn't resume its noise right away. The elf smirked back, popping an eyebrow. "This should prove interesting."

Hazkul Bern's glance flicked to something behind Karnak, and the orc dove and rolled to the side, not wanting to get stabbed in the back. When he popped up in a rather acrobatic move, he saw Merrick, breathing heavily as he ambled into the courtyard.

"Your witch is dead," Merrick said.

Karnak eyed the elf, looking for some reaction.

"Leave it to Chadwa to go out with a bang," Hazkul mused. "Ironic, considering how insufferably quiet she was. I bet she—"

"Oh, no." Merrick stopped him, shaking his head as he chuckled. "That wasn't her."

The revelation made the elf twitch.

"She was already dead. That was one of our new friends taking out a whole slew of geldrins and assassins."

Karnak's frame swelled as he stood straighter, taking a few steps to the side.

Hazkul Bern glanced at the orc and shifted his own stance, not wanting to allow the pair to flank him.

"Interesting how we've come back to this. Just you two and me. What a strange fate we share," the elf said.

"Your fate ends now. All of this ends now," Karnak growled.

The elf laughed. "How foolish. Karnak, I thought we went over this. The wave is coming. And the one who controls the wave does not like disappointment. Ventohl may have been small in his schemes, but he won't be happy about its loss."

"We'll kill the sorcerer, too," the orc snarled.

"Too?" Hazkul Bern shook his head in amusement. "I don't plan to die today," the elf scoffed. "It seems to me that our fates are intertwined now, and it will be quite fascinating to see where this goes. Wouldn't you agree?"

Merrick and Karnak both charged the elf as he whipped a smoke bomb from his cloak. The bomb exploded into thick clouds, knocking the pair to the ground. They sat up, each hunched over in coughing fits.

"No!" Karnak roared.

The orc looked around angrily, seeing no sign of the elf assassin. Hazkul Bern had vanished again.

Chapter Thirty-Seven

Calrok by the Sea

Smarlo strode past the gathered guardians, waiting solemnly for news. Their crowd had grown over the days since the battle of Calrok. The orc mage stepped through the doorway into Healer Kitia's home, where the healer orc performed her most amazing work. Ellaria and Healer Kitia sat together, talking quietly.

"Where is he?" Smarlo asked.

"He's still in there," Healer Kitia said, pointing. "We'll need someone to retrieve his body. He died in the middle of the night, succumbed to his wounds. Even with this one's help," she jutted a thumb toward Ellaria, "we weren't able to save him."

Smarlo cursed under his breath. He'd hoped the man would survive. "And him?" he asked, nodding toward the other room.

"Still hasn't woken up."

The orc mage pressed a sigh through his gritted teeth. He gingerly prodded at the bloody wrappings on his ear.

"How is your ear?" Healer Kitia asked.

"It's fine," Smarlo said, waving away her concern. Compared to the losses and injuries many others had suffered during the battle, he felt the loss of half his ear was a minor inconvenience. "Let me know straight away if he wakes."

"We'll send Taglan running to you."

Smarlo nodded his approval of the plan and swept out of the home. Many of the loitering guardians looked up at him as he exited. The orc mage did his best to hide his frustration and hurried off to the Calrok mage library. He turned down a cobblestoned street, thankful for the solitude it provided. He relished the brief time when he could be alone with his thoughts before returning to constant discussions.

Since the battle ended, the library had become headquarters for leaders of the various gathered groups. Over the last few days, they'd discussed the casualty and readiness statuses of each group.

Belguv had reported they'd lost several Scar Squadron members, leaving their wyverns without riders. The commander planned on heading to the *Spinefish Tavern* to enlist any who were willing. Smarlo had no doubt they would be able to pair each of the wyverns with a new rider. The city was charged, everyone up in arms and ready to do whatever it took to ensure Calrok stayed safe from their enemies.

Jeslora, the captain of the city watch and a rather large female orc, had reported she'd had numerous orcs already approach her to join the city watch. They'd taken heavy losses in the battle by the docks, which had been waged by not just the watch. Civilian orcs had sprung from surrounding homes and buildings, joining the fray to repel the Kelvurian forces from the sea.

The city watch and the Talon Squadron had cleared the ship, which they learned from the captain's log was named the *Harbinger*. They also learned that the stone-like creatures were called geldrins. Having warded off the attack on Calrok, Smarlo was already making plans to use the *Harbinger*. But they still had much to finish before any attempts to cross the sea could be made.

On top of all the other activities, King Genjak was flying in from Ruk with several of his counselors. Smarlo knew the council well, but it seemed a daunting task to host the king's staff while the orc mage still tried to put the pieces of Calrok back together.

As the library came into view, Smarlo's steps shortened, an unusual reaction to one of his favorite places in the world. He didn't mean to slow down, but the orc was not looking forward to sharing the bad news with the rest of them, especially High Commander Mattness. After fighting side by side with the woman, he had a deep respect for her. It was painful for him to be the one to tell her.

The windows of the library were open, and Smarlo's ears caught the sound of the unending discourse within. He closed his eyes and dabbed at his wrapped ear while he took a couple of slow breaths.

Alright, he thought. *Let's get this over with.* The orc mage opened the door and slipped inside.

Garron opened his eyes at the stirring noise. His gaze met the wide eyes of the deep gnome, sitting across the bed from him. Ezel's little brows were raised expectantly, and Garron suddenly realized why.

"Hey now," the man said, stepping from his chair and pressing lightly against Pernden's shoulders to keep the king from sitting up too fast.

"Where am I?" Pernden croaked. He grabbed at his side.

"Don't you bother with that," Garron said. "You don't want to twist your bandages. Healer Kitia doesn't take any nonsense. She reminds me of an orc version of Dona."

Pernden returned his cousin's grin with a weak smile. Garron took a cup from the side table and lifted it for his cousin. The king sputtered as he choked down some water.

Suddenly, Ellaria stepped into the room.

"You're awake!" she started.

"I guess so," Pernden said, sheepishly. "Was it ever in question?"

"The sword wound you took was terrible," the woman said. "It appears you're as stubborn as Orin. Must be a family trait," she teased, with a sideways glance at Garron.

Pernden eyed his cousin. "Were you wounded?"

"No," Garron said, shaking his head. "A couple of nicks and scrapes, though I thought we were done for down in the mines. The whole ceiling was crashing down around us, but Ezel conjured us a protective barrier. As stalactites and massive slabs of stone fell upon us, they struck the magic barrier instead and fell away. It was amazing. I've never seen anything like it."

The king turned to the deep gnome and said, "Thank you."

The genuine solemnity with which Pernden expressed his gratitude, struck Garron deep within.

"I'm sorry," Garron said. "I should have been up above. Maybe I could have met Jolan near the docks. You almost died and—"

"The orc healer's not the only one who takes no nonsense." Pernden shot a tired smirk at him.

"Cousin—" Garron started to say.

"You were doing what you needed to do, and I was doing what I needed to do. This was not your fault," the king said, scrunching his face in pain as he shifted in the bed.

"And he's going to live, anyway," Ellaria cut in. "But he's going to need a lot of rest."

She started shooing Garron and Ezel out of the room, but Pernden stopped them.

"Wait," he said. "Did we defend the city?"

Garron breathed a laugh. "We did."

"Is High Commander Mattness alright? How did our orc friends fare? Did we take any prisoners? What happened to the ship?"

"There will be plenty of time to catch you up on all those things," Ellaria said sternly. She pressed against Garron's shoulder to usher him out of the room.

"Garron?" Pernden called weakly.

The man looked back at his cousin, lying in the bed. The king's eyes were wide with worry. Garron glanced to Ellaria, who sighed and rolled her eyes. She nodded her permission, but he knew he better keep his answer quick. He looked to his cousin.

"Rocktail?" Pernden asked.

Relief flooded Garron. "Alive and well, cousin. Now, get some rest. King Genjak is on his way from Ruk. You'll want to be well-rested for his arrival.

"And there are no prisoners to question?" King Genjak asked.

Smarlo winced at the orc king's question, taking a quick glance at High Commander Mattness who gritted her teeth angrily. Smarlo's eyes fell back on the king. The younger orc still had the same quiet strength Smarlo remembered, but he'd grown more comfortable speaking up when he thought it was important.

"We had a man-kin," Smarlo said, tentatively. "He was a traitor from Whitestone who fled with the sorcerer before. It seems he was leading the attack from the sea."

"You had?" Genjak asked.

Smarlo scratched at his once-long ear. "Yes. He was mortally wounded. Healer Kitia wasn't able to save him."

"How do we know he was leading the attack?"

"Well," the orc mage explained. "We captured their vessel and read the logs. Also, we had several witnesses from the Griffin Guard and the folks down by the docks suggesting the same thing."

"And there were no survivors in the mines?" Genjak asked.

"No," Smarlo admitted with a disappointed sigh. "The miners have been cleaning up the cavern in the Gert Section of the mine for the last three days, and they haven't found a single geldrin survivor. A couple of ghouls have been put down. They have no language and would prove useless in interrogation."

The orc king rose from his seat and paced in thought. He walked over to a shelf loaded with tomes and scrolls and absently thumbed the corner of a copy of *Mountainstead Reflections: A Treatise on Cutting Mountain Cities* by the old goblin architect Biq Lendrak. Everyone sat in silence, waiting for the orc king to speak. When he finally turned to address them, he had an air of authority Smarlo had never seen in Genjak before, and for the first time, the orc mage saw a proper king of Drelek.

"Smarlo," he addressed the mage directly. "You will remain as the interim Gar of Calrok until such a day as we learn of the true fate of Gar Karnak. If he is gone, I will install you as the gar in a more permanent fashion. Belguv will lead the Scar Squadron in Karnak's absence."

Belguv grunted from the corner of the room, placed a thick orc finger to his brow, and gave a slight bow, acknowledging the honor the king bestowed upon him.

"My King," Smarlo said, blinking in confusion. "I can't stay in Calrok. I must lead the mission across the sea to find Gar Karnak."

"You have performed your duties admirably here in Calrok in his stead. But now you also must take up the mantle of Master Mage of Calrok. Do you not think you have enough tasks on your plate already?" Genjak asked, though his question was rhetorical.

Smarlo didn't care whether the king intended the mage to answer. "I can't just leave him out there. Calrok needs its gar!"

Genjak looked to the side where a large orc sat, thick with deceptive layers of fat hiding strong muscles underneath. Gar Klentja sat up with a pensive look on his face. He was one of Genjak's most trusted advisers, and rightfully so. The orc king was originally Klentja's second-in-command when he was with the Borok Squadron.

"Smarlo," the large orc spoke kindly. "By your own account, there is already a squadron of the Griffin Guard that has sailed across the sea to find Karnak." The mention of the name forced Klentja to slow down. He cleared his throat and continued. "We all want to bring him home. But we don't know if he's even out there. You told us you haven't been able to communicate for some time with the troop that left. You can't leave Calrok when we have so little information about what's going on out there."

The mage leapt to his feet, his anger getting the better of him. He ripped the Shell of Callencia out of a pocket in his robes and tossed it to the table in front of him. "Does that really matter?" he spat.

"Smarlo," High Commander Mattness said, attempting to calm him. Her respect for the orc mage had grown greatly through their service together.

"No," he waved to her. "What does it matter, really? The sorcerer has attacked us twice now. Granted the first time was more deceptive in nature, but he brought a dragon into Tarrine and pitted Drelek orc against Drelek orc, forcing us to fight one another."

Smarlo paused and looked around the room. No one said a word. Mattness shrugged her shoulders at him, as if to indicate that he wasn't wrong.

"Then he kidnapped my best friend. A gar of Drelek. Even after taking Karnak, he still attacked Calrok. This won't end. Who knows how he'll try to finish us next time. What if he has more dragons at his disposal? What then? How long will we be able to withstand him? Does the sea ever withhold its waves? No. They crash upon the stone relentlessly. Eventually, even the hardest of stone crumbles."

An orb of light flickered into existence a couple inches above the Shell of Callencia. It blinked wearily.

"Your shell is lit," King Genjak pointed out.

Smarlo waved it off, his tone changing. "It's been doing that. Argus thinks its Lanryn attempting to reach us from across the sea." The orc mage let out a long sigh and straightened himself. "I'm sorry. Perhaps I'm tired. Maybe even hungry. Shall we get some food and reconvene tomorrow? Perhaps King Pernden will have some thoughts as well."

King Genjak didn't say anything at first. He inspected Smarlo, and the king's features softened. "We will work this out, my friend. You have fought hard. I know this hasn't been easy on you."

Smarlo appreciated Genjak's compassion. It seemed genuine, but the orc mage was too flustered to accept it fully.

Suddenly, the blinking orb steadied and sent shimmering reflections off the abalone shell.

"Hello, Tarrine. This is Lanryn. Can anyone hear me?"

Smarlo dove for the shell and, in his haste, fumbled the thing away from himself. High Commander Mattness picked up the shell, quickly trying to get it back to the orc mage.

"Blast," Lanryn's voice said from the orb. *"Alright, what else can I try ..."* the elf murmured to himself.

"Wait!" Smarlo said, finally retrieving the shell from Mattness. "Lanryn, we hear you! This is Smarlo."

"Smarlo?" he replied. *"Is it really you?"*

"Yes!" the orc mage declared with a hearty laugh.

Everyone in the room leaned closer, listening in.

"I cannot believe it. I have been trying everything I could think of to get the shell to work."

"Well done, my friend!" Smarlo exclaimed. "You've done it. How is everyone? Did you find Gar Karnak?"

Everyone in the room held a collective breath, waiting for the elf's reply.

"By my ears," Lanryn said. *"Do I have a story for you!"*

Garron smiled as he strode into the room where Pernden was healing. *How many times did he visit me in the dungeons?* he wondered. His cousin had been so good to him, even though Garron didn't deserve it. Though he never would wish harm on his cousin, he was glad to have an opportunity to reciprocate with Pernden.

He grinned as he took the seat next to the bed. *How many times did he sit in that chair next to my cell and talk with me?* Garron was happy to sit in silence and merely be present for his cousin. Even if he didn't feel like there was anything he could do.

"You know, you're not as quiet as you think you are," the king said, peeking through squinted eyes.

"Oh, is that right?" Garron whispered back. "Or are you just bad at resting?"

"All I've been doing is resting," Pernden said with a frown, opening his eyes all the way. "Ellaria won't let me do anything else."

Garron smirked. "She can be pretty persistent."

"That's one word for it."

"She just wants to see you well. And she is very good at healing," Garron said with a shrug. "Look at me."

As soon as he said the words, he regretted them. He wasn't the same man he was before his encounter with Jaernok Tur, and he didn't believe he ever would be. No amount of magic healing would be able to fix him completely. But to his surprise, his cousin looked at him, pressed his lips together, and nodded approvingly.

Perhaps, Garron thought, *he doesn't think I'm hopeless after all.*

"Alright," Pernden said, raising a hand in surrender. "But I'm going to the library tomorrow to meet with the others. I can't lay in here doing nothing while they're discussing our next course of action."

"Speaking of that," Garron said. "I have word of Nera."

"Is she back?" Pernden asked, sitting up quickly and instantly regretting it.

"No. We received word from Lanryn through the shells."

"What did he say? How is the mission going? Is Nera alright?"

"Yes. Nera's fine."

Relief swept over Pernden, and his entire body relaxed. "Good," he said quietly, more to himself than to Garron.

"They found Merrick and Karnak, but there was a battle."

"A battle? Did they make it?"

"Yes. But I have much to catch you up on."

"Well," Pernden said with a sheepish grin. "I'm not very tired. I could do with some conversation."

Garron smirked, looking both ways to make sure Ellaria wasn't behind him, and leaned in to relay everything Lanryn had told them of the events in Kelvur. As he did, a pit grew in Garron's stomach. Knowing the battle didn't bring about the sorcerer's demise plagued the man.

Just as he felt the repelling pull of the dark tongue, he sensed Jaernok Tur's wickedness in the world. Garron didn't know why Ellaria's healing magic couldn't rid him of that spur deep within, but he was starting to believe that slaying the orc sorcerer might be the only way to remove it. He would do almost anything to see both tasks through.

Chapter Thirty-Eight

Pyre of the Path

Shorlis sat on a stone in the shade of a tree that had avoided the carnage of the Battle of Ventohl. His eyes were closed, but his mind was wide open. He heard others, going about the tasks that were set to them by their respective commanders. Shorlis did not have a commander, but he had helped where he could when it came to the cleanup efforts. Though, Javelin and the Talon Squadron both seemed quite experienced with such operations.

As he inhaled the evening breeze, he could almost imagine the place as peaceful. It was nothing like the Shoals, of course. There was no sea scent in the breeze. He couldn't taste the salt in the air. The chelon knew if he opened his eyes, he'd see the menacing smoke that always covered the sky near the Crags. He filled his lungs, feeling them expand within his shell, and let out a deep resigned sigh.

"That was a big sigh," a woman's voice said from nearby.

The chelon eased one eye open to look at Captain Nera.

"Hello, Captain," he greeted her quietly.

"Nera is fine," she said with a smile. She pointed to the large rock on which Shorlis sat. "Mind if I join you?"

"Please," he said, with an inviting gesture.

Though the chelon had sat alone with the intention of meditating, he had no misconceptions about his struggle to do so. Perhaps her company would be better.

"We received word from home," Nera said.

"From Tarrine?" Shorlis asked in surprise.

"Yes," she replied with a nod. "Lanryn took some of the suggestions that Enkeli the wizard gave him and was able to boost the magic of the shell to reach across the sea."

"That's ..." Shorlis paused. He wasn't really sure what it was. He'd never read about such magic, nor did he remember any tales from his father that spoke of such things. "It's amazing," he said finally.

"Agreed," Nera mused. "I don't know how they do that. It's a wonder."

Her gaze seemed far off, and she seemed unlike herself.

"Is everything alright?" Shorlis asked the woman.

"The man I love was attacked in the midst of a battle," she said, softly. Then she added quickly, "He's alive. He was injured, but it sounds like he's healing."

Shorlis placed a green hand on the woman's shoulder. "I'm sorry," he said.

"It's alright," she continued. "I just didn't expect they would be fighting a battle back home." She huffed a laugh. "Then again, I didn't expect the battle we fought here, either. We really weren't sure what we'd face here in Kelvur." Her bewildered look shifted to an amused and annoyed grin. "I knew those boys wouldn't behave themselves without me there."

"I hope he heals quickly," Shorlis said, with a kind smile.

"I have no doubt. He's well looked after by a friend of mine. Besides, he's too stubborn to let an injury keep him down for long." She paused and smirked at the far-off vision. The smirk soon faded, and Shorlis wasn't sure what to make of the woman's countenance. She continued, "It got me thinking of things differently. I almost lost him, and I wasn't even there with him."

"He could have lost you in this battle, just as easily," Shorlis pointed out.

"Sure," she admitted. "But this time it felt different. I don't like being so far away from him. Before, we were always together. Even if we were in the middle of a skirmish, I always knew he was nearby."

"I don't know how you do it," Shorlis said, quietly.

He fell silent and felt the guardian adjust her seat to view him.

"How are you holding up?" she asked.

"I can't stop thinking about Chol," he admitted. "When we took the mining camp, everything happened so fast. We were fighting for our lives. When I used *Menthrora* on Commander Chol, it was like the staff drew out all the rage within me, and that magic ripped him apart. It was almost like I could feel his pain as it happened."

Nera nodded thoughtfully. They sat in silence for a long while, resting under the tree. They gazed over the grounds of the ancient castle. Dusk was beginning to show its telltale signs, painting the smoky sky with pink and orange tints. Many of the folks that moved about finished their tasks and headed toward the pillared area of the castle.

For a moment, Shorlis forgot Chol. The scene was rather serene, and he was glad for Nera's silent presence. The chelon's mind filled with visions of Ventohl in its prime. What would the city have looked like back then? He thought of how much life there must have been when it was first built. He wondered, *How many of the cities that my father visited are ruins now?*

"Come," Nera said to him, patting his arm. "We should get to the ceremony. Merrick said it's quite beautiful."

Shorlis nodded to her and slid from the rock. The chelon figured he could use all the beauty he could get.

Merrick leaned closer to Ralowyn as they watched the Javelin vigil for their fallen warriors. "That new pile is the pyre of the path. They make that one at the end to remember all who have fallen in the past."

They watched with a shared solidarity as the Javelin children dropped the flaming bundles in a singular pile at the end of the rows. Nelan leaned forward, the old dwarf's white beard dangling in front of his face.

"The pyre of the path is also a promise," he whispered to them. "As they throw those torches into a new pile, they promise to never forget those who died so they could live. And they promise to live their lives for each other, not letting their predecessors' sacrifices be in vain."

Merrick nodded thoughtfully. "It's their way of saying they're with each other."

"Precisely," Nelan said, leaning his balding head back.

The flicker of the firelight twinkled in Merrick's glassy eyes. The implications of the ceremony were made all the more poignant by the fact that Karnak and Captain Nera stood at the front to either side of Vorenna. The sight was more than just warriors coming together to mourn their dead.

It was warriors from clans across Finlestia rallying together for a common purpose, united against a singular enemy that threatened to wipe them all out.

The thought of the war to come gave Merrick pause. He couldn't help but think how far he'd come. He was still that same huntsman who'd left Tamaria so long ago. In that moment, he felt more. He didn't think less of himself for his beginnings but recognized he was no different from most of the people gathered in Ventohl. They were all far from home. Most of them had never expected or wanted to be warriors. Farmers, fishermen, huntsmen, blacksmiths, tanners, cooks, fathers, mothers, sons, and daughters—the list went on. And yet, they were all there, brought together into a wild war.

"Now, eat with your families. Eat with your friends," Vorenna said to the gathering. "If you've lost both, come see me, and I will find you new ones."

Merrick watched as the gathering began to disperse, several people surrounding others, embracing them and bringing them into the fabric of their own families. The huntsman's eyes fell upon a small child, kneeling near one of the pyres, likely hidden from the view of most of the gathering. From Merrick's spot, he saw the child perfectly well. He was a small boy with curly brown hair, and his body shook as he cried.

The huntsman's chin quivered at the thought that the boy would be missed by the dispersing crowd. He tried to wave several groups over, but none of them heard the huntsman over the noise of their own conversations. They were already engrossed in the comforting of others.

Merrick suddenly felt desperate for the little boy and ran down the steps. When he stopped next to the little boy and saw his exposed toes, the huntsman realized he was a halfling. His pathetic cries broke Merrick, and he bent down next to the tiny fellow and placed a hand on his back. The halfling looked up, his hazel eyes glossed with tears. The two stared at each other for only a second, but it felt as though time froze.

Suddenly, the little halfling jumped from his knees and buried himself in the huntsman's chest. Merrick hugged him close, tears streaming down his face and dripping off the stubble on his chin. There they stayed for a long while, hugging one another and letting their tears flow.

The sight of Merrick and the little halfling wrenched Karnak. Thoughts of Gernot and Tanessa flooded his already charged emotions. The big orc sniffed and clenched his jaw to suppress the wavering breath that left his lungs.

"You're a part of us now," Vorenna said next to the orc gar.

Karnak glanced at the barbarian woman and straightened himself.

"We're all in this together," Karnak agreed.

The barbarian leader of Javelin smiled quietly. "No," she said, watching Merrick and the halfling. "It's more than that. Our families are growing. Everything has changed. You have come across the sea and brought a new hope to our lands. And both of our worlds have gotten a lot bigger. The events of the last several days have changed the course of Kelvur and Tarrine forever. Finlestia is a wide world, and this is only the beginning."

Karnak wrinkled his nose a couple of times trying to work the emotion out of his face. He raised his arms and stretched his shoulders, tightening the black knot of hair on the back of his head.

"Only the beginning," he mumbled to himself. When Vorenna eyed him curiously, he continued, "I feel like we're in the middle. We're in the grinding."

"What do you mean?" she asked pensively.

"When grain is on the stem, it isn't much good to us, but at least the birds can eat it. It's only through the grinding of the grains that we can make bread," Karnak said. "The grind will continue for a while before we can see something good come from this. This is far from over. We'll never be able to rest until the sorcerer is dead."

"Are all orcs such poets?"

Karnak turned on her, confusion written all over his face. When he saw her wry smirk, he realized she was teasing him. The long silence that hung between their frozen stares became hilarious to him, and a hearty laugh rumbled through his mighty body. The two of them laughed, Vorenna slapping a strong hand on the orc's big shoulder muscles several times.

"Come," she said. "Bring your family to dine with Nelan and me."

The way she stopped to admire the old dwarf drew another curious glance from the orc gar. "Nelan? Really?" he asked quietly.

"Mmm," she nodded. "Isn't he magnificent?"

Karnak inspected the old dwarf. The last remaining wisps of white hair on his balding head splayed out wildly. His long white beard was impressive enough, though, the orc thought, and Karnak had to admit, the dwarf was sturdy for his age.

"Give me a moment," the orc gar said with a chuckle. "I will gather them."

Ralowyn stroked the little halfling's curls as he snuggled in Merrick's arms. When the little one hadn't immediately perked up for dinner, the elven mage worried. Merrick had convinced the halfling to eat in short order when Nelan started dishing out some of his famous—at least among Javelin folks—cobbler hot off the skillet.

The little halfling's eyes had widened to twice their size as did, Ralowyn was sure, his empty stomach. That was also when they were able to get a name out of the poor boy. "Kippin," he'd said. The elf thought the name fit him perfectly.

She smiled contentedly as she looked at the people gathered around the campfire. Coal sat, unusually quiet, between Merrick and Karnak, while the big orc talked with the other leaders: Nera, Vorenna, and Nelan. She didn't doubt there would be many more discussions in coming weeks. Since Lanryn had been able to reach out to their friends in Tarrine, the leaders would be developing plans to bring more forces to Kelvur to face the sorcerer's armies.

Ralowyn couldn't see another way. But then again, she also did not fancy herself a master tactician. She would leave much of the planning to the others. When she was called upon to protect them, though, she would do so with every ounce of energy she could muster.

Her eyes fell on Merrick. The huntsman sat quietly, also taking in the scene. He was always so good at that. It was one of those things that surprised her. He had the ability to live presently wherever they found themselves. The man never seemed to lose his quiet strength—or at least, she had never seen him lose it. It was one of the things she loved about him.

"Excuse me, Ralowyn?" Shorlis asked.

The elf looked to the chelon with a kind smile. He'd been sitting so quietly next to her that she had almost forgotten he was there. The stark contrast between the quiet side of the campfire and the boisterous side was amusing.

"Yes?" She prompted him onward.

"Nera ... Captain Nera," he corrected himself. "She said you might be able to help me learn to wield the magic of *Menthrora*."

The chelon's words came out tentatively, almost like a child asking someone for help. Ralowyn couldn't tell if Shorlis was embarrassed, but she sensed his trepidation rose from a deeper place.

"Learning the magics of enchanted artifacts is no easy task," she said honestly.

"I am not afraid of work," Shorlis insisted. "I am willing to learn whatever you would teach me."

She smiled at the chelon. "I do not doubt it. What I am trying to tell you is I may not be able to teach you how to wield *Menthrora*. That is something you must learn on your own." When the chelon's gaze fell to the ground, she continued. "However, I can teach you some of the foundational knowledge of magic."

Shorlis perked up. "You can?"

"That, I can do. You will need to learn how to apply those foundations into practice with *Menthrora* yourself."

The chelon seemed satisfied with the answer as he replied with, "Thank you," and turned back to the campfire, lost in his own thoughts.

Ralowyn's slight hand shifted from the brown curls atop Kippin's little head and landed softly on Merrick's shoulder. Her fingers gently played with his shoulder-length hair. He shot her a smile before gazing upon the snoring halfling in his arms.

"He is out," Merrick said with a chuckle.

"He is," she agreed. "With everything going on, I forgot to tell you."

"Tell me what?" the huntsman asked.

"No one wanted to go near the witch's body after the battle was over. So, I was the one to wrap her remains. As I was preparing her, I found something."

"What? A curse? Are you alright?" Merrick's eyes narrowed as he tried to inspect her in the flickering firelight.

"No," she said, rubbing her hand on his shoulder comfortingly. "I am quite alright. But I found something I thought you might like to have back."

From a concealed pocket in her garments, she produced a stone and crystalline figure of a falcon.

"Valurwind," he whispered. A great relief swept over his face, and the elf thought the man's eyes glossed.

Ralowyn handed the statuette to Merrick, and the huntsman thumbed the cool stone.

"Thank you," he whispered. "I wasn't sure I'd ever see her again. Did we find Karnak's axe, *Dalkeri*?"

"I did not, nor have I heard of another finding it. I would have assumed to see it during the battle. A mighty weapon such as that would not be idly tossed away."

"No," Merrick agreed. "I worry if the sorcerer got his hands on it. It's hard to imagine what kind of destruction he could dole out upon the world with *Dalkeri*."

The prospect made Ralowyn shudder, though not enough to be noticed by the others. She sensed there was more to all of this than any of them had yet to figure out. And it was that mystery that worried her.

EPILOGUE

The fetid stench of molten earth stung Hazkul Bern's nose as he slipped through a corridor of the Fell Keep. He moved from shadow to shadow, appearing in the dim, sickly glow between them for only split moments. He was like a ghost. No geldrin would spot the assassin. He knew he could be upon any of the guards and kill them before they even knew they were dead. But that wasn't his plan.

If he were honest with himself, he wasn't entirely sure he knew what his plan was. He'd never been to the Fell Keep or this far into the Crags, for that matter. After losing everything at Ventohl, his initial instinct was to come here. His instincts had rarely failed him in all his life. Though he'd found himself questioning many things recently—something he very much disliked. For years, he had been sure of himself, and he didn't like this new feeling.

Hazkul came to a large arched window. It looked out upon the lava flow of one of the deep wounds that marred the earth in the Crags. The orange tinted light radiated with the heat, bathing the assassin in its molten glow.

The elf reached into his pocket and thumbed at the pouch of seeds he always kept there. It seemed a trivial thing. Maybe even an ignorant thing. *What kind of an assassin would choose the life of an orchardman anyway?*

He lifted the pouch in front of him, debating whether to throw it into the burbling magma below. The bag flitted sideways as the smoky winds wafted putrid air past. He couldn't do it. *One does need something to strive toward.* He replaced the symbol of the elusive skill in his pocket and continued down the hallway.

The Fell Keep was a maze, but the elf assassin had all the time in the world. There was no rush. He wasn't sure what he was going to do when he saw the sorcerer anyway. There were plenty of options. He wasn't entirely convinced Jaernok Tur wouldn't be able to sense his presence with some sort of spell, but if Hazkul was able to sneak up on the sorcerer, maybe a good assassination was in order.

Reporting what happened in Ventohl to the sorcerer was another option. Though Hazkul wasn't sure whether the sorcerer's rage would be targeted at the unbelievable gall of the nomad warriors or himself. He wasn't inclined to find out the hard way.

No. Hazkul Bern's plan was to find Jaernok Tur, wherever the sorcerer was in this wretched castle. Then he would watch and listen. Maybe he'd be able to discern what kind of mood the orc was in, then he could formulate the next phase of his plan.

A groan rumbled through the corridors, shaking the foundation stones of the castle. It was deep, as though it came from the earth itself. *What in Finlestia?* Hazkul wondered.

He slipped down a side passageway that led him to a series of stairs. This area of the castle was surprisingly devoid of geldrins, which made it easier for the assassin to move quickly. He ambled down some stairs and turned into a hall that led to a brightly lit archway.

Hazkul drew near and hid in the shadows of the carved arch. A large stone platform lay just outside the doorway, overlooking an enormous lake of burbling mud. Steam belched from bubbles exploding off the surfaces. To Hazkul's dismay, he found the sorcerer in the middle of the great platform, carrying his twisting black staff in his stone hand and the orc's magic axe in the other. The sorcerer's attention rested upon the terrorscape that was the Crags.

Assassination? Hazkul pondered. If the sorcerer didn't know he was there, it would be easy enough to sneak up on him.

Another grumble resonated all around, forcing painful vibrations in the elf's keen ears. He realized where the terrible rumbling originated. It rose from the burbling lake. *Maker ...* Hazkul thought in terror.

A voice boomed over the entire area, sending bubbles to the top of the lake like a boiling pot.

"Jaernok Tur," the voice said, shaking Hazkul to the bone. "It is time for you to give yourself over to me as completely as the others."

"Master," Jaernok Tur replied with a whimper. "I am the only one left of my kind."

A low growl shook the stone beneath their feet.

"Do you forget your purpose? I will make you something new. Something better," the voice said.

"Y-yes, Master," Jaernok Tur stammered and stepped closer to the edge.

Hazkul Bern watched in horror as the orc raised his staff and the magic axe, clanging them together. The mud swelled and rose in a boiling wave. The liquid ran off in sheets as a mountain grew before them—but it was no mountain. Great wicked black eyes appeared, and Hazkul felt as though his legs had become statues. He wanted to run. He wanted to hide. Nonetheless, he peered, frozen in his spot in the archway.

Kilretheon the Red!

451

The mud mountain shifted in an impossible way as Kilretheon, the monolith dragon, pulled an immense claw from the fuming mud lake. It hovered over the sorcerer, boiling mud dropping in globs onto the stone floor. Jaernok Tur looked tiny under the shadow of the giant claw.

Another moan rumbled the world around Hazkul. "I can already feel it," the booming voice said, with a satisfied air. "My strength is returning."

Jaernok Tur's knees trembled underneath him. To the sorcerer's credit, he held the weapons together high above his head.

The tip of the great claw touched the weapons, and a loud crack rang out. Suddenly, a loud rippling of power began to *verve,* illuminating the scene in a strange hue of orange and black magic, swirling in a maniacal dance. The light grew brighter until Hazkul had to lift his hands to cover his eyes, for he could not bring himself to look away.

Everything finally went quiet, except the perpetual bubbling and cracking of rock that was ever present in the Crags. Hazkul uncovered his eyes and saw that the battle axe had been discarded to the floor. The sorcerer struggled to hold the staff with both his stone hand and his orc hand. The staff was no longer black but a swirling orange and black. It vibrated uncontrollably, shaking Jaernok Tur to his core.

"Now, let go," Kilretheon's voice boomed, accompanied by a beastly snarl.

Suddenly, a powerful explosion blasted a wave of energy that knocked Hazkul Bern down and rattled the walls of the Fell Keep. He was surprised to find himself flat on his back. Something slid to a stop, hitting his foot. When he heaved himself to his knees, his hand landed on the mighty battle axe. Or at least, what used to be a mighty battle axe. The stone that had imbued its magic to the weapon was ripped away, leaving a great crack down the middle.

Hazkul looked up, and his eyes widened as he watched the horrifying scene unfold before him.

Jaernok Tur screamed and roiled as his body shuddered. The orc sorcerer grasped at the staff as cracked stone rolled over his entire body, replacing anything that was left of the orc's pale green skin.

Hazkul couldn't believe his eyes. *That's what happened to the orcs!*

Jaernok Tur shivered and heaved as though he was going to vomit.

"Good," Kilretheon said, as the newly formed geldrin sorcerer stood wearily to his feet. "Now that you've let go, I've reshaped you into something greater. And now, I can make you a master over death."

That was the last thing Hazkul Bern heard as he sprinted through the corridors of the Fell Keep. He glanced at the battle axe he carried. He wasn't sure why he'd grabbed it. Frankly, he wasn't sure *when* he'd grabbed it. He wasn't sure about a lot of things. He used to be so sure of everything. He used to know that *he* was a master of death.

After seeing Jaernok Tur cowed by the ancient dragon Kilretheon the Red, Hazkul Bern didn't think he understood anything anymore.

He ran on, his many years of muscle memory speeding him through the hallways in silence. His instincts had taken over. Those instincts had rarely failed him in the past, and now they told him to run as fast and far as he could.

ACKNOWLEDGEMENTS

Thank you for reading my book! I hope you had as much fun exploring the land beyond the sea as I did writing this adventure. If so, please leave a wonderful review. Reviews are the lifeblood of indie authors like me. The more positive reviews we have, the more likely it is that others will pick up the book as well.

A lot went into this book and I've had some great encouragement and love from folks along the way. But I would be remiss if I didn't thank a few very specific people for helping me on this journey.

First of all, Crystal. You were the first to dive into the world of Finlestia and then you had to wait longer than anyone else to get your hands on this one. But I'm thankful you did. Thank you for your continued love, friendship, and encouragement.

Joy, thank you for making me a better writer! I'm so glad this one went so much smoother. You're making me better with each book.

And finally, my wife Brittany and our kids, you guys have been so patient as I've sailed through another book in this series. Your love and patience mean more to me than anything else.

ABOUT THE AUTHOR

Z.S. Diamanti is the award-winning author of the *Stone &
Sky* series, an epic fantasy adventure and the result of his great
passion for fun and fantastical stories. He went to college
forever and has too many pieces of paper on his wall. He is a
USAF veteran of Operation Enduring Freedom and worked in
ministry for over 10 years. He and his wife reside in Colorado
with their four children where they enjoy hikes and tabletop
games.

You can get the *Stone & Sky Preludes Series* of stories for
FREE at zsdiamanti.com

Connect with him on social media: @zsdiamanti

CONNECT

CONTINUE THE ADVENTURE!

Read the third book in

The Stone & Sky Series

Available
June 2024

ORDER NOW!

Good reviews are vital for Indie Authors. The importance of reviews in helping others find and take a chance on an indie author's book is impossible to overstate.

If you enjoyed this book, would you help me get it in front of more people by taking a minute to give it a good review?
I can't tell you how thankful I'd be.

Check out this link for the best places to review this book and help me get it to more readers who love good books just like you and me!